OTHER BOOKS BY GARY WATSON

Fifteen Minutes of Fame

The Second Chapter of a Bad Dream

A QUICK TRIP BACK HOME

GARY WATSON

authorHOUSE®

AuthorHouse™
1663 Liberty Drive
Bloomington, IN 47403
www.authorhouse.com
Phone: 833-262-8899

Published by AuthorHouse 06/10/2021

ISBN: 978-1-6655-2837-5 (sc)
ISBN: 978-1-6655-2838-2 (e)

Print information available on the last page.

This book is printed on acid-free paper.

ACKNOWLEDGEMENTS

First and foremost, my readers who constantly encourage me to give them more stories

My wife Suzanne who allows me to barricade myself in my study and write for hours on end

My daughters Kelli and Hayley. Two of my biggest supporters

My grandchildren, Tandy, Clinton and Madolyn who brighten my days and help me relax when the words aren't flowing

My dear, dear friend Wes Tallon for editing this book and making wonderful suggestions about the story

The thousands of people I have met through the years who have been the inspiration for many of my stories and characters

Danielle Cherry, my wonderful publicist who helped the world know about my book

ACKNOWLEDGEMENTS

1

A single bead of sweat dripped down the bridge of Kris Keller's nose. He started to wipe it away with his long sleeve but stopped when he realized his white dress shirt was already as drenched as if he had just completed a water-skiing competition on Lake Allatoona. The scorching August sun, unencumbered by a cloudless sky, was bearing down on Kris and the two dozen other reporters and cameramen like an alien death ray. Perched behind the barrier established by police on Swisher Street a mile south of downtown Atlanta, the news media had no shade and no place to escape the energy-sapping heat. Dry cleaners were going to make a killing off the garments that would come their way when this episode was over.

"Why couldn't this jerk have picked a cooler day to rob this bank? Like January or February? Or at least March," panted Patrick Cannon from Channel 12 who was standing next to Kris. Compared to the way his friend Patrick was sweating, Kris looked as cool as a Frosted Orange from the Varsity Drive-In.

Another perspiring reporter from the struggling daily paper running a distant second to Kris' employer, the Atlanta Advocate, joined the conversation. "It's been two hours since the police turned off the air conditioning in the bank. It's got to be as hot as hell in there. How long can this go on?" This reporter looked like he had just stepped out of a sauna.

"My editor called a couple of minutes ago," Kris replied. "He's been told the Mayor is headed here – in a helicopter. Something must be about to happen. How often have you known our Mayor to get personally involved in something?" Kris flipped a drop of sweat off his nose with his right index finger.

Like a guardian angel, an Emergency Management staffer for the City of Atlanta came by distributing 16-ounce plastic bottles of cold water which the crowd stuck behind the barricade guzzled in seconds. A young radio reporter, already drenched with sweat and knowing his audience would not see him when he gave an update, poured his water over his head and let out a sigh of relief. Feeling slightly refreshed, recipients of the water resumed their vigil, waiting for the Mayor's arrival and some action at the small, isolated branch of Atlanta Family Bank that was housed in a hundred-year-old historic building in a portion of the city that was undergoing a significant revitalization with new residences and shops replacing dilapidated housing and shuttered stores.

Marlon Turrentine was a wormy undersized white man with a ragged Atlanta Braves cap situated on long, stringy dirty brown hair. He was wearing cheap dollar store sunglasses, baggy blue jeans and sneakers that looked like they had been picked out of a trash can. Turrentine, in a zipped-up gray windbreaker on a day when the temperature was supposed to hit 95, had entered Atlanta Family Bank shortly after the lobby opened at 9 a.m. He had handed the bespectacled middle-aged female teller closest to the entrance a computer-generated note directing her to place loose currency on the counter so he could inspect it and stuff it in his own bag and avoid the dye bomb. If successful with the robbery, he needed to spend some of the money on significant dental work, a haircut and personal hygiene. He smelled. His caper was going according to plan until a muscular health club owner, in the bank to deposit the previous day's receipts, decided that he would be a hero and take down the little shrimp without much difficulty. And he could have probably done that had Turrentine not pulled a stolen .9 mm from his belt and shot him between the eyes. As the body dropped to the carpeted floor, the bank's two tellers, the branch manager and two customers screamed, horrified that the rattled Turrentine was going to start shooting at them. Instead, he scooped up the money that had been placed on the counter and bolted for the front door but stopped and retreated inside as two City of Atlanta police cars, dispatched following the silent alarm set off discretely by a younger teller, screeched to a halt in front of the bank. With the angry, agitated and extremely nervous Turrentine pointing the .9 mm at the back of her head, the branch manager, showing an outward calm, locked the front doors and the standoff was on.

After an hour of alternating calm and cantankerous and futile negotiations with Turrentine, police shut down power and water to the building thereby eliminating air conditioning and turning the bank into an oven. They expected Turrentine to give in to the heat and their pleadings and surrender but the plan backfired. Rather than forcing surrender, the increasingly unbearable heat stoked Turrentine's agitation. Realizing he was already facing the death penalty for murder and armed robbery; his demands became more outrageous, and he threatened to kill the hostages. He finally told police to end their babbling and listen to him. He wanted a helicopter to land in front of the bank to carry him away. He was explicit in his instructions. He didn't want a police helicopter or even a traffic copter from one of the TV stations. He wanted a chopper from a charter company that specialized in sight-seeing and business trips. One that had plenty of speed to get him out of the area fast. If the police did not comply, he would start shooting a hostage every 15 minutes, starting with the young blonde teller who was trying not to cry was but wasn't being successful. In his warped thinking, Turrentine believed his demand would get more attention if he threatened to kill a sweet young thing rather than a middle-aged matron with no looks and not much personality.

The police wanted to play hardball. They had no intention of meeting this preposterous demand, but an unexpected revelation changed their minds. Atlanta Mayor Alexander Robertson's daughter, home from the University of Virginia, was working a summer job as a teller at the bank. She was the sweet young thing. No one was going to harm his only child and by God, if that meant giving the bastard a helicopter, then that's what the police department would be commanded to do. Police tried to reason with the Mayor, telling him there was not enough room for a chopper to land safely, but there was no convincing him, and he was making the delivery in person.

Kris and the other media corralled 50 yards away across the street from the bank looked skyward as the unique sound of the helicopter became audible. "This is going to be interesting," Kris said to no one in particular. "There's not much room to land that baby. Those power lines are awfully close to the street." The noise got louder and louder and within two minutes the copter was hovering over the narrow street in front of the bank after three news choppers were ordered to evacuate air space around the bank.

The gang behind the barricade, most of whom had reported on countless police matters of all sorts and were accustomed to seeing as many unfortunate endings as happy, collectively held their breath. The chopper pilot – an Army veteran who had flown extraction missions in overseas combat zones and was now SkyHawk Air Services' go-to guy for high-paying business clients – skillfully executed the landing of the helicopter. Before the rotors stopped spinning Mayor Robertson quickly hopped out and headed straight for Police Chief Todd Daniels who was in the department's mobile command center communicating with Turrentine via phone. "He's coming out with a hostage," the Chief explained. "He's promised he won't hurt anyone else, as long as he gets on that helicopter safely."

"Give him free passage," the Mayor barked. "Then as soon as I know for certain Julie is all right, have our sharp-shooters take out the son of a bitch!" Two Atlanta Police marksmen who had served as snipers in the military were positioned atop nearby buildings with their aim directly on the front door of the bank.

"What if he takes a hostage with him on the chopper?" Chief Daniels asked.

"He damned well better not get that far," the Mayor snapped.

Staring directly at the bank, the Mayor grew silent. At that moment he did not care about his job, the citizens of the good city of Atlanta, failing infrastructure and budgets that had too much cash going out and not enough coming in. Nor was he worried about collateral damage. He was not concerned about anyone or anything but Julie, a daddy's girl if there ever was one.

Kris and his colleagues behind the barricade were sweating and waiting. "I don't have a good feeling about this," Kris said, again to no one in particular. "I don't believe they're simply going to let this guy waltz out of the bank, hop on to a helicopter and get away so easily. Someone is going to get hurt. Hopefully, it will only be the robber."

"Maybe they will let him waltz away," Patrick Cannon spoke up after sliding his cell phone into the pocket on the left side of his soaked gray dress slacks. "The word my newsroom is getting is the Mayor's daughter is one of the hostages. He wants to make sure she's not hurt. He has given orders to let the guy come out, get on the chopper and fly away."

Kris looked at Patrick in disbelief. "Out of all the banks in Atlanta, this guy picks the one the Mayor's daughter works at. Maybe this is his lucky day. But I still don't think they're going to let him go." Kris nodded in the direction of one of the nearby buildings where a sliver of one of the shooter's helmet and the barrel of his rifle could be seen. "My bet is he doesn't make it to the chopper."

"We're about to find out," Patrick said. The Mayor and Police Chief were coming out of the command center. SWAT team members and the marksmen started backing away. "Marcus, get that camera rolling," Patrick urged his Channel 12 partner.

Police cleared the path with the Mayor and Chief standing to the side halfway between the bank and helicopter. The Mayor had his hands to his sides, his fists clinched tightly. Nothing happened for five minutes. "He's coming out," the Chief announced as he noticed movement at the door.

"The bastard thinks we've ordered our men to stand down. Get ready to give the order. As soon as they have a clear shot, take him down," the Mayor instructed.

"Yes sir!" Through his mouthpiece, the Chief gave the order to shoot on his command.

"Damn him!" the Mayor mumbled in a voice so low only the Chief could hear. "He's coming out with Julie!"

Wormy little Turrentine, still wearing his Braves' cap, sunglasses and windbreaker, had his arm wrapped Julie's throat and the .9 mm pointed at her head. He had such a grip on her she was having difficulty breathing and walking. Turrentine was drenched in sweat. Julie was gasping for air.

"Mayor, our shooters have a good look. They can take him out," the Chief whispered. "All I've got to do is give the order. All I've got to do is wiggle the fingers on my right hand."

"No!" the Mayor snapped. "I will not take that chance! Not with Julie!" He lifted his right hand and made a circular motion, the signal for the pilot to rev the chopper's blades.

Julie spotted her dad as Turrentine dragged her toward the helicopter. "Daddy!" she said softly, unable to generate much volume with an arm wrapped around her throat. Suddenly realizing who his hostage was, Turrentine smiled wickedly at the Mayor who took a step forward but halted when Chief Daniels grabbed him by the arm.

An excruciating minute later with the Chief still waiting for the Mayor's order, Turrentine and Julie were at the copter. Knowing that no one was going to risk injury to his precious hostage, Turrentine began taunting the Mayor. Holding Julie by her long blonde hair, he pushed her toward her dad but then pulled her back, stuck the .9 mm in her ribs and pushed her into the copter. He followed her, slammed the door shut and stuck the gun to the pilot's head, demanding that he get that damn machine off the ground and the hell out of there!

"That's not part of the deal you bastard!" the Mayor bellowed and broke for the copter before Chief Daniels or anyone else could stop him. The helicopter was already five feet off the ground when the Mayor jumped and grabbed on to the left landing skid. With the Mayor being six feet, three inches tall and a solid 245 pounds, the helicopter began swaying as he struggled to kick his leg over the skid.

Behind the barricade, Kris felt his heart pounding in his chest. The Mayor years earlier had been a three-year starter at linebacker for the University of Georgia but now he was out of shape and was lacking in flexibility and there was no way he could kick his leg over that skid or hold on for very long. Kris had this terrible feeling that Mayor Robertson's term in office was going to be cut short by a 150-foot fall to the Swisher Street pavement.

"This isn't good! This isn't good!" Kris cried as he watched the Mayor struggle to hang on which was preventing the helicopter from gaining altitude and causing it to sway from side to side. The news helicopters, positioned at a safe distance, were feeding the events live to their audiences. Thousands of metro Atlanta residents were watching in live horror, some of them already with tears welling in their eyes.

Julie, hysterical at her father's plight more than her own, brought her hand down in a hard-chopping motion across Turrentine's forearm to knock loose the handgun that was still pointed at the pilot's head. Instead, the gun discharged, mortally wounding the pilot and causing the helicopter to flail out of control. Losing altitude, one of the copter's blades contacted a power line causing a shower of sparks and sending the machine crashing to the street. On impact it exploded, sending hundreds of pieces of shrapnel hurtling toward stunned onlookers who had no chance to seek cover. Kris saw the tail rotor heading straight at him and he threw up both arms to shield his face. At the same moment he felt the sharp pain in his left upper arm, he heard Patrick scream. Attempting to protect his face and head, as Kris had done, Patrick had raised his arms and the catapulting blade severed his right hand.

"Oh God!" Kris exclaimed, watching Patrick writhe and scream in pain on the pavement. He was so focused on Patrick he did not notice the dozen other people around him who had taken hits of varying degrees. Dropping to his knees, Kris did the only thing he knew to do. He clasped Patrick's arm slightly above the wrist as tightly as he could with both hands to stop the bleeding. Marcus, the Channel 12 cameraman, was groggily getting to his feet. His only wound was a minor scrape across the cheek from a bolt that had been blasted loose by the explosion. His camera had shielded much of his face. Marcus was fortunate. A few more inches and the bolt would have drilled him fatally in the forehead.

Patrick continued to flail, making it difficult for Kris to maintain his grip. "Marcus!" Kris screamed, "Sit on him at the waist. Take off your belt so we can use it as a tourniquet."

With considerable difficulty because of Patrick's agonized flailing, Marcus obeyed and managed to get the belt looped around Patrick's wrist. "What do we do now" Marcus asked, wiping blood off his cheek.

"Wait for help. Lots of it," Kris said softly after taking a deep breath. He took a moment to get his first look at the carnage. Black smoke was billowing high in the sky from the blazing helicopter, and bodies, some not moving and others rolling and crying in pain, were scattered up and down the street.

"Kris, are you all right? That's a nasty cut," Marcus asked.

Kris looked down at his left arm. His once-white sleeve was solid crimson. "It's just a little scratch," he joked weakly. Kris passed out 10 seconds later as the air filled with the sirens of approaching emergency vehicles.

2

A reporter's job is to report the news, not be a part of it, but that's the position Kris was in. He was part of the story, a number, a statistic, one of the eighteen people who were injured to varying degrees during the helicopter explosion. Two others were killed, including Police Chief Daniels who was within feet of the copter when it hit the ground. Those two were in addition to the Mayor, his daughter, Turrentine and the chopper pilot. Chief Daniels took a knife-like piece of shrapnel directly into the heart; the other had a projectile bolt drill a hole in his head, the fate Channel 12 cameraman Marcus Smith had narrowly avoided. Injury-wise, there were numerous cuts and bruises, flesh wounds of varying degrees from projectiles from the explosion and a few broken bones, occurring as the spectators scrambled to avoid the flying debris. Three people had second and third degree burns from fireballs from the explosion and had been taken to the burn unit at Grady Memorial Hospital, one of the best in the southeast. A half-dozen other medical centers in the Atlanta area had been mobilized to accept the injured.

Patrick Cannon lost his right hand. Doctors considered trying to reattach it since it had been recovered at the accident site, but it was mangled, and bones broken because it had been stepped on multiple times during the chaos. Kris and Marcus were being hailed as heroes because their prompt attention likely saved Patrick's life. There were similar stories of heroic efforts of people neglecting their own injuries to help others, including a rival reporter who was frequently at odds with Kris, but who had worked with Marcus to curtail Kris' bleeding.

Kris was fortunate. In throwing up his arms to shield his face, he had exposed the brachial artery which runs down the underside of the arm. The hurling rotor blade had missed that artery by fractions of an inch. A direct hit on that artery would have meant Kris would have bled to death in moments, leaving anyone helpless to do anything to save him. The close call with the artery made the litany of small cuts and bruises Kris had sustained inconsequential. He was out of the emergency room in four hours after a tetanus shot, forty stitches in his left arm, and a prescription for a thirty-day supply of antibiotic pills that were only slightly smaller than a marble. He had also been given a prescription for Percocet which he had no intention of using. The ER doctors told him to chill out for a few days, something else he had no intention of doing.

Kris was completely comfortable conducting interviews, but he was totally uncomfortable being interviewed. In the hours and days following the helicopter tragedy, he was having cameras stuck in his face, pocket tape recorders shoved near his nose and print reporters scribbling down his responses to their endless questions. He did not want to be questioned, but he was all too familiar with sources being uncooperative as he was trying to get information for a story. He did not want to be one of those jerks, so he grudgingly but cordially answered all questions from everyone who was asking. He felt uncomfortable watching himself being interviewed on the local TV stations and seeing his name in the newspaper in the body of a story rather than as a byline.

There were some questions he refused to answer. He did not mind talking about the chaos of that day, the heroic actions of others – he tried to deflect any talk of him being a hero – or the amazing response of the City's emergency and medical response teams. What he would not be drawn into a discussion about was the handling of the robbery and hostage situation by the police and Mayor. He was not about to get sucked into any type of political debate as to whether there would not have been such a tragic ending had the situation been handled differently. That would be for people with a higher pay grade for him to decide, but he did hope he would get to report on their findings.

Kris thought continually about Mayor Robertson's actions. Trying to hop onto a helicopter taking off was not heroic; it was stupid, a suicide mission. Kris tried to put himself in the Mayor's shoes. Would he have done the same thing? He did not have children, but would he have put his own life on the line if Julia had been his child? No matter how many times he pondered this, Kris always came up with the same answer. Of course he would!

Mayor Robertson was not universally liked; that was not possible in a city the size of Atlanta and with the problems it had. Some media outlets in the city were trying to make the incident on Swisher Street a referendum on the Mayor's term in office. Kris would have none of that and considered anyone who tried to do so a journalistic scumbag. Kris was a believer in good, hard-nosed reporting but he also felt that cut-throat competition to get a story that no one else had made too many reporters go far past the tenants of ethical reporting. Kris believed the focus now should be on the City Council President being sworn in as Mayor, and what her immediate actions would be.

The most tragic part of the story was the loss of Julie Robertson and Joe Pitcock, the helicopter pilot. Julie was truly a good kid, an Honor Student at UVA in pre-med and very active in her Atlanta and Charlottesville communities. Unlike her father, she had no taste for politics or government, and directed her efforts to endeavors like literacy and feeding the hungry. She was a young person with the potential to impact lives and change the world.

Joe Pitcock was a true patriot, a third-generation soldier who had saved hundreds of lives by extracting them from harm's way. He had been shot down twice, surviving both but breaking a leg in one and suffering a shoulder wound from anti-aircraft fire in the other. He came home with the Purple Heart and the gratitude of all the soldiers he had rescued. Two years earlier, his tour of duty ended, and he had returned to the Atlanta suburb of Sandy Springs and gone to work for SkyHawk Air Services. Friends said he had a girlfriend and was getting ready to propose.

Research on Marlon Turrentine showed he had been in and out of trouble with the law his entire life. He was thirty-four years old and had been arrested for everything from loitering to simple battery to drug possession. He had never held a steady job and had no permanent place of residence. There were records that several charities, churches and social service agencies had tried to help him, but he wasn't receptive. The courts and other agencies could not or would not keep him off the streets, and the result was that innocent people had died.

Two days after the disaster, Kris visited Patrick Cannon. Patrick was in amazingly good spirits. His stay in the hospital would not be lengthy and he had already been assigned to one of Atlanta's premier occupational therapy clinics. Patrick was watching the Atlanta Braves play the New York Mets on the TV anchored on the wall across his bed. "Their bullpen is bad," Patrick mumbled about the Braves.

"How are you feeling?" Kris asked, not sure what to say or ask.

"I'm not available to pitch the ninth," Patrick smiled weakly as he held up his bandaged right arm. The sight almost made Kris sick to his stomach.

"You look a little pale," Patrick said.

Words lodged in Kris' throat. Patrick noticed Kris staring at the spot where his right hand should have been attached to the wrist.

Patrick assured Kris. "I am fine," he said. "The Good Lord has chosen to keep me alive. Missing a hand is only a minor setback."

"Does it hurt?"

"Only when I laugh," Patrick joked.

Kris didn't respond.

"No, it doesn't hurt," Patrick continued. 'They have some wonderful medicine here."

Kris was wearing a long-sleeved white dress shirt so Patrick couldn't see the stitches. Doctors had suggested Kris use a sling, but he wanted no part of that. "What about you? Are you O.K.?" Patrick asked.

"Yeah, I'm O.K. The arm hurts and I'm sore all over but I'm O.K."

Patrick squirmed and sat up in the bed. "You saved my life, man. How can I ever repay you?"

"Don't worry about that. You do not owe me anything. I just did what any self-respecting hero would have done," Kris kidded.

Patrick turned serious. "I mean it Kris. If you ever need me, I will be there. You can count on it."

"I know. I appreciate it. What is management at Channel 12 saying about all of this?"

"All the right things so far. They have promised to pay whatever bills our group insurance does not cover. We will see. I don't know that I have ever seen a one-handed TV reporter."

Kris glanced at the TV. A Braves' relief pitcher had just allowed a three-run homer. "I see what you mean about the bullpen," Kris groaned.

"What about you?" Patrick asked. "Are you ready to go back to work?"

"I want to go back to work but I'm a little shaky. I may take a few days off. The doctors want me to. The paper is pressing me to take it easy. I suppose I can do that. I am not sure what I'll do during that time, but I should be able to find something to do."

"I'm sure Emmy won't mind you taking some time off. I bet she can keep you busy. The station has told me to take my time getting back. That's good because I am going to need some help trying to figure out how to do things with this stump and my left hand. But I believe they might want me back quickly. It would be great for ratings. Everyone will want to tune in to see the one-handed guy."

His friend's humor about the situation impressed Kris who did not see anything funny about Patrick's situation.

3

Emmy Owens knew Kris' thoughts were elsewhere. He was uncharacteristically quiet and had hardly touched the chicken parmesan which was one of his favorite entrees. Emmy took a sip of her sweet, iced tea and studied Kris' pale face. His eyes were weak and tired. "Is your arm hurting?" she asked.

"It's hurting."

"Have you taken a pain pill?"

"No, and I'm not going to. They mess up my mind. Besides, it's not the physical pain that is bothering me."

"What do you mean?"

"The doctor said I was less than a quarter-inch from slicing an artery and bleeding out, right there on the street. I didn't but Patrick lost his hand. Why did he lose his hand while all I got was a fixable gash? We were within inches of each other. Why did we survive the explosion while people around us died or were severely injured?" Everything about Kris at that moment – his eyes, body language, tone – told Emmy he was agonizing over those questions. Time, rather than separating Kris from the events of that day, had made him more introspective. His interest in going back to work had been replaced by a hesitancy, a doubt.

Emmy got up from the small wooden table in the cramped dining nook of Kris' apartment and stood behind him rubbing his shoulders. Her long blonde hair was pulled back into a ponytail. She was wearing a form-fitting white t-shirt that showed the outline of her bra and tight blue jeans that clung to her long shapely legs. She was barefoot. Her fingernails and toenails were painted a subdued crimson and a two-carat diamond engagement ring sparkled on her left hand. "Baby, I can't answer your questions," she started. "No one can. Just be thankful that no more people were killed. It could have been much worse. And be thankful that God spared you and Patrick.

He obviously has a plan for both of you. Both of you will heal and be able to go back to work."

"I wish He would reveal that plan to me. I don't know if I can go back to work. Is reporting what I am supposed to be doing? I don't know if I can handle it, the next time I'm told to go on a police call. I keep replaying that day over and over in my mind. I wake up seeing that chopper blade coming straight at me – and then I wake up in a sweat."

Emmy continued to rub Kris' shoulders. "You will be fine. It just takes time," she said assuredly. "You were born to be a writer, Kris. It's in your blood. I can't imagine you doing anything else. And I think Atlanta is just the first stop for you in what is going to be a great, great career. You are going to be a nationally known journalist who writes best-selling novels on the side. You're going to be famous – and rich."

With his right hand Kris carefully reached back and touched her left hand which was resting on his shoulder. "Don't get carried away," he gently chided her. "For now, I've got to concentrate on getting in the frame of mind to go back to work. I can't stop thinking about Patrick. Channel 12 is so image conscious. They cater to a young audience. Are they going to want a fifty-five-year-old, gray-haired, slightly overweight one-handed reporter? In fact, even without this injury, I am surprised they have stuck with Patrick this long. He may have given his last report for Channel 12."

"They won't be that heartless, that cruel. Patrick…"

Kris interrupted her. "Don't count on that. Compassion takes a back seat to ratings. There might be an initial spike in the ratings when he comes back because of the morbid curiosity of people, but my guess is they will dump him as soon as it is conveniently possible to avoid a discrimination lawsuit and not create a public relations nightmare."

Emmy continued. "Patrick will be all right. He's a pro. Someone will hire him. He's a great reporter. He's got the awards to prove it. Come on. Let's get all of that out of our mind. Let's sit on the sofa. I'll clear the table and do the dishes later."

Emmy softly kissed Kris and led him to the sofa in the den of the 900 square-foot apartment in Midtown Atlanta. They sat down and she snuggled her head on his right shoulder reminding him, "You know people are calling you a hero, don't you? If you and Marcus had not acted so quickly, Patrick would have bled to death. You ignored your own injury to save him."

"I am not a hero. Do not give me so much credit. I did not realize I was cut. I was so focused on Patrick. I cannot tell you what a sickening sight it was to see blood gushing from that stump on his right arm. That could have been me. The people who died – that could have been me. And I cannot stop thinking about Chief Daniels too. He was a good guy, always extremely helpful to me."

"I hate that this is bothering you so much. I wish there were something I could do. I wish there were something I could say."

"I could have been killed Emmy. I didn't think about it much for the first few days afterwards but as things settled down, I realized what all had happened. I could have died, Emmy," Kris repeated. "The chopper blade could have decapitated me, and I can't get that out of my mind! That's not in a reporter's job description unless you are embedded in a combat unit." He looked down at his bandaged upper left arm which was hidden by his standard white long-sleeved dress shirt that was rolled up to the elbows. Like Emmy, he was wearing jeans and was barefoot.

Emmy felt a shiver run through Kris' body and she softly stroked his chest. "But you are still here! That's the important thing. Don't be in a rush to get back to work. Take some more time off. Let's get away for a long weekend. Your editor won't mind. Find a counselor to talk to through the paper's Employee Assistance Program. Plus, you can get your mind off all of this by helping me pick out some more things for our wedding and reception."

"No. I will leave that to you and your parents. I need to get back to work. I've got to get out of this funk and the best way to do that is to get back to work. I don't back down from challenges and trying to get back into a normal routine after all of this is going to be one."

"You can do it, but don't think you have to do this by yourself. I'll be with you every step as will your friends and co-workers." Emmy rubbed the back of Kris' neck. "Just remember. You were born to be a reporter, a writer. You still have great stories to share with the world."

"It's all I ever wanted to do. I love being in the middle of things. I love knowing what's going on and bringing down the crooks and bad guys. Or at least I did until I almost got killed by a stray helicopter blade."

"Don't kid yourself. You still do. And I know all the ideas you have for novels. Why don't you get started on that?"

"Maybe, but right now reporting is paying the bills. Besides I'm not in much of a creative mood right now."

Emmy sat up, smiled at Kris and rubbed his cheek with the back of her soft hand. "It will come back. I just want to see you happy, energized and chomping at the bit again. I know it's easier said than done, but you can move past this Kris. Things happen for a reason."

"I'm not sure Patrick would agree with that."

"I want to see you in a better frame of mind for another reason," she said softly while rubbing her index finger down the middle of Kris' chest.

"And that would be..."

"We haven't made love in several days. I want to make love to a hero."

They started to kiss but Kris' cell phone on the end table next to the sofa rang. Emmy gently pushed Kris back and retrieved his phone and answered.

"Some guy named Lonnie Jackson. Says he's police chief in Fort Phillips."

"Lonnie? Crap! What has Vance done now?" Kris sat up and took the phone from Emmy. Kris sighed before half-heartedly asking, "Hey Lonnie. What's going on?"

"Hey hero. We saw you down here on the news. How's the arm?"

"It hurts. I wouldn't be able to whip your ass in one-on-one basketball tonight, but I will be fine. What's going on?" Kris knew Lonnie Jackson was not calling to check on his health.

"That was awful about the Mayor and his daughter."

Kris and Lonnie had never been partners in small talk. Kris wanted Lonnie to get to the point of the call. "What's going on Lonnie? What's Vance done now?"

"I've got some bad news for you."

"I figured as much. What is it this time?'

"I'm sorry Kris."

"Spit it out Lonnie."

"Kris, Vance is dead. He committed suicide. He shot himself."

"Damn it!" Kris screamed. He bit his bottom lip almost hard enough to puncture it and looked at the ceiling.

Emmy asked, "What's wrong?"

Kris didn't answer. He stood up and walked to the far side of the room. He looked down at the floor before finally asking Lonnie, "How? Where? When?"

"A couple of days ago. At your house, in his bedroom. Stuck a .12-gauge shotgun to his forehead and pulled the trigger. Don't worry Kris. We've cleaned up the mess."

"Why didn't you call me sooner?"

"Just found his body earlier today. The exterminator who was doing the monthly treatment found him. You know Vance never locked the door. It's a good thing the bug man came by. Otherwise, no telling when we would have found him. You know how bad Vance was about disappearing and being gone for days at a time. No one would have thought anything about not seeing him for a while."

"I know. I lived with him for 18 years."

"Is there anything I can do Kris?"

"No, not now. Have you called my sister?"

"No. I thought you would want to call Becky yourself."

"Thanks. I will. There is one thing you can do. Let Montgomery's Funeral Home know I'll be there tomorrow to make arrangements."

"Will do. I'm sorry Kris. I am really sorry. I think deep-down Vance was a good guy. He just never could defeat his personal demons. Are you all right?"

Kris lowered his head and was silent. He finally responded to Lonnie. "Yeah, I'm O.K. Thanks Lonnie. I appreciate it. I'll see you tomorrow."

Kris returned to the sofa and fired his phone into a fat decorative pillow. Emmy sat beside him and again asked, "What's wrong?"

"You were telling me to take a few more days off," he started. "Looks like I'm going to be doing that but not to help you with the wedding. My old man killed himself."

"Oh no Kris! How awful! I'm so sorry Baby!" She hugged him softly to avoid hurting his bandaged arm.

"That's so damn typical of him!" Kris said angrily.

Emmy leaned away from him and asked, "That's a strange thing to say. What do you mean?"

"Because as usual he was only thinking of himself. He gave no thought about what this would do to me or Becky or other people. He never gave any thought to what his behavior was doing to other people. All he was interested in was being with his drinking and gambling buddies. Someone, usually me, had to come behind him and clean up the messes he made. He was the most selfish son of a bitch I ever knew."

"This isn't the time to be saying those things, Kris."

"Why not? It's the truth. He's gone now and again he's left a mess for someone else to clean up."

"But he was your dad."

"Biologically only."

"Don't you have any feelings for him?"

"You want the truth? No, I don't have any feelings for him. On second thought, I do. But they're all negative. Being blunt, I hate his guts. Becky is the same way. I bet she doesn't even come to the funeral. She shouldn't. There's no reason for her to travel across country for the funeral of someone she doesn't love or respect."

Emmy put her hands on her knees and sighed. "I'm sorry Kris. I am. I'm sorry that you never made peace with your dad. I'm afraid that this is going to eat at you. More so than what happened on Swisher Street a few days ago."

"I don't think so. Regardless, I've got to go to Fort Phillips tomorrow. I hate to ask this Emmy, but can you go with me? I don't think I'm up to driving that far yet."

"Of course I'll go with you. I'll call the leasing office first thing in the morning. I'll stay with you as long as you need me. Besides, it will be interesting to see your hometown. You have told me so little about it and what you have told me is mostly bad. I just wish we were going under different circumstances."

Kris smiled weakly and caressed her ponytail. "You're the best. I love you," he whispered. A tear welled in the corner of his right eye, but it was for the pain in his left arm rather than the man who had just blown his brains out.

4

Kris didn't say a dozen words on the two hundred-and-twenty-five-mile drive to Fort Phillips, a stale community of 1,600 hugging the Alabama border deep in southwest Georgia. He was not happy about having to make this trip. His visits home had been as infrequent as a curse word uttered by a Southern Baptist preacher. In the ten years since he left Fort Phillips to attend the University of West Georgia, Kris had returned home five times – once to bury his mother, once to be a pallbearer at the funeral of a high school classmate, and three times to bail Vance out of trouble. It wasn't that he didn't like the town. The people had always been kind and gracious and proud of the local boy who made good, and his high school days had been filled with good friends, academic honors and a spot on the All-Region basketball team as a shooting guard his senior year. The problem was Kris' recollections of his father's drunken binges, week-long disappearances and gambling addiction far outweighed the good memories. But as Kris had frustratingly learned since leaving home, he could never be totally divorced from his father's demons. That is, until now, when he was headed home to get Vance's butt out of a mess one final time.

Emmy was driving. Early in the journey she had tried to engage in chit chat. They were not too far down the road before she realized Kris was absorbed in his own thoughts. Wisely, she turned up the radio, took in the scenery in a part of the state she claimed to know little about and allowed Kris to ponder silently about his father, the explosion in Atlanta or whatever other demons of his own he was battling. She suspected most of Kris' thoughts were consumed at this moment with Vance. Kris had yet to share many details about his father, but she knew enough to understand their relationship was big-time dysfunctional. Since getting the call from Lonnie Jackson, Kris' mantra had been, "All I want to do is get this over with."

Continuing to try to make innocent conversation, Emmy asked Kris about Fort Phillips and the origin of the name. She could not think of many towns with *Fort* in the name. Fort Myers in Florida and Fort Collins in Colorado were the two that came to mind. She had vacationed once on Sanibel Island near Fort Myers and had once worked with a guy who graduated from Colorado State University in Fort Collins. Fort Worth and Fort Wayne were two others that slowly came to mind.

Kris readjusted in his seat and began explaining, "It goes back to the Civil War. Sometime around 1859 or 1860, a group of fifteen families pooled their meager resources and purchased land in the southwest part of Georgia. The soil was fertile, and several small creeks offered a good water supply. Life was good for them. Their gardens flourished, there was plenty of wild game to supply meat, and all the families helped each other build their houses."

Kris paused momentarily as they drove past a large pasture filled with cattle. He resumed his story. "The war started, and the village got word about what Sherman had done to Atlanta, and that he was headed south and was going to destroy everything in his path. The families were determined they were not going to give up what they had worked so hard to build without a fight. They constructed watch towers and fortifications with trees hewn from the abundant forests."

"Well, you know communication wasn't the best in those days and was as slow as molasses, and it took a long time for the settlers go get the word that Sherman had headed east to Savannah and wouldn't come within one hundred miles of them. But they were proud of their efforts to protect their property and decided to name their little community Fort Phillips. They got the *fort* part from the fortification walls they built and *Phillips* from Jacob Phillips, the man who had taken the lead in organizing the protection. Thus, the name Fort Phillips. All of this is on a historical marker on the outskirts of what is now the town of Fort Phillips. The marker is on the banks of Maple Creek."

Emmy smiled. "An interesting story," she said, keeping her eyes on the narrow two-lane road.

"There's more," Kris said. "The newspaper in Fort Phillips is the *Sentinel.* It got its name from the people in the village who stood vigil watching for the Yankees. They were sentinels. Some of those people were ancestors of Mr. Carter Floyd, owner of the Sentinel and my mentor. He's a man I to whom I owe a great deal."

Obeying the 35 miles per hour speed limit, they cruised into Fort Phillips with Kris directing Emmy straight to Montgomery Funeral Home which was two blocks from the main business district or more appropriately, what was left of it. They were greeted by Mickey Montgomery, two years Kris' elder who was now handling much of the day-to-day operations of the business for his father who had finally decided to enjoy life after 35 years of dealing with dead people. Mr. Montgomery had always joked that the dead people were easier to deal with than their relatives.

"Good to see you, Kris. I am sorry for your loss," offered Mickey in his most professional funeral director manner. He led them to an office which had once been a study in the massive, two-story converted old house that had been in the Montgomery family since the turn of the century. Mickey tried to start a "long time, no see" conversation but Kris wanted no part of it. Kris introduced Emmy as his fiancée and asked if they could get on with the business of planning his father's burial. Mickey, who was also the elected county coroner, wanted to know more about the helicopter crash and the tragedy at the bank.

Trying not to let his agitation show, Kris said bluntly, "It should have never happened. The Mayor had no business trying to play hero. Had he stayed out of the way and let the people do their job, several people – including himself and his daughter – would still be alive." With the remarks, Kris realized he was doing what he pledged he would not – be a critic of the way the situation at the bank was handled.

"You're right. But who is to say we wouldn't have done the same thing if it had been our daughter? My little girl is only two but there's nothing I wouldn't do to keep her safe." Adding a little out-of-place humor, Mickey added, "Of course, since high school I have lost a lot of my vertical jump. There's no way I could leap high enough to grab the skid of a helicopter taking off."

Kris moaned and was silent a moment before replying. "Maybe so, but I've got a couple of years before I have to worry about taking care of kids," Kris replied, winking at a smiling Emmy. Kris noticed Mickey sneaking frequent peeks at Emmy. Mickey had always been an admirer of the female figure which made his marriage to Fallon Holloway, who was chunky and had no figure, difficult to explain. Of course, Mickey was no hard body himself and Fallon was likely the best he could do and not even his family's money had helped him in his wifely pursuit.

"I guess they keep you busy up in Atlanta. We don't see you down here very often. How long has it been?" Mickey asked.

"More than a year. When Mom died. I guess 18 months. There's no reason for me to come back here…except…business like this."

"I understand but we miss you. I think Karen in particular misses you," Mickey admitted. Emmy shot Kris an inquiring look but he ignored her.

"I think about you guys on occasion, but I don't miss anything else about this place. I shouldn't say that. The people here have always been great to me. But the truth of the matter is, once I take care of Vance this final time, I doubt that I will ever return here – unless someone else dies or I sell the house and have to come back to sign papers."

"Don't say that," Emmy scolded.

"It's all right," Mickey quickly replied. "I don't blame him. I don't blame anyone for wanting to leave, especially the way things have been around here over the last few years."

Kris glanced at his watch. "I need to go ahead and take care of this," he said. "What's the cheapest, quickest way we can go?"

"Kris!" Emmy responded, much like a mother would when her child has said something improper.

"Cremation. It is relatively inexpensive, and we can still have a nice memorial service. Vance's body has not been returned by the state crime lab yet. Standard procedure for this type of situation but we can go ahead and make all the arrangements for the cremation and a memorial service."

"Why do we need a memorial service?"

"Vance did have some friends. I know they want to pay their respects."

"All right. Let's do it. How about tomorrow?" Ten o'clock?"

"That's pushing it. And what about Becky? She needs time to get here."

"She's not coming but she sends her regards."

"She's not coming for her father's funeral?"

"Nope. She had another appointment. I think she's getting her hair done."

Emmy glanced at the floor and shook her head. Looking up, she ordered in a voice just the slightest bit elevated, "O.K. Kris. That's enough. I'm sorry Mr. Montgomery. It's just that Kris has been through a lot lately." She patted Kris on his thigh. Kris didn't say anything but his look back at Emmy made it clear he didn't like her scolding him.

"It's all right, Miss Owens. I understand. Let's don't rush this. Kris, let's make it day after tomorrow at 10 a.m. That way we will be able to get the word out. I know there are a number of people who will want to attend."

"If they can get away from their card games," Kris mumbled. Emmy wanted to slap him.

Mickey started explaining, "One service we offer is a video. You select photos of your dad, your family, whatever you want, and we will make them into a nice keepsake that we will show during the service."

"We'll pass on that," Kris said immediately.

"No, we won't," Emmy replied emphatically. "We'll get you some photos Mr. Montgomery."

Kris didn't say anything knowing better than to argue with her. "I guess we can go to the house and see what we can come up with," he conceded.

"What about a pastor?" Mickey asked.

"Who in town talks the least?"

"James Riley at the Christian Church."

"He'll do."

"Music?"

"*Ninety-nine Beers on the Wall*, perhaps."

Emmy was fuming at Kris' insensitivity but she kept quiet.

"I don't think so," Mickey replied.

"*The Old Rugged Cross, Amazing Grace.* You know. A couple of the old favorites."

"O.K. I'll talk to Mrs. Johnson. She will be glad to play two or three on the organ."

"What is this going to cost?" Kris asked as he pulled his checkbook out of the right back pocket of his jeans.

"Did you father have insurance?"

"Hell no! Of course he didn't! He wouldn't even pay our utility bills much less set aside some money for insurance."

Mickey knew prices for everything off the top of his head and quickly produced a bill which Kris immediately paid with a check. Mickey explained, "After the cremation I'll give you Vance's ashes."

"Don't bother," Kris replied hatefully. "Give them to the animal shelter for kitty litter."

At that moment, a high-powered laser beam couldn't match the intensity of Emmy's stare at Kris. "You'll have to forgive Kris, Mr. Montgomery," Emmy apologized. "First the helicopter incident and now this with his father. Kris just hasn't been himself lately."

Kris stared back at Emmy, not sorry for what he said.

"It's O.K.," Mickey said in a calm, comforting tone. "I understand the Keller family dynamics."

The conversation ended. "It's good to see you," Mickey said sincerely after escorting Kris and Emmy to the front door. "You know what? I would love to get you out on the basketball court one last time for a game of one-on-one or HORSE. I would like one more chance to finally beat you before you say goodbye to this place forever."

"Sorry. I'm on the disabled list. Kris pointed to his arm.

Kris and Emmy slipped into her black BMW X5 and he gave her directions for the short drive to the Keller homeplace. "You have to forgive your father at some point Kris," Emmy urged. "Otherwise, it's going to make you miserable. Do you realize how ugly you were at the funeral home?"

"I guess I was. I just want to get this over with, get back to Atlanta and get married."

"By the way. Who is this Karen who is still pining for you? Have we ever talked about her?"

"Karen? We spent a lot of time together, had some good times. It was never very serious though. We always knew I was going off to college to get away from here and she was going to stay."

"Sounds like you may be over her a lot more than she's over you."

"She's married to Lonnie Jackson. Besides, I have the girl of my dreams."

They reached the small wooden house on Sims Street where Kris and Becky grew up. Vance's fifteen-year-old red Ford Ranger pick-up was parked in the cracking concrete driveway. The truck had a few visible small scratches, but otherwise it appeared in decent condition. The neighborhood was filled with modest, single-story houses that had been built in the 1960s and 1970s. Vance obviously had not been keen on upkeep. The grass was high and needed cutting; the house needed a coat of white paint and the left side of the roof had a patch of loose shingles. "I hate to see the inside," Kris moaned. "I hate to show you this place," he admitted to Emmy with embarrassment.

"Don't worry," she assured him. "It's part of your past. That's all I see it as. A part of your past."

Kris sighed as they stepped inside but he was shocked and pleasantly surprised. Other than being a little dusty, the house was presentable. Totally out-of-date and somewhat piled up but presentable. The lone bathroom was clean. The kitchen appliances were clean, but Kris was certain they were as old as he was. The refrigerator had none of the current bells and whistles and was opened by pulling on an inch-diameter pole that ran up and down the top third of the door.

"Can we see your room?" Emmy asked.

He led her down a narrow hallway past Becky's old room and into his. The first item Kris noticed was the police scanner perched on his dresser. "I wonder if this still works," Kris thought aloud. He blew dust off the top of the scanner and clicked the power knob. The crackling static and frequently difficult to understand voices of dispatchers filled the room.

"What is that?" Emmy asked.

"The sounds I went to sleep with every night," Kris smiled.

The room was typical teenage boy with dirty crème-colored drywall covered with posters for the Atlanta Braves, Georgia Tech Yellow Jackets and University of West Georgia Wolves. A half-dozen basketball trophies were on the top of a chest of drawers. An old nicked, scratched queen bed took up most of the space in the room. Every piece of furniture was as old as Kris. "The room is the same as when I left for school," Kris admitted, shaking his head.

"You were quite the stud, weren't you?" Emmy smiled. She pulled Kris toward her and kissed him.

"Miss Owens, are you trying to seduce me?"

She kissed him again. "Maybe. I think it would be very sexy to make love in your old room."

"But my arm…"

"I'll go easy on you. It's not your arm I'm interested in." They sat down on the bed and Emmy started unbuttoning his shirt. She gently pushed Kris down on the bed and crawled on top, being careful not to hurt his arm. Things were about to get interesting when they heard someone at the door clearing their throat.

"I hope I'm not interrupting anything," Lonnie Jackson smiled.

Emmy and Kris scrambled to sit up on the bed and straighten their clothes. "We were resting a few minutes. It has been a long day," Kris explained, totally irritated that Lonnie had simply walked into the house without knocking, calling out or giving any type of warning.

"I was driving by on routine patrol and saw the car. Nice car by the way."

"Thanks," Emmy replied.

"I figured you must have stopped by. Good to see you, Kris." Lonnie walked toward Kris who stood up, shook Lonnie's hand and introduced Emmy.

"I'm sorry about Vance. I wish there was something I could have done but I had not seen him in a week before this happened," Lonnie said.

"As messed up as his life has been, I don't guess we should be surprised. Do we have any idea why he would want to do this?"

"No. No note, no reason. Have you seen the bedroom? Come on."

Kris did not want to see the spot where his father had taken his life, but he dutifully followed Lonnie. Reluctantly, Emmy accompanied them. Other than a sizable, discolored spot on the hardwood floor there was no indication of what had taken place.

"I don't understand," Kris said solemnly as he studied the unsightly patch of flooring.

"No one understands when someone takes their own life," Lonnie said sympathetically. "Unless the person leaves a note, all the survivors can do is speculate about a reason."

Kris shook his head in opposition to Lonnie's comment. "That's not what I meant," he said.

"What *do* you mean?" Lonnie asked, scratching his head.

"The shotgun. It's the shotgun. Of all the methods Vance could have used to end his life, why did he choose a shotgun? Vance never owned a gun. I don't think he ever fired a gun of any type. Some of his buddies were hunters, but he never wanted any part of that. I am certain this room was a bloody mess, so again I ask, why the shotgun?" Kris ended as he surveyed the entire room.

Emmy put her hand over her mouth and left the room.

Lonnie shrugged his shoulders. "I don't have the answers to your questions," he said. "I can't tell you why Vance used a shotgun any more than I can tell you why he killed himself." Lonnie paused again before continuing. "You know as well as I how easy it is to get your hands on a gun. You can steal one, or even better, you can walk into any pawn shop and purchase any type of gun – pistol, rifle, shotgun.

As for knowing how to use a gun, well, that is easy. All you have to do is make sure it is loaded and pull the trigger."

Kris didn't verbally respond but a nod of his head indicated his agreement with Lonnie.

"Do you have the shotgun?" Kris asked Lonnie.

"I do," Lonnie responded.

"Have you tried to track down where it came from, how Vance got it?"

"No. I didn't see any reason for that. Where the gun came from was not important. What is was used for *was* important." Lonnie paused again. "I will tell you this. The serial number was sanded off the shotgun. That makes me believe Vance stole it."

Kris quickly rebutted Lonnie's theory. "Vance was a lot of things, but he was not a thief," Kris said emphatically.

"How can you say that for certain? You haven't been around here in ten years."

Not wanting to get into an argument with Lonnie about what appeared to be a half-ass investigation of Vance's death, Kris dropped the subject.

"Thanks for cleaning up," Kris said, trying to end the conversation.

"You are welcome. When is the funeral?"

"Day after tomorrow, 10 o'clock. Just a short memorial service."

"Are you are going to be around for a few days after the service?"

"As few as possible."

"There's bound to be some loose ends you need to handle relating to Vance…."

"There are *always* loose end with Vance," Kris interrupted.

Lonnie started over. "Have you stopped to think there might be a few people who want to see you?"

"No. I haven't thought about that. I just want to get this over."

"You've still got that chip on your shoulder, don't you? Too good for this sad little town."

"Don't start this again Lonnie. You and I have been through this before. Besides, you should be happy I'm gone."

"Yeah, I guess I am. But the fact remains there are some people in town who would like to see you. Karen in particular."

"We'll see. I do appreciate you cleaning up the mess here. Thank you. Send me a bill if necessary."

"Not a problem. I've got to get back to the office. I'll see you at the service."

Kris nodded.

Lonnie started to walk out but stopped. "Vance loved you; you know that don't you?"

"He had a hell of a strange way of showing it."

"He's dead Kris. Cut him some slack."

"I'll see you at the service," was Kris' brief reply. Lonnie left and Kris started back to his room, but he was met by Emmy in the hallway.

"What gives Kris? These people are trying so hard to be nice to you, but you are being a total ass."

"I just want to get this over with."

"Well let's try to be civil for a couple more days. Then it will be over, and we can leave."

"I'll try. I promise. After we look for the photos for that stupid video, there is one person here I really want to see and want you to meet."

"Karen?"

"No. Her father."

Emmy absolutely wanted to meet anyone who could get Kris out of his snit.

5

Rummaging through the Keller home place, Kris and Emmy discovered two shoe boxes full of family photos on a dusty metal shelf in the musty, cluttered unfinished basement. After two major sneezing spells, Kris was ready to quickly and randomly grab a handful of the photos, take them to Montgomery's for the memorial video, and mark one more chore off his bothersome list. Emmy would have none of that. She wanted to look through the two boxes slowly and meticulously, for her own benefit as much as Kris'. She hoped the photos would provide more insight into this brooding, unforgiving man she would soon be marrying. Perhaps they would offer some clue, some key, that she could use to help release Kris from his family albatross. Generally, Kris was cheerful and positive despite some of the vile events and people he had to report on. His character switched 180 degrees when anything came up about Vance.

Emmy wiped away as much of the dust as she could with her hand before taking the boxes upstairs where she cleaned them off with paper towels and set them on the bare wooden kitchen table. Kris joined her, reluctantly at first, but relaxed as they began sorting through the photos. Most of them featured Kris and Becky, from kindergarten all the way through their senior years in high school, in numerous poses and activities, and that brought back nice memories and faint smiles from Kris. His mother, an average-looking woman with a warm face that masked the heartache her husband had put her through, was in a few of the pictures, none from the months leading up to her fatal stroke 18 months earlier. Vance was in even fewer, making the task of finding some suitable for the video difficult. Emmy was saddened when she realized that out of the six or seven dozen photos, only five showed Vance with his children. She was impressed with how handsome Vance was in his younger days when most of the photos that included him were taken. Kris looked a lot like his father, with thick brown hair, penetrating brown eyes, a teasing half-smile and a sleek athletic body.

As he studied the photos of his dad, Kris felt empty, his eyes on the verge of misting. How sad it was that Vance, a socially awkward loner who had little formal education but could do many hands-on chores well, had totally wasted his life and sinfully neglected his family. Kris' pity quickly turned back to the ever-present bitterness. He could not get past the fact that Vance had been a lousy husband and father. "Enough of this!" he abruptly ordered Emmy. At this point, she knew better than to protest. With her making a few quick suggestions, Kris grabbed up each of the photos that included Vance and delivered them to Montgomery's. With that out of the way, Kris' demeanor changed dramatically as Emmy steered her car to the office of the Fort Phillips Sentinel, owned and operated by Kris' mentor Carter Floyd.

Little had changed for the better in Fort Phillips since Kris left, and that included the Sentinel office on Main Street, which was lined with old, in need of repair storefronts, many of which were already shut down or in danger of shutting down. The newspaper office needed painting ten years ago and it needed painting now. The *Fort Phillips Sentinel* lettering on the front window was peeling and needed touching up, but it still looked wonderful to Kris. His happiest times in his hometown came when he was working for Mr. Floyd all through high school, reporting on everything from recreation league basketball to middle school beauty pageants on the Fourth of July. "Come on," Kris invited Emmy as he softly grasped her hand and in gentlemanly fashion led her from the car into the Sentinel office. "I want you to meet the man who was more my father than my father."

No one was at the old metal desk tucked away in the corner of the small reception area, which Kris thought was unusual. Mr. Floyd was a stickler for having a smiling face to greet everyone who came to the office to renew their subscription or bring news about the birth of a grandson or the calling of a new preacher at one of the little local churches. Kris' soft *hello* did not bring a response. His second *hello*, much louder, elicited a *Coming!* from the back office.

"Can I help...Kris? My god!" Karen Jackson exclaimed as she came around a corner into the reception area. She headed directly for him and embraced him in a hug so tight that none of the local high school wrestlers could have escaped. A sharp pain shot through his injured arm. "It is so good to see you!" she smiled widely, finally letting go. Kris wanted to rub his arm but didn't.

"You too," Kris replied. He thought Karen looked weary.

"I'm sorry about Vance. We were all shocked."

"Thanks. The memorial service is day after tomorrow. Ten o'clock."

"How long has it been since you've been home?"

"A long time. Since Mother died."

Tired of waiting for Kris to introduce her, Emmy spoke out. Extending her hand to Karen, she announced, "Hi. I'm Emmy Owens. Kris' fiancée."

"Karen Jackson." She quickly shook Emmy's hand, hardly looking at her, and returned her attention to Kris. "Come in the back and sit down. We've got a lot of catching up to do."

"We came by to see your dad. I want Emmy to meet him."

"You haven't heard?" Karen asked, visibly surprised at Kris' comment.

"No. What?" Kris replied.

"Dad's not doing well. Seventy years of smoking finally started getting to him. He started smoking when he was eight, you know. His heart and lungs are about to give out. He could go at any time."

"I'm sorry, Karen. I didn't know. If I had, I would have been to see him sooner." Kris was visibly upset. Emmy put her arm around Kris' waist. Even though she had never met Mr. Floyd, that seemed the least she could do to comfort Kris.

"Dad's not having a particularly good day today, but I know he would want to see you. If you're going to be around for a few days, go by the house and see him."

"Absolutely. So..." Kris started to ask, gesturing with his right hand, "...who's taking care of the Sentinel?"

"Come on. Let's sit down," Karen suggested as she led Kris and Emmy to a closet-sized breakroom in the back of the building. She pulled a Diet Coke out of the minifridge for slender Emmy and Classic Cokes for herself and Kris as they sat down at a small round table which was every bit as old as the furniture in Kris' bedroom in the house on Sims Street.

After they had all taken a few sips of their beverages, Karen began bringing Kris up to date. A new bypass had taken practically all the traffic away from the downtown stretch of Fort Phillips, killing several businesses and putting others on life support. There had been no need for the bypass, but the local state legislator got it built as a favor to a prominent landowner who thought the new road would enhance the value of acres of vacant land he owned.

Once, decades ago, Fort Phillips was a thriving little town anchored by Simpson Slacks Manufacturers. There were a couple of smaller men's suit manufacturers, clothing outlet stores and mom and pop shops of all types from shoes to apparel to five and dimes. The bulk of the population worked at Simpson Slacks and made a decent living. But if you were short of money and needed new clothes to wear to a special event, you could go to Mrs. Burrell's dress shop and she would hook you up with some credit, on your promise to pay out of your next check. The town slowly began to die, however, first because of cheap imported foreign goods, big box stores in nearby larger towns and then the bypass. Now, the heart of Fort Phillips had been reduced to pawn shops, antique stores, Amigo's Mexican Restaurant, Pete's Hamburger Place and Granny's all-you-can-eat home style buffet.

"It has hurt us too," Karen said of the Sentinel. "Advertising is way down. I'm the staff. Me and a couple of part-timers. That's all we can afford. I would really like to shut this place down, or sell it, but I can't. That would kill Dad faster than all his physical problems. In the meantime, it's killing me. I'm working myself to death."

"I can see," Kris nodded in agreement, realizing he probably should not have made that comment. Karen seemed hurt by Kris' reflection on her appearance. "Any signs of improvement? Is Fort

Phillips growing any?" Kris asked, trying to quickly divert the conversation in another direction.

"No. Bainbridge is doing all right and so is Camilla but not us. This place is as dead as a doorknob. The only positive thing to happen here lately is that some type of distribution center, I think, moved into the old Simpson Slacks plant. That brought some new property tax revenue to the town but that's about all. They are not involved in the community and didn't hire anyone locally. We see their trucks come and go in and out of the building, but they are unmarked. What they saw in that old place is beyond me. It's about to fall apart and they have made no improvements."

Emmy was suddenly having trouble catching her breath, feeling a bit claustrophobic in the tiny room and being the third person in a two-person conversation. "Excuse me," she requested as she slid away from her chair. I need some air. I'll wait out front, Honey. Take your time."

"Are you O.K.?" Kris asked, touching her arm.

"Yes," she smiled weakly. "I'm just feeling a little flushed. Go ahead and finish your conversation." She walked out of the Sentinel office, and even though the August air was stagnant and muggy, it sucked into her nostrils much easier than the newspaper stench inside. Emmy sat in the car, turned on the air conditioning and began to think like Kris. She was ready for all of this to be over with.

6

Kris emerged from the Sentinel office 45 minutes after Emmy. Her irritation with him boiled over immediately. "It's bad enough that you left me out in this hot sun to bake," she fumed. "Worse than that, I suddenly became invisible! From the second Karen came hopping into your arms, it was like I fell off the edge of the earth. You weren't even going to introduce me. And she hardly acknowledged me! It was embarrassing, Kris!"

"I'm sorry," Kris responded meekly. "How long have you been out here?" He glanced at his watch.

"Too long. I've burned a quarter of a tank of gas keeping the air conditioning on in the car so my makeup wouldn't run."

"You could have stayed inside."

"Oh no I couldn't. That tiny room and the newspaper smell were getting to me. I would have passed out."

"I'm sorry," he repeated. "We had a lot of catching up to do. I wanted to know more about her dad, and she wanted to know about the bank robbery and the helicopter crash – and my arm." Kris gingerly rubbed over his bandaged wound.

"Did she want to know anything about me?" Emmy asked, her irritation obvious.

Kris started to laugh at Emmy's frustrations but thought better. "You're over-reacting, big time," he told her. "And do I detect just a hint of jealousy, Miss Owens?" Kris smiled at Emmy and lifted her chin with his index finger.

She sighed. "Maybe. I'm tired and I'm hot and I'm hungry. Let's get something to eat."

"Good idea. Mexican, an all-you-can-eat country style buffet or Pete's Hamburger Place. Pete's got a guarantee. If his burger isn't the greasiest you've ever eaten, you get your choice of an extra-large bottle of Rolaids or your money back."

"Let's try our chances with Mexican."

"O.K. It's two blocks down on the left. Let's leave the car here and walk. I'll give you a grand tour of the Fort Phillips business district."

Emmy quickly shot down the idea of walking, pointing out that not only would her makeup start running, but she would begin to perspire as well. "I'll drive slowly," she told Kris. They inched past a ladies' boutique that was vacant and a small furniture store that was having a going out of business sale. Amigos seemed to be in the same sad plight. Only two other couples were dining at a time the place should have been full.

They sat in a booth toward the back of the restaurant. Kris started munching on chips and salsa while Emmy went to the ladies' room to freshen up. To her, the restroom was dark, depressing and unsanitary and she did her business as quicky as possible. She was going to complain about the condition of the restroom to Kris until she had her first bite of chips and salsa. "It's stale," she grumbled. Catching the attention of their waiter Roberto – his name was embroidered on his blue shirt – Kris requested more fresh chips. Emmy ordered her usual – cheese nachos and a margarita while Kris ordered Combo Dinner Number Three and a Bud Light. "There's no tequila in this drink," Emmy groused.

Happier with the fresh chips and a replacement drink with more booze, Emmy settled in and apologized to Kris for being so edgy. He quickly rebuked her. "I should be the one apologizing," he readily admitted. "I'm sorry. I do admit it was nice to see Karen. In fact, I'm surprised myself at how much I enjoyed seeing her."

Emmy squirmed uncomfortably in the patched red vinyl seat. "So, do I have a reason to be jealous? Has this trip brought back old feelings? She is a pretty girl, Kris, with that curly brown hair and hazel eyes. Maybe ten pounds too heavy, but I'd say she's still hot."

"I didn't pay any attention to how she looked," Kris said with a shrug of the shoulders.

"Bull hockey!" Emmy bellowed. She realized how loudly she had blurted out and looked around to see if anyone had noticed. They had not. "You gave her the once-over, from her painted toenails to that one stray curl on the very top of her head, and with a quick glance at her boobs in between. Don't tell me you didn't notice how she looks."

A big smile stretched across Kris' face, and then he started laughing. After a second, Emmy started laughing too.

Still smiling, Kris reached across the table and gently took hold of Emmy's hands. "I love *you*!" He stated emphatically. "You have no competition. From the moment I first interviewed you for that real estate article, you had me hooked. I'm bewitched, bothered, bewildered, however you want to describe it."

His admission made Emmy smile. "Hmmm. Good title for a song. Someone should write it. I feel the same way, Kris, and I readily admit my first glimpse of you made me want to go to bed with you. Right then, right there!"

"In other word, I'm just your sex object."

"Do you have a problem with being my boy toy?"

"Oh no, and please believe me. I have no interest in Karen," Kris said emphatically. He paused as Roberto delivered their dinner. They both took first bites and were pleased although Emmy pointed out the cheese on her nachos was just a tad too spicy. Pausing after taking a swallow of his beer, Kris explained, "And as for Fort Phillips, I don't hate this place, but my thoughts about my dad cannot be separated from the town, so my thoughts about this town tend to be bad, tend to make me angry. It shouldn't be that way, but it is."

"What happened between you and Karen?"

"Do you really want to know?"

"Yes, or I wouldn't have asked."

"Karen and I were boyfriend and girlfriend through most of high school. We were close. I'm not going to lie to you about that. Her dad had our lives all planned out. Karen and I were going to get married; Mr. Floyd was going to retire, and Karen and I would take over the Sentinel, raise some cub reporters, and live happily ever after. Well, I love Mr. Floyd and I would not be where I am in my career if it weren't for him, but I never had any intention of staying here and running the Sentinel. No way, no how. And the way the town is now?

Well, it makes me sad, but it also makes me realize I made the right decision to leave."

"But did you love Karen?"

"Uh, maybe. I don't know. We were both young. I am not sure we really knew what love was. Honestly, it was harder for me to leave Fort Phillips because of Mr. Floyd than Karen. I owe a lot to that man."

"You and Karen parted peacefully?"

"I didn't say that. She got mad and upset and we yelled and screamed at each other. From the very beginning she knew what my plans were, but when it finally came time for me to leave, she didn't take it very well. I went to the University of West Georgia. I had an opportunity to play basketball there, but I started stringing for newspapers in the small towns close to campus and never had time to be part of the team and the practice and traveling it required. I left Fort Phillips and Karen stayed here and helped her dad and ended up marrying Lonnie Jackson which I thought was interesting because in high school, she would not give him the time of day. She started telling some of her friends that she settled for Lonnie, that he was the next best thing left in Fort Phillips and a poor second to me. Needless to say, that didn't make him happy. Sure as heck strained my relations with Lonnie. He and I were never big buddies but we played a lot of ball together."

"I can see where that would not set well with Lonnie," Emmy said, her eyes studying Kris' face.

"But I do care enough about Karen to want to know what's going on with her and her father. That's why I took so long back at the Sentinel, and that's why I've got to go by and see Mr. Floyd before we go back to Atlanta."

"I understand. I want to meet him."

"I want you to meet him. Where do you want to stay tonight? At one of our zero-star motels or at my old house?"

Emmy paused, taking another bite of her nachos. "Well, I think it could be creepy staying at your house, considering what your father did there, but at the same time, I'm not attracted to the other lodging options. I believe it might be just a step above sleeping outdoors in a tent."

"We'll go to the house. We'll stop at Fast Mart on the way and get some snacks and soft drinks."

"It will be kind of neat, sleeping together in your old room. But you know I believe in ghosts and spirits. I'm afraid your dad's spirit may still be wandering around that house, wanting to make peace with you. Will you cuddle me and hold me close?"

"But Miss Owens," Kris said in mock seriousness. "Ghosts or no ghosts, I'm afraid you may try to take advantage of me."

"You can count on it. I will make you forget about Karen in an instant," Emmy quickly responded before stuffing a nacho in her mouth.

7

Later that evening at the Keller house, Emmy violated her sacred rule of not eating after 7 p.m. Long-time neighbor Alice Hunter brought over an iced pound cake with her *I'm sorry about your father* speech. Kris did not buy her sympathy. He knew Mrs. Hunter had no use for Vance, and had bad-mouthed him for years, even trying to persuade Kris' mother to leave him. But Kris graciously accepted her regrets – and her pound cake – and spent 15 obligatory minutes briefing Mrs. Hunter on his career and impending marriage and asking about her two grown children who had also left Fort Phillips. Her children seldom came back to visit, a matter that did not please Mrs. Hunter and didn't interest Kris. She finally left, and Kris and Emmy immediately attacked the pound cake, devouring large slices as they watched the cable TV broadcast of the Atlanta Braves blowing a ninth inning lead and losing to the Pittsburgh Pirates. Kris smiled as he recalled Patrick Cannon's gripes about the Atlanta team's bullpen. Emmy finished her piece of cake and one more forkful but resisted the urge for a second whole slice. Kris consumed a second and part of a third and washed it all down with Coke.

Tired from the long day and with their bellies full of pound cake, Kris and Emmy prepared for bed. Kris stretched out in his usual t-shirt and boxer briefs, and Emmy, contrary to her earlier pledge to get intimate, looked the part of a long-time wife in her bland cotton shorty pajamas rather than a skimpy selection from her large cache of enticing lingerie. They were cramped in Kris' queen bed with little room to move, but Emmy quickly forgot any notion about ghosts and spirits and went soundly to sleep. Kris was restless, thinking about the next two days and eager to discharge his last responsibility to his father.

Having tossed and turned for hours, Kris had been asleep for about twenty minutes when the community fire siren atop City Hall interrupted the silence of the hot summer night. His eyes popping open, Kris stumbled to the nearby dresser and turned up the volume on the police radio scanner, another reminder of his father. With a scanner, the teenage Kris always had a heads-up on Vance's activities, knowing the police had rounded him up again and would soon be calling the house. He began dressing, waiting for a dispatcher to announce the location of the fire.

"What are you doing?" Emmy asked groggily while sitting up in bed.

"There's a fire somewhere in town. I'm going."

"You've got to be kidding!" Emmy mumbled, running her fingers through her hair. She looked at the small alarm clock she had placed on the night table next to the bed. "It's 2:30, for Christ's sake, Kris. Come back to bed!"

"Can't. I have been chasing sirens since before I started driving. I would go on my bike. It's one of the few forms of entertainment here in Fort Phillips. Besides I'm a reporter. That's what reporters do. We chase sirens."

"Well, I'm not going to join in the chase. I'm tired. I'm going to roll over and go back to sleep. Be careful."

Kris was dressed by the time Emmy uttered her last word and flopped back into bed. He had to listen intently to understand the scratchy news coming over the scanner. The fire was at Dr. Fanning's veterinary clinic near the south city limits. The town's siren was the clarion call for volunteers to scramble to the aid of the inexcusably understaffed city/county fire department. One pumper truck was based inside the city limits; another was in the unincorporated section of the county. The units could not be operated without the assistance of volunteers. Despite his still-sore arm, Kris slid into Emmy's car and drove much faster than he should have to the fire.

Two paid firemen had arrived with the city's one pumper truck, and volunteers were scurrying to roll out hoses and hook them up to nearby hydrants. The county unit was in route. Smoke was already pouring into the sky, but flames were visible in only one small area in the back of the clinic. Parking a block from the clinic so the car would not be in the way of firefighters and law enforcement, Kris started jogging toward the clinic. Responding to the repeated honk of a horn from behind him, Kris had to jump five feet to his right to avoid being sideswiped by a red Dodge Ram that came zooming by. "We've got to get them out!" screamed Dr. Fanning as he popped out of the truck. He took a step toward the clinic, but Fire Chief Norman Bosworth stopped him.

"We can't go in there right now. We've got to evaluate the fire a little more," Bosworth explained to the frantic veterinarian.

"We can't wait! Those animals are going to die! The smoke will kill them before the fire!" Dr. Fanning responded urgently.

Kris stepped closer to Chief Bosworth and Dr. Fanning to better hear the conversation. A considerable crowd of on-lookers was gathering. Several were adding to Dr. Fanning's plea for the firemen to save the animals.

A fireman in full turn-out gear including mask and oxygen tank extended his arm and waved at the chief from the clinic's front door which had been battered down with an ax.

"All right," Chief Bosworth said, acknowledging the signal. "I'm going to send two men in, but I can't guarantee we can get all of the animals out. The fire is getting worse. I will not put my men in more jeopardy than is reasonable." Flames had started shooting out of the shingle roof in several locations and from the windows that firemen had shattered.

"Send more men in! Those two can't get them all!" Dr. Fanning pleaded.

Kris kept glancing at this watch. Two minutes passed. Then three. Then four. Finally, the two firemen, both holding a dog under each arm, staggered out of the clinic. They passed the animals to on-lookers and, with the chief's permission, went back in. Despite the efforts of the other firemen, the blaze was becoming more ferocious. They were losing the battle.

"You're not going to get them all out! Dr. Fanning screamed. "Please send more men in!" The crowd, horrified with the realization the helpless caged occupants of the clinic were about to die, again yelled out in support of his increasingly urgent request.

"Franklin! Go!" the Chief ordered one of the firemen hosing the blaze. A husky young man stepped out of the crowd and took the hose as Franklin disappeared into the clinic.

"You need at least one more man" Dr. Fanning yelled at Chief Bosworth.

"I don't have another! We've done all we can do!"

A little girl, six or seven years old with short red hair, had arrived with her dad. "My kitty is still in there!" She cried running up to Chief Bosworth. "Someone please save my cat!"

Kris looked at the little girl. His mother had been a cat lover and had always had one or two at the house. Also, strays seemed attracted to the Keller house and they ended up being well-fed permanent residents. For Kris, that was a fond memory of Fort Phillips.

"I'll go!" Kris yelled impulsively and started running for the front door of the clinic before anyone could stop him.

"Kris! You fool!" screamed Chief Bosworth. "That's suicide without a mask and protective gear!" Kris had already raced into the blazing building.

The smoke was blinding and the heat intense. Kris knew sucking in the super-heated air would be deadly so he held his breath. Crawling on hands and knees he followed the sounds of crying cats. Three firemen, arms full of barking dogs, passed Kris without seeing him. His eyes were watering uncontrollably and the skin on his face felt like it was about to peel off, but he was determined to make it back to the last couple of animals. The pitiful meowing of cats got closer and closer. Struggling to his feet, with his lungs about to explode, Kris managed to open two cages and grab the cats by the nape of their necks. Hugging the wall, Kris started out. Overcome by the smoke and heat, the cats put up no resistance. Each movement for Kris became more difficult. He could not hold his breath any longer. Taking a mouthful of smoke, he began coughing and was frantic with the sudden realization he could not breathe. He could feel his grip on the cats failing.

As Kris was about to fall face first to the floor, one fireman grabbed him at the arm pits and another took the cats. Thirty seconds later, Kris was outside, flat on the ground, with an oxygen mask cupped over his nose. Taking deep gulps, Kris gradually replaced the smoke in his lungs with oxygen and he was able to sit up as the fire continued to ravage the clinic.

Chief Bosworth came to Kris who was sipping a bottle of cold water. Having watched Kris grow up in Fort Phillips, the Chief gave him a stern, fatherly glare. "Damn it, Kris!" he spouted. "That's the bravest – or dumbest – stunt I've ever seen anyone pull! What in the world possessed you to do that? Do you realize how close you came to dying in there? Are you wanting to be buried with your father?"

"I like cats and you needed help. I guess I suddenly realized that I have spent my whole life standing around watching other people be heroes. The notion just struck me that I couldn't just let those poor animals die."

"That is noble of you, but stupid. To go into a fire like that with no breathing apparatus or protective gear. How you got out of there is beyond me. Looks like you got one or two minor burns but that is it. If you were a cat, you just used one of your nine lives."

It would actually be life number two, Kris thought to himself. The helicopter explosion used up life number one.

Chief Bosworth continued, "Or maybe ole Vance is looking out for you. Goodness knows, you got him out of enough scrapes down through the years."

Holding her still dazed tabby cat tightly, the little girl with the short red hair stepped up to Kris. "Thank you for saving my kitty," she smiled.

"You're welcome," Kris smiled back. He gently rubbed the cat's head.

Dr. Fanning walked up. "Thank you. I and the animals are indebted to you. That's the bravest act I've ever seen." Kris nodded acknowledgement but did not say anything. Kris was indebted to him. Dr. Fanning was a long-time family friend. He had treated many of the Keller kitties at a discounted rate, frequently not charging at all. Dr. Fanning was nearing retirement age. Kris wondered if this fire might hasten that decision.

Dr. Fanning turned and watched as the final portion of roof collapsed. Kris thought back to the helicopter crash on Swisher Street. He had asked himself if he would have acted as Mayor Robertson did if it had been his child who was in peril.

At the animal clinic, Kris had answered his own question. If he would risk his life for a cat, certainly he would do the same for his child.

"If you ever get tired of the newspaper business, I'll hire you in a second," Chief Bosworth told Kris as they shook hands.

"I'm not sure my fiancée would agree to that," Kris smiled, thinking about Emmy who was back at the Keller house, blissfully ignorant of what had been taking place.

8

Kris did not know which was more dangerous - crawling through the veterinary clinic inferno or facing Emmy after she learned what he had done. Ignoring that he was dirty, wet and smelled like smoke, she immediately flew into him about trying to make her a widow before they got married. She reminded him that the helicopter explosion and resulting deaths and injuries had put him in a funk about how close he had come to being killed, and now, only days later, he had unnecessarily put himself in serious harm's way. Kris was beginning to believe that after surviving two close calls, he might not survive her tirade. From her initial anger, Emmy moved to Chief Bosworth's point of view. She did not know whether to praise Kris for his bravery or slap him for his stupidity. And finally, she started crying, realizing how truly close she had come to losing him. "This isn't the life I had pictured," she told him tearfully. "Reporters are supposed to sit at a computer all day, writing their articles and facing nothing more dangerous than a dangling participle. I didn't sign up for all this action and adventure!" Emmy did not tell Kris, but she was starting to get his itch of wrapping things up in Fort Phillips and hightailing it back to Atlanta. This little town was making her boyfriend act strangely.

Saying little in rebuttal, Kris let Emmy vent her justified fears and frustrations and then requested a couple of hours to relax. At her insistence, the police scanner was unplugged. While word of his exploits was spreading through town as fast as the fire ripped through the clinic, Kris had to somehow compose himself and get through the next twenty-four hours and the memorial service for Vance. Mickey Montgomery, considering what had taken place, offered to postpone the service a day, but Kris quickly declined the offer. He wanted to be done with it.

Kris was humbled by the turnout for the memorial service and the seven floral arrangements that had been delivered. Most of Kris' high school classmates who still lived in town came, as well as a few of Vance's friends. And even though he had no use for the friends since they were gamblers and drunks like Vance, Kris did appreciate their attendance and the fact that for a few minutes at least, they were clean and sober. He was also saddened. While everyone offered their condolences, no one talked about what a good man Vance was or that he would be missed. Kris' sense of melancholy was heightened by the memorial video which made him realize the Keller family had always been dysfunctional and never whole. The fact that his sister had chosen not to come put the proper final punctuation mark to his father's life.

As Mickey Montgomery had promised, Pastor Riley of the Christian Church delivered a short, sweet generic message about Vance being free of all his worldly problems, and after Mrs. Johnson played *The Old Rugged Cross* and *Amazing Grace* on the piano, it was over. The small crowd began leaving the funeral home chapel, with a few of the folks stopping to offer Kris one last round of condolences. Karen Jackson, filling out her black dress nicely, gave Kris a hug that Emmy thought went a tad past comforting an old friend. Emmy was also wearing a black dress with black hose and black heels and a single strand of pearls Kris had given her after they had been dating six months. She did not like the kiss Karen planted on Kris' cheek. Karen nodded in approval when Kris told her he and Emmy were going to visit with her father later in the day.

Kris paused one final moment to thank Mickey Montgomery for his help and to get the video memorial, which he expected he would never watch again. Kris softly took Emmy's hand and they walked out of the funeral home. He held open the car door for Emmy to slide into the driver's seat, and before he could get in the passenger seat, a voice from the side of the building called his name. Billy Manley, a friend of Vance's, motioned for Kris.

Manley greeted Kris with a weak handshake. Manley was only 56 or 57, the same age as Vance, but his wrinkled face, tired bloodshot eyes and shaggy salt and pepper hair made him appear more like 65 or 70. His old black suit was threadbare and didn't fit well, but he looked presentable and appeared to be sober.

"Hey Kris," Manley started shakily.

"Hey Billy. I didn't see you inside." Through the years, Manley had been in as many scrapes as Vance, but he did not have a son or other relatives to bail him out.

"I didn't come inside."

"Why? You should have."

Manley grabbed the sleeve of Kris' black suit coat and pulled him out of sight at the side of the funeral home. "Weird things are happening in this town, Kris, weird things," Manley explained, his head swiveling like an oscillating fan as he made certain no one was watching their conversation.

"Like what? What are you talking about?"

"Like the fire at Dr. Fanning's place. That fire was no accident. It was set."

Kris was starting to think Manley may have been drunk after all. "That sounds pretty preposterous, Billy. Why would anyone want to burn down the clinic and hurt so many animals?"

"I don't know, but it wasn't an accident. We've had several other fires lately. None as big as this one, but there's been too many for them to be accidents." Manley continued to scan the area for onlookers.

"I haven't heard anyone else say anything about this. Have you talked to Lonnie Jackson?"

"There's no use talking to him. He says he's investigating, but the only thing he's interested in investigating is the fresh brewed coffee at Fast Mart. As a police chief, he's about as worthless as side pockets on a pig."

"Billy, are you drunk?"

Manley appeared hurt by Kris' question. "I'm sober, Kris. Stone cold sober. If it had only been the fires, I might could overlook them, but there's more. Strange things are going on, Kris. We've had break-ins, a couple of robberies, a hit and run. Hell, things like that never used to happen here. We've had more stuff going on the last few months than in the last ten years combined."

Kris looked back at Emmy and he knew he needed to get to the car. "It's probably just coincidence," Kris started. He hesitated about his next remark but made it any way. "Maybe things like this have been going on all along, and you've just been too smashed to realize it."

"That hurts, Kris. It really does." Manley stopped to light a cigarette and his hand trembled as he lifted the lighter. "Maybe you'll apologize to me after what I'm about to tell you."

Kris rubbed the back of his neck. "Tell me, Billy. I need to go."

"Your dad didn't kill himself, Kris. No way Vance killed himself."

"Come on Billy!" That's ridiculous! Lonnie said Dad blew his brains out."

"Somebody blew his brains out, but Vance didn't pull the trigger."

Kris, not knowing what to think about Manley's theory, got right in his face. "What makes you so sure?"

"Did Vance leave a suicide note?"

"Lonnie said no."

"Have you checked his bank account? Looked to see if his bills are paid?"

"No. Why?"

"Because Vance had started to get his life together." Manley tossed down one cigarette and shakily lit another and drew a hefty puff. "He was drinking less, staying home more, even working a little bit for Buddy Donaldson at the building supply place, generally being more responsible. His frame of mind was the best I've ever seen. Hell, Kris! For the first time in a long time, Vance wanted to live, not die."

Kris dropped his head, not knowing what to say. "I wish I could believe you, Billy," he finally managed to say. "But I don't."

"Believe it. I knew Vance better than anyone in town. I was his best friend."

"You mean his best drinking buddy and gambling buddy?" Kris interrupted.

Manley sighed. "He didn't commit suicide." Billy looked around again and tossed his cigarette butt to the ground.

"Why are you so paranoid about anyone seeing us talk?"

"Because I'm not sure why all of this bad stuff is happening and who's causing it. I'm afraid the same people who killed Vance may decide to kill me too."

"You need to talk to Lonnie."

"I ain't talking to Lonnie. He hates me. He harasses me all the time. I ain't talking to nobody but you. It's up to you to figure out what's going on."

"I don't believe anything is going on, Billy."

Manley wanted another cigarette but the pack was empty. He wadded it up and tossed it away.

"Don't litter," Kris chided.

"Nervous habit. It's almost a ritual. When I get nervous, I smoke, and when I run out of cigarettes, I throw away the pack. Lonnie Jackson says I leave a trail. I don't even realize I'm doing it."

Manley took one more look around. "Kris, Vance was trying to get ready to come see you. He wanted to look you in the eye and apologize for the way he treated you, your mother and Becky. That had really started weighing heavy on him, Kris. It meant a lot to him. He wasn't ready yet, but by God, he was making progress!"

A knot formed in Kris' stomach and all the air went out of him like a balloon that had just been popped. He had no reply to Manley's revelation.

"Find out who killed Vance, Kris. You owe that to your dad." Manley, still looking over his shoulder, started walking down the street, away from Montgomery Funeral Home.

Kris walked back to the car, highly skeptical of Manley's claim of weird things happening in Fort Phillips. They could be passed off as simple coincidences or hallucinations during drunken binges. He was even more skeptical of Vance's supposed desire to make peace and more skeptical beyond that of Vance being murdered. All Kris was certain of is that once again his dad had left a mess for him to clean up. He didn't realize that this could possibly turn out to be the biggest mess ever.

9

Despite Emmy's prodding, Kris did not say a word during the short trip from Montgomery's to the Keller house. His silence continued for more than an hour afterwards. Kris could not get the meeting with Billy Manley out of his mind. Should he believe Manley's theory that Vance's death was not a suicide? If someone did kill him, why? Had he racked up a huge gambling debt he couldn't pay? Cheated someone in a card game? Questioned someone's heritage during a drunken argument? Slept with someone's wife? The first three, perhaps. The last? No way! Vance had never shown much interest in romance and intimacy. Besides, everyone knew the deal with Vance. He would get in trouble and Kris would bail him out, either with some cash or some fast-talking. Why bother to kill the old man when a settlement with Kris would be much more lucrative?

And if Kris did elect to investigate his father's death, where would he start? He was not a detective; he was a reporter. Why should he investigate when the main law enforcement officer in town had chosen not to? What would the people of Fort Phillips think when he started nosing around after being gone so long? Was his father worth any more time and energy? Certainly, the easiest choice would be to head back to Atlanta, check on his friend Patrick Cannon, and get back to work for the Advocate.

But Kris could not shake the haunting notion that Vance was straightening up and wanted to make peace with him. If that was true, then it did not make sense that Vance would have killed himself. And that would leave Kris with no choice. He had to uncover who killed Vance and why.

"Kris?" He felt Emmy's soft hand on his shoulder.

"Hey," he replied twisting on the sofa so he could see her.

"What's wrong Babe? Since we left the funeral home, you have been on another planet. Is the fact that your father is dead finally getting to you?"

He stood up, walked to the back of the sofa and hugged her. "Yeah. Something like that."

"Is there anything I can do to make you feel better?" She asked, rubbing his back.

"Yeah. Go with me to see Mr. Floyd."

She readily agreed and ten minutes later they were at the old two-story plantation style house a mile out of town. Karen and Lonnie Jackson, who had moved in after Mrs. Floyd's death to help take care of Mr. Floyd, greeted them at the front door. "Dad's going to be so glad to see you," Karen said as she led Kris and Emmy to the first-floor bedroom that had been set up for Mr. Floyd.

The room was dark and quiet. Kris held Emmy's hand as they slowly advanced to the side of the bed. Kris was shocked and upset at how frail his dear friend looked. Mr. Floyd's thinning hair was ghost white and his pale skin was hanging off his small bones. He was sleeping and his breathing was labored despite being fed oxygen through a cannula. The nurse who was sitting with him left the room.

"He's sleeping. I shouldn't wake him up," Kris said looking back at Karen.

"Go ahead. He needs to see you. Who knows? This may be your last chance to see him."

Kris squeezed Emmy's hand, let go, and put his hand gently on Mr. Floyd's. "Mr. Floyd. It's Kris."

Mr. Floyd did not respond.

"Mr. Floyd," Kris said louder.

Mr. Floyd slowly lifted his eyelids and initially seemed confused and not aware of who was in the room.

"Mr. Floyd. It's Kris."

His eyes started to brighten ever so slightly, and his lips creased in a small smile. He weakly squeezed Kris' hand. "Kris," he said, barely above a whisper.

Slowly, recognizing Kris brought a spark to Mr. Floyd, and he asked for help to sit up. Karen put her hand over her mouth as tears came to her eyes.

"I knew you would come back," Mr. Floyd said to Kris. "I knew you would come back to save the Sentinel."

Kris glanced at Karen who turned away.

"Do you know why I'm here in Fort Phillips?" Kris asked him.

"Of course," he said, his voice will weak and raspy. "To help Karen with the Sentinel. She really needs your help."

"How are you feeling?" That was all Kris knew to ask.

"I'm tired and ready to give up the fight. But I think I can rest better now that you are here. You take good care of my paper and my daughter. Who is that sweet thing next to you? Is this a reporter you've brought with you to help?"

"You might say that," Kris smiled.

"I'm glad you're here," Mr. Floyd said. His eyes started to close, and he asked for help sliding down in the bed.

"I'll see you later. You get some rest." Mr. Floyd was asleep before the words were out of Kris' mouth.

They left the bedroom. Tears were rolling down Karen's cheeks and Kris was trying not to well up. "You told me he was sick," he said to Karen, "but I didn't expect anything like this."

"I don't think it will be long."

"You didn't tell him the real reason I'm here?"

"You saw him, Kris. Do you think it would have done any good to tell him? I honestly think the only thing that has kept him holding on is waiting for you to come back. You're the son he never had."

"Excuse me, please," Emmy requested. She left the living room and went out on the front porch. Lonnie started to follow her, but Kris asked him to leave her alone. Instead, Lonnie went to the kitchen and popped the tab on a beer.

Kris stood silently for several seconds before asking Karen, "Why didn't you call me?

"What good would that have done? You wouldn't have come."

"Not to run the Sentinel, but to at least see him. You know how much I love that man. I have so much to say to him, and now I may never have the opportunity."

"I know, but your heart's not here. You made that clear a long time ago."

"What are you doing to do, Karen?"

"What do you think? Stay here and take care of Daddy and run the Sentinel. Lonnie's got no ambition. He's content to be the Fort Phillips Chief of Police the rest of his life."

"Can't you sell the paper?"

"It's not worth much right now. Besides, if I sold it, what would I do? Remember, I did not go off to college. I don't have a lot of marketable skills."

"You're selling yourself short," Kris admonished Karen and added, "Let's don't start that right now. I need to talk to Lonnie a minute. First, I want your cell phone number. If there's any change in Mr. Floyd's condition, any, you call me, all right?"

Karen nodded. She called out the phone number which Kris programmed into his cell. He went to find Lonnie while Karen joined Emmy, who was wiping tears from her face, in a white wooden swing attached to the roof of the front porch. "Why are you crying?" Karen asked her.

"I don't know if it's because I'm touched by how much Kris loves your dad, or it's because I'm afraid Kris will decide to stay here."

"Would that be such a bad thing?"

"For me, yes."

Karen locked her fingers together and looked down at them. "Forgive me for saying this," she started, looking up at Emmy, "but you and Kris just don't seem a match to me. You seem a little, uh, snooty, and I think that's rubbing off on Kris."

Emmy resented the remark. "Snooty, no. A little more sophisticated than most people around here, yes."

Karen resented the remark. "Yeah, you're right. We are all a bunch of hayseeds around here."

Emmy did not want the conversation to deteriorate any more. "I'm sorry," she started. "What I said came out wrong. The people I have met here are genuinely nice. It's just that the lifestyle is so different. I grew up in the shadows of Atlanta's skyscrapers. Life's a lot more hectic there. More opportunities, more things to do."

"And exciting?"

"And exciting," Emmy reiterated.

"I still love Kris," Karen said boldly.

"I've noticed. What does your husband think about that?"

"I do all of Lonnie's thinking for him. He's a hayseed, you know."

"Well, Kris and I will be out of here sometime tomorrow, and you and your hayseed husband can go back to doing whatever it is you do around here. Good to talk to you," Emmy said sarcastically. She got up from the swing and walked to the car, got inside and turned up the air conditioner and radio full blast.

While Emmy was fuming in the car, Kris was in the kitchen with Lonnie who had his feet propped up on the table chugging down a beer. Lonnie was a year older and three inches shorter than Kris. He was considerably thicker in the waist than Kris, and his face was marked with the remnants of teenage acne. Lonnie had always tried to be a rival to Kris, but it was not much of a rivalry. Kris always won.

Getting up to retrieve another cold brew from the refrigerator, Lonnie looked at Kris and announced, "Man, you're a tough act to follow."

"You're going to have to explain that to me, Lonnie."

Lonnie took a long swig from his second beer before answering. "The old man loves you. He thinks you walk on water, and the last time I tried that, I almost drowned." He offered a beer to Kris, who declined.

"Don't take it personally." Kris suggested as he sat at the table. "You're in the wrong profession. If you were in the newspaper business, Mr. Floyd would be falling at your feet."

"That's just part of it, Kris, and you know it. The simple fact of the matter is he likes you and doesn't like me."

"He likes you enough to let you marry his daughter."

Lonnie joined Kris at the table. "Karen settled for me. We both know that," Lonnie said. "You left town, so she picked the next best thing. If you had stayed, I wouldn't be anywhere in the picture."

"That's bull, Lonnie. You're not thirty years old yet and you're the police chief in your hometown."

"And we both know how I got this job. Karen's dad lined the mayor's pockets with a huge campaign contribution, which he used for purposes other than campaigning. You've been gone ten years, and there's not a day that goes by that the old man or Karen don't mention you."

"I'm sorry, Lonnie. I don't have any control over that, but believe me, you don't have to worry about me and your wife."

"That's easy for you to say. You're not around to see that blank look in Karen's eyes every day."

"I think I will take a beer," Kris said. Lonnie got up, pulled a beer out and tossed it to Kris who took a couple of big swallows.

"Lonnie, I want to talk to you in your capacity as police chief," Kris started. "Tell me about Vance's death."

"What is there to tell? He blew his brains out with a .12-gauge shotgun."

"Are you sure about that?"

"Hell yes I'm sure. I supervised the cleanup. It was a mess. I puked twice."

"That's not what I mean. Are you sure Vance pulled the trigger?"

Lonnie stood up and gave Kris an intense stare.

"Of course I am! Damn it, Kris! Do not come back into town telling me how to run my department. I have always played second fiddle to you. In high school you were a better shooting guard than me, so I had to play small forward. You were student body president. I didn't even make student council. You go to a fancy four-year college and I go to the community college. I'm sick of it, Kris. I can't do anything about the past, but I sure as heck can make sure you don't run the Fort Phillips Police Department."

"Hey, wait a minute! Hold on big boy! I have no interest in telling you how to do your job. I do have a right to ask questions about my father, and I've been told he was in too positive a frame of mind to take his own life."

Lonnie finished his beer and fired the can into a circular trash container. "I know what's going on. You've been talking to Billy Manley, haven't you? That old drunk doesn't know what he's talking about. The booze and those cheap cigarettes he puffs one after another are killing his brain cells."

"He seemed pretty positive about Vance."

Lonnie got nose-to-nose with Kris. "Let me tell you something, Mr. Big Shot Reporter. The only person who killed Vance Keller was Vance Keller. End of story. Don't you make more out of this than there is!"

"I owe it to Vance to look into…"

"Bullshit, Kris! You never gave a damn about Vance. You hated him, so don't start giving me this crap about you have got to look into his death. Do us all a favor, Kris. Go back to Atlanta and let us poor little country folks get back to our normal lives!"

"Believe me, I'm not going to stay around here any longer than I have to. Thanks for your time, Chief. See you around."

"Damn it!" Lonnie muttered as Kris walked out of the house.

Settling into the passenger seat of the car, Kris said to Emmy, "Sorry you had to wait. I needed to talk to Lonnie a minute."

"I hope your conversation with him was more cordial than mine with Karen."

"Really? What did you two talk about?"

"Nothing important. I did more listening than talking. I truly feel sorry for the people who live here. They are stuck. There's no hope, no future. What about you and Lonnie?"

"I did more listening than talking."

"Well," Emmy said as she pulled the car out of the driveway. "This visit was not a total waste." She pulled a pair of handcuffs out of her pocketbook that was perched on the console between the front seats.

"Where did you get those?"

"I saw them on a desk on my way out of the house. I guess you could say I'm borrowing them."

"You stole a set of handcuffs from the police chief? Damn, Emmy, that's bold." Kris started to laugh.

"Yes, I guess my life of crime starts here in Fort Phillips," she tried to say seriously.

He took the handcuffs from Emmy, held them up and studied them. "Sorry, Honey," Kris said, squirming in his seat. "I'm not in the mood for the kinky stuff tonight."

"Who said anything about kinky stuff? I got those to keep you from getting up in the middle of the night again and doing something stupid like chasing a fire truck."

10

Emmy was not happy with Kris' announcement, but she understood. The morning following Vance's memorial service and their visit to Mr. Floyd, Kris and Emmy were eating their Frosted Flakes with sliced bananas in the Keller kitchen when Kris reluctantly mentioned he needed to stay in Fort Phillips several days to wrap up some of his father's affairs. That was indeed true. Kris had to search for a will, which he was certain Vance hadn't bothered to draw up, check on bank accounts, pay bills, make arrangements to have utilities turned off, and talk to a real estate agent about putting the old house on the market. He did not tell Emmy about his other business. He had to know if Vance had blown out his brains or if someone had done it for him. This was a task that made Kris nervous, and he really wanted to get back to Atlanta, but estranged or not, he owed that to his father.

Kris promised Emmy he would only need a few days to take care of Vance's business, and then they could devote all their attention to wedding plans. She could take her car back to Atlanta and Kris could use Vance's Ford Ranger. Emmy was concerned about Kris' arm, but he assured her it would be fine, provided he did not partake in the pro wrestling matches Saturday night at the American Legion hall. She told Kris he could stay under two conditions – he would not do anything to hurt his arm and he would stay away from Karen Jackson. Emmy saw Karen as much more of a threat to Kris than the masked South Georgia Savage, this weekend's wrestling headliner. Kris' brief reply to both directives was *yes dear*.

As much as she did not want to leave Kris, Emmy admitted she was glad to be headed back to Atlanta. She had experienced as much of Fort Phillips and its residents, one in particular, as she could stomach. Kris piled the breakfast bowls, coffee cups and utensils in the sink while Emmy playfully dropped the handcuffs on the table.

Then she showered and dressed, packed the few things she had brought on the trip, kissed Kris and left. As she drove out of town, she said goodbye with a gesture unbecoming a lady.

Kris was slow to leave the house. With Emmy gone, he deliberately toured each room, which conjured up many memories, some good, some not so good. The door to Becky's room was closed, as it always had been, when she would spend hours writing in her journal. While her few friends were talking on the phone or out flirting with guys, Becky was holed up in her room, writing in that journal. The literary solitude paid off. Her academics and writing skills earned her four years at Mercer University in Macon and following a couple of years at a small lifestyle magazine in New Orleans, Becky landed a prize job as editor of a travel magazine in Portland. Like his sister, various scholarships had paid for Kris' education which was fortuitous. Had it not been for the financial assistance, it is likely neither Keller sibling would have gone to college. Vance certainly did not have anything to contribute, and the salary Kris' mother brought home as a seamstress at Simpson's Slacks could barely cover the essentials like food and mortgage.

Kris ventured into the cramped master bedroom where his mother had slept alone many nights while Vance was out boozing and gambling. He had always admired his mother and at the same time been frustrated with her for her loyalty to Vance. In truth, the family would have probably been better off had Mrs. Keller told Vance to get lost and taken her two children to some other town where they would not have had to deal with the uncertainty of their father's whereabouts or well-bring. The walls of the bedroom were bare, except for two large cheap, tacky landscapes from a yard sale, and a large photo of Vance and Kris standing outside Turner Field, once home of the Atlanta Braves. The long-ago trip to the baseball game and the resulting photo represented one of the truly pleasant experiences Kris ever had with his dad. On occasion Kris would catch Vance staring at the photo. If that photo meant so much to him, Kris often wondered, why didn't Vance take the time to make more moments like that? Looking at the picture, Kris smiled as he remembered how Vance had used it as a stash for some of his gambling money and letters or legal correspondence he did not want anyone to see. Vance never knew that Kris had always known about his taping his stash to the back of the photo. Kris started to look behind the photo, but his eyes caught the stained patch on the floor where Vance had died. That reminded Kris of the job at hand. He panicked when he realized he did not know where the keys to Vance's truck were. Hopefully, they were where Vance always left them – in the ignition.

They were, and after struggling briefly with a balky battery, Kris headed for his first stop, Fort Phillips Community Bank. He knew three-fourths of the employees at the bank and had to stop and speak to all of them before getting to Tonya Adams, the customer representative, a skinny, bony young woman who was a member of his high school class and the top scorer on the girls' basketball team. He had to exchange pleasantries with her for several minutes and hear all about Tonya's two small children and rehash the region championship game she won with a last-second shot from half court before getting down to the business of Vance's account. Kris got his first affirmation of Billy Manley's story. Recently, Vance had made regular deposits, had five hundred dollars and change in a checking account, and had not bounced a check in six months. Kris chose to keep the account open in case Vance had some checks out and provided Tonya with his cell phone number if additional money needed to be deposited.

The next stop was Hometown Pharmacy where Dr. James Harrison had taken care of the Keller family prescription needs for years. Dr. Harrison had taken care of everyone's prescriptions for years. His was the only pharmacy in town. A wide smile stretched across Dr. Harrison's face when he saw Kris, and with no customers to serve at the moment, he came from behind the pharmacy counter. That pleased Kris, who had great respect for Dr. Harrison, a tall, solidly built man with wire rimmed-glasses, silver hair turning white and a smile that immediately made you comfortable.

"It's good to see you," Dr. Harrison started as he sat next to Kris on a short church pew that had been taken out of the old First Methodist Church. "We miss you. I'm sorry that it took your dad's death to get you back home."

"I know. I am sorry I haven't been around. But honestly, since Becky left and Mom died, there hasn't been much to bring me back."

"I understand. Fort Phillips is in trouble, Kris. here's not a business in town that isn't struggling to survive."

"Someone told me Fort Phillips is having some other problems too, like fires and break-ins."

"That is right, but I believe all of that relates to the economy around here. People have lost their jobs or are working short time. There's a lot of frustration. That's manifesting itself by people doing some stupid stuff."

"What's being done about it?"

Dr. Harrison chucked even though Kris had asked a serious question. "Not much. Lonnie Jackson is a good guy, but he's not exactly a ball of fire. But then he doesn't have very many officers to work with either. His department was small to begin with and he's had some men to leave, and the city hasn't let him replace them. Besides, with some of the things that have happened, I don't know if there was anything Lonnie could have done."

"What's going to happen?"

"Fort Phillips is going to be a ghost town. The people who do live here are having to drive 20, 30 miles, even more to find work. A lot of the businesses in town have closed, and others are preparing to close. People are going to be driving to Bainbridge or Camilla or even Thomasville to buy their groceries and get their medicine. The Sentinel is struggling too, you know that, don't you?"

"Karen told me. And I was sad to see Mr. Floyd in such bad shape."

"He won't last much longer. What do you think Karen will do?"

"I don't know. Probably won't stay here."

"I would really hate to see us lose the Sentinel. That would be the final symbol of this town running up the white flag."

"You sound so hopeless. I heard that something opened in the old Simpson Slacks plant. Maybe some other businesses will take their lead and move here."

"Don't count on it. Syndicated Delivery Services – I think that's what they call themselves – isn't contributing anything to the community. Their trucks come and their trucks go. No one knows anything about the company. We're not even sure what it is they do."

"That's strange. Maybe I'll talk to Karen about doing an article on them"

"She's already tried. She couldn't even get in the door."

"That is strange. Most businesses love free publicity. Anyway, I really hope that something will happen to rejuvenate this place. Dr. Harrison, let me ask you something. Did you see Vance in the days before he died?"

"A time or two, yes."

"How did he seem to be doing?"

"I thought he looked great, Kris. He seemed upbeat and in control. Truthfully, I was shocked when I heard he had killed himself."

"Someone else told me that, but Lonnie Jackson is convinced Vance took his own life. I'm not so sure."

"What are you saying Kris?" Dr. Harrison asked with interest.

"I don't know what I'm saying right now, Dr. Harrison. Vance probably did take his own life, but I need to see a few people, ask a few questions."

Dr. Harrison rubbed the right side of his face and looked at Kris. "Please don't take this the wrong way, Kris, but I hope you determine that Vance did kill himself. I wouldn't want to know that his death came another way, if you know what I mean."

"I know exactly what you mean," Kris replied seriously. "I hope Lonnie's right, and I'm sure that will be my conclusion too. But enough about my issues. How are you, Doctor Harrison?"

"I am doing fine," the pharmacist smiled. "I'm going to hang it up in a year or so, either closing the store or selling it. This town has been good to me. I have been able to set aside a nice income for my retirement. We will probably move to Florida. My wife has always wanted to live in Florida."

"Sounds like a plan," Kris smiled in return.

"What about you, Kris? How is your life going? What's ahead for you?"

"Well, I'm getting married. Her name is Emmy Owens and she works for a large leasing cooperation in Atlanta. She finds tenants for everything from warehousing to multi-use high rises. Career-wise, I suppose I will stay in Atlanta a bit longer. It's a great place for a reporter. Somethings is always going on."

"Like bank robberies and helicopter crashes," Doctor Harrison said teasingly.

They chatted a few more minutes with Kris asking about the doctor's son Jeff who was four years older than Kris and was in the middle of a career as a pharmacist with CVS. Kris glanced at his watch and realized he had been there an hour.

Kris and Dr. Harrison hugged rather than shaking hands and Kris felt discomfort in his left arm. His thoughts were in a state of discomfort as well. Why would Vance have taken his own life? Everyone but Lonnie Jackson talked about how well he was doing, and that trend continued later in the afternoon. Kris conferred with the utility companies who confirmed that Vance was current and had paid promptly for several months. The building supply company had hired Vance part-time for loading and unloading lumber and had been pleased with his effort, punctuality and attendance. In fact, Kris had never heard such glowing reports about his dad. There seemed to be no reason whatsoever that Vance would have wanted to put a shotgun to his head at this point in his life.

Drained physically and emotionally, Kris was ready to call it a day, but he wanted to make one more stop. Karen was surprised to see him at the Sentinel and was surprised at his question.

"Do you need a reporter for a few days?" he asked.

"What about Atlanta?" she asked suspiciously. "What about Atlanta and your fiancée?"

"I need time to settle Vance's affairs, and there's a few things I'd like to look into around here, and I would feel more comfortable doing my looking in the official capacity of a reporter rather than a plain old citizen. And as a local reporter, not some snoop from Atlanta."

"You think that me giving you a press card is going to make people ignore the fact that you *would* be a snoop from Atlanta?"

"Probably not, but it would make me feel better."

Karen turned her back on Kris and straightened a small stack of papers on the corner of the desk in the reception area. She started talking before turning back to face Kris. "I know what you're doing. It's Vance, isn't it? Lonnie told me that Billy Manley has been feeding you ridiculous garbage about Vance's death. You simply refuse to believe Lonnie, don't you? This is personal, isn't it? You don't like Lonnie, and if he told you the grass is green, you wouldn't believe him."

Frustrated, Kris quickly replied, "I respect Lonnie and the job he does here. I know it's difficult for him with a small department and not many resources. I'm sure he is overworked. Maybe he overlooked something. That's what I want to make certain, that nothing was overlooked. No one, Lonnie included, has given me any reason, any reason at all, for Vance killing himself. By all accounts, things were going great for him"

Karen looked directly into Kris' eyes for several seconds before answering. "Maybe you are the person overlooking something," she finally said.

"What's that?" Kris asked, surprised by her comeback.

"I think Vance came to a depressing realization – that even though he had turned his life around, he would never have what he wanted most – for things to be right between you and him. He decided that you would always hate him, not being able to forgive him for the years of hell he put you, your mom and Becky through. Vance realized that suddenly he had nothing to live for."

Her theory struck deep into Kris' heart. "That's not true," he said in defense, although he silently admitted she was probably correct,

Karen moved closer to Kris and began rubbing his left arm but stopped when she felt the bandage under the long sleeve of his white shirt. She smiled, “You know I’d love to have you around here, and not just as a reporter. Stay as long as you want, I’ll try my best to give you reasons to stay.”

Kris swallowed hard. He had no response to her comment. He returned to the Keller house and spent a sleepless night agonizing over the possibility he might have been the cause of Vance’s death.

11

Kris' mission had suddenly changed. The notion that Vance may have been murdered was gone. Dwelling on Karen's theory for hours, Kris was ready to concede that Vance had committed suicide. He would talk to a few more people, and if the information kept coming back as it had so far, the doubt would be removed. Vance's anguish over not being able to make peace with his son drove him to death. Guilt was already beginning to gnaw at Kris as was the cold, harsh realization that he would have to carry the guilt with him the rest of his life. Trying to rationalize what had taken place and why, Kris reminded himself he did not know that Vance was ready to try to mend their relationship. The last time Kris had been in Fort Phillips for his mother's funeral, Vance had been the same old Vance, trying to dodge trouble and not willing to take responsibility for his actions and behavior. Still, Kris kept asking the question – had he done all he could to make things right with his dad? No matter how many times he asked, the answer always came back "*No!*"

Unable to shake off his sense of regret, Kris spent part of the morning talking on the phone to his editor in Atlanta, requesting a few more days off, which was granted but not open-ended, and letting Emmy know he had some more loose ends to tie up. She expressed temporary frustration but admitted that a new marketing project aimed at leasing space in a just-completed Midtown Atlanta mixed-purpose high rise would keep her busy in his absence. Playfully, she reminded him again to guard his arm from pro wrestlers. Seriously, she reminded him to guard his heart from Karen and to stop beating himself up over Vance.

His phone chores completed, Kris made the 20-mile trip to the nearest Walmart to buy a single pair of casual khaki slacks, a single pair of jeans, a single pair of walking shorts, a navy-blue golf shirt, t-shirts and briefs and cheap sports shoes to serve him for the next few days. He loaded up on pork rinds, Chex Mix, mini-Three

Musketeers, Coca-Cola and Bud Light. As for regular meals, he had no qualms about eating the fried chicken and okra at Granny's or one of Pete's artery-clogging double cheeseburgers. He would take that over Mexican any day.

Kris spent the remainder of the day looking for Billy Manley who could provide the names of Vance's other acquaintances. What they had to say, Kris surmised, would be critical to his investigation and go a long way in determining the length of his stay in Fort Phillips. Manley, who like Vance had trouble holding a steady job, was nowhere to be found, but the slow-moving clerk at Fast Mart noted that Manley hung out a lot at the city sports complex in the evenings for recreation league softball games and hustling bets on anything and everything. At twilight, Kris, comfortable in his new jeans, shirt and shoes, finally tracked down Manley, who was hugging the Field One outfield fence watching the Prospect Road Baptist men's team pound the Church of God. Manley seemed nervous that Kris wanted to talk, and he requested they move their conversation to the metal bleachers of a field that was not in use. The smoke from Manley's ever-present cigarette could not hide the smell of alcohol on his breath.

Lighting up again and tossing the empty pack away, Manley took a deep puff and said, "This isn't a social visit, is it? You came to talk to me about Vance, right?"

Kris stooped down and picked up Manley's discarded cigarette pack. He started to lecture Manley about littering but didn't. "Why the secrecy?" Kris asked Manley. "What's the deal with us having to lurk in the shadows when we talk?"

"I told you before. I'm afraid the same people who snuffed out Vance will do the same to me."

Kris stuffed the cigarette pack in his pocket. "You're sticking by your story about Vance? You're sure about what happened?"

"I'm as certain of that as I am that you're not here to ask me to be the best man at your wedding," Manley said between pulls on his cigarette.

"That's not what I'm hearing. But I have found out why Vance killed himself."

"And what might that be?"

Kris waited for cheering from an adjacent field to calm before speaking. "He was depressed that he would never be able to reconcile with me."

Manley laughed and tossed away another cigarette butt. "I don't know who you've been talking to, but that's bunch of crap. What you are being told is totally opposite of how Vance felt. He was certain that the two of you could bury the hatchet."

Kris got up from the metal bleachers and looked in the direction of the adjacent field where fans were cheering again. Turning back to Manley, Kris said, "What I've heard makes more sense than your idea that someone killed Vance. I ask you again, why would someone want to kill him?

"That's for you to figure out, Mr. Reporter. That's why I told you all of this to begin with."

"Then give me a lead, a name, a clue."

Manley patted his shirt pocket which was empty. "I don't suppose you have a cigarette," he asked.

"Nope," Kris said but he did give Manley a piece of gum. "It's this way, Billy, I'm going to talk to a few more of Vance's buddies, and unless I hear something different from what I've already heard, I'm going back to Atlanta and try to get rid of the guilt that I'm the one who caused Vance's death."

Manley hopped off the bleachers and stepped close enough for Kris to smell the alcohol again. "You can't do that!" Manley said emphatically. "Look, I do want you to know the real way Vance died, but there's another reason why I told you," Manley paused momentarily, and then nervously admitted, "I'm telling you to protect my own ass too. I want whoever did this caught before they get to me."

"All right," Kris said and then hesitated. "That begs the question. If you can't tell me why someone killed Vance, then tell me why they would want to kill you."

"Hell, by association, I guess. They think that if Vance knew something or had done something, then I probably knew the same shit or had done the same thing."

"Know what? Done what?" Kris asked in frustration. He wanted something concrete.

"I don't know. Let me tell you this again. That's why I came to you. For you to find all of this out."

Kris saw that Manley's hands were trembling. "If you're so scared, why are out at a public place like this?" he asked.

"For exactly that reason. It's a public place. No one can touch me here. It's when I'm alone that worries me. That's what happened to Vance. They got him at home when he was alone."

Kris sat back down on the bleachers and sighed. "I don't know what to tell you Billy. Let's leave it at this. You help me talk to some of Vance's buddies and I'll look out for you. But I've got to tell you, right now I'm pretty much convinced that Vance killed himself."

"Suit yourself. I will take you around to some of Vance's hangouts. I appreciate the offer of protection, but that means you may have to take me with you when you return to Atlanta."

"Uh, I don't think my girlfriend would go for that. We'll get things settled before I leave. I promise. Now when can you help me?"

Manley asked for Kris' cell phone number and told him he would call the next day. After bumming five dollars from Kris, Manley slipped out of sight with the stealth of a spy. Kris, not wanting to return home and spend another night churning a hundred scenarios through his mind, went back to Field One where another game had started. First Christian had already hung up two runs on Mt. Pisgah in the first inning. Mark Stewart, First Christian's coach, immediately noticed old friend Kris who was propped on the fence down the third base line. They shook hands and exchanged a few details about wife and girlfriend. Stewart, tall and muscular and able to belt a softball into orbit, continued the conversation between instructions and encouragement to his team. Remembering Kris' high school athletic accomplishments, Stewart offered to put him on the team right there on the spot, but Kris, mindful of his arm and Emmy's orders, declined. Stewart's next offer got a more positive response from Kris. Seven or eight guys met at the recreation complex gym a couple of nights a week to play pick-up basketball, Kris said he would probably be limited to tossing in a few free throws but promised he would show up. Stewart went back to coaching his team, which ended up winning 20-19 by scoring two runs in the bottom of the seventh inning.

The game's final out was recorded at 10:58, and Kris, not the least bit sleepy, made his way home, hoping a good movie would be showing on one of the cable TV channels. He unlocked the front door, stepped into the den, flipped on the lights and gasped. The room had been ransacked. The old worn sofa had been overturned and the pillows shredded. The drawers had been pulled from a small writing desk and the contents dumped on the floor. Kris' heart started to race. He could hear voices. Someone was in his room. Swallowing hard, Kris shouted, "Who's there?" He didn't get an answer, so he asked again, loudly, "Who's there?" All he heard was his heart beating in his ears. He took three steps toward his room when he heard the stampede start. The intruders were scrambling down a hallway toward the kitchen and the door that opened to the backyard. Kris hustled after them and arrived in the dark kitchen in time to see a tall thick figure shoot out the back door. Another figure, smaller and chubbier, slipped on a small throw rug while trying to make the sharp turn from the hallway into the kitchen, and fell, noisily rolling up against a leg of the kitchen table. Kris quickly dived on top of him, and they wrestled, with Kris screaming as his head bumped against a table leg. The chubby intruder grunted and pushed Kris aside and clumsily tried to get up. Kris, determined that he would not get away, remembered the handcuffs Emmy had left on the table. Kris grabbed the man's right wrist, deftly slapped on the cuffs, and jerked. The chubby man stumbled back to Kris, who locked the other end of the cuffs on the handle of the old refrigerator. The chubby man grunted again and pulled, causing the refrigerator door to pop open, but he was still secured. "Damn it, let me go!" he screamed. Kris pushed him hard against the refrigerator, which moved a good three inches.

"You're not going anywhere, asshole!" Kris shouted at him as he turned on the lights in the kitchen. Pulling his cell phone from the right back pocket of his jeans, Kris bypassed 9-1-1 and called directly to Lonnie Jackson who groggily said he would be there in ten minutes.

"What are you after?" Kris asked the chubby man, who was sweating so much that his black t-shirt that fit tightly against his belly was soaked.

The chubby man tugged hard and the refrigerator flew open again. "You're going to be sorry you did this!" he yelled at Kris.

"*You're* the one who's going to be sorry," Kris shot back as he pushed the fridge door closed.

The chubby man continued to rattle the handcuffs in an attempt to break loose, but he had no success. His wrist was beginning to look red and raw where the cuffs were buffeting against his flesh.

"Don't go anywhere. I'll be right back," Kris said teasingly. He made a quick scan of the house and determined that the den was the only room that had been blitzed. They were apparently getting ready to trash Kris' room when he arrived and interrupted them. He went back to the kitchen where the chubby man was still struggling to no avail. The old refrigerator was holding steady.

True to his word, Lonnie Jackson, accompanied by one of his officers, was at the Keller house in ten minutes. He laughed when he saw the chubby man handcuffed to the refrigerator. "Very good, Kris," Lonnie said. "I'm impressed. That was quick thinking. I'm assuming this is my pair of missing handcuffs."

"Emmy, uh, borrowed them. I just wish I had been able to get the other dude too."

"How are you, Popeye?" Lonnie asked as he tousled the hair of the chubby man who didn't say anything.

"You know this guy?" Kris asked.

"Oh yeah. Popeye's one of our most well-known residents. He's broken into half the houses in town. Who was with you this time, Popeye? BoJo?"

"Popeye? BoJo?" Kris asked.

"Popeye got his nickname because he got his right eye shot out with a BB gun when he was a kid. Our version of Ralphie in *A Christmas Story*. He's got a glass eye. BoJo? That's Bobby Jones, his usual partner in crime."

"What were they looking for?"

"Nothing in particular. Anything they can sell or pawn for a few dollars. This is their job, Kris. You work for a newspaper. I'm a cop. They're petty burglars."

"Let me go, damn it!" Popeye fumed, rattling the handcuffs.

"Hold your horses," Lonnie said, ruffling Popeye's hair again. "We'll get you to your accommodations soon." Lonnie walked back into the den but quickly came back to Kris who remained in the kitchen with Popeye and Lonnie's officer. "Doesn't look like they did too much damage," Lonnie said to Kris. He added, "How's your arm? You didn't hurt it, did you."

Kris realized his arm was aching. "It's all right. I think. Maybe I strained it a little, but I don't think I popped any stitches. I think the only significant item that's messed up in the house is the sofa, and it was about ready to go to the landfill."

"O.K. Well, I'm going to take Popeye with me back to the city jail. Officer Davenport is going to stay here and take a few photos and get some more information from you."

"Thanks, Lonnie," Kris said appreciatively.

"You bet." Lonnie freed Popeye from the refrigerator, cuffed his hands behind his back and started out. He stopped and looked back at Kris. "You know," Lonnie started. "Popeye is harmless enough. But what if it was someone other than Popeye? What if it was someone high on crack who was toting a gun? What if they had pulled that gun on you and started firing instead of simply tucking tail and running out the back door? I could be standing here calling Mickey Montgomery to come pick up your dead body."

"I don't guess I thought of that," Kris said meekly.

"Obviously not. Just like you didn't think before you went into that burning animal clinic." He took a quick glance at Kris' left arm as well. "I don't know what you think you have to prove, Kris, but stop it. Stop it before you get yourself killed."

"Point well taken," Kris replied. He let out a huge sigh of relief as Lonnie tugged at Popeye's belt and led him out of the house.

12

"You did what?" Emmy screamed at Kris through the phone. She was furious about his sudden death wish. Emmy could overlook what happened to Kris outside the bank in Atlanta because he happened to be in the wrong place at the wrong time. Rushing into the animal clinic fire and tangling with Popeye were different. With the animal clinic and Popeye, Kris had made a conscious choice to risk his neck. For five non-stop minutes Emmy went on and on about him taking such unnecessary chances, which made Kris question why he had told Emmy about the break-in to begin with. He realized, too late, that he would have been better off keeping his mouth shut and utilizing the old *what Emmy doesn't know won't hurt her* philosophy. He regretted not taking that approach when Emmy followed up her first five minutes with another mini tirade, listing the reasons he should immediately come back to Atlanta. She even threatened to come back to Fort Phillips, secure him with the borrowed pair of handcuffs and drag him back with her. Kris listened patiently, taking every verbal jab, then calmly told her, "I need to stay a few more days. And Lonnie took back his handcuffs."

"You're starting to have second thoughts about staying down there, aren't you?" she asked. Her ranting had been replaced with sobbing.

"Of course not," he reassured her. "There's just a few details relating to Vance that are taking longer to wrap up than I expected." He was not about to tell her that some of the unfinished business involved untangling Vance's death. An admission that he was on another Don Quixote quest would only set her off again with more reasons for him to get out of the shriveling little town and back to civilization.

"Do you want to call off the engagement?" Emmy asked bluntly.

Kris sensed that she was serious. "No! Heck no! Please Emmy. You are over-reacting. I'll be back in a week. Some of this stuff…I can't simply snap my fingers and make it go away."

"Can you snap your fingers and make Karen go away?"

Kris grunted in frustration. "That's tacky," he admonished her. "Remember, I'm the one invading her space. Karen is my friend. I am concerned about her and I am concerned about her father especially." Kris paused. "I'll be back in a week. I promise. Believe me, I don't want to stay here any longer than I have to."

"If you are not back in a week, I'm coming after you. And if I do that, it won't be pretty."

"Whoa!" Kris exclaimed, holding the cell phone away from his head. "What is this? My prim and proper little Emmy getting angry? I like it! It's kind of sexy."

"Well, sex is out of the question if I'm up here and you're down there."

"If you're trying to entice me to finish up down here, it's working," Kris paused again. "Emmy, what I've have left to do down here is important. Be patient with me. I will be home soon. I promise. I love you."

Much calmer, Emmy sighed and apologized to Kris, admitting that following her grandfather's death, it had taken her family weeks to settle his affairs. Ending the conversation with Kris, she requested, "Please come home soon." And then she ordered, "And don't do anything else stupid!"

"Yes ma'am," he replied before closing with "I love you."

Kris exhaled. "That was an interesting, somewhat one-sided discussion," he mumbled. Taking a Coke out of the refrigerator, Kris was struck by the result of the phone call. He was now on a deadline, with a week to get to the bottom of Vance's death. What was he to do if he didn't have the answer by then? His choices? He could walk away and keep his future wife happy and be tormented for the rest of his life about how his father really died, or he could satisfy his conscience about Vance and risk losing the love of his life.

Trying to drown his anger with the soft drink, Kris quickly gulped down the first can and popped the tab on another. His first gulp of the second soft drink was interrupted by a call on his cell. Billy Manley announced that several of Vance's buddies were involved in an intense card game. Manley offered to direct Kris to the action if he would pick him up in fifteen minutes at the Fast Mart. Given the time constraints Emmy had put him under, Kris readily agreed to Manley's request.

Manley was propped against a tower of barbecue grill propane tanks when Kris steered Vance's Ranger into the parking lot. Manley would not leave until Kris bought him two packs of cigarettes and a six pack of beer. The instant they got into the truck, Manley started to light a cigarette, but Kris would not let him. Denied a smoke, Manley settled on beer instead which set off a series of three increasingly loud burps. Manley had downed two more beers by the time they reached an old gravel road five miles south of town. Swerving like he was on a slalom course to avoid the potholes, Kris headed for an old barn behind a farmhouse that sat in the middle of a treeless pasture. "Now can I have a cigarette?" Manley asked as Kris pulled up next to the barn.

"As soon as you step out of the truck."

Manley started pulling a smoke out of the pack before Kris finished his sentence.

From the outside, the barn looked like hundreds of others that decorated rural areas in Georgia. Manley stopped to light his cigarette before he pulled on the barn door and motioned Kris to enter. "Jesus!" Kris exclaimed. The barn had been gutted and renovated into a cottage that would be perfect for a weekend retreat in the north Georgia mountains or on one of the state's massive fishing and recreation lakes. A fully functional kitchen was tucked in one corner and a regulation pool table occupied the opposite corner. A widescreen television was tuned to the Cubs and Cardinals, and smack in the middle was a card table surrounded by five men flipping chips into a growing pot. The open loft had been converted into a bedroom. All the furnishings looked old and worn, as if they may have been hand-me-downs, but still, for a bunch of guys, it was a palace. Kris almost choked on all the smoke hovering around the card table. "You can light up now," he told Manley, who was already puffing away.

"Our home away from home," Manley said.

"Speaking of home," Kris started, "Where do you live, Billy?"

"Here. There. Everywhere. This place and that. Here sometimes."

"How do you get around? Do you drive? Have a car?"

"Nope. Too shaky. I used to drive, but several years ago I crashed into a tree. Damn near killed myself. Haven't driven since." Manley realized he may have hit a nerve with Kris with the remark about *damn near killed myself.*

The reference to killing oneself didn't register with Kris. He asked Manley, "Who owns this place?" Kris was impressed and envious of the barn.

"Five or six of us. My contribution was, well, minimal. Very minimal."

Kris stopped Manley. "In other words, you just stood around and supervised," he said, poking fun at Manley.

"Yeah, I'm good at that."

Manley resumed. "We bought the barn and three acres from Doug Shaw who got sick and sold his livestock. We all worked on the conversion and contributed the furniture and stuff. I don't have a family, but most of the guys spend more time here than they do with their wives and kids so they decided if that was going to be the case, hell, they were going to make it comfortable."

"What about Vance? Is…was…he an owner?"

"Sort of. He didn't put any money into the place, but he helped with a lot of the work." Manley blew smoke into Kris' face, not on purpose, but not thinking anything about it either.

Kris turned his head and took a step to get out of the smoke. "Damn, Billy, don't these guys feel bad about spending so much time away from their families?" Kris asked.

"Truthfully, no," Manley replied, looking over to the table. "These guys are gamblers, Kris. They have an addiction. They'd bet on how many times a day you piss. They love their families, I think, but they love gambling more. Why do you think we've got the beds here? They want to miss as little of the action as possible."

"That's absolutely damn sick!" Kris shot back. "Friggin' damn sick!"

"You're right. It is a sickness. Considering Vance's history, you should know that."

The blood rushed from Kris' face. Manley was right. Vance had never let his family get in the way of a good card game.

"Come on," Manley motioned. "Let me introduce you to the guys."

Manley introduced Kris as Vance's kid.

Kris' eyes were already watering from the cigarette smoke. He knew three of the men at the table. Another looked familiar but Kris didn't know his name, and the fifth was a stranger. Bruce Morrison, who knew Kris from the times he had brought Vance home when he was too drunk to drive, folded his hand and offered his seat to Kris. "You look more like your old man every day," Morrison said as Kris took his place at the table.

Kris acknowledged with a nod of his head.

"Five card stud," said the dealer, a fat man chewing on an unlit cigar. Kris didn't know him.

Kris waved his hand, declining the invitation to play as he sat at the table. He took a quick glance at the five men. Other than looking like they had not shaved in four days, and reeking of cigarette smoke, they were all presentable. "I'm not here to play," Kris explained. "I came to ask about my dad. Nice place, by the way."

"Thanks," Morrison said. "We're all sorry about Vance. What do you want to know?"

"Lonnie Jackson says Vance killed himself. Manley says Vance had his act together and there was no way Vance would take his own life. I don't know who to believe."

"What are you saying? That someone may have killed your old man?" asked the player that Kris recognized but couldn't recall the name.

"I'm not saying anything right now. That's what I'm trying to find out."

"Actually," Morrison started, "Vance hadn't been hanging around here much lately. He said he was working. He knew that was against our bylaws. We were ready to revoke his membership."

"Vance's only mistake lately was hanging out with that loser Billy Manley. He's a leech, always sucking something out of you," chimed in Chuck McGraw, telephone pole thin with skinny fingers yellow with cigarette stains. Manley walked over to McGraw and playfully smacked the back of his head.

Ronald Rex, once a well-paid manager when Simpson Slacks was in full production, looked as if he were about to speak. Kris was surprised to see him with this bunch, but obviously Fort Phillips' difficult times had hit him hard. "Like Bruce said," Rex started, "Vance hadn't been hanging around here much. I can tell you this. A few weeks ago, my little girl got sick and had to go to the emergency room. We don't have insurance. On the night my girl got sick, I was flat broke. I didn't have a dime in my pocket. Vance gave me some money to help with the bill. I'm indebted to him."

Kris leaned back, pressing his back into the chair. "Let me ask you this," he said. "Do any of you think I might have been the reason Vance killed himself?"

"What do you mean?" Morrison asked as he responded to McGraw's request to bum a cigarette.

"Did he think that I hated him? That I hated him so much I would never forgive him and mend our relationship?"

"He was pretty sure you hated him," Rex agreed, "but I don't think he saw things as hopeless. He seemed in good spirits the last time I saw him. In fact, the night I took my girl to the hospital, Vance told me I should start spending more time with her. As you can see, I didn't take his advice."

"Maybe you should," Kris told him.

Rex did not reply, instead getting up and quickly going to the refrigerator.

Standing behind Kris, Morrison put his hands on Kris' shoulders. "I don't think we can tell you what you want to hear, Kris. Vance seemed to be doing well, but the bottom line is, we couldn't read his mind. None of us knew what he was really thinking. How many other times have you heard of someone killing themselves for no apparent reason? It happens all the time." He softly squeezed Kris' shoulders. "But if you're trying to say someone killed Vance, I think you are way off base, especially in this little town. I don't know of anyone who would have reason to kill him."

Kris got up from the table and smiled weakly at Morrison. "Yeah, you're right, I'm sure. I'm just trying to find some way to keep me from feeling so guilty."

"Don't feel guilty. You did more for Vance than any other son would have done for their father," Morrison said.

Kris replied with another weak smile. "I appreciate that," he told Morrison.

All the card players shook hands with Kris except Rex who hugged him. Rex smelled so strongly of smoke that Kris almost gagged.

Kris waited for Manley to finish a bologna sandwich - Manley called the bologna Alabama steak - he had rummaged in the refrigerator and then they left. Kris was so preoccupied that he didn't say anything when Manley lit a cigarette in the Ranger and tossed the crushed pack to the floor. "What now, Kris?" Manley asked.

"Kris?" Manley asked again when Kris didn't respond.

"Uh, yeah. Hey Billy, throw that cigarette out!"

Manley took one last puff before complying and asked again, "What now, Kris? What about Vance?"

"I'm going back to Atlanta," Kris finally replied. "I have no proof, no reason to think Vance was murdered."

"Other than what I've told you."

"Other than what you've told me. Like Bruce Morrison said: *who in this little town would want to kill Vance?* He was a harmless drunk who liked to play cards - and he didn't play very well. I guess I'll never know why he killed himself. Maybe he didn't have a reason.

Or maybe it was because he really thought I hated him, and he would have been right."

"So, you're going to drop this whole thing, and go back to Atlanta, just like that?"

"Just like that."

"O.K.," Manley shrugged. "But I wouldn't want that guilt on my shoulders for the rest of my life."

"Billy," Kris said sternly, "the only guilt you have is having to ask someone to buy you a pack of cigarettes and a six pack."

"Uh, speaking of cigarettes, can you loan me a ten? I need some more smokes."

Kris fumbled in his pocket and gave Manley all the cash he had on him – a five and three ones. He dropped Manley off at the Fast Mart, went home and showered for fifteen minutes to try to get rid of the smell of cigarette smoke.

13

Kris started cleaning out the Keller house, one of the tasks that needed to be completed before he could return to Atlanta. He quickly realized this was going to be a week-long job, perhaps longer. Vance had straightened up some parts of his life, but not the house, especially the kitchen. The cabinets were filled with pots and pans and other seldom-used utensils, and practically every box, can and jar in the pantry and refrigerator was out-of-date. So were the clothes in three closets. Vance's wardrobe would have been a retro lover's bonanza, and Kris could only shake his head when he discovered that Vance had not given a single stitch of his wife's clothing away. Most of the furniture, although sturdy and still functional, was scratched, scarred and chipped. Three days and a handful of trips to the landfill and First Baptist clothes closet later, Kris was frustrated, tired and discouraged. He had done much but there was so much remaining. He was not close to having the house cleaned out, and he still had to finalize Vance's financial affairs, find someone to make a few minor repairs, and talk to a real estate agent. The house was paid for - Kris had seen to that - and even selling it at a distressed price and paying a commission would bring a nice profit. Kris was eager to get back to Atlanta and Emmy, but he was beginning to think the house was like a crab claw. As soon as he got rid of a pile of old clothes, old food or old odds and ends, it grew back seemingly bigger.

Having been in the house all morning, Kris was beginning to feel like the walls were closing in on him. Besides, his stomach was starting to growl, so Kris decided to treat himself to a delicious grease burger at Pete's. His gut was almost as empty as the tank of Vance's truck, so Kris had to stop at Fast Mart before going anywhere. Billy Manley was at his regular spot, propped against the propane tanks, puffing on a cigarette. Kris did not think that was very smart, but then no one had ever called Manley a Rhodes Scholar.

Kris filled the tank, and on his way in to pay, stopped to talk to Manley. "Billy," Kris started as he pulled his billfold out of his jeans, "you spend so much time at this place they should stick a hose up your butt and use you for a gas pump."

"Regular or unleaded?" Manley asked, eyeing the cash Kris was pulling out.

"With your alcohol content, it would have to be high test," Kris replied. He started into the store, but Manley stopped him with a question.

"How about buying an old buddy a pack of smokes?"

"No cigarettes but tell you what. I'm on my way to Pete's. Come with me. I'll by you lunch." Manley was presentable enough to been seen with in public.

Manley looked out over the parking lot and then through the plate glass window into the store.

"Come on, Billy," Kris started. "Don't tell me you still believe something sinister happened to Vance and that the same thing is going to happen to you. Man, you've got a major case of paranoia!"

"I'd rather be paranoid than dead."

"It's over, Billy. I'm going back to Atlanta. I'm no threat to anyone around here. There's no reason for anyone to get uptight about seeing you with me. You told me what you know, I looked into it, and concluded you don't know what you're talking about. Now do you want a grease burger or not?"

Manley looked around him again before answering. "I guess you're right. A burger would be good."

Kris paid for the gas and then spent the five minutes it took to drive to Pete's trying to convince Manley to get a job rather than being part of the scenery at the Fast Mart and city sport complex. Manley's reply? *Why work if I can talk folks like you into buying me cigarettes, booze and burgers?* Kris thought about giving the speech about self-respect, dignity and purpose, but decided he would be wasting his breath.

Pete's was close to empty when Kris and Manley walked in. Lonnie Jackson and Officer Davenport were conspicuous sitting at a table in the middle of the dining room. "Lonnie," Kris acknowledged as he and Manley walked by. Lonnie, with a big bite of burger in his mouth, nodded.

"I don't like that guy," Manley said to Kris as they sat in a booth.

"Lonnie? You mean the Marshall Dillon of Fort Phillips?"

"Don't make fun of him. He's been harassing my ass like crazy. And I ain't imagining that. I ain't paranoid about that."

"Why would he be giving you a hard time, other than the fact you're an unemployed, uninspired vagrant?"

"Yeah, but I've been an unemployed, uninspired vagrant all my life. Why is he crawling my case so much all of a sudden?"

Kris waited for the young waitress, a high school dropout according to Manley, to bring two Coca-Colas and take their food orders before he answered. "I'm not bosom buddies with Lonnie, so I have no reason to defend him, but my guess it he's taking his frustrations out on you. His father-in-law is dying, his wife is stressed out about the paper, and the mayor and council won't let him hire any new officers. He's got to vent his frustrations some way, and I guess you're it."

Manley took another quick glance back at Lonnie. "If you're expecting me to cut him some slack because of his sob story, forget it," Manley replied. "I just think he's a jackass."

"I can't argue with that assessment," Kris admitted. He and Manley both laughed.

They got their food and were halfway through eating when Lonnie sauntered to their booth. Manley stopped in mid-chew, leaving a big bulge of burger in his jaw. "Bumming another meal off someone, huh, Manley," Lonnie said hatefully. "You're about the sorriest excuse for a human being I ever saw. You know I could put your butt in jail for loitering."

Manley swallowed the big lump of burger and did not say anything.

Lonnie looked at Kris. "You're an enabler. You know that, don't you," Lonnie said. "By feeding this loser, you are enabling him to maintain his sorry, good-for-nothing lifestyle. Why don't you take him back to Atlanta with you?"

"If I did that," Kris quickly shot back, "you would have no one to harass, which means you would have nothing to do since you're obviously not spending any time looking into the fires and break-ins we've had."

Lonnie's stare reflected his anger at Kris' accusation. "Speaking of break-ins," he said, looking directly at Kris. "Judge Landis let Popeye out on bail. A signature bond. The judge knows Popeye's not going anywhere."

"Why? We caught him red-handed, in the act."

"Because he's basically harmless. We know where to find him. Just like we know where to find Mr. Manley, the fine upstanding citizen that he is." Lonnie shot another teasingly hateful look at Manley.

"I think you should leave Billy alone," Kris responded.

"I can't believe you're taking up for this sorry sack of shit. Why?"

"Because he's basically harmless. We know where to find him. He's lived here all his life, and he'll die here."

"Thanks, I think," Manley said.

"Just stay out of my sight, Manley," Lonnie ordered. "And for God's sake, quit throwing away those damn cigarette packs all over town. You leave a trail a blind man could follow."

Lonnie turned to walk away but Kris asked about Mr. Floyd. "He had a bad night," Lonnie said. "He's not going to be around much longer."

"I've got to get back by to see him."

"Yeah, well, you would probably have more time to do that if you didn't hang around so much with our friend here," Lonnie said sarcastically as he patted Manley on the shoulder.

"Mr. Floyd will be glad to see me. So will Karen," Kris responded to Lonnie. The words flew out of Kris' mouth like he had no control over them. It was a tacky remark and uncalled for, but Lonnie had it coming.

The veins in Lonnie's neck were bulging and he appeared ready to take on Kris right there in Pete's, but his walkie-talkie crackled, and he went outside to take the call.

Manley was sweating, even in the air-conditioned hamburger joint. He took a long drink of his Coke. "You and Lonnie don't have any love for each other, do you?" he asked.

"There's always been a little bit of competition between us, most of it coming from him."

"A little bit? I think he was ready to take you apart with his bare hands just then."

"He could have tried, but I would have won. I always do."

"Cocky son of a gun, aren't you?"

"Nope. Confident."

"And I'm confident that the jackass is going to keep harassing me. Are you sure you don't want to take me back to Atlanta with you?"

"No Billy. The last thing Atlanta needs is another homeless person."

14

Playing the part of enabler that Lonnie had crawled him about, Kris gave Manley money for three packs of cigarettes when he dropped him off at Fast Mart. Manley made his purchase and dutifully, like the guards at Buckingham Palace but without the pageantry, took his position at the propane tanks. Kris drove back to his house, not thrilled at the thought of having to resume the overwhelming task of cleaning out the place.

Kris was about to resume clearance efforts in the master bedroom when he was struck with a sudden, severe wave of melancholy. Foregoing the cleaning, he went to the kitchen, pulled out a beer, sat down at the table and started sipping. He was separated from his fiancée and the job he loved. His mother, the glue that had held the family together, was dead, and his father had ended his life in one final selfish act, again leaving Kris to clean up the mess. He had not expected his sister Becky to come cross country for a fifteen-minute memorial service, but she had not even bothered to call. Kris felt alone and helpless, and for the first time in his life, considered getting drunk, but there were only two more beers in the refrigerator, and he didn't want to go back to Fast Mart, especially if it meant seeing Billy Manley again.

More than his family's detachment was bothering Kris. He was sad for his hometown. Years earlier, Fort Phillips had been a vibrant middle-class town, full of people happy with their routine of working at Simpson Slacks and supporting activities at the high school. Then came cheap foreign imports, big box stores and the bypass, and one-by-one, the clothing plants and the little locally owned businesses wilted and died. Kris had managed to escape to a bigger place and a better fate, but he was said for the families and individuals who had chosen to stay and struggle. The most significant addition to the town had been a company that no one knew anything about. As difficult as it was for him to separate his hometown from his bad memories of Vance, Kris was certain this place and its people did not deserve this fate.

Feeling incredibly lonely, Kris pulled out his cell phone and called Emmy. "I just needed to hear your voice," he said tenderly when she answered.

"Hey Babe," she answered back and quickly added, "You sound down. What's wrong Kris? Is something wrong with your arm?" Emmy sounded more concerned, more sympathetic than when they had last spoken.

"The arm is fine. A little sore, but fine. I am just feeling a little down in the dumps, feeling a little sorry for myself. Needing a little moral support."

Emmy hated to hear Kris so forlorn. That was not like him. She wished she could pull him through the phone and give him a big hug. "Is something in particular bothering you?" she asked.

"Yeah. I'm here and you're there."

"I'm glad to hear that you miss me. There is a simple solution to this problem. Come home."

"I wish I could. I have some work remaining. I'm cleaning out the house, and it seems like for every step forward I take, I take two steps backward."

"I understand. Mom and I felt that way after my grandfather died. I guess this means you'll be there a few more days."

"A few. I know I said it would only take a week but…"

"Don't worry about it Kris. I understand." Emmy wanted Kris home, and she wanted him there now, but she did not believe this was the proper time to push him, especially as depressed as he seemed. "Is there anything I can do to make you feel better?" she asked.

"Come back down here."

"That's the one thing I can't do. We're busy at work."

"I know. It was selfish of me to ask. I guess I got that trait from Vance."

"Stop it, Kris! There is nothing selfish about you. Didn't you prove that to yourself with the way you helped save Patrick and rescued cats from the clinic fire? I still can't believe you did that!"

"How is Patrick? I've tied checking on him a few times but haven't had any luck getting in touch."

"He's doing O.K. He is going to physical therapy regularly. Emotionally, he seems amazingly upbeat. The station put him on a leave of absence."

"I'm not surprised. He won't be back at Channel 12."

"But how about you? Are you going to be all right?"

"Yeah. I will be fine. Are you sure you can't come down?"

"I can't. Plus, I don't think Karen would be happy to see me."

"Her father isn't doing well."

"I'm sorry. That is bothering you too, isn't it?"

"It is. A lot of stuff is bothering me right now. I feel like I just need a good cry. Sort of like you females at certain times during the month."

"Try chocolate," she kidded.

They engaged in small talk for another ten minutes before Emmy was called away to serve a client. She encouraged Kris to cheer up and let him know in a sweet but direct manner that she wanted him home soon.

Kris reached into the refrigerator to get another beer but decided not to. He did not want to resume cleaning, but the job was never going to get done if he didn't stick with it. He headed back to the master bedroom but was stopped by his ringing cell phone. Karen's cell number came up. "Dad's dying," she sobbed almost before Kris could answer.

"Lonnie said your dad had a bad night."

"He did, and he's gotten worse. He's dying, Kris. He may not last five more minutes. Can you come over? Please! Hurry!"

Kris did more than hurry. He broke every traffic safety regulation in the books getting to Mr. Floyd's house. Karen and the doctor were at the foot of the bed watching this beloved man take his last short, shallow breaths. Karen, tears streaming down her cheeks, immediately hugged Kris.

With compassion, the doctor said, "There's nothing I can do. I'm going to leave you two with Mr. Floyd."

Karen slipped her arm around Kris' waist and they silently watched the life ebb out of Carter Floyd. Karen was continuously wiping tears from her eyes, and Kris could feel the water welling in his. He bit his lip to keep from crying.

"I owe so much to your dad," Kris admitted, his voice cracking. "He mentored me, encouraged me, pulled some strings to help me get the job in Atlanta. I hope he's proud of what I've been able to do."

"Oh, he was very proud of you," Karen sniffled. "He talked about you all the time."

"He probably talked about me a lot more than Lonnie liked. By the way, where is Lonnie? Shouldn't he be here?"

"He got a call about another break-in. He'll get here as quickly as he can."

"Couldn't he have sent an officer to that? He needs to be here."

"Lonnie doesn't share your admiration of my dad."

"Even if he doesn't, he needs to be here for you."

"I'd rather have you here."

Kris looked into Karen's watery eyes, but quickly looked back at Mr. Floyd. Smiling, Kris started, "I can remember the first assignment your dad sent me on for the Sentinel. I was in the ninth grade. It was the student council talent contest in the high school gym. I even remember the winner. Carrie Fowler did a tap dance. God, she had skinny legs!"

The memory made Karen smile. "Do you remember our first date?" she asked.

Lonnie had quietly entered the house. When he saw Kris and Karen cuddled up at the foot of Mr. Floyd's bed, he stopped at the door of the bedroom instead of continuing in. He watched, and Kris and Karen were oblivious to his presence.

"Do I remember our first date?" Kris asked rhetorically. "Uh, let me think."

"You don't remember?" Karen playfully patted Kris on the upper arm, which elicited a muffled "Ouch!"

"I'm sorry," she apologized, "I forgot about your arm. Are you O.K.?"

"Yeah, I'm fine. It's healing well, just a little sore. And yes, I do remember our first date. We picnicked at Cooter's Lake. Sandwiches, chips and heavy petting."

Karen looked at her dad, whose mouth was open, eyes glazed and fixed and breathing getting less frequent. Mr. Floyd's soul would soon be free of his tired earthly body. She sighed, wiped a tear away, and told Kris, "We had some really good times together, you and me."

"We did. You know one thing I remember in particular?"

"What's that?"

"You never missed one of my basketball games. Through four years of high school, you never missed a game. Now that's dedication."

"No, that's love. I loved you, Kris. I still love you." She hugged him again and started to kiss him. Kris let her.

Lonnie's rage was building as he watched from the entrance to the room. "The son of a bitch!" he muttered about Kris. He slid his hand down to his waist, resting it on his sidearm.

Kris gently pushed Karen away and looked at Mr. Floyd. "We need to say goodbye to your dad," Kris told her.

Kris lifted Mr. Floyd's hand and squeezed gently. Tears started rolling down Kris' face as he professed, "Thanks for everything. I love you, Mr. Floyd. May God take you into His care."

Carter Floyd took his last breath and Karen started crying uncontrollably. Kris took her into his arms. Lonnie, when he should have gone into the room to comfort his wife, slipped out of the house and sped away, spitting out profanity.

Slowly, Karen cried out and gained a measure of composure. "It's proper that you were here for this moment," she smiled at Kris. "I know in my heart that Dad knew you were here."

Kris nodded in agreement.

Karen took Kris' hand and looked at the floor. "Can I get you to do something for me?" she asked, her head still down.

"Sure. You name it."

Smiling weakly, she said, "Stay here and help me run the Sentinel."

Her request unnerved Kris and he was speechless.

"Not permanently," she said. "Just for a few weeks until I can settle Dad's affairs and decide what I want to do."

"I don't know what to say, Karen. I've got to get back to my job in Atlanta, and to…"

"And to Emmy?"

"And to Emmy."

"Kris, I wouldn't ask you to do this unless I really needed you. I am frightened and I feel so alone. Mom died while you and I were in high school. I do not have any brothers or sisters. There is no one in this town that I can confide in. No one knows me better than you."

"What about Lonnie?"

"Lonnie is worthless. Oh, he's not worthless. I didn't mean that. He doesn't know anything about the newspaper business. He has a difficult enough time being police chief. And as for what he does for me…well, he's not very understanding, not very supportive."

"I can't stay."

"Even if you don't want to do it for me, do it for Dad. I think you owe it to him."

Kris looked directly at Karen, looked at her dad, and then ran his fingers through his hair. The emotional spear Karen hurled had pierced his armor and gone straight to his heart.

"I guess I do," he admitted. "I guess I owe it to your dad, and I owe it to you."

Karen started crying again, not for her dad, but for Kris' surrender. She wrapped her arms tightly around Kris who grunted as pain shot through the tender wound on his arm.

15

Montgomery Funeral Home was packed with people and flowers for the scheduled 5 p.m. to 8 p.m. visitation for Carter Floyd, newspaper icon and beloved Fort Phillips advocate/cheerleader. All the floral arrangements made the place look like a jungle and smell like a perfume factory. Mickey Montgomery had to start directing deliveries to the front porch because there was no space left inside. Donald and Winnie Johnson arrived first, fifteen minutes early, to pay their respect; Lester and Rachel Burton were the last to leave, twenty-nine minutes after eight o'clock. In between, hundreds of people, including faithful Sentinel readers who had not missed an issue in thirty years, business and community leaders, newspaper colleagues from throughout the state and even a few slackers like Billy Manley all filed by the bronze casket to say goodbye. They all said Carter Floyd was a good man with a good heart and an unfailing devotion to the little town that had been so good to him. Conventional wisdom is that anyone, regardless of their status, can be replaced, but the exception to that rule may well have been Carter Floyd in Fort Phillips. The countless moist eyes and soaked tissues in the funeral home was a good gauge of how deeply everyone felt about this man.

Emmy Owens' feelings for Mr. Floyd did not run that deep because she didn't know him. Nonetheless, she was at Montgomery's paying her respects, although somewhat under protest. Emmy had received another call from Kris, asking her to return to Fort Phillips with a suit he could wear to the funeral and a couple of days of casual clothes. For Emmy, Kris' timing - and Mr. Floyd's for that matter - was not good. She was snowed at work, did not want to leave, and did not want to ask for time off, but she did, and her boss reluctantly granted the request. Emmy understood her responsibility to be with Kris, but she wished it could be in some place other than Fort Phillips.

Standing by Kris' side as he greeted one old friend and acquaintance after another - all of whom were imploring him to take over the Sentinel - Emmy had managed to avoid Karen, who was tucked away in another corner, going through the same ritual as Kris. Even in a basic black pantsuit appropriate for a funeral, Emmy was stunningly gorgeous, and she could not help but notice the looks she was getting from both men and women. She liked the attention, but it made her feel uncomfortable at the same time, especially when the sneaky peeks were coming from some creep like Billy Manley. Kris was so busy schmoozing that he had no idea about what was going on.

Slipping her hand out of Kris', Emmy weaved her way through the crowd to the kitchen, which the funeral home tried to keep off limits to everyone but family of the deceased. She pulled a Diet Coke out of a cooler full of soft drinks Mr. Floyd's First Baptist Sunday School class had provided, sat down at the table, and sighed. She was ready for all of this to be over.

Emmy stopped in mid-swallow when Karen walked into the kitchen. They were surprised and not pleased to see each other.

"May I join you?" Karen asked, entering the kitchen and getting her own Diet Coke.

"Have a seat," Emmy said, finishing her swallow, quickly trying to think of a way she could gracefully exit.

"I appreciate you coming today," Karen said, popping open her canned drink.

"You're welcome," Emmy replied politely. "I am sorry about your dad. I am blown away by this turnout. This town genuinely loved him."

"They did," Karen nodded. She was not as attractive as Emmy, but certainly worthy of second looks herself.

"I know how much your dad meant to Kris."

"You're right. They were like father and son."

"Well, with all due respect to your father," Emmy started, "Life goes on. I'll be glad to get Kris back to Atlanta so he can go back to work, and we can resume planning our wedding." She looked directly into Karen's eyes and took another sip of her drink.

Karen's eyebrows arched. "Kris hasn't told you yet?" she asked.

Emmy's eyebrows arched in return. "Told me what?"

"That he's going to stay here and help me run the Sentinel." Karen neglected to tell Emmy that Kris' pledge was to stay short term.

Emmy cleared her throat. "Uh, yes, uh, we've talked about it," she stumbled. "We have an understanding." Emmy could feel the blood rushing to her face.

"You do? Are you going to be staying here in Fort Phillips? I am sorry, but I just can't see you setting up residence here. Way too high maintenance for a place like this."

"I would if that's what Kris wanted me to do," Emmy quickly responded although that statement did not express her true feelings. "But that's not what he wants me, wants us, to do."

"Are you sure? When I talked to him yesterday, he seemed excited about the idea of moving back here. I think he may be here to stay." Karen was enjoying playing with Emmy, watching her uncomfortable body movements and facial expressions.

"Is there some chocolate around here?" Emmy asked, surveying the plate of cookies on the kitchen counter. Getting up from the table, Emmy picked up a chocolate chip cookie and crammed it into her mouth. She could not see the wide smile going across Karen's face.

"Don't worry, Emmy," Karen kept teasing. "My relationship with Kris is strictly business.'

"Yeah, monkey business," Emmy uttered under her breath. "I'm feeling a little sick," Emmy said. "Do you mind telling Kris I've gone back to the house?"

"Not at all. I hope you get to feeling better. You know, there are worse places to live than Fort Phillips," Karen said.

"Yeah, a federal prison," Emmy mumbled as she walked out of the back door.

Karen smiled again, straightened her plum-colored dress, rubbed her eyes to make them red and headed back to the crowd of mourners still at the funeral home. She did not see Kris, and asked Mickey Montgomery where he was. All Mickey could offer was Lonnie had tugged on Kris and they had stepped out on the front porch.

Karen thanked Mickey and started the search for her husband and old boyfriend.

Out on the porch, Kris wiped his forehead with a tissue he had been holding for fifteen minutes. "Thanks for rescuing me," Kris said appreciatively to Lonnie. "It was getting hot in there. Between the heat and the smell of all those flowers, I was starting to feel a bit woozy."

Lonnie pulled a couple of leaves from the shrub in front of the porch. "Don't be thanking me," he told Kris. "I didn't come to rescue you. I pulled you aside to chew your ass out."

Kris stopped wiping his forehead. Puzzled, he asked Lonnie, "What the heck are you talking about?"

"Karen told me you're staying to help run the Sentinel. Kris, you do not have any business here. You do not have any idea of what's going on around here. You need to get back to Atlanta, fast. And by the way, dammit, I want you to stay away from my wife!"

"Gee, Lonnie, that's going to be sort of tough, considering she and I are going to be working together."

While Lonnie and Kris were getting heavy into their conversation, Karen had slipped out the back door of the funeral home and stopped at the edge of the front porch, out of sight, but close enough to hear everything that was being said.

Lonnie leaned on the front porch railing, looked out into the yard, and back at Kris. "I'm not worried about the work. It's the other stuff between the two of you that worries me," Lonnie said.

Kris rolled his eyes in frustration. "My god, Lonnie! How many times do I have to tell you? There is nothing between Karen and me. I am engaged. As soon as Karen can settle her dad's affairs and decide what she wants to do with the Sentinel, I am out of here. I have a wedding to plan, and my boss wants me back in Atlanta. Believe me, I don't want to stay here any longer than I have to."

"Why are you having to stay here at all?"

Kris was silent. He rubbed the back of his neck before answering, "I'm staying because I owe it to Mr. Floyd. And Karen. But mostly to Mr. Floyd."

At the side of the house, Karen smiled and nodded.

"I don't believe you!" Lonnie shot back, his voice getting louder. "I still think you love Karen, and I sure as hell know she still loves you."

"I give up!" Kris said, his voice trailing off. "Obviously I cannot say anything that will penetrate that thick skull of yours, so I'm ending this conversation. I am tired. I'm going home." Kris started to walk off the porch, but Lonnie stepped in front of him.

"I mean it, Kris. Stay away from Karen. Get out of this town before you get hurt. You have no idea what you're getting in to."

"I know I'm getting into a futile discussion with an idiot."

"I'm a good mind to pick you up and personally carry your ass out of town."

Kris' frustration was turning into anger. "You throw me out of town? You and who else? You've never got the best of me in anything."

Lonnie slid his hand down to his sidearm. Kris noticed and swallowed hard. "I'll see you later, Lonnie," Kris said, trying to get back inside.

Lonnie stepped in front of him again and put his hand on Kris' chest. "Are we clear on everything?" Lonnie asked.

Kris pushed Lonnie's hand away. "Yeah, we're clear," Kris retorted. "Clear as mud. And if you lay a hand on me again, I will knock your damn teeth out!" Kris started walking away before Lonnie, startled at Kris' aggressive warning, could respond.

Tired and frustrated and fighting back a wave of rage, Kris bumped Lonnie, inadvertently, and went back into the funeral home to get Emmy and head home. He did not find Emmy, but Karen found him.

"Where have you been?" she asked.

"Outside, getting some fresh air."

"Everything was getting to Emmy too. She asked me to tell you she was going home."

"Thanks. I am glad we came in separate vehicles. Otherwise, I guess I would be walking home."

"You know I would have gladly given you a ride."

"I don't think your husband would like that."

"Who cares what Lonnie thinks? After all, we are business partners now, aren't we?"

"Yeah, and let's keep it at strictly business."

"Whatever you say, partner." Karen was struggling not to show her pleasure with the conversation she had heard outside between Kris and Lonnie.

Realizing why he was at Montgomery's in the first place, Kris felt ashamed of himself. He took a deep breath, composed himself, and asked Karen. "Are you holding up all right? Are you going to make it through the rest of this visitation and the funeral tomorrow?"

"I am fine. Just tired. I am ready to get all of this over."

"Good," Kris said. He took her hand and squeezed it softly. "I'll see you tomorrow."

She clenched his hand, pulled him toward her and hugged him. Karen put her mouth to his ear and whispered, "I love you."

Kris backed away, smiled weakly, and repeated, "I'll see you tomorrow." Walking out of Montgomery Funeral Home, Kris wondered if he was really doing the right thing by agreeing to stay in Fort Phillips.

16

While Kris was making his way home, Emmy was at the Keller house trying to relax after the trip down from Atlanta earlier in the day and the unpleasant meeting with Karen at the funeral home. Stripped down to black panties and bra, Emmy was sitting at the kitchen table sipping on a cup of decaffeinated coffee, haunted by the notion that Kris might be staying in Fort Phillips, and hurt because he had yet to tell her. She tried to drive the notion out of her head, but Emmy, seriously, for the first time, was starting to doubt their future together.

She used her last sip of coffee to down two Tylenol PM and went to the bathroom to wash off her makeup. The hour was early, but she was ready to go to bed. She did not want to wait up for Kris. All she wanted to do was crawl in bed, pull the covers over her head, and hope that when she woke up, she *and* Kris would be back in Atlanta, and life would be blissfully like it was before the phone call came that Vance Keller had died.

Staring into the mirror over the bathroom sink, Emmy realized how tired her eyes were. She turned on the water, soaped up a good lather on her hands and, with head down, started scrubbing her face. Having rinsed off the refreshing lavender soap, Emmy looked into the mirror again and gasped as she got a glimpse of the chubby man's face in the mirror. Before she could scream or make any kind of movement, the intruder wrapped his arm around her throat and started dragging her to the bed in Kris' room. He was holding Emmy with such force that her feet were a couple of inches off the ground. He flung her on the bed and quickly straddled her at the waist, almost knocking the breath out of her. With one hand, he held Emmy's arms above her head and started tugging at her bra with the other. He leaned down to kiss her, and she turned away. The alcohol smell on his breath almost made her sick. Too frightened to cry or scream, Emmy closed her eyes as she felt her bra pull away from her breasts.

"You damn son of a bitch!" Kris screamed as he took a running leap from the doorway of the room and landed solidly on the chubby man, knocking him off Emmy and on to the floor. Having to stay on the bed a moment to catch her breath, Emmy watched as Kris and the chubby man wrestled. Landing a lucky punch to the jaw, the chubby man staggered Kris and was about to pick him up by the shirt and bash him against the wall when Emmy whacked him in the back of his head with one of Kris' basketball trophies. The chubby man went down in a heap, and Kris wasted no time binding his hands and feet with some old neckties from his closet.

"I knew there was a reason I didn't throw those trophies away," Kris said, observing the bloody Most Valuable Player award Emmy was still holding. Rummaging through the closet, Kris found an old Georgia Tech football jersey he put on Emmy who was shaking uncontrollably. "It's O.K. Baby," he reassured her, "It's O.K." Kris let her go long enough to call Lonnie Jackson and clutched her tightly again.

Kris readily recognized Popeye, the earlier intruder whom Lonnie had termed a *harmless petty thief.* There was nothing harmless or petty about Popeye's actions this night. If Kris had not interrupted, Popeye would have raped Emmy at the least and more than likely killed her afterwards. Emmy had stopped shaking but tears were still streaming down her cheeks. Kris helped her dress in brown sandals, jeans and a red short-sleeve shirt and held her until Lonnie and Officer Davenport arrived. Popeye was just beginning to move and make groaning noises.

"Get this asshole out of my house!" Kris screamed at Lonnie while gesturing toward Popeye.

Lonnie leaned down, grabbed Popeye by the hair and studied his face. Popeye's eyes were glazed, and he had no idea if he was in Georgia, Alabama or Alaska. Emmy had belted him solidly with the trophy. Wiping blood from his hand with a handkerchief, Lonnie asked a non-responsive Popeye, "Getting handcuffed to the table wasn't enough for you?"

"Why did he come back? What's he after? There's nothing in this house worth taking," Kris asked. He looked back at Emmy who was still sitting on the bed with a distant, hollow look in her eyes.

"Beauty is in the eye of the beholder," Lonnie explained. "Something that you believe is worthless can bring a few dollars at a pawn shop. On the other hand, he may have taken it as a personal challenge to break in again, since you caught him the first time. I admit, Popeye does have a bit of a mean streak in him." Lonnie glanced at Emmy. "And if you had taken a few more minutes getting back from the funeral home, his revenge would have been really sweet."

"By God, this is the last time this son of a bitch will get in my house! If he does, I will kill him! He shouldn't be here now, if you and your judge had kept him locked up like he should have been!"

"Cut out the chest-thumping!" Lonnie snapped back as he helped his officer pull Popeye to his feet. A second officer had arrived and assisted with getting Popeye, who was still groggy and a dead weight, to the squad car. "You do not go around in my town telling people you're going to kill them…or knocking out their teeth!"

"Maybe that's what people around here need to do. Take matters into their own hands. You sure as heck don't seem to be doing a particularly good job protecting them!"

"Does she need to go to the hospital?" Lonnie looked at Emmy again and asked her, "Do you need to go to the hospital?"

Sniffling, she answered softly, "No."

Lonnie looked at Kris. "I know you're upset…"

"That's an understatement!" Kris interrupted.

"Let me do my job. Why don't you and your girlfriend go back to Atlanta where the real crime is."

"And where the real law enforcement officers are."

"Yeah, We're just a bunch of Barney Fifes down here. Don't know our butts from a hole in the ground."

"Just keep this creep away from us! I mean it Lonnie. I'll do whatever it takes to keep us safe."

Lonnie glared at Kris, "I'm tired of you mouthing off, damn it! I am tired of you ruining my life. It's like we were back in high school."

Both men were ready to escalate their war or words. Kris was about to continue the verbal jousting when Emmy urged him, "That's enough Kris! Drop it!" She wiped a tear off her cheek.

"Your girlfriend is smart…and pretty," Lonnie started "I'm going to need a statement from her, but I'm not going to ask her for it tonight. The two of you come by my office in the morning and we'll take care of it."

Kris' only reply was a quick, "O.K."

Lonnie walked to Emmy who was still sitting on the bed, put his hand on her shoulder and said, "I'm glad you're all right. Come see me in the morning." She nodded affirmatively.

With Lonnie gone, Kris gently guided Emmy to the kitchen and poured them both cups of coffee. "I'm so sorry this happened," Kris told her.

"You're sorry? You're not the one who almost got raped."

"It won't happen again," Kris assured her.

Emmy tucked her head and began fumbling with the diamond engagement ring on her left hand. "You're right," she answered, "it won't happen again." She slipped the ring off her finger and dropped it on the table.

Kris was stunned. "What are you doing?" he asked.

With head still down, Emmy started, "It's obvious that, at this point, you love this town and the people here more than you love me." She looked at Kris. Her eyes were full of tears.

"That's crazy!"

"Is it? Karen told me you're staying here to help with the Sentinel. Which do you love the most, Kris, that newspaper or Karen?"

"Neither," Kris said frantically. "I love you, Emmy!"

"Prove it. Come back to Atlanta."

"I'm going to…just not right now."

Emmy managed a weak smile. "See what I mean," she said, wiping another tear from the corner of her eye. "I almost get raped by some fat freak and that's still not enough to get you away from this place."

"All I need is a few more days."

"And I'm not willing to give you a few more days. Unless you are ready to go back with me now, tonight, I don't see that we have any future together."

"You're not being fair."

"Maybe not, but that's the way it is. What's it going to be Kris?"

He tried to talk, but no words came out. "I, uh…"

Emmy got up from the table. "I'm going to get together the few things I brought and leave. Tonight."

Kris got up with her. "You can't leave," he said. "You've got to go by the police station in the morning and give Lonnie a statement."

"I don't have to," Emmy said, making her way to Kris' bedroom.

"They won't have a case against him, not unless you give a statement and then come back to testify."

Emmy started stuffing items into an overnight bag. "What do I care? I don't plan on ever seeing that monster or this town again."

"Please don't leave, Emmy," Kris was about to cry.

"It's funny, Kris. When we first came down after we found out about your dad, I could not believe the negative attitude you had about this place. All you wanted to do was take care of business and get out of here. A quick trip back home. I was urging you to be more tolerant. Now, I am the one wanting to leave, and you're telling me to be more tolerant."

"I had no intention of staying here. Some stuff just happened," Kris said, putting up a weak defense.

"Well, when you take care of your stuff, come see me. Then we'll decide if you and I have a future."

Emmy picked up her bag and walked out to her car with Kris following, begging her not to leave. "I can't believe I'm doing this," she said. "But you left me no choice."

She drove away, leaving Kris standing in the driveway, rubbing his aching arm, wondering how in the world he had managed to mess up his life in such a short amount of time.

17

Slouched at a desk in what used to be Carter Floyd's cramped office in the back of the Sentinel, Kris was in the third day of a three-day bout with depression. He had tried calling Emmy a hundred times, but she would not answer or return his calls. He desperately wanted to talk to her, even though he was not sure what he would say. He could not shake the sickening image of Popeye straddled over Emmy, tearing away at her underclothes, getting ready to violate her. Traumatized over the incident as any woman would be, Emmy had begged Kris to get her out of town and he had refused. He had brushed off the woman he loves and intends to marry to stay behind and assist an old girlfriend. Kris knew he had made the wrong decision. He could tell Emmy he was sorry, but that would sound awfully hollow, especially considering he was still in Fort Phillips. Kris wanted to leave, but some invisible, irresistible force would not let him. Was it his devotion to Mr. Floyd? Did he subconsciously want to take on the challenge of running the Sentinel? Was Billy Manley's theory that Vance did not kill himself still in the back of his mind? Deep down, did he still love Karen? Or was it all those factors combined? Kris did not know. He did not have a clue, and the knot in his stomach indicated he was not anywhere close to coming to a conclusion.

Making matters worse, the editor at the Atlanta Advocate was not thrilled with Kris calling him a second time and requesting more time off. Kris was a good reporter, certainly, but not so valuable for someone to make an open-ended promise to hold his job. Kris was perilously close to losing Emmy and his job - if he had not already. In a few short days, all he would have left from his time in Atlanta was a used engagement ring and forty stitches in his left arm.

Besides being depressed, Kris was angry because Emmy was not around to press charges or serve as a witness and because Lonnie, on advice from the District Attorney, had released Popeye a second time. Kris was flabbergasted authorities would not retain a degenerate who had caused the town grief through multiple break-ins and had now graduated to attempted rape. Kris saw that was one way his hometown had changed. Ten years ago, the police and chief prosecutor would have put Popeye in jail and thrown away the key. Now they all seemed in cahoots. Billy Manley was right about one thing. Strange stuff was going on in Fort Phillips.

Kris had promised to help Karen with the Sentinel, but as he sat at Carter Floyd's desk, he did not know what to do. Flipping through old copies of the Sentinel, he had concluded the paper's days were numbered. There was no real news in the newspaper. Ninety percent of the articles in every issue had been submitted by a civic club, school class, church or couples announcing their engagements. Reports about the city council, school board and courts and law enforcement were infrequent and lacked details. Advertising through the eight pages was skimpy. Kris knew the Sentinel could not be paying its bills without having to dip into its financial reserves, which would no doubt soon be gone. Then, Karen would have no choice but to fold the newspaper, a fate Kris did not want to accept. He did not blame Karen for the paper's plight. Considering she had been running the paper by herself, Kris thought she had done an admirable job.

The financial aspect of the newspaper business was not Kris' strong point, but he could offer his reporting and editing skills. Perhaps by improving the editorial content, Kris could generate a few more subscription and ad sales, thereby buying the Sentinel a few more weeks or months. Hopefully, Karen could find an individual with deep pockets or a company to make a respectable offer for the paper.

Trying mightily to get his mind off his other troubles, Kris was jotting story ideas down on a legal pad. There was no shortage of topics that needed to be covered - the town's economic woes, the recent rash of break-in, fires and other suspicious activities, the reluctance of police and prosecutors to aggressively go after all the Popeyes in Fort Phillips, and the mysterious delivery company that had moved to town when all other businesses were shutting down or leaving. Kris had plenty to keep him busy. The problem was, all those stories would take time to investigate and develop, and he was praying that he would not be around long enough to get started on most of them, much less finish.

With his gaze fixed on the list, trying to decide which assignment to tackle first, Kris did not see Karen walk into the office. She startled him by admitting, "You look good sitting there at Dad's desk."

"I wish I was half the newspaperman he was," Kris replied, slowly looking up. Karen looked fresh and appealing in a knee length printed skirt, sleeveless white knit top and white sandals with two-inch heels. Her outward appearance gave no indication of the difficult times she had been through with her father and the Sentinel.

"You will be, in time. In fact, you are close already. You had a good teacher," she smiled.

"Yes, I did," he smiled back.

"You look sad, Kris," Karen said. She approached him and rubbed the back of his neck.

"I am bummed out," he admitted. "I treated Emmy terribly, I've put my job in Atlanta at risk, and I am not sure how much I can help you."

"You're helping me by just being here."

"What are you going to do? You are going to try to sell the Sentinel, aren't you?"

"Yes, but I'm afraid that may be difficult. Everyone knows what terrible shape this town is in. And you know as well as I do the newspaper business as a whole is suffering. The Internet and ten thousand cable news networks are killing us."

"Someone will buy it. Hopefully sooner than later."

"Are you in that much of a hurry to leave here?"

"I must. I have too much at stake. I should not have come here, Karen. I should have sent Mickey Montgomery a check and let him take care of Vance without me ever setting foot in Fort Phillips."

"That's absurd Kris, and you know it."

"All I know right now is that I'm a candidate for a nervous breakdown."

"Let me see if I can help," Karen placed her hands gently on the back of Kris' neck and began massaging. He lowered his head and allowed her to continue. Closing his eyes, he forgot about his troubles for a moment.

"That feels so good," he said.

Karen leaned down and whispered in his ear, "I can think of something we can do that will feel even better."

He softly took her hands and pushed them away. "I don't think so," he said.

Frustrated, Karen asked, "Why fight it, Kris? You know it's supposed to be."

"No, I don't know that at all. I've got to try to patch things up with Emmy and you're married to the town's police chief."

"We could make things work."

"Let's stick with trying to make things work here at the Sentinel. I've been looking over a list of possible story ideas. What do you think about me trying to interview someone about the new delivery company?"

"Knock yourself out, but you won't get to first base. Now with me, on the other hand, you could hit a homerun."

"I think I'll check out the delivery company, distribution company or whatever the hell they are."

Karen sighed. "Good luck." She started out the door but stopped, "If you won't let me relieve your tension, make a date with your first love – basketball. Lonnie, Mickey Montgomery and some other guys are always playing at the recreation complex. I think they may be there now."

"Playing basketball in the middle of the day in the middle of the week?"

She tapped him playfully on the shoulder. "Never let work get in the way of a good basketball game," she smiled.

"Thanks. I remember Mark Stewart saying something about that to me at the softball games. I'm not sure how much I can do with my arm, but I think I'll show up a little later if they're still playing."

Even though the thermometer on the Fort Phillips Community Bank sign was registering 89 degrees, Kris walked the three blocks to the old Simpson Slacks plant. He was determined to put together some type of story about the current occupant, the mysterious Syndicated Delivery Services, which seemed to have no interest in being a good neighbor or a contributing member of the community. But as he stood in front of the decaying two story building whose walls were murals of flaking white paint and broken windows, Kris' thoughts were in the past rather than the present. In its prime thirty years earlier, Simpson Slacks was the heart of Fort Phillips, employing 250 people and churning out hundreds of pairs of slacks a day that were distributed to men's stores throughout the country and sold in several outlet stores in Fort Phillips. The company had little turnover. A job at Simpson Slacks was coveted. The paychecks weren't that great, but they were steady and dependable. Workers had medical and dental insurance and two weeks of annual vacation wrapped around the Fourth of July. Like the plant, Fort Phillips and its good folks thrived. Everyone had nice cars, nice houses and disposable income to spend in a good variety of locally owned stores and restaurants.

Studying the tired old building that needed to be demolished, Kris was hit with a wave of sadness for his hometown. There seemed to be no hope for a rebirth, a revitalization. He did not know anything about Syndicated Delivery Services, but he already thought of them with contempt for not making an effort to help the town out of its economic grave. Wiping a drop of sweat from his brow, Kris started walking around the perimeter of the massive rectangular building. No cars were in the parking lot. Kris saw no signs of activity. A couple of side doors leading to the first floor were secured with padlocks and looked as if they had not been opened in years. In the back, despite a sign that ordered *No Admittance. Violators Will Be Prosecuted*, Kris rattled two large, locked cargo doors. Kris did not feel threatened. He did not believe anyone was around to shoo him away, much less have him arrested.

Looking for some sign of life, Kris continued to circle the building. The place was as quiet as Christmas Eve after all the children have gone to bed. His immediate thought was why would anyone want to purchase this relic? It was about to cave in and judging by what he was seeing and had been told, no repairs or upgrades had been made or were planned. Unless it was being used as a quick-in, quick-out warehouse, he had no idea of its purpose.

Taking the next logical step, Kris went to the front door, which was locked. A letter-size piece of white paper thumb-tacked to the heavy wooden door declared *No Admittance. For Emergencies, Call 555-5555.*

Kris scratched his head. "Hmmm. I would consider this an emergency," he mumbled to himself. "It's an emergency because I need some information for my story." He tugged on the door handle once again, foolishly believing it might open, but when it didn't, he turned away to go back to the Sentinel. Lonnie Jackson had pulled his patrol car in front of the building and was striding toward Kris.

"What are you doing here?" Lonnie barked at Kris.

"Working on a story. Karen told me you were playing basketball."

"That's later. Seven o'clock or so. The folks that run this place, they do not want any publicity," Lonnie said, inching his nose close to Kris.

"How do you know that?"

"Isn't it obvious?" Lonnie asked, pointing to the sign on the door.

"Well, they should know that crap like that only makes a good reporter want to dig harder. Besides, what do you care? Are you on their payroll?"

"No, but by damn, I'm the Chief of Police, and if a place has *No Admittance* signs up everywhere, I'm obligated to make sure there is no admittance."

"I'm going to get in there some way."

Lonnie was becoming agitated, and his breathing was labored. Kris could tell by the look on his face that Lonnie's rage was building.

"Calm down, Dude, before you have a stroke," Kris told him.

Lonnie exhaled. It sounded like air being let out of a balloon, and if by magic, his tension disappeared. Then, after taking a deep breath, he said to Kris. "It's hot as hell out here. Let's go to my car. I need to tell you something."

"If you're going to lecture me about Karen again…"

"No, it's way more than that. Come on."

Reluctantly, Kris followed Lonnie into his creaky city-issued car which should have been replaced three years earlier. Sitting in the air-conditioned vehicle was much better than standing out in the sweltering Georgia heat.

"What do you need to tell me, Lonnie?"

Using the sleeve of his uniform shirt to wipe his forehead, Lonnie started to speak and then stopped, as if he had changed his mind.

"What is it, Lonnie?"

"You cannot tell anyone else what I am about to tell you. If I do see you about to tell someone else, I'll have to kill you."

Kris moaned. "Geez, Lonnie. That line is so old and lame. Is that the best you can come up with?"

"No, I mean it. If you start to tell someone, I'll have to kill you."

Kris decided to play along. "My lips are sealed," he said, pretending to be serious.

Looking straight ahead rather than at Kris, Lonnie started, "You know that I was never the brightest student at good ole Fort Phillips High School."

"That I remember. Coach had to stay on your ass about your grades to keep you eligible to play basketball."

Yeah, and in particular, I hated world geography. Why the hell would I care that coffee was Columbia's biggest export?"

"O.K.," Kris replied, puzzled where Lonnie was going with this.

"And international affairs? All I want to know about international affairs is when the World Cup is being played, and if England beat China in another of those boring1-Nil matches."

"Get to your point," Kris urged. So far, everything Lonnie had said was of no interest to Kris.

"I have been told there are governments in different parts of the world that are not friends of the United States and they do everything they can to undermine our diplomatic and humanitarian efforts."

Kris wondered if Lonnie had been body-snatched. He had never heard him talk so concisely about such worldly matters. At the same time, Kris had had enough. "O.K. Lonnie. You've lost me. What does all of that have to do with Fort Phillips and us sitting in front of the old Simpson Slacks building?"

"Let me finish." Lonnie glanced briefly at Kris and then resumed looking straight ahead. Both he and Kris had cooled considerably thanks to the air conditioning. "Our government is supporting guerilla movements in certain countries. The goal is for the guerillas to overthrow sitting regimes and replace them with leaders who are, uh, more receptive to American overtures. Coups, they call it, right?"

"Right," Kris replied. His head was spinning. It was about to start spinning even more.

"Syndicated Delivery Services is a private, third party contractor for the U.S. government. Their job is to get certain uh, resources to the guerilla forces."

"Damn!" Kris proclaimed loudly. "Let me guess. Some of those resources are being warehoused here." He pointed back at the old Simpson building.

"Exactly. I haven't been inside, but I'm guessing you'll find guns, ammo, explosive devices, who knows what else. But I guarantee you it's some serious shit."

Kris shook his head in disbelief. "Why here in Fort Phillips? Why in this old building that's about to fall apart?

"Because it has to look like our government has nothing to do with all of this. They tell me it would be a worldwide public relations disaster if it was revealed that the U.S. was playing a role in the overthrow of sitting governments. That's why they use a contractor like Syndicated and a place like Fort Phillips. If the coup attempts are discovered, our government can disavow any knowledge and claim it's all the doing of a radical, extremist group using a legitimate business as a cover. There is to be no connection whatsoever between the U.S. government and Syndicated. No paper trail, no breadcrumb trail, no nothing. Ignorance is bliss."

Kris was silent as he tried to digest everything Lonnie had told him. He watched several cars drive by. "Now I understand why Syndicated Delivery Services has no interest in being a part of the community. If someone around here did discover what Syndicated's business is really about, there would be a hell of a lot of questions to answer. Questions more serious than why they aren't reaching out to help the community."

"You catch on fast, Mr. Reporter."

"How did you learn all of this? I was joking when I asked if you were on their payroll, but I'm thinking you *are* probably on their payroll."

"I am. They didn't want to put up an elaborate security system or have armed guards or anything like that. That would seem very suspicious, so they figured they could pay the local country bumpkin police chief to make sure no one does any snooping, and no one would pay any attention to that. It would simply look like he was doing his job, running his regular patrol."

"I expect they are you paying you well. All cash, all under the table."

"I know what I am doing is wrong, but times have been hard. They money has really helped me and Karen."

"Does she know what you're doing?"

"No, and hopefully she will never find out. This gig won't last forever. Syndicated will finish this mission and move on to whatever the government has in store for them next."

All Kris could do was look at Lonnie, partly in disgust, partly in admiration and partly because Lonnie's story was difficult to believe. "Heck, Lonnie. You are smarter than I've been giving you credit for. Being involved in a plot of global magnitude is impressive."

"See why I said I would have to kill you? Please don't go doing anything stupid with this information I've given you. Up to now my job has been easy. Sure, some of the local people have asked questions, tried to be nosey, but heck, everyone around here is so busy trying to keep their heads above water, they don't have time to dwell on what some strange company is doing. Yeah, it's been easy until some big city reporter arrives in town and starts…"

Kris stopped Lonnie. "I understand, Lonnie. Your secret is safe with me. But as a reporter, I do have a curious disposition."

"Yeah, and you know what curiosity did to the cat."

"Is there anything else you need to tell me?"

"Yeah. I'm glad you are here to help save the Sentinel. But Kris, stay away from this building and stay away from my wife dammit! Do that and you and I will get along just fine."

"Yes sir. Got it."

"Now for the important stuff. Be at the gym tonight. I'm ready for you to leave town, but not before I kick your ass on the court."

"I'll be there. What makes you think you can win?"

"There's a first time for everything."

18

Thinking he had just read a chapter out of a Tom Clancy novel, Kris slowly walked back to the Sentinel office. Ever suspicious as a reporter, it sounded to Kris as if Lonnie had been well-trained to tell the Syndicated Delivery Services' story. Lonnie's explanation had been far too poised and precise. Another question was on Kris' mind. Why would anyone trust Lonnie Jackson with sensitive information about a massive covert operation that had worldwide implications? In high school, other guys quickly learned not to share their date details with Lonnie. He would have it broadcast over the entire campus before the end of sixth period. Kris doubted Lonnie's confession was truthful, but if it wasn't, then what was the truth? It all sounded preposterous, but Kris also knew the U.S. government, military and intelligence agencies were involved in all sorts of meddling and subterfuge around the world. Kris had the sickening feeling that it was going to be all but impossible to find out anything meaningful about Syndicated Delivery Services and what they were doing. Despite Lonnie's warning, Kris' catlike curiosity wouldn't let him back away.

Back at the Sentinel, Kris retrieved a Coke from the refrigerator in the break room, went to his desk and leaned back in his chair. He started researching Syndicated. Kris took a deep swallow of his soft drink and started making phone calls. Locally, he did learn Syndicated had purchased a Fort Phillips business license but had not joined the county Chamber of Commerce or civic clubs which was the first requirement in corporate civics 101. Water and power services had been paid a year in advance with no more than a company name and post office address provided to the utilities. Kris could find no information about the company on the Internet, and the Georgia Secretary of State's office had no information on an incorporation for Syndicated Delivery Services. When he dialed the phone number on the notice on the front door, a recording of a male voice said, *we are unavailable at this moment.* There was no cordial *Your call is important to us* or directions to leave a message. Just *We are unavailable at this moment.*

"That's interesting," Kris said to himself. "They definitely don't want to be bothered."

Kris tried another approach. Dan McKenzie was a college buddy who came from a military family and had worked his way through the ranks to a semi-important public information job at the Pentagon. They talked on the phone probably six times a year and Kris had Dan's cell number. Even though he stayed busy, Dan usually answered his phone and did this time when Kris called at 6:25 p.m.

"Mr. Keller. How are you doing, sir?"

"Not bad. Yourself?"

"As usual, up to my neck in bureaucratic bullshit, but all in all, not bad."

"I feel for you. I am so sick of Washington politics. Sometimes I think we would be better off with a dictator rather that all those bozo senators and representatives whose only job is to get re-elected. They don't really care what's best for the country. They just want to stay in office."

"Preach it, brother! But enough about the ills of Washington. How's Emmy? You guys are getting married soon, right?"

"Uh, change in plans. A long story. We'll talk about it later."

"I'm sorry to hear that. Listen, I have a meeting in ten minutes. What can I do for you?"

"I have a crazy, crazy request."

"I get those all the time. Shoot."

"I'm working on a story and I want to see if it has legs."

"O.K."

"Don't laugh, but I've been told by a source, and I don't know how reliable this source is, that we are involved in attempts to overthrow several governments overseas."

McKenzie started laughing.

"You promised me you wouldn't laugh."

"As a general statement, what you just said is probably correct. We have our hands in other people's business all over the world. Unfortunately, the type of information you are seeking is way, way above the propaganda that I am directed to churn out every day."

"You can't blame a guy for trying."

"Since when did you get involved in this kind of stuff? I mean, isn't this sort of story way out of your league?"

"Absolutely it is, but Dan, there may be a connection between my little backwoods hometown and the question I asked you. I want to know what the connection is. That's how I got involved."

McKenzie had stopped laughing and turned serious. "That sounds like a huge stretch but who knows? The world is going crazy now, Kris, and I don't totally disbelieve anything I hear. At any rate, one thing I appreciate about you is that you always double and triple check your sources and you never publish a story until you are certain it is 100 percent accurate. You know we have missions going on all around the globe and the majority of them are classified and so secretive that you will never hear about them. Frankly, I don't want to know about them because they're sinister, illegal and the truth about them would scare the shit out of me. But for you, my friend, I will make some calls and do some asking but I am so low in the pecking order I doubt I will be able to come up with anything which is probably just as well for both of us. I believe the less we know, the better off we will be."

"I really appreciate you trying to help me." McKenzie's description of the way America carries on its missions unnerved Kris. He told his friend, "In trying to help me, please don't do anything that's going to put you at risk."

"Don't worry. I'll be fine. What little you've told me so far is totally non-specific. What exactly is it you are needing to know?"

"A company called Syndicated Delivery Services. Can you see if they are a government contractor?"

"I suppose they're involved somehow in what you're investigating?"

"Yes. They have a presence here in Fort Phillips. That's the connection I am talking about. What I've been told is that our government wants the overthrow of certain foreign governments and that Syndicated is delivering military-type resources out of a warehouse here in Fort Phillips in support of these efforts. I'm not interested in uncovering any scandal involving our government or military. I'll leave that to *Sixty Minutes* and the *Washington Post.* All I'm really trying to do is find out is what a private government contractor would be doing in an old, dilapidated warehouse in my speck-on-the-map hometown."

"Gotcha. If something like that is going on, it will be near impossible to find out. As far as this Syndicated Delivery Services, well, you know we only have about seven million third party contractors working for us."

"I know and I hate to ask, but I'm running out of leads."

There was a pause and Kris could hear McKenzie taking a deep breath.

"Give me a few days and I'll get back to you," McKenzie said. There was a hint of irritation and hesitation in his voice. "Glad to do it for you, Kris, but be careful. If there is any truth to what you are telling me, snooping reporters won't be tolerated. Watch your back."

"Will do."

They ended the conversation. Rather than convincing Kris to steer away from the story, McKenzie's warning had made Kris more determined to learn the truth about Syndicated. But for the moment that could wait. Kris left for his house to change and then steered Vance's Ranger to the recreation complex.

19

When Kris arrived at the city gym, another aging brick building in need of a facelift, four guys were already on the court tossing up shots that seldom went through the net. Mickey Montgomery and Mark Stewart immediately greeted Kris, introduced him to Randy Hall and Tony Collier and handed him a basketball. Starting slowly to determine how his arm would feel, Kris arched up ten free throws without missing. He was aiming at number eleven when, out of the corner of his eye, he noticed Lonnie walking into the gym. Kris went through with the shot, which rattled on the rim twice and dropped to the court. Trying to ignore each other, Kris continued shooting while Lonnie grabbed another basketball and went to the opposite end of the court. Kris went through another stretch of nine good free throws before Mark suggested the group split into two teams of three and start playing.

"I think I'm going to be a spectator," Kris said. "I'm not sure my arm is up to playing."

"What's the matter?" Lonnie quickly blurted. "Afraid of getting your butt beat, Mr. All Region?"

Bouncing the ball once, Kris ignored Lonnie's comment and started walking off the court.

"Come on, Kris. Let's see if you've still got it. Let's see if life in the big city has made you soft."

"That's enough," Mickey Montgomery suggested, realizing Lonnie's prodding went beyond playful banter with Kris. He was trying to pick a fight. Randy and Tony, not familiar with Kris or his history with Lonnie, stood around with puzzled looks etched on their faces.

"What about it, Kris?" Lonnie kept on. "You're not turning sissy on us, are you?"

"Cool it, Lonnie!" Mickey Montgomery requested again.

Kris was standing off the court and Lonnie motioned for him. "Let's see what you've got," Lonnie sneered.

"You're an idiot," Mark snapped at Lonnie. "Kris kicked your butt all through high school, and he'll still do it."

"Why don't we find out. What about it, Kris?" Lonnie asked, again motioning for Kris.

"Give it a rest!" Mickey Montgomery said angrily.

"You're afraid, aren't you?" Lonnie asked, laughing at Kris. "You're afraid that I'll beat you."

Kris dribbled the ball twice, stepped out on the court and launched a 35-foot set shot that sailed cleanly through the net. "Let's play," he said calmly. Randy and Tony looked at each other, hooted and exchanged high fives over Kris' definitive response.

"You don't have to," Mark told him.

"No, it's O.K.," Kris assured him. "Mickey, me, and, uh, Tony against Mark, Lonnie and the other guy."

"All right. Half court. To twenty," Mickey announced.

"You can have the ball first," Lonnie offered.

From mid-court, Mickey passed the ball to Kris at the free throw line. Lonnie immediately bellied up to him in a tight defensive position, bumping Kris as he drove toward the basket. Thinking Kris was about to attempt a lay-up, Lonnie jumped, creating space for Kris to drop a perfect pass to Mickey for an easy basket, which drew whistles of admiration from the other players.

Mark passed the ball to Lonnie twenty feet from the basket, and Kris crouched to play defense. Moving his feet quickly, Kris blocked Lonnie from driving to the basket. Glaring at him, Lonnie began dribbling, lowering his shoulder into Kris and knocking him down. "That's a charge! Our ball!" Mickey yelled.

"Hell no! It was a block on Kris!" Lonnie shouted back.

"It was a charge!" Mark repeated. "Give them the ball."

"Some teammate you are!" Lonnie fussed at Mark.

Again, Mickey passed to Kris at the free throw line. The time Kris faked a drive to the basket, got Lonnie off his feet and launched a jump shot that floated softly through the net. Kris got slaps of encouragement from his teammates.

The game continued for fifteen minutes. Kris and Mark were clearly the best players. Lonnie was little more than a banger, playing tough defense and doing a lot of pushing and shoving. His role on the high school team had been to frustrate the other team and get them angry with his rough play to the point they lost their concentration.

With Kris doing most of the scoring, his team built a big lead and was set to try for the winning points. Lonnie, panting for breath, had backed off his defense, leaving Kris with an easy 15-foot shot for the win, but he didn't take it, instead passing to Mickey for an open ten-footer from the opposite side. The shot bounced off the rim and high into the air. Kris broke to the basket, grabbed the rebound and as he put the ball on the backboard, was blindsided by Lonnie, directly on the healing cut on his left arm. Kris hit the floor with a thud, immediately feeling the pain shoot through this arm. "Get that shot out of here!" Lonnie squatted down and yelled at Kris, practically spitting in his face.

Mickey started helping Kris up. "In case you didn't notice," Mickey said, looking up at Lonnie. "The shot went in. You lose again!"

"Son of a bitch!" Lonnie mumbled. He grabbed his towel and keys from the bleachers and stormed out of the gym.

"Are you all right?" Your arm is bleeding," Mickey asked Kris as the remaining players gathered around.

Kris looked at his arm and realized he had popped a stitch. His arm was hurting a lot. He took off his t-shirt and wiped away the blood. "What's with Lonnie?" Kris asked. "He and I have never been bosom buddies, but he definitely seems to have it in for me." Earlier in the day, Kris had thought that Lonnie's revelation about Syndicated Delivery Services might have softened the tension between them. The pick-up game had proven otherwise.

"I don't know. He has been acting strange lately. Seems very frustrated. Part of it is he is jealous of you, Kris. You have always been better than him, in everything. The one thing he got that you didn't was Karen, and now he's got this notion that you've come back to take her away from him."

"I've tried to get it through his thick head I have no interest in Karen," Kris said, dabbing the shirt against the wound on his arm. "I promised I'd help her with the Sentinel until she decides what to do with it, then I'm outta here."

"Just be careful," Mark warned. "Karen leads Lonnie around by the nose. She may think she can do the same with you. I think - no, I know- she would drop Lonnie in a minute if she thought she could get you back."

Randy and Tony left, leaving Kris, Mickey and Mark. "Is there any chance of you staying in Fort Phillips?" Mickey asked.

"Not a chance."

"Not even if I save you a spot on my softball team?" Mark quickly offered.

Kris laughed. "It's tempting."

"So, what can Atlanta offer you that Fort Phillips can't?" Mickey asked tongue-in-cheek.

"Emmy Owens," Kris replied with emphasis.

20

"What are you doing here?" asked Emmy, surprised to see Kris walk through the door to her office.

Disappointed with her greeting, Kris asked, "Don't I get a hug?"

Emmy stayed seated at her desk momentarily, and reluctantly, got up and gave Kris a sisterly hug, which disappointed him even more.

She backed away and asked again, "What are you doing here?"

"You wouldn't return any of my phone calls, so I had no choice but to come back to Atlanta to see you. Besides, I had to go by my apartment to get my toothbrush and I was running out of underwear."

Emmy did not crack a smile at Kris' attempt at humor. "This really isn't the way I wanted to start my day," she said seriously.

"Can't we talk?" he requested.

"I'm not sure we have anything to talk about."

"Please." Kris was asking with the lost puppy look in his brown eyes as much as he was with his voice.

Emmy did not respond. Any concern she had once had about Kris' injury or his well-being seemed to have evaporated.

"Please," Kris repeated. He had been away from Emmy only a few days but had almost forgotten how beautiful she was. Her off-white pants suit and three-inch heels made her look six feet tall.

Emmy sighed and glanced at her watch. "I've got an appointment in thirty minutes. Let's go to the break room."

Sipping on cups of coffee, they sat down at the small round table. Everything about Emmy indicated she did not want to be with him and Kris realized that.

"Are you mad at me?" he asked.

"Mad? Perhaps that is not the proper word. Disappointed? Frustrated? Sad? I think those words better describe my emotions at this moment," she admitted before taking another sip of coffee.

"What have I done that's so bad?"

Emmy started to put down her coffee cup, arched her eyebrows and replied, "Do you really have to ask that?"

"Tell me."

She set down her cup hard enough on the table that a drop of coffee popped out. Emmy leaned toward him and looking straight at him, explained, "You dumped me, Kris. You dumped me for Fort Phillips, for Karen and for whatever other attraction there is down there."

"No, I didn't. I simply had to stay longer than anticipated to finish up some business."

A curvy bleached blonde in a short skirt, tight silk blouse and black hose walked by and perkily chirped, "Hey Kris. How are you doing?"

"Good Marilyn. You?"

"Better, now that I've seen you." She took a quick glance at Emmy, and looked back at Kris, telling him, "Maybe I'll see you later."

"Maybe," was Kris' short response.

"She's hot for you, you know that," Emmy told Kris.

"I haven't noticed."

"Pleeease," Emmy groaned. "You're not that dumb. Maybe you ought to take the little tramp up on her offer about later."

His frustration growing, Kris announced, "I'm not interested in anyone else. I love you." From his shirt pocket, he carefully pulled out the engagement ring Emmy had given back, placed it on the table and slid it toward her.

"Are you ready to come back home?" she asked.

"Not today."

With her right index finger Emmy slid the ring back toward Kris and told him, "Then I'm not ready to take this back."

"We can't negotiate, reach a compromise?"

"Nope."

"I'm going to get you back."

"We'll see." Emmy looked at her watch again. "I've got to go, Kris," she said, standing up. "I hope you get things straightened out. I really do."

"So do I," Kris said in a whisper as Emmy returned to her office.

Confused and depressed, Kris remained at the table, not knowing what to do next other than finish his coffee. Marilyn returned to the break room, and sliding a chair away from the table, sat down and crossed her legs slowly.

"You don't look so happy," she said.

"I've got a lot on my mind," is all he said.

"Emmy's been acting strange too. Quiet. Distant. Is everything all right between you two?"

"We'll be fine."

She uncrossed her legs, providing a tantalizing upskirt view. "I'm available if you need to talk. I think I can probably get your mind off your troubles," she smiled.

"Thanks, but I'm going to be leaving town again." He was shocked at how casually Marilyn had been with giving him a peep show. It was slow and with purpose. Obviously, she had had a lot of practice.

Marilyn took a business card out of the pocket on her skirt. "My business and cell numbers are on the card," she said. "If you change your mind and want to talk - or whatever - call me." She got up and rubbed his back as she walked away.

Kris smiled and shook his head. He hardly knew the woman, seeing her only a few times when he accompanied Emmy to work functions and parties. Admittedly, he was a bit flattered by her come-on, but she was not his type. Marilyn's face and body were enticing, almost mesmerizing, and she used them to her full advantage. That was the problem Kris had with her. She looked and acted more like a hooker than a girlfriend.

Finishing his coffee, Kris wanted to make one more stop before collecting clothes from his apartment and heading back to Fort Phillips. He had to check on Patrick Cannon. Kris felt guilty that he had been so wrapped up with his own personal problems that he had neglected to check on Patrick's progress since the helicopter explosion. Patrick was one of the first reporters Kris met when he went to work in Atlanta, and despite a twenty-plus years age difference, they became close friends, sharing tips and leads on stories, attending sporting events and just sitting around, talking for hours about life in general. Along with Carter Floyd, Patrick Cannon had been a positive influence in Kris' life. He was going to be best man in Kris' wedding.

An hour later, Patrick's wife Margaret, was ushering Kris into the living room of their townhouse fifteen miles northeast of Downtown Atlanta. As if someone had flipped a switch, Patrick's eyes glowed at the sight of his friend. They hugged and Kris tried not to stare at the bandaged stump on the end of Patrick's right arm.

"I owe you man," Patrick said, his voice cracking, with his arms still around Kris. "You and Marcus saved my life. I could have easily bled to death on the hot pavement outside that bank."

"But you didn't. You are still around to give the city's politicians and government slackers hell," Kris smiled as they sat down. Kris tried to keep his eyes off Patrick's wound, but he felt as though a magnet was pulling them in that direction.

Margaret handed the men glasses of tea. Patrick took a swallow before admitting to Kris, "I may not be around that much longer. Channel 12 says they eventually want me back, but they've given me a damn good offer, uh, to retire early which means they really do not want me back."

"Oh really?" Kris asked before tasting the tea. "Can they do that? Are you considering it? Can't you file some kind of discrimination suit?"

"Probably, but I don't want to. I have been at Channel 12 a long time, and they have been good to me. It's not like they're kicking me out. Their offer to me is good, Kris, really good. Margaret and I can take the money and go in search of the next great challenge. Our kids are grown and gone, and we have no ties to Atlanta. Heck, as soon as I get doctor's clearance, be fitted for a prosthesis, and go through more physical therapy, we can leave."

Kris shook his head in amazement. His friend seemed in great spirits considering what had recently taken place. "Are you all right? Are you sure you are all right?" Kris asked.

"I'm good," Patrick replied softly. "Oh, I've had some bad moments, no doubt about that. I have felt sorry for myself a few times, but it's like you said. Man, I'm still around. I can still do whatever I want to do, maybe except for playing wide receiver in the National Football League."

Kris laughed and looked at Margaret who had joined Patrick on the sofa. "Is he really doing all right?" Kris asked her.

"He's doing all right," Margaret repeated. "As you can tell, the injury certainly hasn't hurt his sense of humor."

"And you're O.K. with this notion he's got of pulling up roots and searching for another big adventure?"

"Absolutely!" Margaret quickly replied. "I think it would be good for both of us."

"You know what pisses me off the most about this whole mess?" Patrick asked.

Kris thought for a moment. "Let's see. It affects your driving, uh, you have to get someone to cut your steak, uh, you can't play wide receiver in the National Football League."

"Wiping my butt."

"What?"

"Wiping my butt. I have always been a right-handed wiper. Do you know how hard it is to wipe your butt left-handed? Or picking your nose left-handed?"

Kris looked once more at Margaret, this time more seriously. "He's kidding, right, isn't he?" Kris asked. "Is that what's really bothering him?"

She smiled broadly. "He's not kidding. That's what is really bothering him."

"Well, in that case, there must be some type of physical therapy you can take for left-handed butt wiping," Kris said, starting to laugh.

"I've already looked into it," Patrick replied, starting to laugh as well.

"I'm amazed," Kris told his friend. "How can you be in such good spirits? You haven't been depressed? Aren't you in pain?"

"Yes and yes, but that's only temporary. I could have easily gotten my head sliced off instead of my hand. Do you realize how fortunate I am? Do you realize how fortunate you are? You could have lost your hand - or head!"

"Believe me, I've given that some thought."

"Enough about this old one-handed butt wiper. How are you doing? What about your arm? How's Emmy?"

Kris squirmed in his chair across from the sofa where Patrick and Margaret were sitting. "The arm is fine. There's some aches and soreness and some pain when I do stupid things like play basketball, but it's all coming along. The first thing I did yesterday when I got back to Atlanta was have the stitches taken out. As far as the rest of my life, I've kind of made a mess of things," Kris admitted weakly.

The Cannons did not reply, instead waiting for Kris to continue.

"My father died…"

"We heard. We're sorry," Patrick said.

"Thanks. I had to go to Fort Phillips to make final arrangements and take care of some of Vance's business. When I got down there, some strange stuff started happening. Emmy kind of freaked out."

"What happened?" Patrick asked. He and Margaret looked directly at Kris, who debated on whether to continue his story. He paused for several seconds, prompting Patrick to ask again, "What happened?"

"I almost died in a burning animal clinic. My house was invaded twice, with Emmy almost getting raped the second time. And I promised I would stay in town for a short time to help my old girlfriend run the Fort Phillips Sentinel."

"I see. Just everyday stuff," Patrick said calmly. He paused before shouting out, "What in the hell were you thinking, boy?"

"I'm not sure," Kris admitted. "I still don't know why I did what I did."

"What did Emmy do?"

"She handed her engagement ring back to me and returned to Atlanta."

"That's not good," Margaret said, stating the obvious.

"You are certainly right about that," Kris agreed.

"I am sure everything will be all right, now that you're back in Atlanta," Patrick assured him.

Kris ducked his head and did not say anything.

"You *are* back for good, aren't you?" Patrick asked.

Kris still did not say anything.

"Kris..." Patrick started.

"I've got to go back to Fort Phillips. Unfinished business."

"And this business is more important than Emmy?"

Kris smiled uneasily. "That's what's so strange. It's not. But right now, the place has a hold on me," Kris admitted. He did not go into detail regarding the thoughts about Vance, the Sentinel, Mr. Floyd and Karen still swirling in his head.

Patrick got up from the sofa, walked to Kris and patted him on the shoulder with his remaining hand. "Don't mess up a good thing," he told Kris. "Go back to Fort Phillips, take care of that unfinished business - fast - and get back here to Emmy. You get down on your knees if that's what you have to do to get that girl back."

"Yes sir!" Kris responded.

They retreated to the kitchen where Margaret cut three pieces of a homemade lemon meringue pie. Between bites, Kris watched Patrick handle the fork with his left hand. Some clumsiness was evident, but all in all, Patrick did fine. Kris felt better about his friend. Patrick and Margaret, at least on the surface, were handling this huge change in their lives with poise, dignity and a sense of humor.

Kris stayed thirty more minutes, with the conversation ranging from the Atlanta Braves to the latest blunder in Atlanta city government. When the time came for him to leave, Margaret hugged him, thanked him for dropping by, and left Kris and Patrick alone after again assuring Kris that Patrick was doing fine.

Patrick hugged Kris again, patted him on the back, and with eyes misting, said, "I owe you, friend, big time. If you ever need anything, let me know. Especially now. I have got plenty of time on my hands.... uh, hand."

They both laughed.

"As a matter of fact, there is something you can do for me."

"Name it."

"How about doing some research. See what you can find out about a business called Syndicated Delivery Services, especially if they are a government contractor. I haven't had any luck."

"Sure. What's going on?"

"I don't know. They moved into Fort Phillips and have been very secretive. The town's tried to extend its welcome, but this company is not interested. It's just strange." Kris didn't believe it was time to share Lonnie's wild story about Syndicated with Patrick.

"I'll start as soon as you leave. I'm glad to have something to do."

They hugged again. "I love you, man," Kris said, wiping a tear from his eye.

Kris got in the old Ford Ranger he had driven up from Fort Phillips, sighed, and asked out loud, "Why couldn't my Dad have been like Patrick Cannon?"

21

Patrick may not have been depressed, but Kris was. Back at his desk at the Sentinel two days after his trip to Atlanta, Kris was bemoaning his current status. He had already lost his girlfriend, and his job with the Atlanta Advocate appeared to be next. Making a stop at the newspaper while in Atlanta, Kris hem-hawed with his boss, not wanting to give a definite date as to when he would be back. Believing Kris had been given ample time to clear up his father's business, the editor gave Kris two more weeks to wrap things up and get back to work. Even with the threat of losing so much, Kris was not sure he could make that deadline. He was not sure he wanted to. He slipped his wallet out of his back pocket and pulled out Marilyn's business card. "Maybe a night of mindless sex is what I need," Kris said in a voice louder than normal conversation.

"I'm game," Karen offered, slipping into Kris' office. He felt his face turning red.

"Why wait for the night? How about right here in the office, right now?" she suggested. Kris found himself sucking for air. The combination of Karen appearing out of nowhere just as he wished for problem-forgetting sex had Kris gasping.

Wearing a cotton knit white summer-weight sweater and jeans that were a half-size too tight, Karen slinked toward Kris. He could feel his heart starting to beat faster.

"Mindless sex is good," she said seductively. Karen pulled Kris' chair away from the desk and sat in his lap. She put his right hand on her leg and his left hand on her breast. Kris offered no resistance, even starting to slide his hand up her leg.

"I can't do this," he said abruptly.

"Yes, you can. It's going to happen sooner or later, Kris. You know it and I know it. Why prolong the tension? I want it and so do you."

"No," was his weak reply.

She took his hand again and pressed it to her breast. "I feel good, don't I, Kris?"

Their eyes locked and Kris felt his resistance melting away. He quickly jerked his hand away when Lonnie bellowed from the office door, "Does your job description include fondling my wife?"

Kris tried to push Karen out of his lap, but she would not let him. "Kris and I are in a business discussion," she told her husband. "Why don't you go outside and find some crime to solve."

Stepping into the office, Lonnie replied, "That's exactly what I'm doing. I just got a call about a body in the trash bin in the alley behind Pete's Hamburger Place. I thought lover boy might want to go with me, to see that there is actually some news around here occasionally."

Realizing her chance to make love to Kris was gone, Karen got up and winked at Kris. "We'll get back to business at a later date," she told him playfully.

"Son of a bitch!" is all Lonnie said as he walked out of the office. Kris grabbed a note pad off his desk and followed.

Lonnie said nothing on the short walk to the alley where Officer Davenport was already starting to put out crime scene tape. "Who found the body?" Lonnie asked Davenport.

"The cook," Davenport said, nodding to a pole-thin scruffy-faced man with glazed-over eyes standing a few feet away. "He was taking the morning's first load of trash out."

Lonnie opened the side door to the trash bin and peered inside. The body was sprawled on top of a dozen large black trash bags and several flattened cardboard boxes. "Hmmm," Lonnie said, taking a glance back at Kris. "Come take a look."

His reporter's inquisitive nature taking over, Kris readily accepted Lonnie's offer and peered into the trash bin.

Lonnie stuck his head back inside as well. "Recognize the victim?" he asked Kris.

Without hesitation, Kris answered, "Yeah. It's that jerk Popeye who broke into my house." A kitchen knife was plunged deep into Popeye's chest near the heart. His loose-fitting Florida State University t-shirt was covered in blood.

"I don't think you'll have to worry about him now," Lonnie replied.

Kris took another quick look and stepped away from the trash bin. As a reporter he had seen many dead people ranging from shooting victims with barely visible wounds to air travelers splattered into a thousand bits and pieces in a plane crash. Despite trying to maintain a reporter's detachment, he usually felt some compassion, some sadness for the victims and the circumstances that resulted in their demise. He did not have that feeling with Popeye. Kris was glad he was gone and thought it appropriate that he ended up in a trash pile. To Kris, that's what he was - a piece of trash.

"What do you think?" Lonnie asked Kris.

"It's not my job to think. I just report. You're the cop. What do you think?"

Lonnie rubbed his chin. "Let's see. Who would have a motive to kill Popeye? There's his gambling debts, all the houses he's broken into, the fights he's been in. Plus, the fact that he's a son of a bitch. That about covers the whole town. Yeah, we have a whole town of suspects. What about you, Kris? I bet you wanted him dead too."

"I never wished him dead, but at the same time, I'm not shedding any tears. Sounds to me like he's someone only a momma could love."

"Even she didn't like him. She kicked him out of the house several years ago."

"Good riddance is all I can say. Why even bother to look for his killer? They did us a favor."

"Now, Mr. Reporter Boy, you know we don't operate that way. We'll process the scene. Try to find some fingerprints or some type of clue. Killers, especially amateurs, always leave something behind. We'll find out who did this. The problem is, when we do find out who killed Popeye, like you said, most of the town will want to give him a medal instead of prosecuting him."

"I'll throw in a few dollars for the medal."

"I hate to break up this love fest for Popeye," Lonnie said, "but we need to go to work. I will give you a few details for the Sentinel later. Then you can write your story if you can stay away from my life long enough."

"I believe I can do that," Kris told him, and walked to the front of Pete's where Billy Manley was propped against the wall smoking his ever-present cheap cigarette.

"God, those things stink," Kris, waving his hand past his nose, told Manley.

"It's all I can afford. Got a few dollars I can borrow?"

"Sorry. Where have you been? I haven't seen you in a few days."

"Oh, just taking care of some business."

"You mean you got a job?"

"No. I said I was taking care of business. That doesn't mean I got a job." A visible shudder shot through Manley's torso at the mere mention of the word *job.*

Scratching his head, Kris said, "I see, I think," and started walking to the Sentinel office. Manley walked with him.

Manley lit his last cigarette, crumpled the pack in his hand and tossed it away. Irritated, Kris picked it up and stowed it in his pocket.

"I hear you went back to Atlanta a few days ago. I figured you would stay there, especially since you decided not to follow up on what I told you about Vance," Manley said between puffs.

"I did follow up on your theory. There's nothing to it. And I am going back to Atlanta as soon as Karen decides what to do with the newspaper."

"You are? Lonnie thinks you're moving in on Karen, and that you're here for good."

"Lonnie doesn't have the sense to come in out of the rain."

"Or to solve a murder?"

"Yeah, that too."

They reached the Sentinel and Kris started to step inside, but Manley grabbed him by the arm. "I told you what you needed to know about your dad," Manley started. "If you're at peace with his passing, then leave, Kris. This town's going down. There's nothing but trouble for you here."

"Damn, Billy. You make things sound so sinister. Why do a few break-ins and fires have you and the rest of the town so spooked?"

"You're having to ask me that? After your girlfriend almost got raped? Maybe you're the one who doesn't have sense to get in out of the rain."

"Maybe," Kris said, shrugging his shoulders, "but I do have enough sense to get in out of this heat." Before going inside, Kris fumbled through his pants pocket and found a single five-dollar bill he gave to Manley.

Kris stopped at the refrigerator for a Coke before proceeding to his desk. He was three deep gulps into his drink when his cell phone rang. He smiled when he saw the number.

"How's my favorite left-handed butt wiper?" Kris asked Patrick Cannon.

"I've taken a laxative just so I can get more practice. How are things down in Fort Phillips?"

"Interesting. Believe it or not, we just had a murder."

"Stop the presses! What happened?"

"Someone stabbed the town's resident trouble-maker. We'll probably have a parade instead of a funeral."

"I see. Do you need some help reporting on this case?"

"I don't think so. I know the police chief. All I've got to do it let him beat me at basketball and he'll tell me anything I want to know."

"That's good. Speaking of what you want to know, I've been checking on Syndicated Delivery Services for you."

"Good. Tell me."

"The business doesn't exist, Kris. All I have are dead ends. They purchased a Fort Phillips business license and nothing else. No Articles of Incorporation, no chief operating officer. No federal or state tax filings. They do have a fleet of box trucks registered under the business name, but the address listed on the registrations doesn't exist. It's a fake. Whatever business Syndicated Delivery Services is involved with, they're covering it up really, really efficiently. And by the way, I cannot find any database that shows them as a government contractor."

Patrick continued. "The sale of the building was legitimate. Syndicated got it for a steal. The Simpson family obviously was ready to get this pimple off their butt. Sold it for $25,000. The land alone is worth more than that. A Savannah law firm with a shady reputation handled the closing."

"What about on this end? Did a local real estate agent broker the deal?"

"Yes. You probably know there is only one real estate agency in Fort Phillips. A guy named Ralph Hughes represented the Simpsons. Hughes told me something that makes this story remarkably interesting. He never showed the building to anyone. Syndicated purchased the property without ever looking at it. No officer from Syndicated was at the closing. Another law firm from Charleston, with its own cloudy reputation, represented them. It certainly appears they want to operate under a veil of secrecy."

Kris was silent for almost thirty seconds. After Patrick confirmed Kris was still on the call, Kris pronounced, "Well, we need to lift that veil of secrecy."

"Let me help."

"You already have."

"No, let me really help. Margaret's going out of town for two weeks. She and a bunch of her girlfriends have had a cruise planned for more than a year. I am not going to make her give that up. While she's gone, let me come down and help. I will have to get her drive me down, but I would really like to come. I will help you out with the newspaper. I will do whatever you need me to do. And if we can find out the big mystery behind Syndicated Delivery Services, that will be great."

Kris took a final swallow of his drink before answering, "Patrick, you've made me an offer I can't refuse. Besides, how can I deny anyone the opportunity to see fabulous Fort Phillips, Georgia?"

"My sentiments exactly. Margaret is leaving in four days. What if she drives me down day-after-tomorrow?"

"Perfect. See you then."

"Good. One last thing before I let you go. How's Emmy? What about the two of you?"

"Status quo," Kris replied softly. "No progress."

"Sorry to hear that. We'll talk some more when I get there. Thanks, Kris."

The two friends ended their conversation, and reluctantly Kris turned to the small stack of news items on his desk. After thumbing through the stack, he was thankful to have Popeye's murder to work on. Otherwise, the most exciting event for a story was the Grand Jury's recommendation that the tile floors in the courthouse restrooms be replaced.

22

Margaret Cannon wanted to resume preparations for her cruise, so she made a hurried trip to Fort Phillips. She found Kris' house after stopping at Fast Mart for directions, helped Patrick remove his one suitcase from the car and kissed him. She asked Patrick if he was sure he would be all right and then scurried back to Atlanta almost before Patrick had the opportunity to respond. Kris kidded Patrick that as quickly as Margaret dumped him, his missing hand wasn't generating much sympathy, to which Patrick replied just the opposite was true. His devoted wife had practically smothered him with attention since the accident, and frankly, he was ready for a break and so was she. Patrick, keeping a straight face, told Kris that if Margaret had not had the cruise planned, he would have bought her a plane ticket to any place in the world.

Kris was happy to see his friend in such good spirits. They spent fifteen minutes poking fun at each other, exchanging jokes and one-liners. Patrick spit out jokes about one-armed people and Kris responded with small town jokes. After that, they talked for thirty more minutes while downing a couple of beers. Kris, who was still having trouble preventing his eyes from straying to the bandaged stub at the end of Patrick's right arm, explained how the closing of Simpson Slacks and other locally owned businesses had caused Fort Phillips' economic demise. Patrick mentioned what Kris already knew. Fort Phillips was not by itself. Small towns throughout America were suffering, teetering on the brink of extinction due to new interstate highways and byways and megastores that would entice shoppers to drive fifty miles. Little locally owned shops, for years the backbone of American communities, were dropping faster than oak leaves in autumn.

Kris offered Patrick the master bedroom and asked him if he minded staying in the room where Vance had blown his brains out.

Patrick replied that was not a problem unless Kris thought the spirit of Vance might still be hanging around. Kris assured him that was not the case. He was certain that Vance was seated at a card game in Heaven or wherever it was he landed.

Using his good arm and hand, Patrick, with a slight bit of awkwardness, tossed his suitcase on the bed and then asked Kris to take him a tour of the town, which took ten minutes. With the afternoon headed toward evening, they stopped by Pete's, where Patrick quickly consumed a greasy hamburger he praised as the best he had ever eaten. Having to eat one-handed appeared only slightly clumsy for Patrick, and he did not appear to be self-conscious. Crawling back into Vance's Ranger, Kris produced a large bottle of antacids and tossed them to Patrick who made a nice one-handed catch. "My guess is that you'll need those within thirty minutes," Kris grinned.

The next stop, at Patrick's request, was the Simpson Slacks building. Kris pulled the pickup to the curb in front of the building. They remained in the Ranger and observed the old building. "It certainly doesn't look sinister, but it does look sad," Patrick said.

"There's more to this story. I haven't told you everything," Kris said.

"Patrick's eyes widened. "Tell me more," he requested of Kris.

Before Kris could begin, Lonnie Jackson pulled up to the Ranger and rolled down the window of his car. "Kris, what the hell are you doing here?" he asked hatefully.

"Paying homage to a Fort Phillips landmark," Kris said through his rolled-down window.

"I've told you to stay away. Don't you remember our conversation from a few days ago? Do you want me to arrest you for trespassing?"

"Trespassing? How can you arrest me for trespassing? I'm on a public street!"

"Just stay away from this building. Who's your friend?"

"Patrick Cannon. He's here from Atlanta. Have you caught Popeye's killer yet?"

"No!" Lonnie responded quickly. In the dimness of twilight, Lonnie couldn't tell much about Patrick's features or his age. "How in the hell did you let Kris drag you down here?" Lonnie asked.

"I'm giving Kris a hand with a story." Patrick raised his bandaged stump.

"God, what happened to you? Oh yeah, you're the explosion guy, right?" Lonnie asked.

"I didn't know I was so famous."

"Well, if you're smart, you won't stay here long, and you'll take Kris back with you. Now get out of here before I think up some other reason to arrest you."

Kris gently pulled away from Simpson Slacks, starting to laugh at Patrick's snappy comebacks to Lonnie.

"So, who was Wyatt Earp back there?" Patrick asked.

"Lonnie Jackson, the Chief of Police. Did you see his face when you held up your arm?"

"Yeah. Caught him off guard, didn't I? I guess Popeye is the town troublemaker you mentioned, right? And what's the Chief's deal? He was acting like he's a security guard for that place."

"In a sense, he is a security guard for the place. Syndicated is paying Lonnie under the table to keep people – namely me – away."

"O.K. Tell me the rest of the story."

"You're not going to believe this." As they drove around Fort Phillips for the next fifteen minutes, Kris repeated Lonnie's tale of foreign government coups, a warehouse full of guns and instruments of war and a private contractor assigned to deliver those resources.

"Damn! That is one tall tale," Patrick exclaimed. "Do you believe it?"

"Not really, but then there is something strange about this Syndicated Delivery Services that I can't put my finger on. If they are involved in something funny with the government, that would explain why they want nothing to do with the community. It would also explain why you weren't able to dig up any information on them. The government is covering for them."

Patrick nodded in agreement. "Makes sense. If the government wants it that way, no matter how much digging we do, we won't find anything."

They drove past Fast Mart. Billy Manley was in his usual spot, propped against the propane tanks, puffing on a cigarette. Kris continued, "Not all hope is lost. I have a buddy who works at the Pentagon. He's low-level but he has some connections. He's going to get back to me about Syndicated and any foreign government overthrows the U.S. may be involved in."

Patrick chuckled. "Seriously, Kris? Our government is *always* involved in crap like that. Your friend may come back with some information for us but there's no guarantee that it would help us find out what's going on in your building here in Fort Phillips."

Kris could feel his face turning crimson. Thank goodness in the twilight, Patrick couldn't see it. Kris gave himself a quick mental thrashing for being so naïve. Of course Patrick was right. Even if the U.S. was involved in a dozen coups, what are the chances anything about them would filter down to little Fort Phillips in the southwest part of Georgia?

Patrick could tell Kris was deflated, so he offered another glimmer of hope. "We're reporters, Kris. We never give up. And if your friend in Washington doesn't come through, we have one other option."

"And what might that be?"

"We break into Simpson Slacks."

Kris almost steered the Ranger off the road. "We're reporters, productive members of society. We can't do something like that."

"Ah, come on," Patrick teasingly urged.

"Yeah, we could do it just to irritate Wyatt Earp. Let's give it some thought."

"I detect a little personal animosity."

Kris did not respond directly to Patrick's comment, but asked, "Want to meet his wife? She's my partner at the newspaper."

"My goodness," Patrick smiled. "Interesting dynamics you have in this little town."

When Kris and Patrick arrived at the Sentinel, Karen was about to walk out the door. Kris introduced Patrick and noticed she took a quick glance at Patrick's right arm. Karen seemed unconcerned when Kris told her Patrick would be hanging with him at the paper for a few days. Her only comment was, "I hope Kris didn't offer to pay you anything."

Patrick assured her no cash would be involved. They had a final polite *nice to meet you* exchange and Kris escorted Patrick to the small office where he would be working.

Settling into the worn chair behind the old wooden desk in the musty smelling closet-sized office, Patrick told Kris, "I can understand why Emmy doesn't want you here. Karen is fine."

"We're just friends. Old friends," Kris mumbled.

"Yeah, but just how good of friends are you?"

"At one time we were real good friends."

"Well, judging from the way she looks at you, I'd say that friendship still has a good spark to it, at least from her standpoint. Do you know what you're getting into?" Patrick asked seriously.

Kris propped against the door frame of the office. "I don't know," he finally confessed. "You don't know all of the story."

"Again? I don't have all of a second story? I'm listening," Patrick replied, leaning back in the chair, which almost toppled over. Patrick had to do some quick shifting to regain his balance.

Kris almost laughed, but his pensive mood quickly took over again. Restlessly, he sat on the edge of the desk. "I was called down here when my father died. They said he committed suicide. That made me mad because it left me one final mess to clean up. That has been the story of my life, cleaning up after Vance."

"I knew that much about you and your dad. You've told me some of that history before," Patrick said.

"The problem was, when I got down here, this guy, Billy Manley, one of Vance's best friends, hinted that Vance was murdered. Manley said Vance was trying to get his life straightened out, that he wanted to mend things with me, and his spirits were too high to take his own life."

That got Patrick's undivided attention.

Kris continued, "No one else shared Manley's opinion. Certainly not Wyatt Earp, uh, Lonnie Jackson, the police chief, who ruled the death a suicide about as fast as Chase Elliott can make a lap at Atlanta International Speedway. I did some investigating myself and did not find anything to substantiate the claim. I was ready to go back to Atlanta."

"Obviously, you didn't make it back to Atlanta."

"No. Things started happening. Fires, break-ins, Karen's dad - my mentor – died., Karen begged me to stay, Emmy almost got raped and begged me to leave..."

"And you chose to stay."

"I did."

"Why?"

"I don't know. I've asked myself that a thousand times."

"My guess is you still have deep feelings for Karen."

"Maybe. If I do, I'm trying to fight them. But Vance is why I'm still here."

"Are you sure? Explain."

"In spite of what everyone says, despite what I learned myself, I can't get Vance's death out of my mind. I have despised him all my life, and all I should have done was put him to rest, get out of here and say goodbye to this place forever. But damn it, Patrick, it has stuck in the back of my head that perhaps Vance did not kill himself. Even if he was a bum, he was my father, and I can't get rid of this notion that I have the responsibility to find out how he really died." Kris hung his head and cleared his throat.

Slipping out of his chair, Patrick sat down on the corner of the desk opposite Kris. "Sounds to me like we need to do some more investigating," Patrick said.

"I don't need to get you involved in this."

"And why not? Remember, you saved my life. I owe you. Besides, what else do I have to do? Go to physical therapy? Sit around and watch television? Man, I am thankful to be here! For a wide spot in the road in the middle of nowhere, this little place seems to have a lot going on."

Kris raised his head, managed a small smile and admitted, "It's good to have you here. I appreciate your help. I need your help. I'm confused and depressed."

Patrick slid off the desk, walked to Kris and put his left hand on Kris' shoulder. "We will uncover out what's going on," Patrick assured him. "We will determine what happened to your dad. We will solve the mystery about all those fires and break-ins. We'll even find out about our mysterious friends at Syndicated Delivery Services." Patrick paused, looked directly at Kris, and told him, "I can help you with all that. What I cannot help you with is Emmy and Karen. That's between you and your heart."

Kris' smile widened. "Sappy but true," he said of Patrick's remark. "Sappy but true."

23

Kris took Patrick's fatherly talk to heart and started searching his own heart. With thought after thought exploding in his mind like popcorn kernels, concentrating on anything for more than a few seconds was impossible. After two days of agonizing mental debate during which Kris neglected the Sentinel, his appearance, Patrick and everything around him, he recognized a recurring theme. Emmy belonged in his life. Emmy was his future. The job or location were no longer important. They could change and he could be happy. Without Emmy he could not be happy.

The problem was Kris could not reach Emmy to tell her. She would not answer her cell or work phone, and the receptionist answering the main line at Emmy's office would only say she was unavailable. Desperate and down to his last option, he pulled Marilyn's business card out of his wallet. Having lost track of time, he looked at his watch. Since it was a few minutes before 7 p.m., he punched Marilyn's personal number and tossed her card on the kitchen table at the Keller house. Marilyn was surprised, but pleased, to hear his voice.

"Are you ready to take me up on my offer to talk - or whatever?" Marilyn asked pleasantly.

Kris immediately went to the purpose of his call. "Do you know where Emmy is?" Kris asked, his hint of desperation obvious to Marilyn.

"Is that why you called me, to find out where Emmy is?"

"Yeah," Kris said timidly.

"Come to my apartment and I'll tell you personally."

"I'm still in Fort Phillips," Kris told her. "Do me a really big favor, Marilyn, and tell me where Emmy is."

Several seconds of silence followed before Marilyn firmly responded. "Promise me that you'll have dinner with me the next time you are in town and I'll tell you. I promise I'll make the dinner worth your time."

Frustrated, Kris rubbed the back of his neck. "O.K., Marilyn," he relented. "You tell me where Emmy is, and I'll have dinner with you the next time I'm in Atlanta."

"You're not going to like what I have to tell you."

"Tell me, Marilyn."

"She and Kevin Chandler went on a business trip together, to look at some property in Memphis. They're not due back for three more days."

"Will you please get her to call me when she's back."

Marilyn paused again. "I don't think their trip was strictly business."

"What do you mean?"

"They've, uh, sort of been acting cutesy with each other. The new property may not be all they check out."

Kris knew Marilyn was interested in him, and he suspected she was fabricating this story to make him more interested in her. "Come on, Marilyn, shoot straight with me."

"Oh Kris, I would love to shoot straight with you. And I am about Emmy. Trust me. In the case of you and Emmy, absence is definitely not making the heart grow fonder."

"Why is she doing this to me?" Kris, on the verge of a panic attack, asked.

"Do you really have to ask that? She begged you to come back to Atlanta with her and you're still down there. Any more dumb questions?"

Kris lowered his head and bit his lip. "No, I guess not," he said softly, just loud enough for Marilyn to be able to hear.

"I can take a few days off. Would you like me to drive down?" she asked.

"Thanks, but no," Kris quickly replied. "I need to do some work so I can get back to Atlanta. And I promise we'll have dinner."

"Would you like to know what I'm wearing?"

"I'll talk to you later…"

"I still have on what I wore to work today…a short black skirt, seamed black stockings…"

"Bye Marilyn." Kris quickly hung up before the erotic description continued.

"God, what have I done?" Kris asked. He picked up Marilyn's card, and holding it on its edge with his left index finger, flicked it across the room with his right index finger. Had he been playing paper football, the field goal attempt would have been wide right - by a lot. That seemed appropriate. At this moment, his whole life was wide right.

His pity party was interrupted by a knock on the front door. Visitors was exactly what Kris did not want. And no doubt this was next door neighbor Alice Hunter whose visits were becoming daily. The kindly neighbor meant well, and she kept Kris supplied with sweets, but he was not in the mood for a social call, even if Mrs. Hunter was delivering one of her iced pound cakes. Grumbling as he shuffled to the door, he thought about not responding, but lights were on in the house, and Vance's truck was in the driveway. "Hello, Mrs. Hunter," Kris said, before he had completely opened the door.

"Guess again," was Karen's greeting.

"I don't suppose you've got an iced pound cake in that picnic basket you're carrying?" Kris asked.

Karen walked into the house. "No. Why?"

"Because that's what Mrs. Hunter from next door always brings."

"Sorry, but I don't think you'll be disappointed with what I have," Karen said on her way to the kitchen.

"What are you doing here?"

"Lonnie's out saving the world from crime, so I'm alone for supper. I know you left Patrick at the Sentinel to do your work and that you've got to go back for him later, so you're alone for supper. Why should we eat alone? I whipped out a few ham and cheese sandwiches, some macaroni salad and a vegetable tray. I even brought a bottle of wine."

"I'm impressed," he said, watching Karen empty the contents of the picnic basket on to the kitchen table.

Kris poured two glasses of the Merlot while Karen distributed food on their plates. Kris realized he was hungry, having not eaten anything all day but two strawberry Pop-Tarts for breakfast. He quickly gulped down one sandwich and reached for another, which made Karen smile.

Nibbling on a carrot stick, Karen said, "Remember, we used to do this all the time in high school. Even sneaked off with some beer and wine a few times."

Kris chuckled. "Yeah, living with Vance, there was usually some around. He never missed it."

"Do you remember the time we went skinny-dipping at the Cooter's Lake and Mickey Montgomery stole our clothes? And you drove naked back to your house to get us something to wear? Thank God my parents weren't at home to see me come home in a pair of your shorts and your t-shirt."

"Oh, I remember, but I remember that we got even with Mickey. We invited him to our next picnic. Those tuna fish sandwiches he liked so much? They were really cat food."

Karen started to laugh, almost spitting out the sip of wine she had just taken. "I thought I was going to die laughing when he asked for a second."

Kris looked at the sandwich he was eating and then looked at Karen.

"I promise it's real ham and cheese," she said. "I'll even take a bite of it if you want me to."

"That's O.K." he said, taking another huge bite.

Karen smiled weakly at Kris. "That wasn't the only good time we had," she said.

"No, we had a bunch. And I spent so much time at your house I might as well have lived there. Your folks were like my second set of parents."

"And you were like their son."

"Your parents were good people. The best."

"Why can't today be like that again?" Karen asked.

"Your parents are dead."

"You and I, Kris. Why can't we be like that again?"

Kris sighed and looked in the direction of the door leading from the kitchen to the backyard. "It just is not meant to be," he said softly. "I was ready to strike out on my own and you were staying here. A lot of time has passed since those days."

"But there's nothing to keep me here now."

"There's the Sentinel."

"The Sentinel matter is going to be resolved. Wherever you want to go, I will go with you, Kris."

"You're married!"

"Lonnie is no hindrance to what you and I want to do. You and I were meant to be together. I think it was fate that brought you back."

"Fate? I'd call it damn bad luck."

"I call it fate. Why else would your girlfriend dump you? It is over for the two of you, isn't it? That's why you have been in a funk these last few days."

"Seems that way," he reluctantly admitted. "I was ready to go back to her like a whipped puppy, but I just learned that she's off on a not-all-business trip."

Karen took a long sip of her wine. Looking over the rim of the glass, she said, "I am so sorry, Kris. No, I take that back. I am not sorry."

"I'm not ready to give up on Emmy just yet."

Karen got up from the table. "Let me see if I can convince you otherwise." She cupped his face in her hands and started slowly kissing him. He softly took her arms and started to push her away but didn't. He liked the attention. Kris pushed his chair away from the table and Karen straddled him and continued to kiss. His hands slid up her white cotton blouse to her breasts and she moaned. Both were starting to breathe hard. Kris was fumbling with the top button on Karen's blouse when someone knocked on the door again.

"Damn it!" Kris fumed.

"Don't answer it," Karen pleaded.

Kris gently pushed Karen out of his lap. "I've got to," he told her. "If it's Mrs. Hunter she won't go away. But I promise I'll get rid of her fast."

"You better!"

Kris hurried to the door, ready to take Mrs. Hunter's cake and say thanks and good night. He opened the door, but Mrs. Hunter wasn't on the porch. Billy Manley and his smelly cigarette was.

"What are you doing here?" Kris snapped.

"Looking for a loan. Got a few bucks a good friend of your dad could borrow?"

Kris sighed in frustration. "Yeah, let me get my wallet." Kris scurried to his bedroom, grabbed a twenty-dollar bill and headed back. He was irritated to discover that Manley had stepped inside and was rummaging through a drawer in a writing desk in a corner.

"Manley, what the hell are you doing?"

"I, uh, I'm looking for a pen and a piece of paper. I want to write you an IOU."

"You don't have to do that," Kris said, handing him the money.

"I want to show you that I'm good for the money."

"Oh, I know you're good for the money. I'll get it one of these days, maybe when the sun burns out."

"That's harsh, Kris. You hurt my feelings."

"Gosh, Billy. I didn't realize you were so sensitive," Kris said, trying not to laugh.

"I insist on writing you an IOU." Manley pulled open another drawer on the desk.

"Billy, quit snooping!" Kris ordered. "I'll get you a piece of paper. Kris hurried back to his room, found a pen, tore a page from a note pad and returned to Manley, who scratched an illegible note.

"There. I feel better," Manley said, handing the note to Kris. "You got any food around here?" Without an invitation, Manley started walking to the kitchen. Manley had been in the house many times with Vance. He knew the floor plan.

Manley stopped when he saw Karen still sitting at the table. "I'm sorry. Did I interrupt something?" he asked Kris.

"Yeah. We were discussing the North Korean nuclear threat," Kris said.

"Hey, newspaper lady," Manley said.

"Hello Billy."

"Can I have one of those?" Manley, eyeing the two remaining ham and cheese sandwiches, asked.

"We're not through," Kris told him.

"Let him have them," Karen sighed. "I need to get home anyway."

"Are you sure?" Kris asked.

Karen nodded yes. She said goodbye to Manley and started walking to the front door. Kris accompanied her, and she gently reached for his hand. She started with a polite peck on his cheek and followed that up with an emphatic lip lock. Karen rubbed her hand across his cheek, smiled and promised him, "I'll see you tomorrow."

He smiled in return and propped his head against the door frame. What was he doing? Thirty minutes earlier he was trying to call Emmy, ready to pledge his undying love, and yet he had come within an unwanted visitor of cheating on her by having sex with a married woman. Rationalizing, he deemed his actions justifiable since Emmy was apparently off giving one of her co-workers the business. "Damn it! Damn it!" Kris muttered while he beat his hand against the door. The sickening thought flashed through his mind that he was never going to get his life straightened out.

Kris returned to the kitchen, plopped down in a chair at the table and watched Manley devour the rest of the food. "Does Lonnie know you're doing his wife?" Manley asked between big bites of sandwich.

"I'm not doing his wife. I've got a girlfriend."

"Since when did that stop anyone?"

"I don't want to talk about any of this. Shut up and eat."

Manley obliged and was silent for several minutes, which was a relief to Kris, who was completely at war with his emotions. One moment he was ready to hop in Vance's truck and head to Atlanta. The next moment he was telling himself there was unfinished business in Fort Phillips, and perhaps Karen was part of that unfinished business.

Kris retrieved a beer from the refrigerator and quickly gulped down half of it. "I envy you Billy."

Manley's eyes widened. "Me?" he asked.

"Yeah. What do you have to worry about? Your next pack of cigarettes? Finding someone to give you twenty dollars? You don't have a wife or girlfriend - or a job - to frustrate you. Can we swap places?" Kris finished off the beer, crushed the can and tossed it into the trash.

Manley stopped in mid-chew. "You don't want to do that, believe me. You have no idea what's going on in my life. You don't want to know," he told Kris before swallowing the food in his mouth.

"Whatever you've got going, it can't be any more nerve-wracking than the mess I'm in."

"Get out of this place, Kris. Get out fast. I know I'm not one to be giving anyone much advice but trust me on this. Leave! Get out of this place. You don't belong here."

Manley's urging surprised Kris. "Why are you telling me this? Kris asked. "You've been demanding that I stay to find out the truth about Vance's death. Now you're telling me to get out of town."

Manley didn't reply because Kris' cell started ringing. Lonnie Jackson was letting him know a house just inside the east city limits was on fire. Photos of burning houses always looked good on the front page of the Sentinel, Lonnie joked. Kris wondered why he had not heard an announcement of a fire over the police scanner but then he remembered it had been unplugged at Emmy's insistence and he had neglected to turn it back on. But neither had he heard the town's siren beckoning volunteer firefighters.

Sliding his phone back in his jeans pocket, Kris told Manley, "I am getting out of this place. At least for a few minutes. Want to go with me to a fire?"

Manley bounced out of his chair and followed Kris to Vance's truck. They arrived at the burning house in less than ten minutes, just in time to see the roof collapse. The house was gone. Firemen couldn't save it, but the family was not home, so no one was injured. The main objective was to keep the fire from spreading to neighboring houses. With Manley following him like a novice reporter, Kris took several photos before approaching Fire Chief Norman Bosworth for information.

While Kris was getting a lot of *I don't know* from Chief Bosworth, Patrick was at the Sentinel finishing the final two stories for the issue that was to be printed at 9 o'clock the next morning. Neither story would make a ripple outside the city limits, but they were important to Fort Phillips, and Patrick was treating them that way. Thankful to have something to work on and keep his mind off his physical misfortune, Patrick had approached every simple task for the Sentinel with enthusiasm and professionalism. Only occasionally did he think about the high- profile assignments he had been given at Channel 12. For this moment, his world revolved around the Fort Phillips City Council and their decision to buy a new garbage truck. Thirty years earlier his career had started at small newspapers and small television markets, and he was enjoying returning to his roots. He fondly remembered his lessons learned and mistakes made in those early, formative days of his career. In Fort Phillips, the only struggle he was having was keyboarding. He was managing though, even joking about the drumstick he had clumsily taped to his stump to help him peck out his stories.

Searching for the right words to end his city council recap, Patrick flinched when he heard glass shattering. Expecting to discover a brick that some juvenile delinquent had tossed through the plate glass window at the front of the building, Patrick gasped when he stuck his head out of his office. A fireball exploded, sending flames up the old dirty green curtains framing the shattered window. In seconds the entire front wall was covered, cutting off exit from the door. Smoke was already filling the front part of the building and wafting down the hall.

Trying to remain calm but already starting to shake, Patrick used his cell to call 9-1-1. The dispatcher answered, "Collier County 9-1-1. What is the nature of your emergency?"

"The Sentinel office is on fire!" was his swift, short reply.

"Do you have an address sir?"

"No. I've only been in town a few days. This town is not that big. Surely you can find the place!" he bellowed, part out of fear and part out of anger at the question. How could a 9-1-1 dispatcher in this little piss ant town not know the address of the Sentinel?

"I have located the address. I am going to dispatch the county unit as quickly as possible. Are you in danger?"

Patrick did not know much about the community, but he knew enough about geography to understand that a city fire unit had to be closer to the Sentinel than a county unit. What he did not know was there were only two units in the county, the city unit and the county unit, both staffed mostly by volunteers. "Why a county unit?" he shouted at the dispatcher. "And hell yeah I'm in danger. I'm in a friggin' burning building!"

"The city has responded to another call. I will have a unit there as quickly as possible."

Trying to remain calm, Patrick was starting to realize he did not have time to debate the issue with the dispatcher. Smoke was starting to choke off the air. He moved deliberately toward the back door, the only other way out of the building. Patrick pushed the door, but it would not open. He tried a second time and a third, each time with greater force, but the door would not open. Next, he crashed his shoulder into the door, hurting himself, but not budging the door. Something was keeping Patrick from being able to open the door.

His face flush and his breathing labored, Patrick managed to use his phone to call Kris, who had left the other fire three minutes earlier. Again, Patrick's message was short and meaningful, "The Sentinel is on fire and I'm trapped inside!"

Stunned, Kris shouted "Stay calm!" He wasn't heeding his own advice. The speed of Vance's truck and his heartbeat immediately shifted into high gear.

"What's going on?" Manley asked. When the truck jerked forward, Manley's cigarette dropped out of his mouth.

"The Sentinel office is on fire and Patrick is trapped inside!"

"Damn! That's some serious shit!"

"And I'm in a truck that's as slow as you are about filling out a job application!"

"I know a shortcut!"

"Tell me, damn it!"

"About fifty yards ahead, on the right, there's a dirt road. It's rough but it'll cut three or four minutes off your time."

"You just earned that twenty dollars I gave you earlier tonight," Kris said.

"Really? Thanks, man!"

Kris stomped the gas pedal again just as the truck hit a rut in the dirt road. Kris and Manley bounced three inches off the seat. "This would be fun if I wasn't scared to death," Kris admitted.

"What about me?" Manley asked. "I'm about to pee in my pants."

"Hold it. You can use it to help put out the fire."

"Glad to do my part," Manley replied as Kris pumped the gas pedal again.

With his breathing becoming more difficult, Patrick took refuge in the cramped restroom at the Sentinel. He wet a towel and stuffed it into the crack between the base of the door and the floor. Exhausted, Patrick sat on the commode and pondered the irony of his situation. Had he survived the fiery explosion of a helicopter in an incident that generated national headlines only to die in a fire in an obscure newspaper office in an obscure town where no one would notice? *This isn't funny, God,* Patrick mumbled while taking deeper breaths to try to suck the little remaining air into his lungs.

True to Manley's word, the shortcut was bumpy but fast. With Vance's Ranger rattling like tin cans tied on a string, Kris sped into downtown Fort Phillips. "I don't believe this," he said, close to crying at the first glance of the bonfire the front of the Sentinel had become. Two other cars pulled up and the occupants got out, realizing there was nothing they could do. "Where the hell is the fire truck!" Kris cried. He tossed his cell phone to Manley. "Call 9-1-1!" he ordered, not knowing Patrick had already made the call. Obviously, entrance to the building from the front was impossible, so Kris sprinted to the back where his concern for Patrick was momentarily overcome by rage. Someone had wedged a four-by-four post against the door, meaning neither Patrick nor the strongest man in town could have opened it from the inside. Grunting loudly, Kris kicked the post four times before it fell away from the door. The heat and smoke immediately hit him in the face. Recklessly stepping inside, he started screaming for Patrick. The smoke was killing his eyes.

"I'm here!" Patrick shouted between coughs as he exited the restroom. Kris wrapped his arm around Patrick's waist and led him outside. Gasping for air, Patrick collapsed on the ground. Kris, his hands resting on his knees, was sucking for air as well. Slowly, their lungs replaced smoke with air and they, along with Manley, watched the Sentinel's roof cave in. They finally heard the first, faint sound from the siren of the county fire truck.

"Better late than never," Patrick shrugged.

"Are you all right?" Kris asked.

"I couldn't get the back door open."

"Someone had propped a post against the door. You would never have opened it."

Patrick's eyes, still moist from the smoke, widened. "Someone didn't want me to get out?"

"More likely, they didn't want me to get out. They probably thought I was still at work."

"Why? Why would anyone want to kill you?"

"To stop me from snooping around."

Kris and Manley assisted Patrick to an ambulance that had arrived and he was administered oxygen. Relieved that his friend was receiving appropriate treatment, Kris stepped a few feet away. Taking his phone back from Manley, Kris undertook another difficult task - calling Karen to tell her the bad news.

24

The next morning, Kris, Patrick and Karen, who was sniffling and had tears streaming down her cheeks, were standing on the sidewalk surveying the burned-out shell of the Sentinel. Karen's tears were not for the building or its contents. Insurance would cover that. They could be replaced. Her sadness came from thinking about her father and his years of around the clock effort that made the little newspaper such an integral part of the community. She recalled the thousands of birth announcements, wedding engagements, obituary notices and high school sports events that had been published. At some point in time, through one article or another, every person in Fort Phillips had a connection to the Sentinel. Like the first settlers, the Sentinel had always been there to look over the town, to protect it, to be its moral compass, to be there through the good times and bad; reporting on everything from to the Anderson family's Sunday visitors from Knoxville to the city council raising taxes. And like the town, the Sentinel had struggled mightily for the last few years. They were both on borrowed time, and Karen, in something of a sense of relief, viewed the fire as a mercy killing, putting an end to the Sentinel before times got worse.

Silently, Karen continued to stare through misty eyes at the destroyed building. Every few seconds she would put her hand over her mouth as if to contain the full-blown cry she was trying hard to suppress. For minutes, Kris was silent with her, offering support by putting his arm around her waist. They were grieving, like they had lost a member of the family and in a very real sense, they had. Finally, having used up most of her supply of tears, Karen said softly, "I was ready to do something with the Sentinel and move on with my life, but this isn't exactly how I had it pictured."

"Do you think your dad would go out like this?" Kris asked.

"What do you mean?" Karen questioned, wiping another tear from the corner of her eye.

"I mean, do you think your dad would let a fire put him out of business? Hell no! And it's not going to put us out of business!"

"But there's nothing left, Kris, nothing but memories."

"Oh, I beg to differ. There's your dad's legacy. There's your legacy. Heck, there's even my little bit of legacy in this newspaper. That's what's left. We can be back in business tomorrow."

Karen dropped the tissue she was holding and looked at Kris. "I don't understand," she said.

With Patrick looking on and starting to smile, Kris softly took Karen's hands and looked reassuringly into her still moist eyes. "We can set up shop at my house. Printing the paper isn't an issue since the plant is twenty-five miles away. We can do our writing and whatever else we need at the house. All the jerks who torched this place did is inconvenience us a little bit. I'm ready to get back to work.!"

"So am I!" Patrick barked gleefully.

Karen was totally surprised. "What about Atlanta? What about Emmy?

"If it weren't for your dad, if it wasn't for the little newspaper that used to be housed in this building, I would not have my job in Atlanta, and I would not have met Emmy. I have been trying to run away from this town for ten years, and now it's time for me to come back! I refuse to let the Sentinel go down this way!"

"Bravo!" shouted Patrick, shaking Kris at the neck vigorously with his good hand.

Karen dropped her head. She looked back up and tried to smile at Kris but did not do a particularly good job. "That sounds very noble, but I don't know if I've got enough fight left in me. I don't know if this town has any fight left in it," she whispered. "I'm tired. I need a break."

He squeezed her hands tighter. "We can do this, Karen," he said. "We can do this together. You and me and Patrick." He glanced over at Patrick.

"Absolutely!" Patrick quickly responded.

She dropped her head again and looked up. "What about us? You and me?"

"No promises about us. I am not going to do anything to break up your marriage. I do promise that we are going to get the Sentinel back on its feet and find out the person or persons responsible for setting fires and breaking into houses and trying to destroy this town. I am even going to find out who killed Popeye."

"And if Lonnie and I just happen to go our separate ways?"

"What's meant to be will be. Things have a way of working themselves out."

Karen managed a small smile. "I can accept that. So, when do we go to work?"

"Right now." From his wallet, Kris pulled out his credit card and handed it to Karen. "You and Patrick go to the house. Talk about what you will need to get us started and start planning the next issue. I know what our lead story is going to be! I will meet you there later. First thing I want to do is talk to Lonnie about all the crap that is going on around here. Do you know where he is? He called me about the house fire last night but wasn't there."

"Check with the police station. There's been another break-in."

Karen hugged Kris and asked Patrick if he was ready to leave. Saying he needed a moment with Kris about a story idea, Patrick told Karen he would be at her car in a minute. Pulling Kris closer to the burned building, Patrick started, "I'm all for getting the Sentinel back in business. It is a big challenge and I have plenty of time to devote to it, and I am not going to let some fire-setting thugs scare me away. But what about you, Kris. Is this what you really want? What does this do to you and Emmy?"

"I don't know," Kris responded quickly and honestly. "Like I told Karen, what is meant to be, will be. If I am meant to be with Emmy, I will end up with Emmy. All I know is, that right now, this is what I want to do. This is what I've got to do."

"If you're sure."

"I'm one hundred percent sure."

"Then I'm in one hundred percent, too."

"What about Margaret?"

"As long as she knows I'm healthy and busy, she'll be all for it. She's got her own stuff to do and girlfriends to hang out with. I do think it should conveniently slip our minds to tell her about the little incident last night."

"The little incident in which you almost ended like a charred hot dog at a cookout?"

"That's the one."

"I think that is an excellent idea…but are you sure you want to be involved in this mess?"

"I would not miss it for the world."

"Good," Kris nodded. "I can't think of anyone I'd rather have here giving me a hand."

"Well, I've only got one, but it's all yours," Patrick said, holding up his one good hand and his nub.

"And when you and Karen go for supplies, be sure and get some left-handed toilet paper," Kris smiled. They both laughed and hugged. Patrick headed out with Karen, and Kris, after learning Lonnie's location from the police department's secretary-receptionist, steered Vance's truck to the scene of the most recent house intrusion.

Standing out in the yard of the house that sat by itself on a narrow city street, Lonnie seemed surprised to see Kris. "What are you doing here? I figured the Sentinel was out of business," Lonnie said.

"Nope. It is not taking the Sentinel three days to resurrect. We are not skipping a beat. One of my next stories is going to be about all these break-ins. What are you doing to solve all these?"

"Trying to do my job again?" Lonnie asked as he glanced at an initial report one of his officers had completed after talking to the occupants.

"Nope. Just doing mine. What about it, Chief? Any leads?"

"Not on this case, but remember Popeye? I've got a possible lead on his killer." Lonnie started walking to his car.

"Good," Kris said, walking after him. "What can you tell me?"

"Want to know who the suspect is?" Lonnie asked, as he sat on the edge of the hood of his car.

"If you're willing to tell me, I'm willing to listen."

"It's you. You're the suspect," Lonnie announced calmly.

"What?" is all Kris could say.

"You. Your fingerprints were all over the knife that was in Popeye's chest. We matched the prints on the knife with the prints we had on file for you. Seems the Fort Phillips police had to do a background check on you when you applied to be a camp counselor the summer between your junior and senior year in high school."

"I don't remember. That was a million years ago. You're kidding, right?" Kris asked in disbelief.

"Do I look like I'm kidding?"

"You're saying this because you think I've got something going on with Karen, right? Well, I don't, damn it!"

"I'm not the country bumpkin policeman you think I am, Kris. We followed procedure. *Policing for Dummies* says check the murder weapon for fingerprints first thing. We did. Yours matched. Pretty stupid of you not to wipe the knife clean."

"I didn't wipe the knife clean because I didn't use it on Popeye."

"How do you explain your prints on the knife?"

Kris ran his fingers through his hair. "It's a kitchen knife. I probably used it in the kitchen, don't you think? Popeye must have taken the knife."

"Now, why would Popeye have taken a $3.95 knife from your kitchen? Surely you've got something more valuable than that in your house."

"I think he was taking anything he could get his hands on before I interrupted him. Or, someone else took it because they wanted to set me up on this bogus charge about killing Popeye."

"And how do you explain this? He shows up dead days after he breaks into your house and comes close to violating your girlfriend?"

"Coincidence. You said yourself a lot of people in town had motive to kill him."

"Yeah, but you're at the top of the list."

"This isn't funny Lonnie."

"No, it's not. We take murder seriously around here."

Kris' mouth was getting dry, and his heart was pounding harder than a bass drum at the Georgia Bulldog - Florida Gator football game. "I didn't kill him!" Kris said emphatically.

"We'll see. We're still investigating."

"Do I need to get a lawyer?"

"That's up to you. Since the Sentinel seems back in business, I assume I'll know where to find you."

"Yes. Find your wife and you'll likely find me too," Kris said. He knew the remark was rude, almost hateful, but it just popped out.

Lonnie got in his car and before shutting the door glared at Kris. "Why didn't you just bury Vance and go back to Atlanta?" he asked with a sigh. "You've screwed things up royally Kris. For yourself and a lot of other people. You're going to end up like your father."

The remark caught Kris' attention. "What do you mean?" Kris asked.

"He had a habit of fouling up his life. You're starting to follow in his footsteps."

"Vance had nothing to do with this."

"If he hadn't blown his brains out, you would have never come back to Fort Phillips, and you wouldn't be the prime suspect in a murder."

"And you wouldn't be worried about me taking away your wife."

Lonnie grunted. "Get your ass out of here before I arrest you on the spot. I've got work to do."

"Me too. See you on the front page of the Sentinel," Kris said as he walked back to Vance's truck. He took a deep breath, and a shiver went through his body.

25

Kris didn't tell Patrick and Karen that he had become the main suspect in Popeye's murder. He assumed he would not have to. The way gossip spread in the little town, everyone would know within a few days, and he wondered what Karen's reaction would be when she learned her husband had made him the focal point of the murder investigation. He could picture her screaming at Lonnie that he did not know what he was doing, and that he should stick to the jobs he did well like directing traffic at the high school football games. Kris had no doubt that with any matter involving him and Lonnie, Karen would side with him, not her husband. He was not proud or pleased with that, but it was the truth.

That's what concerned Kris about Lonnie targeting him as the prime murder suspect. To prove himself to Karen and the rest of the town, Lonnie could easily become obsessed with putting Kris in jail. But despite being inwardly rattled by Lonnie, Kris maintained a calm façade and was able to put all his energy into collaborating with Patrick on a front-page story about the fires and break-ins and other strange occurrences that were haunting the town. The State Insurance Commissioner had assigned investigators to the fires, which were obviously arson, but little headway had been made relating to identifying suspects.

As for the break-ins, the Georgia Bureau of Investigation agents interviewed by Kris all said the same thing. Those cases were a matter of local jurisdiction and the state would get involved only if asked. Patrick had the task of interviewing Lonnie, whose only printable comments from a thirty-minute question and answer session were his department was working around the clock, and he had confidence the Fort Phillips police would make arrests. Kris was concerned that Lonnie's pre-occupation with nailing him with Popeye's murder would become so strong that the other cases would be neglected. And the truth of the matter was, even if Lonnie was a dedicated detective with no hidden agenda, his department did not have the manpower or training to conduct the type of in-depth investigation that was needed.

The confrontation Kris had anticipated came three days later. "I can't believe you're doing this!" Karen bellowed at Lonnie as he walked into the Sentinel's makeshift office at Kris' house. Kris, who had been talking over a couple of story ideas with Karen swallowed hard and braced himself.

"You can't believe I'm doing what?" Lonnie, acting surprised, asked.

"I just came from the drug store a few minutes ago. Doctor Harrison asked me what I thought about you naming Kris as the prime suspect in Popeye's murder. What the hell are you thinking?" Her eyes were bulging, and she was practically snorting the words at Lonnie.

"I'm thinking that's what the evidence shows," Lonnie responded, trying to sound firm.

Kris knew it was time to leave. He made up an excuse about having to go to the high school for an interview with the principal and left Lonnie and Karen to continue their debate.

Karen threw up her hands. "You've known Kris for years. You know as well as I do that Kris did not kill Popeye, although I would not have blamed him after Popeye broke into his house twice and tried to sexually assault Emmy! Stop this foolishness now!"

"You can't get over the fact that lover boy may not be perfect, can you? That for once, I might be right and he's wrong. You know what Karen? It feels good. It feels damn good that I'm on the verge of nailing his butt for this."

Karen threw up her hands again. "You're clueless! Worse than that, you're hopeless!"

"That's sort of how I've felt about our marriage, especially since he came back."

"Well, you don't have anything to worry about. Kris is going to Atlanta tomorrow, and I expect he will stay. What's to keep him in this town?"

"You. And the fact that he's my main suspect in a murder."

"You won't win, Lonnie. You are not in Kris' league. And if you want you and I to have any chance to stay together, look in another direction for Popeye's killer."

Lonnie turned his back on Karen and then turned back to her. Showing a crooked smile, he told her, "One way or another, Keller is going to be out of our hair. He's either going back to Atlanta or to jail. Do you think he's smart enough to figure it out if I give him the choice?" He looked at her coldly and directly. "I'm tired of people running over me, telling me what to do. I'm tired of you telling me what to do," he said with no emotion.

"Someone has to tell you what to do, Lonnie. It's always been that way."

Now Lonnie glared at her hatefully. "I've had enough of this discussion. I'll see you at home later." He turned to walk out the door.

"I can hardly wait," she mumbled under her breath.

Lonnie turned around and faced her. "What did you say?"

"I said I can hardly wait…for you to get home…so we can have a lovely, delightful dinner together."

Without responding, Lonnie exited the house.

When Kris returned thirty minutes later, Karen was at her small desk, her head buried in her hands. "Are you all right?" he asked.

She raised her head. Her mascara was smudged from tears. "I'm sorry Lonnie is being such a jerk."

Kris pulled up an old chair and sat close to her. "He's only doing his job," he said. "And let's face it. He's got incriminating evidence against me."

"He knows you didn't murder Popeye, but he's so damned determined to do something that's going to make this town - and me - respect him."

"Don't worry. Things will work out. Are you going to be all right for a few days while I go to Atlanta?"

Karen cleared her throat, wiped a tear from her eye and smiled. "I'll be fine. You're going to try to get back with Emmy, aren't you?"

Kris nodded. "I need to talk to her. I'm not sure she needs to talk to me."

Karen got out of her chair, took Kris' hands and tugged gently, suggesting he get out of his chair. "I'll be here when you get back," she smiled, tears starting to trickle down her cheeks. They hugged and might have kissed had Patrick not returned from a lengthy interview with senior citizen and antique car enthusiast Cotton Kincade who had provided a tour of the county in his Chevrolet Impala. After Karen took a few minutes to freshen up, she, Kris and Patrick spent an hour going over story ideas and the Sentinel's shoestring budget. In fact, it was not a shoestring budget. It was more like a flip-flop budget.

26

Armed with substantial ***to do*** **lists, Kris and Patrick arrived in** Atlanta shortly after noon. Patrick had appointments with his surgeon and physical therapist, both of whom were pleased with his progress and attitude and were ready to get him fitted with a prosthesis. Relieved to get those visits completed, Patrick joined wife Margaret at LaFrance, a pricey favorite of Atlanta's restaurant critics. The conversation was badly one-sided as Margaret went on and on about her cruise. Patrick didn't mind. His musings about life in Fort Phillips were rather mundane compared to her babbling about tropical breezes and deeply tanned cabana boys with flat stomachs and chiseled chests. He conveniently avoided talking about the fire at the Sentinel. Describing that would no doubt make her hesitant about allowing him to return to Fort Phillips, which was his big announcement of the night. Margaret expressed a bit of reluctance, due mainly to her concern about his health, but once Patrick assured her that he was doing fine, she quickly gave her blessing. Through their twenty-five years of marriage, Margaret had gotten comfortable with her husband's journalistic wanderlust, and that had been the push for her to develop her own interests such as the cruise. Although totally committed to each other, they thought nothing about being out of town at the same time on different adventures. As soon as Patrick announced his plan to travel back to Fort Phillips, Margaret cracked a big smile and started formulating her own escapade, even asking Patrick for suggestions. They ended the evening with a delicious strawberry cheesecake dessert at the restaurant and more dessert in their bedroom.

While Patrick was receiving good news and enjoying light-hearted conversation, Kris was dealing with issues much less pleasant. His first stop was at the Atlanta Advocate where he reluctantly submitted his resignation. Kris did not think he had any choice. His employer wanted him back, had given him something of a deadline, but he could not come back, not just yet. Too many questions remained to be answered. When his editor told him he was making a huge mistake, both career-wise and personally, all Kris could do was swallow hard and nod his head in agreement. Certainly, he was making a financial mistake. Suddenly he had no income. Kris had some savings and investments he could cash in, but that would not last forever. While in Atlanta he did sell his three-year-old Jeep Grand Cherokee, which was paid for, so that gave him some cash to pocket. Besides, right now Vance's Ford Ranger was all he needed. Eventually, he would have to turn the Sentinel into a money-maker, or at least profitable enough to pay himself and a small staff or find employment elsewhere.

From the newspaper office, Kris went to the bank where he closed accounts and withdrew funds. The next step was his apartment complex where he exercised an expensive escape clause to break his lease. Thankfully, the apartment was furnished, so he didn't have to deal with moving and storing furniture. All he had to do was gather personal items, and that was a difficult enough job, particularly since some of Emmy's belongings and clothes were at the apartment.

He needed to talk to Emmy, but she still would not take his calls, so his only recourse was to try to catch her at her office. After showering and changing clothes one last time in the apartment, Kris left for Emmy's work, trying to sync his arrival at closing time, hoping she would accept a dinner invitation.

When the receptionist told Kris Emmy was gone for the day, she might as well have told him his favorite cat needed to be put to sleep. He was saddened, deflated. He needed to talk to Emmy, to settle things, one way or the other, for good. At the very least, she needed to go by his apartment and pick up her things while he still had a key.

Kris was unsuccessfully trying to convince the receptionist to tell him Emmy's whereabouts when Marilyn walked into the lobby from a back office. He had to look twice to recognize her. Marilyn had toned down her act considerably. Her makeup was light and tasteful; her pinstriped black suit and black heels were worthy of an appearance before a board of directors. She looked great and was obviously pleased that Kris could not take his eyes off her.

"Hi Kris," Marilyn smiled. She extended her hand, which surprised him, but after a brief hesitation, he shook it. "You're looking for Emmy, I guess," she said.

"I am. She's not here," Kris replied, taking another quick glance at Marilyn.

"I hope you didn't come to town just to see her. She's difficult to catch these days, Kris. In and out a lot."

Kris walked away from the receptionist to a corner and Marilyn followed. "No," he said. "I had several things to take care of, like quitting my job, giving up my apartment, draining my bank account."

"Geez, Kris!" Marilyn said in part shock, part surprise. "You are serious about this Fort Sentinel stuff, aren't you?"

"It's Fort Phillips, and yeah, I guess I am."

"And this is what you're wanting to tell Emmy?"

"It is."

Marilyn reached out and rubbed Kris' arm. "I'm sorry," she started. "I'm sorry that Emmy won't give you a few minutes of her suddenly invaluable time, and I'm sorry that you're making such a sacrifice."

"It's not a sacrifice if it's something you want to do."

"Maybe so, but I don't think I could do what you're doing. How long are you going to be in town? If I see or talk to Emmy tomorrow, I'll try my best to get her to call you."

Kris took another full-figure glance at Marilyn. He started to speak but the words caught in his throat. "Uh, can I ask you something," he stuttered.

"Sure," she smiled, surprised at his request.

"Emmy might not be willing to give me a few minutes of her invaluable time, but what about you? Would you have dinner with me?"

Marilyn's smile lighted the foyer "I'd love to. After all, you did promise to have dinner with me, remember?"

"I remember."

With part of her job being to arrange lunch and dinner meetings with clients of the leasing company, Marilyn suggested the Atlanta Landing, a popular steakhouse on the twenty-fourth floor of a midtown hotel. Kris did not know which view he was enjoying the most - the city's skyline or Marilyn. They asked for glasses of Chardonnay, placed their food orders and spent several minutes trying to identify distant buildings. Kris was impressed with her knowledge of the city. That's not all that was impressing him.

"Can I ask you a question?" he said clumsily.

"Another question?" she smiled. "Sure."

"I'm not sure how to say this, but you look different."

"I do?" she smiled broadly.

"Yeah," he answered clumsily. "But a good different."

She smiled. "Thanks. It is a conscious effort on my part. And you are responsible."

"How so?"

"You know I have always admired you from afar, sometimes from not so afar?"

Kris nodded.

"The last time you were here, I started asking myself why I couldn't get a second look from the good guys like you? I have never had any trouble getting men to notice me, but none of them have exactly been husband material. I did some soul-searching and decided that I needed to make a lot of changes, give myself a total makeover."

"It worked. You look great!"

Marilyn's smile indicated her pleasure. "Thank you but looks are only a start. Behavior modification is part of it. I cannot believe some of the awful things I have done. All the upskirt glimpses I have given you and other guys. In case you did not notice, I was trying to seduce you over the phone when you called my apartment looking for Emmy. I'm embarrassed to even talk about my past behavior."

"I've got to admit, the change is amazing. All I can say is, *WOW!"*

A big smile swept across Marilyn's face. "Thank you," she replied.

"I have another question ask."

"A third question? My goodness," she smiled.

Kris waited for the waitress to serve their salads before continuing. "Would you like to come with me to my apartment tonight? Before I have to vacate it?"

Marilyn fumbled the fork she had picked up to start on her salad. She put her hand high on her chest. "I can't believe what I'm about to say," she started. "Thanks, but no thanks. Part of the new me, you know."

Kris turned crimson, not so much over Marilyn's rejection, but the fact he asked the question to begin with. "I'm sorry," he apologized.

"Don't be. I am flattered…and tempted because the old Marilyn still tries to burst out quite often. I still catch myself being a tease or hiking up my skirt, but I am trying hard to be better. As for your offer, like I said, I'm tempted, oh so tempted, but I want some time to work on me some more, and I want you to have some time to work on your issues."

"Ah yes, my issues," Kris said, picking at the lettuce.

Marilyn finished a bite of salad and put down her fork. "You tell me if I'm out of line, because I don't know what's really going on between you and Emmy," she started. "I've just got bits and pieces of information here and there. But I do know this, Kris. Emmy has changed too. She's lost some of her bounce, her spirit, like she's preoccupied with something."

"I can't say I'm surprised, with all the crap I've put her through."

"No, it started before that. Her mind was already wandering. I have no idea what was going on. You know, she and I weren't exactly big buddies, but I was around her enough to notice the change."

"Everything O.K. here at work?"

"Yes. Things have been a little slow, but we have all been battling that. We have some new projects that are helping. I just assumed you two were going through a rough patch."

"I never noticed a difference in her. I should have, but I tend to get caught up in my work."

"If something was bothering her, she should have told you."

"Yeah, she's usually not shy about letting me know what's on her mind. She certainly unloaded on me about Fort Phillips."

Marilyn picked up her fork and started stabbing at her salad. Before sliding a bite in her mouth, she told Kris, "Both of you are good people. I hope the two of you can get your issues worked out."

"Thanks," Kris said meekly.

"And if you ever need someone to talk to, you let me know. And the next time you ask me to go home with you, I may not be so saintly. You have no idea how many times I have dreamed about going to bed with you."

Kris turned crimson again. "The evening's still young," he said.

"Eat your salad," Marilyn directed, and Kris complied. For the next hour he fascinated her with tales of Fort Phillips, about being accused of murder, about almost dying in a burning animal clinic, and rescuing Patrick from the Sentinel fire. His arm, which was healing well, was not a topic of conversation.

Kris spent the next day at his apartment, packing some things and throwing others away. His mind kept wandering to the previous evening with Marilyn, one moment salivating about how fabulous she looked, and the next moment getting knots in his stomach over the revelation that something had been bothering Emmy and he hadn't noticed. He really needed to talk to Emmy. He hoped Marilyn had been able to ask Emmy to call him.

He got his wish. Answering the bell to the door of his apartment, he was shocked, pleasantly, to see Emmy. "I need to pick up my things," she announced.

"Why didn't you use your key?" he asked.

She didn't answer, but handed Kris her key to his apartment, which he accepted silently.

Kris escorted her inside. "I'm surprised to see you. I was hoping we would at least get to talk. You look great." He loved how sleek Emmy appeared in the tailored black slacks, burgundy blouse and black pumps.

"You're really doing it. You're really leaving Atlanta."

"How are you doing?" Kris asked, avoiding her question.

"I'm all right. You?"

"I'm O.K. I've been busy."

"Things are popping in Fort Phillips?"

"You don't know the half of it."

"And I don't want to know. I've made enough trips down there to know all I want to know about Fort Phillips."

"What do you mean trips? You've only been there twice."

Emmy walked away from Kris and started rubbing the fabric on the back of the sofa. She cleared her throat before replying, "Twice is plenty. What is that old joke? I spent a month in Fort Phillips one week in August?"

Kris kept his distance from Emmy. "It's not that bad a place," he said.

Emmy sighed. "Kris, I don't want to start this discussion again. I have an appointment. I need to get my things and go." She started walking toward the bedroom.

Kris took several steps toward Emmy, forcing her to stop. "Is this the point you and I have reached? A polite hello, a short good-bye, and get the hell out?"

"Seems like it." Emmy resumed her walk to the bedroom.

Kris met her at the door frame, forcing her to stop again. "I'm sorry I destroyed our relationship," he said softly, "and I'm sorry I got so wrapped up in my own work and world that I didn't realize something was bothering you."

Emmy squeezed into the bedroom and began placing clothes from the closet on the bed they had shared many nights. "I've never said our relationship is over. It's up to you, Kris. You can come back, and we'll try to make things work. Fort Phillips is not part of the equation. You may be able to go back to the small-town lifestyle but not me. I am a big city girl, remember? I like nice restaurants and theaters and shopping malls. I also like money, a lot, and from what I've seen, there's not much of that in Fort Phillips." She lifted several pairs of thong panties from the middle drawer of a dresser.

"All I need is a little time. That's all I'm asking of you."

"I can't, Kris. I'm not willing to put my life on hold while you go chasing windmills."

Kris sat down on the edge of the bed and smoothed the comforter with his hand. Without looking at Emmy, he said, "Then I guess this conversation is over."

"I guess you are correct." Emmy was struggling to hold all the clothing items she had picked up.

"Let me help you out to your car," Kris offered, taking some of the items from her.

Three armfuls later, Emmy was ready to leave. She slipped on her sunglasses, slid into her car, and, forcing a smile said, "Take care of yourself Kris."

"You, too." Kris watched her drive away. All that was left for him to do was return to Fort Phillips. With no fiancée and no job, he had plenty of time to resolve matters down there.

27

Shuffling out of the Fort Phillips Recreation Center in the darkness of a late summer night after two hours of elbow-throwing, hip-checking, non-stop basketball, Kris was still using a white towel to wipe sweat from his forehead. The regular guys - Kris, Mickey Montgomery, Lonnie Jackson, Mark Stewart and others - had chosen sides four different times for mini-games and Kris' group had won every time. Whether it was a mid-range jump shot, a stick-back of a rebound, or a no-look pass to a teammate for a basket, Kris always made the play that decided the outcome. Kris and Lonnie went at each other hard but cleanly. The cheap shots that had almost brought them to blows earlier were gone. There was still plenty of contact between them, but it was good, hard-nosed basketball. Kris liked that, thrived on it, and in fact, appreciated the passion that marked Lonnie's play.

Kris loved basketball and he loved to play. It was his favorite form of exercise, but more importantly, when he was on the court, he was in another world. For two hours he could forget about Emmy, Karen, Vance and the Sentinel and concentrate on hitting the open shot or heading down court on a fast break. He wished all the decisions he had to make were as simple as the ones that seemed like second nature to him on the court. His arm was still tender, but it was not going to keep him from the sport he loved.

About to reach Vance's truck in a far corner of the 150-space parking lot, Kris stopped when a dirty, dented, old white sedan, its light on bright, headed directly toward him. Almost blinded, Kris stopped. "Damn!" he shouted, realizing how close the car had come to clipping him.

The car's tires smoked as it came to a quick stop and the driver's side window came down. Kris had difficulty seeing a face.

"I need to talk to you," the husky male voice came from inside the car.

"You almost hit me," was Kris' irritated reply.

"I'm sorry. We need to talk."

Kris leaned forward to get a better look, but he still could not distinguish the face. "Who are you?" Kris asked.

"BoJo. Bobby Jones. Popeye's friend."

"BoJo, huh? What do you want to talk about? You want to give me advance notice of the next time you break in my house?"

"Get in the car!"

Kris still could not see the face clearly, but he saw the barrel of the handgun BoJo stuck out the window. "Get in," BoJo demanded again.

Taking a step back, Kris defiantly said, "I'm not getting in the car with you. I don't want Lonnie Jackson finding my body in a back alley in a day or two. You'll have to shoot me here, right here in the Recreation Center parking lot."

"Damn it, Keller! Get in the car!" Kris could hear BoJo cock the gun.

"Nope. I'm getting in my truck and going home."

"Damn it!" BoJo jerked the gun back, rolled up the window, and with the car tires squealing, sped out of the complex, the glass packed muffler providing a noisy exit. Shaking but relieved, Kris stood in the parking lot wondering what BoJo was up to. About to get in the Ranger, Kris stopped when he saw headlights heading back accompanied by the unmistakable noise of BoJo's beat-up old car. Pulling back into the parking lot, BoJo almost hit Kris again.

"He's not going to shoot me. He's going to run over me!" Kris said out loud.

BoJo rolled down his window and held out the gun, the handle facing Kris. "I'm not going to hurt you, Keller. Here. Take the gun. It's not loaded, but you can hold it if you'll come with me."

"What's going on?" Kris asked, totally puzzled by the weird scenario. Not waiting for an answer, Kris, going against good judgment, got in the car.

"This car is really loud," Kris said as they left the park. "And it smells. Cigarettes and booze. Where are we going?"

"We're just driving. I've got some stuff I need to tell you."

"I'm listening."

"Lonnie Jackson is trying to pin Popeye's murder on you, right?"

"Yes."

"I know you didn't kill him. I know because we stole the knife that was used to kill him from your house."

Kris slapped the dash of the car. "I knew that's what happened! All right, who did kill him?"

"I don't know. Things are getting really strange around here, and I want to leave town."

"You can't leave until you tell Lonnie what you just told me."

"I won't have to tell him, because there's other stuff you've got to figure out, and when you do that, I think you'll find the killer."

BoJo was driving too fast. Kris realized that as they zipped past the City Limits sign. "Are you sober?" Kris asked, beginning to have doubt about BoJo's ramblings.

"Dead sober. Listen, the times your house was broken into?"

"Yeah?"

"Somebody paid us to do it."

"What the hell are you talking about?"

"Somebody paid us to break into your house. That is, somebody paid Popeye and he cut me in on it."

"Why my house? Lord knows, there's nothing of value there."

"Somebody thinks there it. Popeye told me he was looking for something. He never told me what it was, but I know he didn't find it."

"Why should I believe any of this? Maybe you killed Popeye. If someone was throwing money at him, maybe you decided you wanted all of it instead of a cut."

"I'm telling you so I can leave town before someone sticks a knife in my chest. I'm telling you so you can figure out what really happened to Vance."

BoJo absolutely had Kris' attention now. "You don't think Vance killed himself?"

"The last time I talked to Vance he seemed fine. But the night before he died, I was driving through town and saw him coming out of the back of the Simpson Slacks building. He seemed like he was agitated and in a hurry. I asked him if he was O.K. He said he was, got in his truck and drove off. I have this sick feeling in the pit of my stomach that someone saw me talking to Vance, and they don't like that."

"How did he get in? That place is shut tighter than a South Georgia liquor store on Sunday," Kris asked, ignoring BoJo's fear for his safety.

"I don't know, but he did." BoJo rolled his car to a stop on a decaying asphalt road that was pitch dark.

"We're at the Tanks, aren't we?" Kris asked, shifting his head to the barely visible large white pipeline fuel storage tanks in the adjacent field.

"Yeah. How do you know about the Tanks?"

"Because back when I was in high school, this is where we came with our girlfriends to make out. Or should I say, this is where other couples came. I never did."

"Bull crap!" BoJo shot back. "I bet you and that Karen girl had some fine times out here."

"Well, you couldn't have picked a more isolated spot to talk. You're not going to shoot me or stab me, are you? Or make sexual advances toward me?" Kris asked jokingly, certain at this point BoJo meant him no harm.

"No. I don't really know you Keller, but from what I've seen and heard, you're an O.K. guy. I don't want you to get arrested for Popeye's murder, and I don't want someone to get away with Vance's murder, if that's what happened."

Kris leaned back against the door on the passenger side of BoJo's car. After several moments of silence in the dark evening, Kris started, "All right. This is what you're telling me. Someone paid Popeye to break into my house to look for something. You don't know what it was, but you know Popeye didn't find it. One thing you took from the house was a knife, that someone used to murder Popeye. Right so far?"

BoJo nodded affirmatively.

Kris continued. "So why did Popeye get murdered? Was it because he didn't find what he was looking for?"

"Don't know. Maybe. Yeah, I'd guess that."

"Or someone didn't want Popeye to be able to tell Lonnie Jackson, me or anyone else that he had been paid to break into my house."

"That makes sense," BoJo said. He swiveled his head as if he expected to discover someone was observing his conversation with Kris.

"So, Vance had something that somebody wanted. And you saw him coming out of Simpson Slacks, a place that no one gets into, and he was upset. Right so far?"

"So far."

"And you're about to leave town because…"

"Because somebody, whoever snuffed out Popeye, is probably going to want to do that same thing to me, because I know they paid Popeye to bust into your house. Popeye can't tell anyone now, but I can, and that makes me expendable."

"And you have no idea who paid Popeye?"

"No, and I'm not sticking around to find out."

"Damn BoJo! Talk about someone throwing you a curve! That's what you've done to me tonight. You've given me a helluva lot of information - information that would be really, really easy to not believe."

Again, BoJo looked out of the car into the darkness and started talking. "I know I ain't got the best reputation in town and I've done a lot of sorry things, but this isn't one of them. I'm telling you the truth. I don't like all the shit that's going on around here. I'm scared."

"I believe you BoJo," Kris, now convinced, told him. "I do believe you are spooked. I do you do believe someone could be out to get you like they did Popeye."

"And that's why I'm hauling ass out of town." BoJo, his paranoia obvious, continued scanning from one side of his car to the other.

"I don't like what's going on here - even if I have been part of the problem. I'm telling you all of this, because if anyone can get to the bottom of it, you can. There's no reason to tell Lonnie Jackson. He's not going to break a sweat about anything but those basketball games you play."

"I appreciate you telling me this BoJo. Is there anything I can do for you?"

"Just find out what's going on. And don't tell anyone we talked."

"I won't. Any idea where you're going?"

"Not yet. And I wouldn't tell anyone if I did."

"You're really frightened, aren't you?"

"I am, and you should be too."

"Frightened? You know what really frightened is? Being here at the Tanks at midnight with your girlfriend when someone comes along and starts shaking your car. Especially after you have been watching one of those god-awful slasher movies."

"I thought you said you never came out here."

"My memory came back."

BoJo grunted. They were silent on the drive back to the Recreation Center. Kris gave BoJo $30 for gas to get him out of town, and then went home for a restless night.

With practically no sleep, Kris struggled to clear his head the next morning. Patrick was so cheerful Kris wanted to slap him. At the breakfast table they guzzled coffee and ate Pop Tarts and talked about the previous evening's Major League baseball scores. Kris wasn't ready to share BoJo's admissions yet with anyone but Lonnie Jackson. Even though Kris shared BoJo's assertion that Lonnie couldn't solve a fifth-grade jigsaw puzzle, much less a murder, he felt obligated to tell him first. Then, if Lonnie ignored the tip in his typical fashion, Kris would search for someone else to listen. For Kris, learning more about Vance's exit from the Simpson Slacks building was now as important as identifying Popeye's killer. If the old building was being used as a depository for military-type resources for some far-flung government coup, as Lonnie had claimed, what was Vance doing there?

Patrick stayed at the house working on several insignificant stories and Kris left in search of Lonnie. He didn't have to look long. Two blocks from the police station, Kris spotted Lonnie directing traffic around an accident. A dirty SUV had jumped the sidewalk, breaking a utility pole and crashing it to the street. Kris pulled into a parking space, used his cell phone camera to take one shot of the SUV and another of the crew removing the pole, and walked over to Lonnie.

"Good job," Kris kidded. "I think you've finally found your calling."

"No wise cracks, please. It's too early in the morning," Lonnie grumbled as he motioned another car through on the one lane that was open.

"Anyone hurt?"

"The driver was banged up a bit. Nothing bad, but he's been taken to the hospital."

"What happened?"

"It was P.E. Rainey. He was not drunk, but he was high on something. We'll wait for toxicology."

"Sounds like you've got one more big problem in this little town. Fires, burglaries, murders, drugs."

"We don't have a drug problem in this town, and I don't need you to tell me what's going on in my town."

"What are you going to do about all the crazy stuff that's going on in my hometown?"

"What do you care about this town?" Lonnie asked brusquely. "You abandoned your hometown a long time ago." Lonnie waved at the crew that finally had the pole off the street. Telling Officer Davenport to finish the accident report and wait for a tow truck, Lonnie started walking to his car, trying to ignore Kris, who wouldn't let him.

"How deeply did you look into the break-ins at my house?"

"As deep as I needed to. You caught Popeye red-handed. What else did I need to know?"

"It would be good if you found out who paid Popeye to break into my house."

Without getting inside, Lonnie slammed shut the car door he had just opened. "What the hell are you talking about?"

"Somebody paid Popeye to break into my house. They were looking for something that belonged to Vance."

"And what in hell would Vance have that was so important?"

"I don't know, but I think you should find out."

Lonnie propped up against his car and folded his arms. "Who gave you this valuable information? Billy Manley?"

"That's not important. What's important is they swore they were telling the truth."

"Oh, O.K. Well, that means a lot around here."

"There's something else."

"Tell me. I can't wait to hear."

"Vance was in the Simpson Slacks building the night before he died."

Lonnie changed his expression to show mock interest. "Wow! That is really big news, Kris. Did you ever stop to think he might have been asking for a job?"

"Not with Syndicated Delivery Services. Not at night. Not at a building that stays shut as tight as the vault at Fort Phillips Community Bank. But whatever went on in there had him upset."

"Yeah, he asked for a job and they wouldn't give him one. That's what had him upset."

"Come on, Lonnie. Tell me what's really going on. Vance didn't go there looking for a job. How did he get in? What was he doing there? Is Syndicated Delivery Services a real company? I can't find out anything about them. And is the Simpson building really full of guns and bombs and everything you need to carry on a war like you claim it is? What have you gotten yourself into, Lonnie?"

Lonnie's face was getting red and the veins in his neck protruding. "You sorry sack of shit!" Lonnie started, loud enough for Officer Davenport to hear. "Mr. Big Shot Reporter. You come back home all high and mighty, snooping, trying to run things, making trouble for all of us. Everything was fine until you showed up. And I told you already. Under a government contract, Syndicated Delivery Services is hauling some serious stuff in and out of that building, and they're paying me to keep smart asses like you away!"

"I'm going to get in that building, somehow," Kris bluntly told him.

Lonnie slid into his car, slammed his door and rolled down the window.

"Leave well enough alone, Kris. None of this is your business. Besides, you have other things to worry about. You're still my prime suspect in Popeye's death."

"Give it up, Lonnie. You know as well as I do that the knife you found in Popeye was stolen from my house. And if I must, I can prove that."

"You may have to, big boy, because I haven't come up with any other suspects."

"I know. Like you haven't come up with any suspects for all the burglaries and fires, either."

"You let me do my job and I won't tell you how to run that crappy little paper. Stay away from Syndicated and the Simpson building. You don't want to mess around with these people. It's the government, for God's sake. Don't make me any madder than I am, or I may just go ahead and arrest your butt on murder charges."

"I'm not making any promises."

"You're just like your damn father. Hard-headed. Will not listen to anyone. I sure as heck hope you don't end up like he did."

"Not a chance. I'm going to find out what really happened to him."

"Knock yourself out. To me, it's completely cut and dried when you find a man with his head blown off and a shotgun covered with his fingerprints right next to him. But what do I know? I'm just a country bumpkin police chief and you're a big city reporter. Or should I say you used to be a big city reporter?" Lonnie rolled up his window and drove away. His response had been as expected. If Kris wanted answers to his mounting questions about Vance, he was going to have to get them himself.

28

Kris' declaration did not come as a surprise to Patrick.

"Let's do it! Details, please!" Patrick responded enthusiastically.

"Syndicated Delivery Services. I want to get in their building. I want to know what my father was doing there. I want to know if his appearance there is related to his death. I want to know if all this ties together with someone breaking into my house, searching for something that belonged to Vance. And I want to know how all of that ties into me being accused of murder by the police chief, who is acting like the head of security for Syndicated."

"We have talked about some of this. It's still making my head spin, but the plot keeps getting thicker. You accused of murder? Vance at Syndicated? Gracious, Kris, that was a mouthful you just spit out."

"There's a mouthful of stuff going on in this little hometown of mine."

"How did you piece all of this together?"

"One of the guys who broke into my house provided me with some important information."

"What did he tell you?"

"He doesn't want to see me nailed for a murder I didn't commit. And he's frightened, so frightened he's leaving town. He's frightened that someone may try to kill him."

"Frightened? Of being killed? I would be frightened too. But by whom?"

"That the same people who killed his buddy will kill him."

"Why did they kill his buddy?"

"That's one of the things I want to find out."

"And you think all of this starts with the old building?"

"I don't know, Patrick, but I don't have any other clues. There's no other place to start."

"What does the police chief say?"

"That I'm stupid and need to let things be. But Patrick, I am starting to get this gnawing feeling that Vance did not kill himself. I just have not been able to make everything fit together. I'm not even close."

Patrick got out of his chair, poured a cup of coffee and doctored it with cream and sugar. He took two long sips and studied Kris' face. "You're serious about this, aren't you?" Patrick asked.

"Absolutely."

Patrick took another swallow of coffee. "Let's do it," he repeated excitedly.

"You don't have to. I am talking about committing a crime, you know. If we get caught, we could be in some big-time trouble."

"You think that possibility is going to bother me? After getting sliced up by an exploding helicopter and almost getting barbecued in a newspaper office? Heck, compared to all of that, breaking into a building sounds about as calm as a Sunday afternoon picnic."

"It won't be a picnic, and depending on what we learn, I'm not sure what will come next."

"I know you well enough Kris, to know that you won't rest until you figure all of this out. That is the newspaper ink you have in your blood. How do you propose to break into the building? Isn't there some type of surveillance camera system? What about security guards?"

"There's no security system. Lonnie told me. Lonnie guards over that place like a gold depository. Come to think of it, whatever is in the building may be more valuable than gold. Lonnie can't solve any of the crimes and fires that are taking place here, but he sure as heck keeps everyone away from the Simpson Slacks building."

"Do you really believe what Lonnie told you about Syndicated being a delivery system for our government's covert missions?

"I don't know what to believe, other than something of great value and importance is in that building. That's why we need to get inside, to see for ourselves. Where's Karen?"

"She called. She had a couple of errands to run and will be in after that. She wanted to know what you did to her husband to get him so pissed off."

Kris grinned. "I told him I was going to break into the Simpson Slacks building."

"You are making this a challenge, aren't you?"

"I could tell him the day and time we're going to do it, and it wouldn't matter. Lonnie's not the sharpest tool in the shed."

"When do we pull this off?"

"I've got to do some think..."

Kris stopped mid-sentence when he heard the front door open, followed by the click-click of shoes on the hardwood floor. "Hello?" asked a soft voice from the living room/makeshift newspaper office.

"In here," Patrick said. Neither he nor Kris made any effort to greet the female visitor. They assumed another Fort Phillips momma had come to submit their daughter's wedding announcement for publication.

"Marilyn?" Kris asked in shock as she slowly entered the kitchen. She looked fantastic in black leggings, a light blue long sleeve cotton pullover shirt and sandals that showed lots of foot. She had her hair pulled back in a ponytail.

"I didn't think I'd have any trouble finding you in such a small town, but I did. I had to ask for directions twice, even with GPS," she smiled nervously and added, "It's a long way down here, and no easy way to get here."

"What are you doing here?" Kris asked clumsily.

"I have the week off. I didn't have anything else to do, so I decided to come see you. I couldn't get you out of my mind. The evening we had dinner...it was special to me...I sensed we were starting to make a connection."

Patrick, himself enchanted by Marilyn's hormone heightening appearance, saw that Kris had been momentarily transformed into a speechless statue. "I'm Patrick Cannon," he said walking over to Marilyn. He extended his left hand, and she shook it firmly, not looking for a second at his right arm. Her focus was on Kris.

She smiled, nodded and introduced herself. Kris was still stuck to the floor, trying to recover his verbal skills.

Patrick took over. "Would you like a soft drink? Some coffee?" he asked.

"A Diet Coke would be nice."

Patrick handed her the drink from the refrigerator and invited her to sit at the table. "I've got to make some phone calls," Patrick said, excusing himself. He glanced at Kris, who had this *please don't leave me alone with her* look, but Patrick left anyway. Finally managing to get his feet to move, Kris sat down as well.

"Surprised to see me?" Marilyn asked.

"I will be less surprised if the Braves ever win another World Series."

"I don't know much about football."

"Baseball. The Braves play baseball."

"Whatever. Are you glad to see me?"

"Sure. But this isn't exactly the kind of place where people generally want to spend their vacation."

"I'll be fine, as long as I get to spend some time with you. I mean what I said Kris. I know it was only one night, but I felt some chemistry between us that night."

Kris recalled the evening as pleasant, but certainly did not feel a connection as deep as Marilyn was describing, especially since she had declined his offer to go to his apartment. "It was nice," he said politely.

She took a swallow from her Diet Coke and told Kris, "I know you're going to ask, so I'm going to tell you before you ask. I think Emmy has moved on with her life. She doesn't mention you, isn't sitting around waiting for you to call. She's heavy into work, is gone a lot. I think she's been out on several dates."

"Thanks for the good news," Kris said, a trace of hurt obvious in his voice.

"I'm sorry. I thought you'd want to know."

"I do. It's just hard to stomach. This all happened so fast."

"I know. And the big reason I came to see you is to help you pick up the pieces, to start over. I'm not ashamed to say I'm trying to catch you on the rebound."

"I don't think I'm such of a catch right now, but you…wow! I really like the way the new you looks!"

"Thanks," she smiled widely. "I hope there will be other things about the new me that you will grow to like."

Kris smiled back at her and looked around the room. "I really appreciate you coming down, but this isn't a very good time," he started explaining. "We're struggling to keep this paper afloat, and there's some personal stuff about my father I still have to settle. I am not sure how much time I will have to spend with you, and besides, I am probably about to get involved in some things I shouldn't get involved in. I mean some serious, illegal-type stuff."

Marilyn's eye brightened. "Really? Sounds exciting! Now I definitely want to hang around for a while. Remember, it wasn't that long ago that I was playing up my bad girl image."

"It would be better if you didn't hang around here. Fort Phillips Jail accommodations are not exactly enticing, especially for a pretty girl like you."

Marilyn propped her arms on the table and leaned toward Kris. "I'm here and I'm staying. Even if you don't want me to. I can get a room at a motel close by. This town does have a motel, doesn't it?"

"Yes, but they are just a slight cut above the jail."

"I'll survive. I promise to stay out of the way. Just give me a little of your time. That is all I ask. Besides, it sounds like you might need someone to make bond once you are incarcerated."

"Could be," he agreed with a hint of seriousness in his tone. "Look, if you're determined to stay, you can stay here. You can use my sister's old room. It may be a little awkward because there's only one bathroom and the house is doubling as the newspaper office, but you're welcome to stay."

"Thanks. That sounds like a nice arrangement…to begin with. I know a little about what happened with your dad, but there is obviously a lot I do not know. Fill me in."

Somewhat reluctantly, Kris began. He repeated some of what he had told her during dinner in Atlanta, but added more detail this time. Marilyn's interest grew with each sentence about everything going on in Fort Phillips. Her jaw dropped when Kris explained why he was a murder suspect, and she could feel her skin becoming clammy as he revealed his increasing doubts about the official declaration that Vance died by his own hand.

"You weren't kidding when you said a lot was going on," Marilyn said, rubbing her arms to make the goose bumps go away.

As Kris and Marilyn continued their conversation, Karen greeted Patrick in the living room/office. "Who's our visitor?" she asked. The Honda in the driveway has a Fulton County tag. It's not Emmy, is it?"

"No, it's not Emmy," Patrick said, looking up from his laptop screen.

Karen didn't wait for more information from Patrick. She moved quickly to the kitchen and was not happy with what she saw.

"Hey Karen," Kris said, not getting up from his chair. "This is Marilyn Parker, a friend from Atlanta."

"Hello," Karen replied in a not-so-pleasant voice as she studied Marilyn from head to toe.

Marilyn got up from the table and extended a hand to Karen, who reciprocated weakly. "I've heard a lot about you." Marilyn told her.

"Really?"

"No, not really, but isn't that what you're supposed to say?"

Kris had to suppress a giggle. Karen didn't think the remark was funny.

"What are you doing here?" Karen asked, getting straight to the point.

"I have a few days off. I came to see Kris."

"Why? I did not know you were such good friends. And why would anyone want to come to Fort Phillips if they didn't have to?" Karen asked, her displeasure evident.

"Oh, Kris and I are relatively new friends, wouldn't you say?" Marilyn asked, glancing at Kris.

With a sheepish look, he nodded in agreement but did not say anything.

"Besides, I was getting tired of taking my vacations at Hilton Head and Daytona Beach," Marilyn said with a straight face.

Again, Kris had to muffle a giggle.

Karen was miffed. "Kris and I are business partners. And friends. Incredibly good friends…from a long way back," she said.

"I know."

"Very, very good friends," Karen repeated.

"I know," Marilyn repeated.

"Marilyn's going to stay here at the house for a few days," Kris said, drawing a disapproving stare from Karen.

"I promise I'll stay out of the way," Marilyn said.

"Please do. We have work to do. I have work to do."

"By the way," Kris interrupted, "the printer called with a question about this week's press schedule. Can you give him a call back?"

"All right," Karen said, quickly exiting the room but not before stopping to take another look at Marilyn.

"Nice to meet you too," Marilyn waved as Karen left. "Hmmm. Not exactly a Chamber of Commerce greeting from her," she told Kris.

"Actually, she's genuinely nice. She's just got a lot on her mind right now."

"And obviously, you're one of the things on her mind."

"She wishes we were back in high school."

"Do you?"

"Yeah, if I could play high school basketball again. Seriously, I'm happy with the way things are now. Well, sort of."

Marilyn scooted close to Kris and smiled. "I hope I can make you happy over the next few days. What do you do around here for a good time?"

"For a female? The aerobics class at the recreation center."

"I can hardly wait. What about eating places?"

"The nearest decent place is thirty miles away. I will treat you tonight. How about that?"

"We'll go dutch."

"No. I'll pay. Let me help you get your things from the car. Like Karen said, we do have some work to get done."

"So do I," Marilyn replied with a teasing smile.

Kris helped Marilyn get settled and he went to work, scurrying throughout the town, gathering information on several routine, boring articles for the next edition. He passed the charred remnants of the Sentinel office and the animal clinic, where rebuilding efforts were already underway, and admitted to himself that the perpetrators would probably never be caught. Nor would Popeye's killer. Kris still had the unnerving thought in the back of his head that Lonnie, desperate to make a name for himself and gain the respect of the town and his wife, would arrest him and press the District Attorney for an indictment. He was also beginning to have the feeling in his gut that Vance's supposed suicide and Popeye's murder were connected. Unfortunately, he had no idea about how to prove that.

As Kris was about to leave City Hall after gathering some information on a Budget Committee meeting, his cell rang. Kris answered, got in the Ranger and turned on the air conditioning on the hot September day.

"Hey buddy, what's up?" Dan McKenzie asked from his office in the Pentagon.

"Just another day in paradise. How are things in our nation's capital?"

"You know how it goes. You get one fire put out and another pops up."

"I know exactly what you mean." Kris thought McKenzie's reference to fires was ironic, considering what had been occurring in Forth Phillips.

"The last time we talked, things sounded a bit bumpy with you and Emmy. How's that going?"

"Too long a story to tell. Did you come up with some information for me?"

McKenzie went straight to the point. "Sorry, Kris, I didn't. I tried, but I just don't have the pull to gather the type of intel you were requesting. However, I did look into this Syndicated Delivery Services you asked about. There is no record of them being a federal vendor or contractor. Looks like from our end, they don't exist. But that doesn't mean we don't have something going with them."

"I figured as much. Thanks for trying." Kris and McKenzie continued the conversation briefly. They both promised to try to hook up around the holidays, but Kris knew that wouldn't happen. Kris sat in the Ranger drumming on the steering wheel. The mystery of Syndicated Delivery Services kept getting deeper and deeper.

29

For Kris, following his call with McKenzie, the remainder of the day moved quickly, and he and Marilyn headed out in her car on their dinner date. A bit overdressed for the trip to the family steakhouse in Camilla, Marilyn was even more enticing than she had been on her arrival earlier in the day. Kris readily admitted to himself he could easily forgo being a gentleman and get down to basics with Marilyn. He would not press the issue, but if she showed an interest, well…

On their way out of town, Kris gave Marilyn the complete ten-minute tour of Fort Phillips, including the Recreation Center and the Simpson Slacks plant which, as usual, was dark and deserted. Continuing the drive to the steakhouse, Kris told Marilyn about the old Fort Phillips, when the sewing machines at Simpson Slacks were humming, everyone had a steady paycheck, local businesses were always full of shoppers and life was good. Marilyn could not relate to life in a small town, but she easily detected Kris' sadness as he talked about the demise of his hometown. In the quietness of Marilyn's car as Kris steered beneath the cloudy southwest Georgia sky, Kris admitted regret that his rage at his father had caused him to be estranged from the town for ten years.

They settled at a table for two at the half-full Big Beef Steakhouse, a national chain where the food was good, but not great, plentiful but not expensive. Marilyn grazed on salad and cottage cheese while Kris opted for sirloin steak and baked potato. Through their polite conversation, Kris kept his eyes glued on her. He was fascinated by the transformation. With a simple change of wardrobe, a lighter touch of makeup, and a shift in attitude, Marilyn had gone from the cliched office tart to a sophisticated, mesmerizing woman of class and style. By becoming less sexy, she had become sexier. Given the opportunity, he would sleep with her without hesitation, but for now, all they could do was engage in small talk and debate on whether they would make a trip to the dessert bar.

Giving in to temptation, Kris selected a calorie-filled slice of strawberry cheesecake while Marilyn settled on one macadamia nut cookie. Before stuffing a piece of the cake in his mouth, Kris told Marilyn, "I think you know a lot more about me than I do about you. How about filling me in."

Her smile indicated she was pleased with Kris' interest. "We definitely don't have hometowns in common," she stated. "You grew up in this little, out of the way town where everyone knows each other. I grew up in Houston and went to a high school with 3,000 students. Dad worked at the space center. Mom was a housewife. I have older brothers. One is in medical school; the other's an engineer with his own firm. I come from a family of high achievers."

"I'm impressed," Kris said, swallowing his last bite of cheesecake. "Sounds like a nice family. How did you get to Atlanta?"

"Followed my college boyfriend. We both graduated from the University of Houston, and right off the bat, he got a great job offer from a high-tech company in Atlanta. I really didn't know what I wanted to do, but I figured that with my degree in marketing and a minor in insurance, I wouldn't have much trouble finding a job in a place like Atlanta, but I did have trouble. A lot of it."

"What happened to the boyfriend?"

"He dumped me. We moved in together, and less than a month later, he dumped me for some bimbo he met at work. Suddenly there I was with no job and no place to stay. It hurt at first. It hurt a lot, but I didn't have time to sit around and mope. I had to find a job fast. It was not easy. I went for a dozen interviews and did not get a single call back. I was a nervous wreck. As I said, I come from a family of high achievers and I was not achieving. I could not understand what I was doing wrong, and then I started thinking about the other women I saw in most of the offices. I started comparing myself to them and realized my skirts were not short enough and my blouses were not tight enough. I didn't think situations like that really existed, but was I wrong!"

Kris leaned forward and said, "Let me guess. You started showing more leg and cleavage and voila, a job!"

"Voila, a job!" Marilyn repeated.

"As for me, all people were ever interested in was my sentence structure and punctuation skills," Kris complained in a fake whiny voice.

"It was humiliating at first, but the bad part is," Marilyn said, choosing to put down the last piece of cookie she was about to eat. "I started enjoying it. I was an honor graduate at UH, and no one ever paid me any attention. I raise my skirt four inches, and men are slobbering all over me. I liked the attention. I decided it was my teen rebellion, just a few years late. I had men wanting to take me places, and give me things...of course, they came with a price, and I'm not proud of that at all."

Marilyn dropped her head, and Kris realized she was embarrassed. Kris struggled to think of something to say that would lighten the moment. He finally offered, "Sometimes I think that is what this whole country is built on - looks over intelligence, style over substance."

"Maybe, but I regret getting caught up in that game. It's not me. I haven't felt good about myself for a long time, and that day in the break room when I let you see up my skirt was the last straw. I realized that any man worth having would not be tempted by that. I realized that to get the attention of a decent man like you, I had to be myself, my smart self, my moderately conservative self that refuses to allow skirts so short they show butt cheeks."

Kris smiled broadly. "I have a confession too," he said. "I *was* tempted! A lot! I like butt cheeks. I'm not that decent. In fact, I'm sitting here right now, lusting after you."

His admission surprised Marilyn. She didn't blush, but her face brightened. "I'm glad to hear that," she smiled. "Perhaps at some point, but not now. It's not the right time for either of us."

"I know. I know. We must get to know each other first. God! I can't believe I brought out that tired old cliché," Kris moaned.

"That's why I'm here. So we can start the process of getting to know each other," she smiled. "Although I don't think Karen is going to be very happy with that."

"Karen has no claim on me. I am her friend, and she needs me to help her out of a bad situation with the newspaper. That's my only interest in her."

"Are you sure?"

"Totally."

"Good. In that case, I'm really looking forward to the next few days."

"Me too," Kris replied.

30

A light rain was falling when Kris and Marilyn left the steakhouse. Three miles down the dark road, the light rain had turned into a downpour and Kris contemplated pulling off the road. Before he could find a suitable location, he noticed the high beam headlights approaching from the opposite direction. The car was coming much too fast for the weather. Defensively, Kris got ready to slip his foot on the brake pedal. Marilyn mentioned the car needed to dim its lights.

Kris, hoping the car would reciprocate, dimmed his lights. The car kept coming. Continuing to slow down, Kris used his left hand to shield his eyes from the bright lights. Now, two cars, filling both lanes of the highway, were headed straight toward Kris and Marilyn. "My God! What are they doing?" Marilyn screamed.

With his foot tapping the brake, Kris started slowly veering off the right side of the road. The two sets of lights were about to blind him. "Pull over, Kris!" Marilyn pleaded.

As Kris pulled over on a narrow patch of shoulder, the two approaching cars were side-by-side. The car in Kris' lane veered to the right, bumping the other car, which somehow managed to stay in the road. The two cars bumped a second time, a third and a fourth, with the final bump sending one car veering off the road, down an embankment and into a thicket of pine trees. The remaining car came fishtailing by, missing Kris and Marilyn by inches and throwing up water as the driver gained control and sped away.

"Oh my God!" Marilyn, her hands shaking, cried. Kris, his hands frozen to the steering wheel, sat motionless.

Swallowing hard and exhaling, Kris asked Marilyn if she was all right.

"I think so, but I could really use the restroom," she admitted nervously.

"I've got to check on the people in that car. Stay here and call 9-1-1. Is there a flashlight in your car?"

Marilyn directed Kris to the trunk. Ten seconds after getting out of the car, he was drenched. With the flashlight in hand, Kris carefully inched down the embankment toward the car, which had rolled over. Its crushed hood was resting against two small pine trees and the driver's door was pinned shut against the ground. Shaking from the pelting rain and apprehension, Kris did not expect to find anyone alive.

Nearing the wreckage, Kris heard a man's frantic desperate pleading. "Help me! I'm hurt! Get me out of here!"

The rain was getting heavier. Peering through the spider-webbed, heavily damaged windshield, Kris, even with the flashlight, could not see anything inside the car. "How many people are with you?" Kris asked.

"Just me. I'm hurting! Get me out of here!"

"Try to stay calm. We've called for help. An ambulance will be here shortly," Kris tried to reassure the driver.

"No! I don't want an ambulance. They'll take me back to Fort Phillips, and I don't want to go back! Please get me out of this damn car!"

Kris tried to wipe the rain from his face, but as soon as he did, he got pelted by more. Surveying the crushed car, Kris told the man, "I don't think I can get you out by myself."

"Keller?" the voice from inside the muddy white car asked.

"Yes," Kris responded in total surprise.

"It's BoJo. You've got to get me out of here! I'm hurt. I think my arm's broke, and I may have a couple of broke ribs. Damn, I'm hurting!"

Kris continued to study the car and wiped more rain from his face. "Can you crawl up to the passenger door?" he asked BoJo.

"No! I'm hurting too much. And this damn seat belt is stuck! You've got to get me out. Don't wait on the rescue people."

"I'm afraid I'll hurt you more."

"Don't be! Get me out, damn it!"

Kris looked at the car again and studied. "O.K. Can you cover your eyes?"

"Yes."

"I'm going to kick this windshield out. On the count of three, all right?"

"Yeah! All right!"

Kris lifted his foot, ready to ram it through the weakened windshield when he was stopped by Marilyn's voice. He turned to see her slip and fall face first, sliding halfway down the embankment. He rushed to pick her up, and immediately admonished her, "You should have stayed in the car," he said.

"It may be a while before help arrives," Marilyn said, wiping mud off her chest. "The dispatcher told me there are two accidents in other parts of the county."

"It doesn't matter," Kris told her, wiping a small clump of dirt off Marilyn's cheek. "BoJo wants us to get him out."

"Who's BoJo?"

"I'll tell you later." He took Marilyn's hand and led her to the car. "O.K. BoJo. Here we go!" Kris took a deep breath. "One! Two! Three!" His initial kick didn't work because he was having difficulty maintaining his balance because of the car's position on its side. Three more kicks finally caved-in the windshield. Kris felt a sharp sting around his right Achilles tendon. He shined the flashlight in the car and was able to see BoJo still in his seat, tugging on the seatbelt, trying to get it to release.

"The damn seatbelt is stuck!" BoJo complained. Kris managed to get his head and upper body inside the car through the hole left by the destroyed windshield. The airbag had not deployed. He tugged on the seatbelt but it would not budge.

BoJo groaned. "There's a knife in the dashboard. Can you get it?"

Kris twisted, awkwardly, and felt a twinge in his back, but he was able to pop open the dash. A three-inch pocketknife, along with a flask, fell out. In the cramped space, any type of movement was difficult, but Kris managed to reach the knife and open it. Struggling, he cut through the seatbelt with BoJo constantly complaining about how long the process was taking. The task completed, Kris backed out of the car, and instructed BoJo to try to get out on his own. Moaning and maneuvering with pain, BoJo was able to get his head and shoulders through the windshield space. Like a doctor assisting with the birth of child, Kris grabbed at BoJo's shoulders and started easing him out of the car. When BoJo was halfway out, Marilyn started gently tugging at him as well. With BoJo screaming with all the air remaining in his lungs, Kris and Marilyn stretched him out on the wet undergrowth. Rain was pelting him in the face. "We've got to get you to the hospital," Kris told him.

"There's one in Moultrie about thirty miles east of here. That's where I want to go."

"Why not Fort Phillips?" Kris asked. "We can have you there much faster."

"Because the same thugs who ran me off the road will be back there waiting for me."

"O.K. BoJo, we'll do it," Kris told him. "We need to get you up and out of the rain."

"Let's go," BoJo said. He tried to sit up but screamed in pain. Slowly, carefully, Kris and Marilyn managed to get BoJo to his feet. He immediately clutched his right side.

"Can you make it up the embankment to the road?"

"I'll make it!" BoJo grabbed at his side again. With Marilyn holding him by one arm and Kris by the other which Kris was certain was broken, BoJo started up the slippery embankment. He slipped once, bumping his right knee when Marilyn lost her grip. Agonizingly slowly, they proceeded up the embankment, finally arriving at the road. Marilyn opened the back-driver's side door and. Kris helped him in. BoJo rested his head on the back of the seat and moaned, "God! This hurts!"

Both filthy and soaked, Kris and Marilyn boarded, and they headed slowly down the highway toward Moultrie. "Are you gonna make it?" Kris asked BoJo, and added. "I can't go fast in this rain. I don't want to put you in your second accident of the night."

"That back there wasn't an accident, was it?" Marilyn asked.

"Who's she?" BoJo asked.

"A friend," Kris quickly replied. "It wasn't an accident, was it?" Kris repeated. "Someone intentionally ran you off the road."

"Do you know how damn ironic it is that you rescued me?" BoJo asked Kris.

"What do you mean?"

"Because the creeps did this to me because of the stuff I told you."

"Explain, please," Kris said without looking back. The rain was falling so heavily Kris had to keep his eyes on the road.

"Lonnie Jackson found out that I had talked to you. Before I could leave town, he came to see me. It was a strange conversation, man. When I told him you didn't kill Popeye, he acted like he didn't give a shit. Same thing when I told him someone paid Popeye to break into your house. You know what he seemed most interested in?"

Kris didn't reply, but Marilyn asked, "What?"

"Who is she?" BoJo asked again.

"A friend," Kris replied again. "What got Lonnie's attention?"

"He almost freaked out when I said I had told you about seeing Vance at the Simpson Slacks plant right before he killed himself. He wanted to know every word, every damn word about what I told you. Can't you drive any faster? My arm and side are killing me!"

"I'm going as fast as I can under these conditions. Why would Lonnie be so interested in that?"

"Hell if I know. But I do know for damn sure that it is all tied in with what happened to me a few minutes ago, and it will happen again if I go back to Fort Phillips. If I were you, Keller, I would get the hell out too. You've rattled somebody's cages about something."

Kris knew that already, but he still asked BoJo, "Who's cage have I rattled?"

"That's for you to find out. As soon as I get patched up, I'm outta here!"

By the time they reached the Community Hospital in Moultrie, the rain had slowed to a drizzle. It took both Kris and Marilyn to get BoJo, slumped and wobbly, into the emergency room. Two other people, a young man and an old woman, neither of whom appeared to be sick or injured, were in the waiting area. BoJo, fussing every second, had to wait twenty minutes for triage, and ten additional minutes for a registration clerk. He started pitching a fit when the clerk began asking him questions about insurance, which he did not have. Kris and Marilyn kept their distance as BoJo got more and more irritated. After a phone call and a discussion with the shift supervisor, the clerk completed the paperwork and cleared BoJo for treatment. The only information BoJo offered was that he had been in a single car accident. He didn't say a word about intentionally being run off the road.

Kris and Marilyn located restrooms and cleaned up as best they could. Kris found a vending machine and got cups of coffee. While they waited on BoJo's diagnosis and treatment, Kris called Patrick with a brief description of what had transpired. Patrick, first and foremost relieved to learn that Kris and Marilyn were not hurt, wanted more details, but Kris said it was all too complicated and he would fill him in the next morning.

"So, do I still look sexy? Are you still lusting after me?" Marilyn asked teasingly as she sipped from the coffee cup she was holding with both hands. Her wet hair was combed straight back and all her makeup was off.

"Absolutely," he nodded. "You shouldn't have gotten out of the car. You ruined your clothes, and you could have slipped and broken something yourself." Feeling a twinge in the back of his right leg, just above the ankle, Kris pulled up his pant leg. He had a two-inch scratch that was still bleeding slightly.

"Kris! You're hurt!" Marilyn said with concern. "Let me call for a doctor." She started to get up out of her seat.

"No, no," he said, softly grabbing her by the right arm and returning her to her seat. "I'm O.K. This is just a little scratch. Nothing serious."

"Are you sure?"

"He patted his left arm. "After getting forty stitches up here, I think I know what a serious cut is," he smiled.

"Well, you were very brave. You could have been seriously hurt rescuing BoJo. Was that his name?"

"Yeah. His name is Bobby Jones. BoJo."

"And what was he talking about, the things he had told you?"

"He's one of Fort Phillips' resident delinquents. Always in some type of trouble. He told me that he and his buddy were paid to break into my house with orders to find something my father had. I don't know what they were looking for. There is doubt as to whether my father killed himself. BoJo is trying to tie my father's death to a visit he made to this mysterious new business in town. Our police chief learned BoJo told all of that to me, and for some reason, that flew all over the chief, who has claimed from the very beginning that my father committed suicide. By the way, the police chief is the husband of Karen Jackson, the lady at the house who gave you such a frosty reception."

"I'm confused," Marilyn admitted before taking another swallow of coffee.

"Join the crowd. Instead of finding answers about all this stuff, I'm getting more questions. I don't know what's going to come of all of this. You might want to think about heading on back to Atlanta."

"No way!" Marilyn shot back, sitting straight up. "No way I'm going to leave you here with all of this strange business going on. It sounds to me like you need someone to cover your back."

"You need to leave. It may get a bit treacherous around here."

"I'm not afraid, Kris. I am a big girl. I can take care of myself. Besides, this is my vacation. This is like one of those mystery cruises you go on, minus the cruise."

"You're not afraid?"

"No," she said, tossing her empty cup into a trash can.

"Well, I am." He tossed his cup into the trash and went back to the vending machine for a second cup.

They tried to make small talk about other matters, but they were tired, and slowly they both started drifting in and out of light sleep as they waited on BoJo. Four hours later, he came riding in a wheelchair back from the treatment area with his two broken ribs wrapped and his fractured arm in a cast. Refusing to go any further than the waiting room in the wheelchair, BoJo walked shakily with Kris and Marilyn to her car.

"Thanks, man. I owe you," BoJo said. "I guess it was my lucky night."

"We need to find out who did this to you."

"You can find out. I'm getting as far away from here as I can. I'm calling a friend to pick me up."

"What about your car?"

"You can get it towed. The bank was about to take it back any way."

"I need to ask you something, BoJo. Do you think my father killed himself?"

BoJo looked away from Kris to compose his reply. Turning back around, BoJo said, "You figure out some of the other shit that's going on in Fort Phillips, and I think you'll have the answer to that question."

"You don't want to stay around and help me?"

"Hell no man! Can I use your cell phone to call my friend? And do either of you have twenty dollars I can borrow?"

Kris had twenty-seven dollars and fifty cents after paying for dinner and he gave it all to BoJo who used Marilyn's phone to call his friend. At his insistence, they left him at the hospital and started the drive back to Fort Phillips. Marilyn had a dozen questions she wanted to ask but was too tired. They could wait until the next day.

31

Back at home after a long stressful, tiring night at Moultrie Community Hospital, Kris had trouble sleeping. Unable to shut off his mind about BoJo's close call and everything else that had been going on in Fort Phillips, Kris would doze a few minutes, wake up, doze a few more minutes and wake up again. Realizing that getting any meaningful rest was a lost cause, Kris chose to go ahead and get up at 6:30 a.m. The soothing smell of coffee brewing aided him with that decision. Patrick was already at the kitchen table, looking relaxed, refreshed and ready to start the day as he contentedly sipped on his coffee.

"There ought to be a law against looking as perky as you do this early in the morning," Kris grumbled as he shuffled past Patrick on his way to the coffee maker. Kris was wearing a white cotton t-shirt and unbelted jeans. He was barefooted.

"I'm alive. That's all that matters," Patrick replied cheerfully.

"You've got a point, but right now, I'm too sleepy to figure out if I'm alive or not."

"Yeah, I want to hear about last night. You didn't say much during your phone call. You ended up taking this BoJo guy to the hospital?"

"Making a long story short, someone tried to kill him. They ran his car off the road and down an embankment. He's lucky. He came out of it with a broken arm and a couple of busted ribs. I think he is probably saying what you are. That being alive is all that matters."

"Who would want to kill him? From what you have told me, he seems rather worthless and not worth the trouble for someone to snuff him. What in the heck is going on in this little town?" Patrick asked, getting up from the table to refill his cup.

"I don't know, but we're about to find out," Kris said as he sat down. "And you and I are going to have to do the finding. Lonnie

Jackson's not going to help. In fact, last night BoJo told me something remarkably interesting about Lonnie."

"Let's hear it."

"BoJo told Lonnie two things – that I did not stab Popeye, and that Vance paid a visit to the Simpson plant shortly before he died. BoJo said Lonnie just shrugged at the news that would clear me, but he went ballistic when BoJo mentioned to him he had told me about Vance. Something is going on in that old building, Patrick, that I believe is behind a lot of the crap that is going on around here. We've got to get in there."

Patrick calmly sipped his coffee, looked Kris squarely in the eyes, and said matter-of-factly, "As we previously, ah, discussed, let's break in."

"That's the only way we're going to get in," Kris said in agreement.

"What about tonight? We are supposed to have some more heavy rain. It will be dark. We will have good cover. Are you sure there aren't any surveillance cameras?"

"I am sure. Are you sure you want to be part of this mission?" Kris asked Patrick.

"Try keeping me away," Patrick said.

"Me too," Marilyn said as she entered the kitchen in a silk lavender bathrobe.

"You're supposed to be asleep," Kris fussed.

"The coffee woke me up. Any left?"

"A little," Patrick said. "I'll make some more."

Marilyn emptied the pot and Patrick started brewing the second pot. "You didn't hear any of the conversation Patrick and I had," Kris ordered.

"I heard every word of it. What time tonight do we go into action?"

"There's no *we* to it," Kris insisted. "You're going to stay here and watch the Lifetime Channel or HGTV."

"I don't think so," Marilyn responded firmly. "Not after last night. Not after I got muddy, soaking wet, ruined my two hundred-dollar shoes and let you see me without any makeup. Not after I spent a zillion hours with you at that hospital waiting on some strange character named BoJo. Not after I've heard a little about the strange goings-on around here."

Frustrated, Kris looked at Patrick. "Help me out with this," he begged Patrick. "Tell the woman she can't be a part of this."

"You can't be a part of this," he said teasingly.

"You're not very much help," Kris fussed at Patrick.

"I'll stay out of the way, but I'm going. I can carry your break-in tools."

"Break-in tools?" Kris asked before he started laughing. Patrick laughed too. "All right," Kris relented. "You can carry our break-in tools, but you're not going in the building with us. You have to stay outside and be our lookout."

"Cool. We'll need some kind of code word I can use to let you know if I see someone coming."

Kris and Patrick were grinning broadly. "No one's going to see us, but we'll come up with a code word just in case." Kris sounded serious but he wasn't.

"I'll come up with a code word during the day," Patrick offered, going along with Kris' shtick, "but right now I've got to get ready for work. Got a busy day today, checking on the Lions Club meeting and the city's new schedule for garbage collection. Really big stuff." Patrick smiled, rinsed out his cup, placed it in the drying rack and left the room.

Kris and Marilyn continued to drink their coffee. He studied her face. Even early in the morning, without any primping, Marilyn was easy on the eyes. He readily admitted to himself he was becoming more and more sexually attracted to her, and, to a lesser degree, emotionally attracted and attached. Kris shifted nervously in his chair and started talking to her like a concerned brother. "We've joked about break-in tools and code words, but this is serious business," he said. "We're talking about breaking the law. We could get arrested and thrown in jail. Is this how you want to spend your vacation?"

"If I'm with you, yes."

"I wish I could talk you out of this."

"You can't."

"I don't know what we're going to uncover. I may be next on someone's list. They may come after me like they did BoJo."

"All the more reason you need me around. With all due respect to Patrick, you may need another helping hand."

"That's bad," Kris groaned. Taking a last swallow of coffee, Kris was ready to finish dressing even though he had little on his newspaper agenda for the day. Marilyn stopped him as he walked by the table. She hugged him softly and kissed him lightly on the cheek. "I want to be with you, whether it's breaking into an old building or sharing a bed," she whispered.

Caught off guard by her tease, Kris smiled and left the kitchen. Marilyn sat back down at the kitchen table, sighed and gazed into her coffee cup. She closed her eyes and was about to nod off to sleep.

"I'm surprised to see you up so early after the late night you had," Karen said on her way to the coffee maker.

Marilyn's eyes popped open. "How did you hear about last night?" she asked Karen.

"My husband is the police chief. He gets paid to know what's going on. Can't you see that bad things happen to people who have any association with Kris? His dad. Patrick. Popeye. BoJo. His girlfriend."

"I'm not his girlfriend, at least not yet."

"I was talking about the other one. And honestly, I don't think you're his type."

"And you are?"

"Yes. He and I have a history to prove it."

"Ancient history. You're close to Kris, and nothing has happened to you."

"Nothing's going to happen to me. You, on the other hand, would be wise to get out of town."

Karen was making Marilyn uncomfortable quickly. Marilyn took a long slow sip of her coffee to give herself time to collect her thoughts. With her heartbeat quickening, Marilyn got up for more coffee, but the pot was empty. Taking a deep breath, she hoped her voice would not give away how nervous she was. "Look," she started, looking directly at Karen, who reciprocated. "I don't know what kind of game you're playing, or what kind of game this whole freakin' little town is playing. But Kris is about to find out."

"There's nothing to find out. What Kris needs to concentrate on is getting his own life together."

"That's one reason I'm here. To help him."

"He doesn't need your help. He and I will work things out."

Marilyn slammed her cup on the table and threw her hands up. "Whatever! Don't you have to deliver some newspapers on your broomstick or something like that?"

Karen glared at Marilyn and warned, "You can't win a fight against me. You're wasting your time trying."

"Bitch!" Marilyn uttered under her breath as Karen left.

After taking a few minutes to compose herself, Marilyn showered, dressed and started thinking of a way to pass the day, given her limited options in Fort Phillips. Although she had not admitted it to Kris, she was apprehensive about his plan to break into Syndicated. With her limited knowledge of recent events in town and of what Kris actually knew, Marilyn was concerned that he was about to embark on a wild goose chase that could only get him in trouble. Karen bothered her too, a lot. She feared that Karen did indeed have some type of hold on him, which would render her efforts to earn Kris' affections fruitless. Marilyn was not ready to give up just yet, but she did need something to clear her mind. Her solution was to go shopping. Shopping always cheered a girl up. Surely, she thought, there had to be some place to shop in reasonable driving distance.

While Marilyn was off in search of stores, Kris was on his search for Billy Manley. He found Manley at the predictable spot - propped up against the propane tanks, a cigarette dangling from his mouth, in front of Fast Mart.

"Sounds like you had a busy night," Manley said, tossing a crushed cigarette pack that Kris caught.

"Yeah. You have some bad drivers around here. Tonight's going to be busy too. That is why I am here. I want you to go somewhere with me." Instead of tossing the cigarette pack to the pavement, Kris wadded it into his jeans pocket.

"I'll have to consult my social calendar. Where are we going?"

"You'll see."

"Better be inside. Otherwise we are going to get wet," Manley noted as he looked at the dirty clouds that were accumulating.

"You'll be fine. I'll make it worth your time with a carton of cigarettes."

"I'll settle for that. You wouldn't happen to have five bucks on you, would you?"

Kris fished in his pocket and pulled out a ten for Manley. "Be at the house around 11 tonight. You got a way to get there?"

"I'll be there. That is late man, past my bedtime."

As Manley opened another pack of cigarettes, a tow truck carrying a beat-up white sedan with a crushed roof moved slowly past Fast Mart. The police car following the tow truck stopped abruptly, and with tires squealing, peeled into the parking lot in front of Kris and Manley. Lonnie Jackson, looking none too chipper, got out of the car.

"Where's BoJo?" Lonnie asked Kris.

"I have no idea."

"You took him to the hospital last night, didn't you?"

"Yeah, and I left him there. He called someone to pick him up. He didn't say where he was going. All he said was he wanted to get the hell out of Fort Phillips. He told me about his visit with you."

"BoJo's like a lot of other people around here. He needs to mind his own business. That includes you."

Manley, his head swiveling from Kris to Lonnie as he watched their verbal sparring, said nothing.

"Trust me," Kris said, "all I intend to do is mind my own business. It just so happens that my business is apparently intertwined with the business of some other folks."

A few small raindrops fell and then a few heavier ones. Fifteen seconds later, the sky opened sending Lonnie to his car. "Don't make me do something I don't want to," Lonnie said before slipping back into his car and squealing away.

“He’s a real pleasant person, isn’t he?” Manley asked facetiously.

“He’s a jerk,” Kris replied. “See you at 11. Don’t’ stand me up,” Kris said.

“No chance. I can’t wait to see what you’re up to,” Manley responded. He flipped his half-smoked cigarette onto the asphalt, and the rain quickly extinguished it.

32

At ten till eleven, Kris was pacing the floor. Marilyn, half-asleep, was curled up on the sofa, and Patrick was studying investment tips on the Internet. Kris, eager for Billy Manley to arrive, was nervous but certain he was doing the right thing. He was convinced that whatever was going on inside the Simpson Slacks plant had some connection with the outbreak of crime in Fort Phillips, and probably Vance's death. He was just as convinced that Lonnie Jackson was not going to lift a finger to help get to the bottom of what was going on. Lonnie had already admitted to taking secret cash from the government or some nebulous agency to keep people away from the old building. But as convinced as Kris was there was a connection, his big fear was that he would get inside the building, and not find any evidence to corroborate his theory.

At a minute till eleven, Manley knocked on the front door, and instead of waiting for someone to come to the door, he walked in. Kris immediately told him to toss the cigarette he was smoking. Beads of rain dotted Manley's dark green windbreaker jacket.

"How did you get here?" Kris asked.

"Lonnie Jackson dropped me off."

Kris' heart sank. "You got Lonnie to drop you off? Crap, Billy, that was dumb."

Manley was puzzled by Kris' reaction. "Lonnie was on his way home. It wasn't out of his way. What did I do wrong?"

"Nothing," Kris sighed. "Have a seat Billy."

Marilyn slowly sat up on the sofa and Patrick read the last paragraph of an article on mutual funds. Kris, sitting down next to Marilyn who yawned widely, announced, "O.K. team. Here's what we're going to do. We're sneaking into Syndicated Delivery Services for some clues about all the strange stuff going on here."

Patrick and Marilyn already knew what was about to transpire, but Manley was stunned. "You're crazy!" he complained. "And why are you including me in this plan?"

"Because Patrick, Marilyn and I don't have a clue about how to break into a place. I figure you've had some experience."

"Well, uh, yeah, I admit I've picked a few locks and busted a few windows, but why are you doing this?"

"Because I'm bored," Kris responded.

"Wouldn't it be more fun if you and the girl just made out?" Manley asked glancing at Marilyn.

"Probably, but that wouldn't tell me anything about how Vance really died, and that's what I hope to get with this little illegal activity tonight."

"You're crazy!" Manley repeated. "You're not going to find anything! Don't do this!"

"You're beginning to sound like Lonnie Jackson," Kris said.

"Don't insult me. I don't want to be a part of this."

"All right," Kris responded calmly. "We're going to do it with or without you. I thought this would be a good way for you to make a hundred bucks."

Manley's eyes widened. "A hundred bucks? Now? In advance?"

Kris stepped into his bedroom, pulled five twenties out of his wallet, came back and handed them to Manley.

"What are we waiting for?" Manley asked, stuffing the bills into his pocket.

"I need to pee and change clothes," Marilyn said.

"Hurry up!" Kris and Patrick said together.

For ten minutes as they waited on Marilyn, Kris and Patrick had to listen to Manley question what they were about to do. Kris finally ordered him to the kitchen to find a beer and a snack just to keep him quiet. Kris was pacing the floor again and Patrick told him, "You know, Manley may be right. We may get in the building and not find anything. What do we do then?"

"I don't know," Kris said, his voice trailing off. "If we don't, maybe it will be time to move on."

Marilyn came back and immediately got everyone's attention. She was black from head to toe - long-sleeved black turtleneck shirt, black jeans, black boots that came to two inches below the knees and her hair tucked under a black baseball cap. "I went shopping today," she smiled playfully.

"Obviously," Kris noted.

"I feel like Wonder Woman in black."

"You look more like a prison guard," Patrick remarked, suppressing a laugh.

"O.K., let's go," Kris said. "We'll take Vance's truck. Marilyn, you sit in the cab with me, Patrick, you and Manley lie down in the bed."

The rain was light but steady and the sky, with clouds hiding the stars and moon, was as black as Marilyn's outfit. Kris covered Patrick and Manley with a blue plastic tarp for the short ride to the plant. Kris maneuvered Vance's truck through the deserted streets of Fort Phillips and all the way to the back of the Simpson Slacks building without meeting another vehicle.

Kris pulled as close as he could to a small heavy side door secured by a bulky padlock. Reaching into a sturdy black plastic trash bag he had taken from the truck, Kris said, "I brought these to help. Surely we can get the lock off with these." One by one, Kris pulled out a hacksaw, bolt cutters, a hammer and two flashlights.

"Those are nice, but this may work better," Manley said. He took a single key out of his jeans pocket.

"Where did you get that?" Kris asked.

"I have keys to most of the businesses in town."

"How did you get them?"

"Don't ask. As for this key, remember Clayton Justice? He was custodian for Simpson Slacks a long time. Not long after the plant closed, I won this key from him in a card game. It's a master key. Opens every door and unlocks every lock in this whole damn building - provided they haven't changed the locks, and it doesn't look like they have. I never thought this key would be worth anything, but I kept it, just in case I needed a place to call home for a few days."

"That's why we brought you along," Kris said. "All right, Billy, do your thing."

"Hurry up. I'm getting wet," Marilyn fussed.

With Kris shining light on the lock, Manley slowly inserted the key but did not get any results. Wiggling the key and taking it out and reinserting it several times did not help. "This thing is really stiff. It has probably been years since it has been opened. We need some kind of lubricant."

"I didn't bring any. I didn't realize we had a key," Kris said in an irritated tone. He looked directly at Manley.

"I may be able to help," Marilyn offered. She scurried back to the truck, searched through a small purse she had brought despite Kris' objection and returned to Manley. "Try this," she said.

Manley started laughing. "Sweet Slide Intimate Lubricant for Women?" Kris and Patrick started laughing too. The darkness prevented them from seeing Marilyn's face turn red.

"Like the Boy Scouts, my motto is *Be Prepared,"* she smiled. Manley coated the key with the lubricant and inserted it in the lock. After three seconds of curse words and twisting the key, Manley got the lock to pop open.

"That's why we brought you along," Kris said to Marilyn as he slipped his arm around her waist.

"What now boss?" Manley asked.

"I'm going in. The rest of you stay out here and be on guard. If you see anyone coming, get the hell out of here!" Kris ordered.

Kris disappeared into the building. Without the flashlight, he would not have been able to see his hand in front of his face. Making his way through the huge plant in the dark would take some time, especially since he did not know what he was looking for.

Fifteen minutes later, Patrick, Marilyn and Manley had taken refuge from the rain in the truck. He's been in there a long time," Marilyn fretted.

"You make it sound like he's having surgery," Patrick said.

"It is surgery, sort of. Exploratory surgery," Manley offered.

"Damn! A car's coming!" Patrick warned as he saw the beams from headlights flash around the corner.

Manley turned his head just in time to see the car come around the corner of the building. "It's the cops!" he said.

"How do you know?" Marilyn asked.

"Who the hell else would it be?"

"Get out of the truck!" Patrick told Marilyn "Go hide behind the garbage bin. This may be trouble."

She quickly obeyed. The dome light in the truck was burned out, not giving the approaching car a clue that someone was slipping out.

"I told you this was a bad idea," Manley said nervously.

"Keep your mouth shut. I'll do the talking," Patrick ordered.

The police car pulled up next to Vance's truck and Lonnie Jackson and Officer Davenport stepped out. Patrick rolled down the truck window.

Lonnie used his flashlight to look in the truck. "What the hell are you two doing here?"

"Making out," Patrick replied quickly.

"It's late and I'm tired and I'm wet. I do not want any smart-ass answers. Where's Keller?"

"Haven't seen him," Patrick replied.

"He's in the building, isn't he? After I told him to mind his own business, he went and did it anyway, didn't he? This is the very reason I decided to ride around after I dropped Manley off at Keller's. I smelled a rat, and the scent led me here."

"I don't know where Kris is, Chief. We're looking for him too," Patrick said. That was sort of the truth. He did not know exactly where Kris was in the building.

"What do you know about this?" Lonnie asked Manley, shining the light directly in his face.

"I'm just along for the ride."

"All right, Officer Davenport. Take these two-night owls to the jail and hold them. I will figure out what to charge them with later. I'm going in for Keller so I can arrest his sorry ass for breaking and entering and trespassing. I'll drive the truck back to the station."

Manley and Patrick offered no resistance. Manley was shaking. Patrick was calm on the outside, but his stomach was churning.

"You've gone too far this time, Keller!" Lonnie growled as he entered the building. Crouched behind the trash bin, Marilyn was engulfed in silent panic. Trying to remain calm, she decided to stay put and wait to see if Lonnie came out with Kris.

Inside, Kris had completed his sweep of the first floor, finding only hundreds of scraps of cloth fabrics, battered worktables and three dozen old, outdated industrial sewing machines. A nauseating, overpowering stench made breathing difficult. Using the beam from the flashlight to guide his way, Kris carefully moved up a steep set of stairs to the second floor. The small flashlight did not generate much illumination in the cave-dark room, and initially, all Kris noticed was more fabric scraps and pressing tables. Swiveling the flashlight from side to side like a searchlight, Kris moved cautiously as he strained to see through the darkness. The decades old wood floor creaked with his every step. Sweating and feeling more and more like he was about to throw up, Kris was about to leave but directed the flashlight for one last look into a corner. "What's this?" Kris asked, moving closer to several shadowy objects.

The narrow beam of light fell upon a complex network of tubes, flasks and barrels. "My God! I don't believe this!" he said aloud. Kris' newspaper had worked with federal law enforcement and prosecutors in Atlanta on dozens of articles about the methamphetamine epidemic sweeping the country. Because it was dissected by several major interstate highways, Atlanta had become a distribution point for shipping meth all along the east coast. What Kris was looking at now, in the darkness of the old Simpson Slacks building, was a super lab, capable of producing millions of dollars of the deadly, addictive drug. Kris stood rigidly in awe of the magnitude of the setup. He remembered the feds talking about how elaborate and uniform these super labs were, almost like franchises. There were not a lot of them, and most were in Mexico or out west. This lab had four "bubbling 22" globe-shaped flasks, the signature feature of the super lab used to cook the mixture. From what he had read and been told, Kris guessed the setup could produce thousands of doses of meth.

Kris shined his flashlight behind the lab set-up. Lined up on a back wall were dozens and dozens of file-sized boxes. "What the hell?" Kris asked as he moved slowly in the direction of the pyramid of boxes. Swallowing hard, he lifted the top of one of the boxes. Its contents were hundreds of dime bags of pills, powder and herbs. "Damn!" Kris said to himself. "This is what Syndicated Delivery Services is all about! They are making meth *and* distributing every other illegal drug known to man. Heroin, cocaine, marijuana, ecstasy, Molly, GHB. Shit! No wonder they are so secretive. No wonder they don't want anyone meddling in their business. I can't imagine there's a larger illegal drug outfit than this east of the Mississippi. These boxes represent millions of dollars!" Kris stood silent in disgusting awe of this monstrous enterprise.

Suddenly, the entire second floor was bathed in light. "How about a good look at everything," Lonnie said, moving his hand away from the master light switch on the wall at the top of the stairs. With his other hand, he slid his pistol out of its holster. Outside, Marilyn was shivering more from nerves than the steady rain. Kris had been in the building too long, and she did not like him being in there alone with Lonnie. She thought about going inside but decided waiting would be the better choice. "Come on out Kris, come on out," she urged, wiping rain off her face.

Rather than turning to face Lonnie, Kris held his position, continuing to study the lab, which was far more sophisticated and productive than the makeshift setups found in basements and bedrooms. "Well, Lonnie. You've really done it this time." Turning around, Kris stared at Lonnie. His emotions toward Lonnie were all over the place – anger, disgust, even a twinge of pity. "This isn't some government or military operation. There are no weapons or explosives here to be shipped out to guerillas interested in overthrowing governments. It's all about illegal drugs! The manufacture and distribution of illegal drugs! Is getting involved in all this your way of trying to impress your wife, this town, me? I feel sorry for you

Lonnie. You've really messed up this time. You've done some stupid things in your life, but this time, you are way in over your head!"

Lonnie took a step in Kris' direction. "Oh, I don't know about that. I would say my situation isn't nearly as dire as the predicament you are about to be in."

The two men were standing ten feet apart. "I do have to hand it to you, Lonnie," Kris started. "You couldn't tell me you were protecting an illegal drug operation that has the capability of killing thousands of people and wrecking far more lives, so you make up this wild story about storing and delivering resources for guerilla troops trying to overthrow foreign governments. And you know what? You almost had me believing you!"

"Oh, I didn't come up with the story. Someone did that for me. But yeah, most people, when you tell them the government or military is involved, they will leave you alone and go about their business. The last thing they want to do is get tangled up with the feds. But not you, Mr. Big Shot Reporter. You had to keep snooping and look at the mess you're in now."

"But Lonnie. I wasn't snooping," Kris said, his words dripping with sarcasm. "I was just going about my business. That's what reporters do."

"Want to know the rest of the story? All the fires and break-ins we have had? These people paid for those to happen. They figured if everyone was so concerned about all of that shit, they wouldn't pay much attention to what was going on in here."

"Well, it worked."

"Want to know something else? They paid me to be the inept small-town police chief who couldn't solve a case if someone handed him the clues on a Thanksgiving turkey platter. The more I bumble those cases, the more the town gets mad at me, wanting my hide, and that keeps the focus away from here. A nice plan, don't you think?"

"Only one thing about that," Kris said, finally looking at Lonnie in disgust. "Why did they waste their money paying you to be inept? It comes so naturally for you."

"Make all the smart-ass remarks you want, but this is one time - finally - that I'm going to get the best of you."

"And how is that?"

"Their plan was working fine until you showed up and started snooping around. Everyone expected you to take care of Vance's last rites and get the hell out of here as quickly as possible. No harm, no foul. But no, you had to be Mr. Big Man from Atlanta. Why couldn't you have left well enough alone and stayed away like I asked?"

"So, what are you going to do, Lonnie? Kill me?" Kris turned back to look at the meth-making equipment and the cache of boxes.

Lonnie moved closer to Kris. They were so close Kris could see Lonnie's nostrils flaring. "Because of your snooping, these people are going to shut down their operation. You are costing them a ton of money, Kris. A ton of money. A lot of inconvenience. They are not happy. They make people pay. They do not like witnesses or snitches. I did not think twice about sticking that knife in Popeye. It was good riddance. BoJo should be gone too but the men I paid to do him in messed up the job. They may go after him; they may not. As for you, Kris, they want me to torch this building - with you in it." Lonnie sucker-punched Kris in the stomach and then in the back of the head with his gun, sending Kris groggily to the floor. Grabbing Kris by the wrist, Lonnie dragged him to a nearby two-inch exposed water pipe and handcuffed him to it. He retrieved a red plastic five-gallon container from behind a wood storage chest and started splattering gasoline on the wooden floor.

"It didn't have to end this way, Kris," Lonnie sighed. "All you had to do was bury Vance and go back to Atlanta and we all would have lived happily ever after."

Shaking his head, Kris tried to look at Lonnie, but his eyes would not focus. "I didn't bury Vance. I had him cremated," Kris said. His remark had nothing to do with his immediate plight. "Why are you doing this?" he asked Lonnie.

"Money, of course. Money is always the reason."

"If it's money you want, I'll write you a check. Just get me out of these handcuffs," Kris suggested, shaking his shackled hand and rattling the water pipe.

"That's funny. Do you really believe you can match their deep pockets? I'm sorry Kris. I really am. On second thought, no I'm not!" Lonnie pulled a small box of matches out of his shirt pocket, lit one, looked at it for a second, and tossed it into one of the puddles of gas. Thin lines of flame instantly covered the floor. Lonnie started to walk out but stopped and turned to Kris. "And by the way, Kris, I am sorry about what I had to do to Vance, but I just do what I'm told." This time Lonnie did walk out.

"You son of a bitch!" Kris screamed.

Her eyes fixed on the side door, Marilyn saw Lonnie scurry out of the building. He crawled into Vance's truck and quickly drove away. "Kris, you need to come out," she said nervously. Apprehensive that Lonnie or one of his officers might still be close by, Marilyn remained huddled behind the trash bin. She alternated quick glances for approaching headlights with glances back to the building.

Marilyn's gut told her something was not right. Kris should have come out with Lonnie. Whether he had been arrested or given a chewing out to leave, Kris should have come out with Lonnie. Clutching a flashlight, she hurried into the building. The glow from the flames above lighted her way to the stairs. She began yelling for Kris before she reached the stairs and he yelled back at her. The upstairs was filled with scorching, soaring flames, but in his haphazard scattering of the gas, Lonnie had inadvertently left a clear path to Kris.

"I've got myself in a bit of a jam," Kris said with deep breaths.

"I see." Marilyn tugged at the handcuffs, but obvious to her and Kris, they were not going to pop open.

"The bolt cutters," Kris panted. "Did Lonnie take them? Are they still outside?"

"I don't know. I think so."

"Go get them. That's our only chance."

The heat was growing more intense by the second, and the clear path to Kris was growing narrower. In her haste to go down the stairs, Marilyn made an awkward step and almost fell. Pain shot through her ankle, but she could not let that stop her. Hobbling slightly, she got to the door and found the break-in tools. She grabbed the bolt cutters, nervously dropped them, picked them up and began the journey back to Kris.

Reaching the top of the stairs, she noticed the path to Kris had all but vanished. She put her arms in front of her face and rushed to Kris, hopping over two small lines of flames. Kris' breathing was labored. He stretched the handcuffs taut and asked Marilyn to try to cut them in the middle. Groaning and straining, she tried and was unsuccessful. She flipped the cap off her head and stopped to take two deep breaths and wipe her forehead. "Try again. Try harder," he requested calmly.

"What if I can't?" she cried. A tear trickled down her cheek.

"You can do it," he reassured her.

She wiped her forehead again and placed the bolt cutters on the handcuffs. Grunting, she pressed with all her strength on the two handles. No luck. She tried again and again and stopped to wipe her eyes that were burning from the smoke. She and Kris were both coughing.

"Keep trying," Kris urged. He had the fleeting thought that he was about to die, and Marilyn was as well because of him.

Crying uncontrollably, Marilyn mustered all her strength and pressed on the handles again. And again. Her eyes bulged with surprise as she felt the metal of the handcuffs give way. Kris scrambled to his feet and grabbed Marilyn's hand. Hopping over flames and protecting their faces with their arms, they made their way through the room to the stairs and out the building. They both spent two full minutes sucking the cool moist air into their lungs. The rain was a heavy drizzle.

His breathing finally back to normal, Kris cupped Marilyn's face in his hands. "Thank you," he smiled before hugging her.

She couldn't reply because she was still sucking air into her lungs.

"You not only look like Wonder Woman, you are Wonder Woman tonight!" he told her.

"Can Wonder Woman have a kiss?" she asked between gulps for air.

Smoke and flames were shooting out of the old roof. The flames were so intense the rain was having no effect on them. Kris kissed Marilyn. Her face was soot-stained and wet. They held each other for several minutes until they finally heard the sirens from the city's fire truck.

"I've got some unfinished business, but I don't want to leave you alone," Kris said.

"You go ahead. I'll be fine," she smiled. "Remember, tonight I'm Wonder Woman."

He squeezed her hand and began sprinting toward the front of the building where the fire truck was pulling up and spectators were gathering. Kris started searching the crowd and spotted Lonnie in the middle of the street, directing traffic away from the scene.

Kris confronted him head-on. "You son of a bitch!" Kris screamed. "Your attempt to kill me was like everything else you've ever done. Half ass! You screwed up! You're gonna wish you had killed me because I'm going to beat the shit out of you!"

Kris lunged and smacked Lonnie in the stomach with his shoulder. Entangled, they landed on the rough street with Kris getting an immediate nasty scratch on his arm just below his healing wound. Kris slugged Lonnie in the jaw, grabbed him by the shirt collar and raised him up. "Before I beat you to a pulp, you son of a bitch, tell me! Tell me why you killed Vance!" The crowd suddenly stopped watching the fire and turned their attention to the fight, gathering in a large circle.

Lonnie didn't answer and he made no attempt to fight back. Kris raised his fist to hit him again. Karen, who had elbowed her way through the thick crowd, begged Kris, "Don't hit him again. Let him go!"

Kris started to go through with the punch but stopped. He let go of Lonnie's collar, leaving Lonnie on all fours. Glaring at Karen, Kris said, "Your husband killed my father! The son of a bitch. If I don't kill him first, he's going to jail!" Karen started crying. A middle-aged lady who attended church with Karen was in the crowd. She put her arm around Karen's shoulders and unsuccessfully tried to console her.

Lonnie rose to his knees while Kris was facing Karen. "I told you back in the plant I was going to get the best of you this time, and I meant it," Lonnie said between gasps for air. He took his gun from its holster, and rather than pointing it at Kris, stuck it deep in his mouth and pulled the trigger. Amid horrified screams from the crowd, Lonnie's lifeless body fell to the pavement. Kris hurried to Karen and she buried her head in his chest. This time Lonnie had not fouled things up.

33

All Kris knew to do was hold Karen. She had held up through Lonnie's funeral and the public humiliation as word spread of her husband's involvement in a major drug scheme, but now was the difficult time when all the friends and sympathizers had come and gone, leaving her alone to agonize over everything that had occurred. Kris had hardly left her side for two reasons. First, he was her friend. Second, he was overwhelmed by guilt that he was responsible for Lonnie's death. True, Lonnie, by his own actions and decisions had put himself in harm's way, but Kris was tormented by his own behavior. He had allowed his rage to overcome his judgment, confronting Lonnie in the street in front of an audience, rather than quietly working behind the scenes with law enforcement to bring Lonnie to justice. Obviously, his momentary lapse had created a situation for which Lonnie saw only one satisfactory conclusion. Kris did not believe for a moment Lonnie feared going through the legal process. It was the wrath and ridicule of the town he did not want to face, so he took the easy way out.

Between Karen's quiet times and her uncontrollable crying spells, she and Kris had talked. Time and again she assured him that she did not blame him for Lonnie's death, but her absolution did little to make him feel better. He wanted to talk about what had happened. She wanted to talk about what was going to happen. Many decisions remained to be made. What was she going to do with the Sentinel? Was she going to stay in Fort Phillips? She had made that decision and the answer was no. The remaining question was where would she go? And she had made it emphatically clear that wherever she went, she wanted Kris with her.

Kris had managed to give a non-committal response or change the subject when Karen talked about their future. He honestly did not know how he felt about her. He had so much on his own plate to resolve. He still had feelings for Emmy and believed the last chapter in their relationship had not been written. He had to decide about his career and work. Certainly, he did not see a future in Fort Phillips. And then there was the matter of Marilyn, this woman who, practically out of nowhere had come into his life and saved his life. Two months ago, he knew her in passing as a co-worker with Emmy. Now his attraction to her was growing by the minute. Graciously, she had stayed in the background, giving Kris plenty of time to spend with Karen and plenty of time to answer the hundreds of questions posed by law enforcement.

Agents swarmed the town within hours after Kris called the regional GBI office with his revelation about the activities inside the Simpson Slacks building. Preliminary investigation had not uncovered much. None of the Syndicated box trucks had been located. Speculation was they had been disposed of, burned or dumped into a body of water. The FBI was assisting, scouring their databases for known drug syndicates and cartels, but identifying the group that had set up the meth lab would be difficult, because as Lonnie had described, they generally do not leave any evidence or witnesses. As for other individuals who may have been paid to stage the fires and break-ins and kill BoJo, investigators were not having much success. Agents interviewed the likely candidates in town, and there were lots of them, but they all pleaded ignorance. Either they truly did not know what had been going on, or they were giving Academy Award acting performances. As for the money Lonnie claimed he was getting for his involvement, it could not be located. Perhaps he had stashed it in an out-of-the-country account or a shoe box buried in the backyard, but he had been smart enough not to deposit it in his personal account or leave it at his house or the police station.

The little town was still buzzing about everything that had taken place, and for that reason, Karen had been a recluse. The first time after the funeral that she did venture out, the pathetic looks and talking behind her back quickly convinced her to take refuge in her house. With the town eager to read how the owner of the Sentinel would report on her husband's escapades, the newspaper set a record for sales. Kris was thankful to have Patrick to write these stories. His friend did a splendid job of reporting, sticking strictly to the few facts that were known, not once interjecting speculation, rumor or personal sidebars into the articles.

Kris had spent the afternoon with Karen at her house. They did not talk much but she did a lot of crying. Exhausted after several sleepless nights, she finally dozed off on the sofa as darkness fell on the town. Kris covered her with a light throw and waited on Marilyn who was bringing supper. He watched for her out the front window so she would not have to knock or ring, which would likely wake Karen.

Kris and Marilyn quietly slipped into the kitchen where they unloaded the picnic basket she had prepared. "You look tired," Marilyn told him as she distributed turkey sandwiches, potato chips and carrot and raisin salad.

"I am," he admitted, "More emotionally than physically."

"How's Karen?"

"Same as me. Very tired."

Karen poured Diet Coke out of a two-liter bottle into two ice-filled glasses. "What's going to happen to her, Kris?"

"I don't know. I do not think she knows. I do know she is not going to stay around here. Why should she?"

Marilyn bowed her head, rubbed her glass with her fingers, and, looking up, asked Kris, "What's going to happen to us? You and me?"

He stopped chewing his bite of sandwich, took time to swallow, and admitted to her, "I don't know. There are so many things I am uncertain about. I cannot get my father out of mind. I don't think there's much doubt now that he was murdered by Lonnie but why did Vance have to die? I need to know what involvement he had in this whole meth mess. And," he admitted honestly," there's Emmy. I need to make peace with her. I hope she and I are not finished…" he continued. His statement drained all the color from Marilyn's face. "But if we are finished…" he continued, "…but if we are finished, I still want to say goodbye to her, to try to end it on good terms."

Marilyn managed a weak smile, trying to convince herself that surely Kris and Emmy were finished. "That's a nice gesture," she said. "I wouldn't expect less from a class act like you."

He smiled back. "I appreciate that, but right now I feel like a jerk. One reason I feel like a jerk is I haven't had the opportunity to thank you for what you did. You saved my life. What you did was very brave, going into that burning building. We could have both ended up dead."

"But we didn't and that's what's important. It really felt strange, Kris, like I did not have control of my own body, like some higher power was guiding me. I think I need to start going to church again."

"I know I do but thank you again for what you did. And, as for you and me, well, all I can tell you for certain is that I want to get to know you better."

"That's a start." This time her smile was much more animated.

Karen, looking very listless, shuffled into the kitchen and poured a glass of water. Kris told her, "I was hoping you would sleep longer."

She sat at the kitchen table. "I can't get my mind to turn off. I am haunted by the image of Lonnie, on his knees in the middle of the street, with that gun in his mouth. That popping noise when the gun went off is something I will never forget. I get sick to my stomach every time I think about it, which is often." Karen gave Marilyn an unfriendly glance.

"I probably need to go," Marilyn offered.

"Finish your sandwich," Kris said.

"She probably has things she needs to do," Karen said.

"Let her eat," Kris insisted. "She prepared all of this."

"Thank you," Karen replied without a trace of sincerity.

The bell to the front door rang. Kris hopped up quickly, saying, "I'll get that. You two continue this charming discussion."

He left the kitchen, rudely leaving Marilyn in an awkward, uncomfortable position. She took a bite of her sandwich, but her stomach was in such a knot there was no way she was going to be able to swallow it.

"When are you going back to Atlanta?" Karen asked.

"In a few days. I got an extension on my vacation," Marilyn responded nervously, awaiting Karen's response.

"You're wasting your time here. I'm claiming Kris."

"Have you told him that?" Marilyn finally managed to get the bite of sandwich down by chasing it with a big swig of Diet Coke.

"He knows. Besides, I have a plan."

Marilyn did not want to continue the conversation, so she was relieved to see Kris return with Mickey Montgomery. Marilyn offered Mickey a sandwich, but he politely declined. He was delivering the guest book from Lonnie's service and a dozen or so sympathy cards that had been dropped off at the funeral home. More importantly, he wanted to check on Karen. After a few minutes of small talk, including the news that Eula Lee Garrett, one of the town's oldest residents, had died in her sleep the night before. Mickey said he needed to leave to make one more visit before calling it quits for the day, but not before he told Karen to take care of herself.

"I'll walk you to the door," Kris said.

"So will I," Marilyn said.

The three reached the front door. "I'll see you back at the house," Marilyn told Kris as she gently squeezed his hand.

"See you later. Bye, Mr. Montgomery," she smiled, leaving Kris and Mickey in the living room.

"You two have something going?" Mickey asked.

Kris vigorously shook his head. "Just friends."

"Well, she's sort of gaining hero status around here. Everyone knows how she saved you from that burning building."

"She deserves that status. She did save my life. And I'll find an appropriate way to thank her."

"I bet you will. What about Karen? She looks bad."

"I'm going to take care of her. I think she'll be fine once she gets some sleep."

"I can't believe Lonnie was involved in that whole mess."

"People do stupid things, especially when money's involved."

"You're right about that. I just know I will be glad when all these federal and state agents leave town. That makes me extremely uncomfortable."

"Me too, but they've still got some questions to answer. One being, why did Lonnie have to kill Vance?"

"Speaking of Vance, I've been meaning to tell you," Mickey said. "I got his ashes back from the crematory. Things have been so busy, I just forgot to let you know."

"Thanks. I'll come by in a day or two to pick them up."

"There's something else I've been meaning to tell you," Mickey said, almost secretively.

"What?" Kris asked, his curiosity aroused.

"When we picked up his body to take it to the crime lab…"

"Yeah, go ahead," Kris requested with increasing interest.

"He was clutching a crushed cigarette pack in his right fist. I had never seen Vance smoke. I don't know if it means anything, but I wanted to tell you."

Kris did not say anything in reply, trying to hide the thoughts going through his mind.

"He did smoke on occasion, especially if he was nervous," Kris finally replied. He had lied to Mickey. Vance had a lot of vices, but smoking was not one of them.

The two men shook hands and Mickey left. Kris stood at the door, running his fingers through his hair. He had a good idea where the cigarette pack came from, and he was going to talk to the one person who could tell him about it.

34

Billy Manley had disappeared. Fruitlessly searching for two days, Kris checked at all of Manley's hangouts, including the barn, and inquired with all his cohorts as to his whereabouts, but no one had seen him or heard from him. Perhaps Manley had left town, but Kris was more concerned he had met the same fate as Popeye or was a target like BoJo. Either way, Kris feared he had lost the opportunity to learn why Vance was clutching one of Manley's cigarette packs when he died.

But just as he was about to give up hope, Kris spotted Manley, smoking a cigarette, propped up against the propane tanks at Fast Mart. "He must be needing some money," Kris mumbled, relieved to see Manley safe and eager to question him about the cigarette pack.

Stepping out of Vance's truck, Kris joked with Manley about his disappearing act.

"Had some business to take care of," Manley said, taking one last draw off his cigarette and flipping it away with his right middle finger.

"Where did you go? What kind of business?" Kris asked, even though he knew he would not get an answer.

"Just business. Out of town." Manley took the last cigarette, lit it and wadded the pack and tossed it to Kris who caught it and squeezed it in his fist.

"I want to ask you about this," Kris said, opening his fist and displaying the crumpled pack.

"That?" Manley asked.

"Yeah. I got some interesting news from Mickey Montgomery."

"What?" Manley asked, appearing to not have any idea what Kris was talking about.

"That Vance was holding one of your crushed cigarette packs in his hand when he died."

"So?" Manley asked Kris. Kris noticed a sudden change in Manley's body language. "I had been over at Vance's house. He probably picked up the pack after I tossed it. Everyone picks up after me. Even you," Manley said, using his index figure to point at the pack Kris was holding.

Kris waited for a mother and her two small daughters who were sipping soft drinks through straws to leave the store and get settled in their car. "My question for you, Billy, is why would Vance have been holding one of your cigarette packs when he killed himself? Better yet, how could he have been holding the gun or pulled the trigger while he was holding your cigarette pack?"

"How the hell should I know?" Manley asked, his voice cracking. He flipped the lit cigarette in Kris' face, and began running clumsily toward the back of the store. Kris, an ash stinging his eye, easily caught up with Manley, grabbed him by the collar of his shirt and slammed his back against the side wall of the Fast Mart building.

"Tell me what happened to Vance, damn it!" Kris demanded loudly, not bothering to see if anyone was looking. They were not.

"I don't know," Manley replied, his voice cracking again. His entire body was shaking.

Kris pushed him harder against the wall. "Don't bullshit me, Billy. You and I are going to have a little Come to Jesus meeting. We're not leaving here until you tell me what happened!"

"You're not going to slug me, are you? Like you did Lonnie?" Manley was terrified, as if he knew Kris was about to send him to his Maker.

"Not if you tell me what happened." Kris tightened his grip on the front of Manley's shirt.

"O.K., O.K.," Manley agreed, "But let's at least go behind the store."

Kris dragged him behind Fast Mart and out of public view. "Talk!" Kris ordered. He still had Manley by the shirt collar.

Manley could not stop trembling. He tried to speak but the words would not come out. The furious stare Kris was giving him made Manley know he somehow had to talk. Finally, he started. "The people making the meth were paying several of us to stir things up, to make trouble to keep the heat off them. I took Vance with me to the plant one night to see if he wanted to get in on the action. Hell, man, it was easy money! Not a lot, but enough to buy lots of cigarettes. I kept bumming money off you and other people so no one would know I was getting paid."

Kris loosened his grip on Manley. "Everyone keeps saying *the people.* Who are *the people*? I want some names. Some real blessed names!"

Manley vigorously shook his head. "I don't have any names. I talked to one guy face-to-face twice. Don't know who he was. He was just an average-looking guy. I think he was getting his orders from someone else. There's still a pay phone here at Fast Mart. The only one left in town. If Lonnie didn't tell me what to do, someone would call me on the pay phone and give me instructions and tell me where I could pick up my money."

"Go on," Kris said, regaining a firm grip on Manley. Kris' face was getting flush and his heart beating faster.

"I took Vance to meet the guy at Simpsons. That was the second time I had seen him or talked to him. Well, Vance picked a hell of a time to get all moral and ethical. He said he wouldn't be a part of it, and in fact, got all pissed off that he had even been asked. He stormed all huffy out of the building. I went after him and asked him to reconsider. He wouldn't and said he was going to do something about it. He knew asking Lonnie Jackson to do something about what was going on would be a waste of time so he said he was going to write you and tell you what was going on, that you would know what to do. He was going to tell you that, and that he wanted a second chance with you."

Kris hung his head and bit his lip. His grip on Manley softened slightly. "He got murdered because he wouldn't have anything to do with all of this crap!"

"I didn't have any choice."

"What did you say?" Kris asked, his eyes focused on Manley with the intensity of a laser.

"I said I didn't have any choice."

"Any choice about what?"

"Lonnie told me to kill Vance. He told me that she had ordered him to kill Vance. The instructions to him were to make it look like a suicide. But the wimp didn't have the guts to do it. Lonnie didn't have a problem with killing Popeye, but he said he couldn't kill Vance; that it was too personal. Lonnie didn't have the damn guts to do it, so he made me do it! It was either me or Vance. One of us was going to die; me for bringing Vance to the plant, or Vance for knowing what was going on and refusing to be a part of it. I put the shotgun barrel to Vance's head and pulled the trigger. Do you have any idea how sick that made me? I killed my best friend! I felt like doing the same thing to myself but was too much of a coward. Then, after the exterminator found Vance, Lonnie was first on the scene. He took the gun so no one would discover that Vance's fingerprints weren't on it. I was nervous as hell the night I did it. I was smoking like a chimney. I guess by habit I must have tossed away one of my cigarette packs and Vance grabbed it. I'm sorry, Kris," Manley quivered, on the verge of hysteria. He started blubbering like a child.

"You bastard!" Kris screamed. He tightened his grip on Manley's shirt with both hands and almost lifted him off the ground. He wanted to choke the life out of Billy Manley. Instead, he pressed him against the wall again, and asked, "You're the one who told me to look into Vance's death, that it wasn't a suicide. Why did you do that?"

"Do you really have to ask that? To take the heat off myself. I figured if I told you to look into Vance's death, you'd never think I had anything to do with it. Knowing how you felt about Vance, I thought you would just say to hell with it and go back to Atlanta." With wide, horrified eyes, Manley added, "But, I wanted you to know that Vance really had turned his life around. He was getting ready to try to make up with you and he was going to start by writing you a letter."

"I never got a letter," Kris said, his own voice starting to quiver.

"I don't know if he ever sent it. I looked for it at your house that night. So did Popeye. So did BoJo. That's why they broke into your house, to find the damn letter. That's why Popeye got killed and BoJo almost got killed, because they never found the letter, and when Popeye kept getting caught, there was too much of a chance he would start running his mouth. Depending on what was in the letter, it could have caused some serious shit!"

"This is unbelievable, you wormy little bastard!" Kris was about to cry. Tears were welling in his eyes.

"What are you going to do to me?" Manley had not made any attempt to break free from Kris.

"I'm going to take you to the GBI." Glaring at Manley, Kris had a flashback about one of Manley's confessions. "You said *she*. You said *she* ordered Lonnie to kill Vance."

Wide-eyed, Manley asked, "Did I say *she*?" He kneed Kris in the groin and slapped Kris' hands away from his shirt. As Kris bent over and tried not to vomit, Manley frantically started running away in the direction of the street in front of Fast Mart. Trying to catch his breath and fight off the pain, Kris first heard the squealing of brakes and then a solid thud. Wobbling to the front of the store, Kris looked to the street. Manley was sprawled on the pavement, having been hit by a gravel truck.

Kris hurried to Manley as did the clerk and two customers from inside Fast Mart. The truck driver was already bent over Manley.

"I couldn't help it! He ran right out in front of me!" the middle-aged driver with a full beard and tobacco-stained teeth said. The driver was shaken and gasping for breath.

Kris searched for a pulse and couldn't find one. Manley was not breathing. Kris and one of the Fast Mart customers administered CPR until a rescue unit arrived in seven minutes, and then paramedics took over. They loaded Manley in the ambulance and headed for the hospital. They should have headed straight for Mickey Montgomery's place. Manley was dead.

35

Kris followed the ambulance to the hospital where he met GBI and FBI agents and told them of Manley's confession about Vance's death. He was shaken by Manley's demise, not because he and Manley were bosom buddies, but because it meant Manley would not be available to provide more information about the awful activities at the Simpson Slacks building. Kris was haunted by another realization. Why did Vance not put up a fight when Manley came to kill him? From what Manley said, Vance apparently offered no resistance. Everyone Kris had talked to said Vance was in a good frame of mind, so why was he such a willing participant? Sadly, Kris knew he would likely never have the answer to that question, and he would have to struggle with it for the remainder of his life.

Finished with his statement to the authorities, Kris went straight home to search for Vance's missing letter. He had yet to talk to Patrick and Karen who were out of town getting the next issue of the Sentinel printed, and Marilyn was probably out shopping, giving Kris plenty of freedom to search and inspect every nook and cranny, cabinet and drawer in the house. Thirty minutes of relentless searching uncovered nothing. He made another sweep through the house, stopping in every room, trying to think of some place he had not looked. Surveying Vance's room, Kris' eyes stopped on the photo of him and Vance at Turner Field and he remembered how Vance used to stash items behind it. With anticipation, Kris pulled the photo off the wall. Nothing was taped to the back. He took the back off, hoping something might be between the back and the photo. Nothing. "Damn it!" he yelped, more out of frustration than anger. Had Vance not gotten around to writing the letter? If he had written it, where was it?

His search was interrupted when Patrick and Karen arrived together. Having stopped at Fast Mart for gas, they were stunned at the news about Billy Manley. Kris sat down with them at the kitchen table and slowly and meticulously explained what happened, including Manley's declaration that, while he may have pulled the trigger, Lonnie had given the orders for Vance's execution. Restlessly, Karen sat and listened, her face getting paler by the minute and her eyes filling with tears. Finally, she pushed away from the table, knocking over the chair she had been using and rushed out of the kitchen and on to the front porch.

Without saying anything else, Kris followed her. Karen was sitting on the steps, her head buried in her hands, sobbing. Kris nudged beside her and put his arm around her. "I'm sorry," he said. "I am so sorry you are having to go through this."

"It's so embarrassing," she sniffled. "I'm humiliated."

"No one's blaming you. I think everyone in town feels sorry for you."

That was the wrong thing for Kris to say. Karen immediately shot back, "I don't want that either. I don't want anyone's sympathy or pity. I don't want them to be looking at me and saying *Poor Karen.* I just want them to leave me alone."

"They will. They're just not used to this type of thing happening in their town."

Kris realized he had put his foot in his mouth again. Wide-eyed Karen snapped at him, "And you think I am? This is my town too, remember? I've lived here all my life, unfortunately."

"Maybe you should take a vacation. Get out of town for a while."

"I want to do more than that. I want to leave for good, and I want you to go with me."

Her request caught Kris' breath. "I think you may need some time alone," he said, giving his best off-the-top-of-his-head reply.

"All of this will be tolerable if it means you and I can be together. Otherwise, I don't have much to live for."

Kris grabbed her firmly by the arm. "Don't say that," he told her, wiping a tear from her cheek. "Your whole life is ahead of you. There's so much for you to do, to accomplish."

"I don't care about any of that now. All I want to hear is that you'll leave this terrible town with me."

In silence, Kris turned his head away from Karen. He felt cornered. Rubbing his hands together, Kris took a deep breath, and with his head hanging, started, "Before we can think about that, I need to ask you a question." He raised his head, looked directly at Karen and continued, "I hate to ask this, but I have to. How much did you know about Lonnie's involvement in all of this?" He gritted his teeth waiting for the explosion.

And he got it. "I can't believe you asked me that!" she shouted, jumping up from the steps. "You come out here, put your arm around me, trying to console me, I assume, and the next thing, you're accusing me of being a part of this whole sordid mess. God, Kris! I can't believe this!" Tears started streaming down her cheeks and she tried to wipe them away with the palms of her hands.

Kris felt like a creep, but he had to ask the question. Perhaps he could have asked it at a better time, but at some point, he had to ask. He started explaining, "One of the things Manley told me was that Lonnie's order to have Vance killed came from a female. You're the only female I know who was in Lonnie's life."

"Well, I can damn assure you, it wasn't me!" Karen shot back. "Maybe the mayor's wife, the school nurse, the waitress over at Pete's. How the hell do I know who it was? All I know is, it was not me, and I am mortified, absolutely mortified, that you could think for a second, a half-second, that it was me! My God, Kris, you know me better than that!"

Feeling about three inches tall, Kris meekly said, "I'm sorry, but I had to ask."

"No, you didn't!"

"Someone had my father killed, Karen, and I've got to find out who."

"And I'm the first person you think of?"

"Based on what Manley told me, yes."

Karen turned her back to Kris. "Get out of my sight, please. Go away!" she ordered.

"Uh, this is my house," he pointed out.

"I feel like I'm going to be sick!" Karen put her hand over her mouth, hurried to her car in Kris' driveway and sped away. With the knot in his own stomach growing larger, Kris prayed that Karen would not do anything irrational.

Kris went back inside and, looking for sympathy, told Patrick what he had done. Instead of sympathy, he got a lecture about how insensitive he had been. Patrick agreed questioning Karen about her possible involvement was legitimate, but the timing was atrocious. Marilyn, entering the house upon returning from looking in antique shops in nearby Sylvester, got in on the tail-end of the discussion and wanted to know what was going on. Reluctantly Kris repeated the entire story of Billy Manley's demise and his assertion that a female had been dishing out orders. Expecting to be lambasted by Marilyn as well, Kris was shocked, but relieved when she said, "It was a question you had to ask, and to my way of thinking, the sooner the better." Patrick didn't say anything out loud, but he understood Marilyn's position. Eliminating Karen would give her a clearer path to Kris.

The remainder of the day was thankfully uneventful and Kris, not the least bit sleepy with a thousand negative thoughts and images swirling in his head, went to bed after the 11 o'clock TV news. Stretched flat on his back and pondering about who was going to make funeral arrangements for Manley, Kris watched as the door to his room creaked and slowly opened. He started following the shadowy outline as it made its way to his bed. He wasn't threatened by this intruder.

Marilyn sat down on the edge of the bed and put her hand on Kris' chest. He put his hand on top of hers.

"I've been worried about you, tonight. I wanted to check on you," she whispered.

"I'm all right," he answered.

"I bet I can make you think about something else." Marilyn leaned into Kris' face and started kissing him slowly and tenderly. He reached up and began rubbing her hair, eliciting a soft moan from her. Marilyn rubbed his chest and continued a downward descent with her hand. "My strategy is working," she said with a smile that was not visible in the dark room. "Feels like I definitely have you thinking about something else."

"Yes, you do," Kris admitted. He placed his hands on the thin cotton camisole covering her breasts which generated another soft moan.

Marilyn laid on top of him. "I've wanted to make love to you for the longest time," she admitted.

"I've been thinking a lot about you lately," he admitted in return, gently rolling Marilyn over so he was on top. Kris' cell phone on the stand next to his bed started vibrating, but he was not about to answer. He and Marilyn celebrated the evening, and drained, lay next to each other in his bed.

"Thanks. I needed that. I am very relaxed now. Hopefully, I can go to sleep," Kris told her.

"My pleasure. Can I sleep with you tonight?"

"I'm not going to kick you out of the bed!"

"Good, because we may not be through."

That possibility was fine with Kris and he kissed her. His cell phone vibrated again, and this time, despite Marilyn urging that he ignore it, Kris answered when he saw the number was Karen's. Before he could say hello, Karen started sobbing, "I'm desperate, depressed and I think I'm going to take this whole bottle of sleeping pills the doctor prescribed."

Kris, still naked, hopped out of bed and started dressing with one hand while holding his cell phone in the other. "Put those pills down, right now!" he ordered. Kris realized he may have used too harsh a voice. In a much more reassuring tone, he requested, "Put the pills down. I'll be there in ten minutes."

"I don't know," she said between sobs.

Kris tossed down his phone and almost fell back on the bed while trying to put on his jeans. Marilyn, slipping into her skimpy night clothes, asked, "What in the world is going on?"

"Karen. She's threatening to overdose on sleeping pills. I've gotta go!"

"Do you need me to go with you?"

"No," Kris said as he tucked a white golf shirt into his jeans. Forgoing socks, he slipped on his shoes and said, "I'll call as soon as I find out what's going on."

Marilyn watched Kris practically sprint out of the house. Sitting on the edge of the bed, she sighed. She and Kris had just enjoyed a wonderful session of lovemaking and were about to snuggle into each other's arms for the night. Now, instead of having that sweet time on his mind, Kris was in a panic, on his way to rescue his old girlfriend. Marilyn was concerned about Karen's well-being, but totally frustrated with her sense of timing and Kris' willingness to run off to her. Expecting Kris to be gone the remainder of the night, Marilyn took a sleeping pill herself and returned to her room.

Coaxing every ounce of horsepower out of Vance's old truck, Kris got to Karen's house in eight minutes. The house was dark and quiet, so quiet Kris could hear his heartbeat in his ears. He swallowed hard and started up the stairs to the master bedroom. A dusty, dim flicker of light coming from the bedroom helped Kris through the darkness. He called Karen's name but there was no answer. He called for her again and still did not receive a reply. Kris was struck with the horrible thought that Karen had chosen to use a measure swifter than sleeping pills to end her life. He took a deep breath to try to slow his heart down as he stepped into the bedroom.

"Hello," Karen said seductively. Naked, she was propped up by her right arm, her legs folded under her.

Kris exhaled in relief. "You don't look very depressed and distressed to me," he said, not stepping any deeper into the room.

"I lied," she smiled.

"And why did you lie?"

"To get you here with me, by yourself."

Kris held his position. "And why do you want me here, just the two of us? To discuss the sad state of the clothing industry in Fort Phillips?"

"What do you think about my clothing situation?"

"Oh, I can tell you there's nothing sad about it."

"How about coming closer so you can get a better look." She patted the bed.

Kris went halfway to the bed. "You scared the crap out of me. I seriously thought you were going to do something stupid," he chided her.

"Well, I am depressed," she admitted. "I do need someone to talk to, and I really would like to make love. It's been a long, long time."

"You and Lonnie…"

"He was terrible. I liked my vibrator better."

Kris managed a fake cough. "I think I need to go," he said, taking another look at her.

"Don't go," she pleaded. "I do want to talk to you. I want to apologize." Again, she motioned for Kris to sit on the bed.

Relenting, he sat on the edge of the bed and, starting at her toes, ran his eyes all the way up her legs. "What do you want to apologize about?"

"The way I reacted when you asked me about knowing Lonnie's involvement in the meth set-up. You knew Lonnie. You knew he wasn't smart enough to get involved in something like that without someone giving him orders. It was a legitimate question, and I'm sorry that I jumped all over you. But I didn't know, Kris. I swear."

"I believe you, and I'm sorry I asked. Yes, I knew Lonnie, but I know you as well, and I know you couldn't get messed up in anything like that." He smiled at her.

"Thanks," she smiled back and fell back on the bed, totally exposing herself to Kris.

He gulped. "I wish you wouldn't do that," he said, having to clear his throat.

"Why? Don't you like what you see?"

"That's the problem. Yes. I like what I see. Very much."

"It's yours." She rubbed her hand along the side of her leg.

Kris surveyed her body and silently compared it to Marilyn's. Karen's legs were longer and more shapely; Marilyn's breasts fuller. Facially, they were both extremely attractive. Kris was tempted, but the timing did not seem right. Lonnie had not been gone long enough for Kris to be bedding his wife. "Not tonight," he said softly.

"Please Kris. I really need some intimacy tonight."

"Karen…I…"

"Please, Kris." She took his hand and tugged but Kris did not budge. She tugged again, harder, and this time Kris gave in. Still clothed, he settled on top of her and they began kissing. She tenderly undressed him, and forgoing preliminaries, they made love. "I love you," Karen whispered in his ear.

With Kris stretched out on his back, Karen laid her head on his chest. Without looking at him, she said, "I want you to go away with me. I have decided to close the Sentinel. I want to go somewhere and make a new life for myself. I want you to be a part of it."

He had been running his fingers through her hair but stopped. "You're closing the Sentinel? I cannot believe that! What would your father think?"

She raised her head and looked at him. "I can't think about Dad now. I have to think about myself. There is nothing to keep me here. Mom has been dead for years. My Dad died. Lonnie was messed up in all sorts of sordid activities, killed himself and humiliated me. Don't you think I've been through enough to deserve a new start?"

"There's no denying that, but to close the Sentinel?"

"I've thought about it a lot. That is my decision. And I want you to go with me."

"Where?"

"I don't know. A thousand miles from here. A million miles from here."

Kris shifted and sat up in the bed. He gently rubbed her cheek with his hand. "I can't make any promises now. I can't be much good to anyone else until I get some of my own issues resolved."

"Like Emmy?"

"Yeah, like Emmy. And Marilyn. And Vance."

"Vance? Vance is gone. There's nothing you can do."

"That's the problem. There is nothing I can do. He wanted to make peace with me, for us to have a new start, and I was not around to let him. He allowed Billy Manley to kill him without resistance. The guilt I'm feeling is hanging over me like a July rain cloud."

"It shouldn't. Down through the years you did more for Vance than any other son would have done for their father. Let him go, Kris, and get on with your life."

"It's not that easy. It's just not that easy."

Karen kissed Kris. "I'm really relaxed now. Let's get some sleep. We'll talk about the future - our future together - in the morning."

Karen was asleep in seconds. Kris was physically drained and relaxed, but his mind was in turbo drive. Just weeks ago, his life was close to perfect. Now it was totally falling apart, just like his hometown.

36

Kris slept little during the night and was wide awake at 6 o'clock the next morning. Moving slowly and deliberately to not awaken Karen, Kris quietly slipped out of the room and returned to his house. He brewed some coffee and drank a couple of cups while he continued to replay recent events in his mind. Realizing he was driving himself crazy. Kris began scanning the Internet to catch up with what was going on in the world. Recently Fort Phillips had been his world. He felt like he was beginning to lose touch with reality. He needed a good dose of Congress' most recent squabbles, the latest Hollywood gossip and the National League baseball standings to help remember there was life outside southwest Georgia.

The number one item on Kris' agenda for the day was to call Emmy early, before she started seeing clients outside the office. He had to see her again, to be able to look into her eyes to judge how she really felt about him. His gut feeling was they were finished. If that was the case, he wanted to hug her one last time, say goodbye and move on. If Emmy was not interested, Kris knew he had two other ladies who were extremely interested, butt-naked interested.

The problem was getting Emmy to take his call. By consistently not answering to begin with or abruptly hanging up when she recognized Kris as the caller, Emmy was emphasizing her desire to not have anything to do with him. He realized the time had come to be devious. His plan was to call, using a fictitious name, and ask to talk to Emmy about assistance in locating lease space. There was no guarantee that she wouldn't hang up again, but hopefully she would realize how desperate he was to see her and grant him a brief audience. At the same time, the notion struck Kris that he was pathetic. Did he care enough about this woman to stoop to such low tactics to beg her for a few crumbs of her time? His conclusion? Yes, he was pathetic, and yes, he did care enough for her to make one last attempt to talk to her face-to-face.

At 8:15, with Patrick and Marilyn still in their rooms, Kris called the leasing office and identified himself as George Andrews from Birmingham who was looking for office space in Atlanta, and a business associate had told him Emmy could help. The receptionist must have been new because Kris didn't recognize her voice, but she cheerfully declared Emmy would be pleased to talk to him. She transferred the call to Emmy's office. Kris could feel his palms start to sweat, and he began to hope she wouldn't answer.

"Hello Mr. Andrews. This is Emmy Owens. How may I assist you?" was the perky greeting. Kris hated bubbly early morning salutations.

"Hello, Emmy," Kris said, choosing not to carry on with the charade.

"Kris?"

"Yes. Please do not hang up. I won't take but a minute."

"What do you want?" she asked, the surprise of his call obvious in her tone.

"I want to see you. Maybe take you to dinner. I guess we need to say goodbye."

"How are you? How's your arm?" Kris didn't detect much sincere concern in Emmy's voice.

"I'm O.K. My arm's O.K., but a lot has happened."

"I know. I've seen some TV reports and Marilyn has been keeping in touch with the office. Is she still down there? Is she one of the reasons we need to say goodbye?"

"She's still down here. If you are asking if she's any threat to you, the answer at this moment is no. If you are saying there's no chance for you and me, then the answer is yes."

"I've never considered Marilyn a threat. Fort Phillips. Karen. The newspaper business. They are my competition. If we do say goodbye, that will be why. Not Marilyn."

"Are you saying there's hope for us?"

Silence was the response to Kris' question. "I think it's too late for us, Kris. Too much has happened. I've moving on. I'm leaving town at the end of the week."

Kris lowered his head, closed his eyes and bit his lip. Emmy was telling him what he needed to hear, but hearing it was still painful. "Where are you going?" he asked.

"Away from here. I'm still finalizing plans."

"I would still like to see you," he told her in a soft voice. "Can I come up?"

"I don't know Kris."

"Please. I will not pressure you. I will not ask questions. Just one last meal with a good friend."

"If that's all…"

"That's all."

"O.K. Day after tomorrow. Meet me at The Orchid at 7."

Kris bit his lip again. "You would have to pick The Orchid," he said. "One of our favorite places."

"Then, you choose. Or we can just call it off."

"No," he responded emphatically. "The Orchid is fine. I'm looking forward to seeing you."

"You too," was her reply, which Kris knew was false. She hung up before he could say anything else.

Kris sighed. Now that he had the date he so desperately wanted, what was he going to say once he sat down with Emmy? Was there anything left to say? Could he do anything other than make more of a fool of himself than he already had? Confused and forlorn and desperately needing to clear his mind, Kris changed into shorts and sneakers and began a long, painful slow jog on the streets of Fort Phillips. Badly out of shape despite the basketball sessions at the recreation center, he did not let shortness of breath and an aching side stop him. Ten miles and almost three hours later, sucking air and barely able to put one foot in front of the other, Kris returned to his house convinced that seeing Emmy one last time was the right thing to do.

Patrick was working at his computer, finishing the lead story for the next Sentinel, when Kris came dragging in. "You don't look so good," Patrick said.

"Just a little winded."

"Just a little winded? Back in high school, this guy we called Lard Butt was in my physical education class. The coach made Lard Butt run a 440 after he smarted off about something. Lard Butt finished, but I thought he was going to die. He did go into the bathroom and puke for five minutes. That's what you look like."

"I bet he didn't mouth off anymore, did he?" Kris asked, still breathing hard.

"No, and I bet you don't ever repeat whatever it was that sent you on this death march."

"I talked to Emmy," Kris said as he melted into the chair next to Patrick's desk.

"Oh," Patrick nodded. "I assume the talk didn't go so well?"

"You assume correctly. But I am going to see her day after tomorrow. Want to go to Atlanta?"

"Sure. I will ride with you. I guess I do need to see my wife. My doctor, too. Any chance of you two patching things up?

"I'd say the odds of that happening are only slightly better than me getting a contract to be the shooting guard for the Atlanta Hawks. Has the mail come yet?"

"Just arrived," Patrick replied, reaching for the small stack of envelopes on the corner of the desk. "Most of it is junk. There is one item here, however, that looks interesting." Patrick handed Kris the letter-size white envelope.

Kris glanced down at the address on the letter and looked at Patrick. He looked at the letter again and noticed the return address. Now, Kris' eyes were glued to the letter.

"This is it," Kris said calmly, as much to himself as to Patrick. "This is the letter Vance sent me, the letter Popeye and the drug hooligans were after. Vance got the address wrong. I lived on Jonas Street in Atlanta. He sent it to Jones Street. The Post Office could not deliver it, so they returned it to the sender. This thing has been floating around in postal purgatory for weeks."

"Are you sure you want to open it? Sometimes letters tell you what you don't want to know."

"I want to open it," Kris said. He carefully unsealed the envelope and unfolded the single piece of paper inside. Kris started reading the hand-written words. He didn't say anything but lowered his head and closed his eyes a couple of times. Patrick didn't say anything, allowing Kris to concentrate on the reading.

Kris raised his head, letting Patrick see the tears rolling down his cheeks. "You're right, Patrick," Kris said. "Sometimes letters tell you what you don't want to know."

37

Kris was uncomfortable sitting alone while waiting for Emmy to arrive at The Orchid. His discomfort was compounded by members of the wait staff coming by to say hello and asking about Emmy. They all knew Kris and Emmy, their favorite drinks, their favorite entrees and the table they preferred. Kris answered their questions about Emmy by saying she was fine and would arrive shortly. She was late, and Kris' jitters were growing with each passing minute. He was beginning to ponder the possibility that he had been stood up.

Twenty minutes beyond their scheduled meeting time, Emmy arrived. He was glad to see her but at the same time he wasn't. No coward's way out now. No leaving before she arrived. They were about to be face-to-face. Time to put all their issues on the table.

On this night, Emmy was Miss America gorgeous. Her shoulder-length blonde hair glistened in the soft restaurant light and her sparkly low-cut black dress provocatively offered glimpses of the side of her breasts. Her makeup provided a soft, pale, almost angelic hue to her face. Captivated by her elegance, Kris could feel his resolve to say what needed to be said melting away.

Kris got up from the table and helped Emmy to her seat. "You look great!" he told her nervously. He was encouraged that she had dressed so elegantly for their meeting. If she had dressed so elegantly to gain his attention, she had succeeded.

That thought was quickly shot down. "Thank you," Emmy answered. "I wore this to an important meeting. That's why I am late. I didn't have time to go home and change. You, uh, you look, uh, tired."

Her remark deflated Kris, but knowing she was correct, replied, "I am tired, but I'm glad to see you. Thanks for coming." He was nervous, even more nervous than when he proposed.

"How was your drive up?" Emmy asked as the waiter dropped by to get their drink orders. They both requested glasses of Chardonnay and placed their food orders without having to study the menu. Kris, although not the least bit hungry, ordered prime rib. Emmy asked for lobster. She said if she was going to break her rule of not eating after 7 p.m., it would be for the most expensive item on the menu.

Kris took a sip of his wine before answering, "The drive was fine. I have a proposition for you," he said.

"I'm not interested," she quickly replied.

"Please," Kris requested, his body all but quivering.

"What?" she asked, pulling her glass down from in front of her face.

"Let's don't talk about what has taken place over the last few weeks. Catch me up with what's going on in Atlanta. Let's just enjoy a nice evening."

"Fair enough," she agreed, and through dinner and dessert they did enjoy a pleasant conversation about many topics, none of them of any relevance. And while the evening was cordial, Emmy's body language and expressions clearly indicated she would rather be dining with one of Atlanta's homeless people than Kris.

Even with a second bottle of wine, the conversation started to wane, and Emmy became increasingly restless, constantly shifting in her chair. After sneaking three glances at her watch, she announced, "I need to leave."

Kris surveyed the half-full restaurant. "Since this is obviously our goodbye," he stated, "can I ask you one last question?"

"I suppose," was her irritated answer.

Kris looked around at the diners again and making eye contact with Emmy, asked, "How in the world did you get mixed up with Syndicated Delivery Services in Fort Phillips?"

Emmy's face froze as if she had just seen a five-car crash on Atlanta's Downtown Connector. "You're more tired than you realize. You are out of your mind. You're delusional," she replied unevenly.

"You might as well come clean. Vance sent me a letter telling me all about your involvement. He saw you at the old Simpson plant. He described you to the last detail. He said you identified yourself as my girlfriend, and that I was in on this scheme, and I had suggested he join in. He didn't believe you. I never had any faith in him, but he had faith in me. Vance's letter was enough to convince me, but on top of it, Billy Manley told me Lonnie was taking orders from a woman. It's you, Emmy, I know. What I don't know is why."

As Kris had done, Emmy glanced around at the restaurant's guests and then used her hand to hide a fake laugh. "Why did I do it?" she asked. "Why Kris, I did it for us."

Kris cocked his head. "You're going to have to explain that."

"You're a newspaper reporter. I lease and manage properties. Do you think those jobs are going to pay for the kind of lifestyle I want? Remember Kris, I am a big city girl, a spoiled rotten only child, Daddy's Little Princess who gets whatever she wants. I am a Mercedes-Benz, Versace kind of girl. The kind of cash these people are throwing at me is unbelievable."

"You never said anything to me about being unhappy with our finances. Weren't we doing everything we wanted to?" Kris was stunned at her confession.

"I never said anything, but it was constantly on my mind. The more you and I were together, the more I realized bling-bling means a whole lot more to me than it does to you. In my job, I am never going to make big money, and neither are you in your job. Our only hope for wealth was for you to write that novel you keep talking about and it turns out to be a New York Times best seller. So, when this opportunity came along, I did not see any reason to say anything, because you would never learn of it and we would have all the money we needed."

"How did this, uh, opportunity come along?" Kris was having as much trouble digesting this sickening confession as he would with a tough ribeye at a cheap café.

"I confided to some friends my job wasn't paying enough. They sent some people to me who were wanting to lease a property that would be off the beaten path and would not draw much attention. From the beginning they flashed big cash. I would have leased them my parents' house for what they were offering. I would have sold my soul for what they were offering. I would have done practically anything for what they were offering." She smiled and shrugged her shoulders. "I guess I did do practically anything. I gave the order to have someone killed. Anyway, back to how I got involved. I had heard you talk - make that complain - so much about Fort Phillips, that I suggested we look there. One weekend while you were busy with assignments, I drove down and saw the old Simpson Slacks plant. It was perfect. Far enough away from Atlanta, but close enough to good roads for easy distribution. They liked the old building so much they bought it."

"And they bought you too."

"They did. I'm not ashamed, not with the way my bank account looks now."

"Wasn't it enough just to broker the sale? Why did you get involved any deeper?"

"They quickly saw I was something of a mercenary. They asked if I would be interested in coming up with a plan that would keep the rhubarbs in Fort Phillips away from the plant. I formulated the idea for the fires and break-ins to divert attention. Some of the locals were more than willing to cooperate. Vance wasn't. On one of my trips to the building, Vance showed up, said he was just roaming around. We were in the middle of setting everything up and I talked to him about joining us. He wouldn't. Later, Manley brought Vance back to the plant to show him the operational set-up and Vance pitched a fit. That's when I knew Vance had to go."

"So you had him killed."

"I'm sorry about your dad, sort of. You know what? I thought I was doing you a favor by getting rid of Vance. How many times did you come to me, looking for sympathy for all the times Vance screwed up? You are just like you dad, do you know that, Kris? Stubborn and hard-headed. All Vance had to do was join our little game, keep quiet and he would still be alive, have all the gambling money he could ever want, and you and I would be rich and preparing to be married. I did love you, Kris. I really did, and maybe I still do. I don't know. But that idiot Manley went soft and had to tell you Vance did not kill himself, and you, despite your disdain for your father, had to hang around and check out Manley's story. Things really started going south from there. Karen moved in on you which totally frustrated me, and then Popeye tried to rape me when all he was supposed to do was burglarize your house and find Vance's letter. The damn fat pervert! After that, Popeye had to go and so did I. By then, I had seen all I wanted of Fort Phillips, and I realized that too much of your heart was still with your hometown and your little high school sweetheart. And, like I said, I realized money is a lot more important to me than it is to you."

Kris was trying to prevent his body from shaking. "This can't be true," he said, his voice trembling. "I'm going to wake up from this nightmare."

"Believe me, it's real. I have the Benjamins to prove it. You really messed things up, Kris. My clients thought they had the perfect set-up for a very profitable long-term arrangement. But you got in the way, spoiled their plans, and because of you, people died."

Her words stabbed Kris as much as the knife that was found in Popeye's chest. He was silent and for several moments and looked at Emmy with moist eyes and his lips trembling. Finally, he managed to say in an obviously sarcastic tone, "I guess this means the wedding is off." He wanted to see Emmy's reaction.

"Yes, that is absolutely accurate. Sorry Kris."

"What happens now?"

"I leave town, probably leave the country. I can picture myself lounging on Natadola Beach in Fiji or LaConcha in Spain sipping on a Pina Colada or another scrumptious adult beverage. I have enough money to allow me to kick back and relax on a beautiful beach for a long, long time. You? I guess you go back to the Centennial and replace Mr. Floyd as the town legend. Honestly, I don't care what you do."

"It's the Sentinel, not the Centennial." Kris paused, took a deep sigh and half-heartedly smiled at Emmy. "Mmmm. Sounds like you have already been scouring travel brochures, planning your foot loose and fancy-free life." Kris paused again, took another deep breath and asked, "Tell me, Emmy, do you expect me to let you simply walk out of here like nothing ever happened? You killed my father, Emmy. You're a murderer!"

"I didn't pull the trigger, and Lonnie Jackson and Manley are dead so they can't testify that I gave the order. And yes, you're going to let me walk out of here. You know why? Because, despite what I have done, you still love me. Despite what I have done, you would rip my dress off right now and fuck my brains out. I'll admit Kris, there is one thing I'll miss about you. You were a damn good lover!"

"I'm a damn good liar too. When I first called you about tonight, I honestly did want to see you and either end things or take the first step toward getting back together. Then I found Vance's letter, and all I could think about was nailing your enticing butt to the wall. I'm wired Emmy. This whole conversation has been recorded. See the couple at that table…and that table? They're GBI agents, and I expect that they'll be coming over any second now to arrest you."

Emmy's jaw dropped and her eyes mirrored her disbelief. "You could you do this to me?" she asked, her lips trembling and her hands shaking.

"How could you do this to me?" Kris, his own hands shaking, retorted.

Two pairs of GBI agents rose and headed to Kris' table.

"I have another confession," Emmy said weakly as she wiped a tear from her eye.

Kris was silent as he waited for Emmy to continue speaking.

"I'm pregnant, Kris. You're going to be a father."

Before Kris could think of a response and with Emmy saying nothing else, she rose from the table. Emmy followed the GBI agents out of the restaurant without making a scene. The exit was so swift and quiet that the other diners and staff had no clue as to what was going on. Kris felt glued to the table and thought he was going to vomit at any moment in the middle of the fancy restaurant. His legs felt so rubbery he wasn't certain if he could walk. Kris wanted to cry, but instead he quickly guzzled down two full glasses of wine.

38

After a restless, sleepless night in a downtown Atlanta hotel that had jacked its rates because of a huge dental convention that was in town at the World Congress Center, Kris picked up Patrick for the journey back to Fort Phillips. Patrick, holding a cup of coffee in his good hand, had just settled into his seat when Kris, struggling to maintain his composure, began laying out the details of the night before. Stunned and saddened at the revelation about Emmy, Patrick did not know what to say. He had always been a huge Emmy fan, frequently declaring that she and Kris were so right for each other - a perfect match, a perfect couple. Patrick had struggled to understand how two people who seemed to be so in love could unravel so quickly and be so unwilling to compromise and talk things out. What started out as a seeming disagreement over Kris' need to stay in his hometown temporarily had somehow evolved from a relationship issue into a sordid tale of illegal drugs and murder. And now Patrick was being told by the man who loved Emmy that she was a schemer, a criminal, a cold-blooded bitch who had orchestrated to have someone killed.

Kris kept on talking, going over the same details four and five times. Patrick, knowing this was Kris' way of coping, sat quietly and listened as the scenery shifted from urban to suburban to rural. Kris' voice cracked several times, but he never cried. Patrick was trying not to cry as well, wondering what Emmy's fate would be and how Kris would deal with everything he had been through.

"There's more," Kris said after a long silence.

"I'm listening," Patrick offered.

"Emmy's pregnant."

"Jesus Kris! Pregnant? How do you feel about this?"

"I don't know. Maybe numb is the best way to describe how I feel."

"What about Emmy? How does she feel?"

"I don't know. She told me just as GBI agents escorted her out of the restaurant."

"She had to be on birth control."

"Of course she was. Experts say birth control is 99 percent effective. I guess we belong in the other one percent."

Patrick shook his head, took a sip of coffee and with hesitancy, asked, "The child? It's yours?"

"It is."

"How can you be certain? Emmy hasn't been the most truthful person these last few months."

"I'm sure. I have no reason to doubt Emmy about this. Besides, my gut instincts tell me the child is mine. But I do admit this is a real punch to the gut."

"Wow!" Patrick said, shaking his head again. "That's some way for a child to come into this world, with its mother in prison or about to go to prison."

"That won't happen. I'll see to it that Emmy stays out of prison long enough to have the baby."

Patrick leaned over and patted Kris on the thigh. "You still love her, don't you?"

"Do you still have one of those bite-size Three Musketeers?" Kris asked, looking straight ahead at the road.

Realizing that subject was not going to be discussed, Patrick peeled the candy and handed it to Kris who stuffed it in his mouth.

"I do know one thing, Kris. You will be a great father."

"Thanks."

"Any preference? Boy or girl?"

"Not at all, although I imagine that my college alma mater might need a really good shooting guard or small forward in about 18 years."

Kris' answer elicited a smile from Patrick. There was one other item he knew for certain about Kris. The boy loved basketball.

Patrick took a deep breath, exhaled, and asked, "What's next?"

"Lord, I don't know Patrick. I truly don't know. There are still so many loose ends to tie up in Fort Phillips and now I have a baby - and Emmy – to think about.

"You still love her, don't you?" Patrick asked again.

Kris requested another Three Musketeers.

39

Ten miles out of Fort Phillips, Kris finally calmed down and quit talking. Patrick, hoping to offer some comforting advice, suggested, "Besides learning you are going to be a father, there is something else to be thankful for."

"I can't wait to hear this," Kris said, keeping his eyes on the road.

"The good thing is, you found out about Emmy's adventures before you got married. That, my friend, would have certainly caused some complications."

"You're right about that," Kris said. He and Patrick were quiet as they reached Fort Phillips. Kris broke the silence by confessing, "Actually, something else good came out of this mess."

"And that would be…"

"I learned that Vance really had turned his life around. He was doing well. I just wish he and I had been able to talk." Kris' lip trembled and he had to wipe a tear off his cheek. With his good left hand, Patrick gently patted him on the leg.

Arriving at Kris' house, Patrick announced, "I have some more interesting news for you."

"Please make it interesting good news. I've had about all the bad news I can take."

"It is good news. I'm buying the Sentinel."

"You're what?" Kris asked in disbelief.

"I'm buying the Sentinel. Karen made me an offer I could not refuse. She's practically giving it to me."

"How did this come about?"

"She brought it up several days ago, and honestly, I was intrigued by the proposal from the very beginning. I have not been in Fort Phillips long, but I really like the town and the people. I know times are hard now, but I think we can bounce back. I like the involvement I can have in the community. Plus, I know my television career is over."

"What does Margaret say about this?"

"You may find this difficult to believe, but she actually likes the idea. We talked about it for hours last night. She comes from a relatively small town, and she is excited about the idea of living in a small community again where everyone knows each other, and neighbors are good neighbors. She even got this wild idea about opening a little antique shop, or maybe a bakery. That is something she has always had in the back of her mind. I know I won't make much money with the Sentinel, but with my retirement package the station is offering and the insurance settlement for the accident, we're set, pretty much for life."

"Well, I'm proud of you, I think. You and Margaret will be great additions to Fort Phillips. I can't imagine anyone I would entrust the Sentinel to more than you."

"You are kind to say that. Now, my friend, I have a business proposal to present to you."

Puzzled, Kris asked, "And what might that be?"

"Margaret and I want to buy Vance's house."

"Seriously?"

"Yes. We can continue to use it as the Sentinel's office. The City Council has already said they will give us a zoning to operate a business out of a home. I believe they would have given me anything I asked for. They are desperate to save the Sentinel."

Despite spending the first eighteen years of his life in the house, Kris had no significant emotional attachment to it. He was delighted to hear Patrick's proposal. "Yes, we can talk business," Kris said, trying to sound serious. "As long as you're not one of those cut-throat flippers who will give me an insulting lowball offer."

"Oh, I believe you will be delighted with my offer."

"And you are certain this is what you want to do?"

"Yes, we are absolutely, positively certain."

"Well good. Just make certain my name is spelled correctly on the check."

"Mr. Keller, you drive a hard bargain."

As happy as he was for Patrick and Margaret, Kris flipped the conversation. "Now that she's selling the Sentinel, did Karen say what she's going to do?"

"Other than leave Fort Phillips, no. She did say something about you going with her. I didn't have any response to that declaration."

"Good, because there's no truth to it."

"What are you going to do, Kris? You know you can stay at the Sentinel for as long as you want, but I don't think that's what you want, and I think that would be a severe waste of your talent."

"I have a much deeper appreciation for my hometown than I did several months ago but it's not where I want to be. You are right. I need to spend some time deciding what I want to do, and I can't do it here. I need some solitude."

"Are we going to put anything in the Sentinel about Emmy?"

"Why not? It should boost the paper's readership. But it's your paper. The decision is yours."

"It's not my paper yet, but I'm with you. Why not? People have heard all about it already. Word gets around. I know it is my obligation as a journalist to report this story. Some people will be appreciative that I write the story, while others will be upset. We need to get all of this out in the open and then move on. This town and its people need time to heal. Moving forward, there will be other big issues and events for us to tackle."

Kris chuckled. "Are you sure about that - more big events and issues? Remember, this is Fort Phillips. Nothing ever happens here, except for an illegal drug enterprise moving in and almost destroying the town. Prior to that, the biggest news I can remember is when the high school's star quarterback got suspended from the region championship game for hiding a skunk in the principal's office."

"I hope that meant the game wasn't a stinker." Patrick and Kris both laughed.

Kris, twisting his head so he could look at Patrick, smiled and said, "You're a good friend. No, I take that back. You are more than a good friend. You are a good father. That's how I see you - as my second father."

He was humbled by Kris' confession. He wanted to say something appropriate and profound in return, but the words stuck in his throat. He finally managed to playfully say, "Thanks for the compliment, but you make me feel so old."

40

As Kris and Patrick stood outside talking in front of the temporary Sentinel office, Karen was inside and not having difficulty verbalizing to Marilyn. "Are you still here? When is your vacation over? Don't you realize you're wasting your time making a play for Kris?" Karen asked hatefully. She dropped a large green canvas tote bag on the kitchen table.

Taking a 16-ounce can of lemon tea out of the refrigerator, Marilyn shut the door with a bit more force than necessary, popped the tab on the can, and responded, not hatefully, but sternly. "I still have a few days, and no, I don't think I'm wasting my time going after Kris. In fact, I think he and I are coming along quiet well." Marilyn wanted to leave the room, but Karen continued talking.

"Kris and I are going to be together, and if you could have seen the way we made sweet love the other night, you would realize that."

Marilyn peered at Karen over the rim of her soft drink can. "What night was it you and Kris made love?" she asked.

"Tuesday night. It was wonderful Like it was meant to be!"

"That's interesting," Marilyn responded with a teasing smile. "Kris and I made love that night. It was wonderful. Like it was meant to be!"

Marilyn's admission caught Karen off-guard, and her facial expression showed it. "No you didn't! Don't lie about it!"

"Why would I lie? We had just finished when you called with your little soap opera about the pills. I could have told Kris you were putting on a show, but he wouldn't have believed me."

"Well, I hope you enjoyed it, because that's the only time you two are going to make love."

"Oh, I wouldn't be so sure of that. He certainly seemed to enjoy it." Marilyn took a long swallow of her tea.

"I think I can guarantee it won't happen again. I have a plan to bring Kris and I together."

"And what might this plan be?"

Karen started reaching into the green tote bag and for a moment Marilyn's heart stopped. Was Karen going to pull out a gun and shoot her right there? That would certainly take her out of the picture.

Instead of pulling out a gun, Karen pulled out five stacks of crisp hundred-dollar bills. "This is my plan," she said, "I'm willing to pay you $100,000 to leave Fort Phillips and leave Kris alone."

Marilyn's eyes grew wide at the sight of the cash. She looked at the money and then looked at Karen. "This isn't about money," Marilyn retorted. "This is about Kris and I. I think we can have a nice life together." Marilyn was not going to admit it, but she was severely tempted by the cash.

"Oh, bullshit!? Karen snapped. "Everyone has their price! What is yours? I'll give you a hundred and fifty thousand!" She pulled out two more stacks of bills.

Marilyn could feel moisture collecting on her skin. "You can't bribe me," she answered, her voice lacking the bravado it had earlier in their conversation. The cash was so tempting.

"All right, here's the deal!" snapped Karen. She pulled out more stacks of cash. "Two hundred thousand dollars. I'll give you two hundred thousand dollars to get out of my way!"

"And if I refuse?"

Karen reached into the tote bag again. Marilyn wondered just how high she would go. This time, Karen's hand came out of the bag holding a small pistol. "If you don't take the cash, I'll put a bullet in your head and take your body to a place where it will never be found!"

Marilyn was now in a full sweat and her heart was pounding. "You would really do this, wouldn't you?" she asked Karen, but she already knew the answer.

"In a heartbeat," was Karen's quick reply.

Marilyn looked at the cash. It was a life-changing amount. "So, is this the deal?" she asked Karen. "I get the cash, get out of town, and that's it? You won't come looking or me or do me any harm?"

"No. I just want you out of my hair."

Marilyn took a deep breath and squeezed her drink can, bending it slightly. Again, she looked at the cash. She cleared her throat. "I'll do it!" she said.

"You're a smart girl," Karen smiled, nodded her head and put the pistol back in the bag. "Here's what I want. You leave town fast. No goodbye, no hugs, no nothing. All you do is leave Kris a note, explaining to him that you do not think you and he are meant to be together, that it just would not work out. Tell him you know that he loves me, and I love him, and we should be together. Now, that is not a bad way to make a quick two hundred thousand dollars, is it?"

"I can't believe I'm doing this," Marilyn whispered. "I like my chances with Kris, but two hundred thousand dollars?"

"A good choice," Karen replied with a cocky smile.

Marilyn sighed. "I guess you win." She started picking up the stacks of cash.

"I thought you would see things my way, so I brought this." Reaching into the tote bag again, Karen took out a pastel paper shopping bag. She unfolded it, opened it, and handed it to Marilyn. "Get that money out of sight before Kris gets back," she ordered.

Marilyn started dropping the money into the bag. She looked up at Karen and asked, "Where did you get this money? I know your dad had some money, and you're getting insurance money for the Sentinel fire, but where did you get the kind of money to be tossing around two hundred thousand?"

"When someone gives you two million dollars in meth to distribute and sell and you don't have to report it to the IRS, well, two hundred thousand is pocket change."

Marilyn dropped the last stack of cash on the table, and for a moment she thought about calling off the deal. She did not want any part of drug money. But when she quickly remembered her other option - getting shot - she put the last stack of money in the bag.

"If you have two million dollars, giving me two hundred thousand sounds paltry. Perhaps I should raise my price."

Kern slipped her hand back in the tote bag and started pulling the gun out once more. "Don't get greedy," she snapped at Marilyn.

"So, you were in on all this from the beginning?" she asked Karen.

"They paid me to look the other way as the newspaper editor. The easiest money I have ever made. Have you heard the news about Kris' ex-girlfriend? She was in on all of this. It seems that the same people who paid me paid her. She has been arrested."

"Emmy?" Marilyn asked in disbelief. "You are lying!"

"No, I'm not. I didn't take orders from her; had no idea she was involved. But apparently she was giving orders to Lonnie and other locals involved in this little operation. She ordered Lonnie to kill Kris' father."

Marilyn's legs were turning to jelly. She had had her fill of Karen Jackson and Fort Phillips. Marilyn stood up and said sarcastically, "Karen, it's been a pleasure doing business with you." She took the pastel bag containing the two hundred thousand dollars.

"Same here," Karen nodded as the glow of victory spread over her face.

"I guess I'd better go pack."

"Guess you better. Kris and Patrick should be back soon. I will give you until tomorrow. It would be suspicious if you left now, in the middle of the day. Pick your spot tomorrow to leave."

Marilyn went to her room and started thinking of ways to say goodbye to Kris and spend two hundred thousand dollars. Karen went to her desk in the makeshift newsroom and started thinking about sharing the rest of her life with Kris.

41

“Where’s Marilyn?” Kris asked Patrick who was pecking out an article for the next Sentinel.

“She left while you were out running errands this morning. She told me to give you this.”

Puzzled, Kris glanced at the envelope and asked Patrick, “What do you mean left?”

“Like for good. She was packed. You didn’t know she was leaving?”

Kris shook his head, sat down, opened the envelope, unfolded the single sheet of paper and started reading. Without looking up, he told Patrick, “She’s gone. She said she does not see the two of us working out, and that it is better for her to leave before one of us gets hurt. She wished me the best and said she hopes Karen I can build a relationship.”

“That’s nice of her, I guess,” Patrick said, taking a momentary break from his work.

“It’s not nice. It is strange. I never pictured Marilyn as a quitter, someone who would give up that easily. She and I were just starting to have a connection. For her to bail out now is just strange, very strange.”

“Talk to her.”

“In her letter she asked me not to. She says she’s ready to move on with her life.”

Patrick rocked back in his chair. “Buddy boy, your girlfriends are dropping like flies. First Emmy, now Marilyn. Better hope you can hit it off with Karen, or it’s strike three for you.”

Kris folded the letter and put it in the pocket of his jeans. “I’ve got some things to do today,” he told Patrick. “I’m not sure when I’ll be back.” Kris’ voice was weak.

“Are you all right?”

"Yeah, I'll be fine. There's just some personal matters I have to handle. I can't process this information about Marilyn until I take care of these other matters."

Patrick went back to composing his story and Kris went out to Vance's truck. Earlier that morning, he had picked up Vance's ashes from Mickey Montgomery. Paying some type of tribute to his father had become important to Kris. Struggling to come up with an appropriate manner to scatter Vance's ashes, Kris' thoughts kept coming back to Cooter's Lake. He remembered the fishing trip he and Vance had made to the lake the day after high school graduation. It was, sadly, one of the very few times Kris could remember spending any quality time with Vance. It was, sadly, one of the few fond memories Kris had of his father. Taking Vance back to this special place, even if it had only been special for a few hours on a single day, was important to Kris. He needed closure.

Traveling down a ruddy dirt road, Kris pulled Vance's truck to within twenty feet of the six-acre lake which was surrounded by a mixture of hardwoods and pines. The wind was blowing enough to cause the water to ripple. For an hour, Kris sat in the truck, gazing at the water and replaying his life. Concluding that his life had basically been a waste, he started to cry. He had yet to do anything significant to leave his mark in the newspaper business, and from a personal standpoint, his life was a train wreck. His mother was dead, his father was dead, his sister was three thousand miles away, Lonnie Jackson and Billy Manley had died because of confrontations with him, and the woman he had selected as his bride-to-be was going to jail. In the solitude of his surroundings, Kris decided that with so much going wrong in his life, he could make one thing right. He opened the truck's dash and retrieved Vance's letter. Kris quickly scanned the first lengthy, disjointed paragraph which chronicled Emmy's involvement with Syndicated Delivery Services. Tears were gathering in his eyes, which made reading the final few sentences difficult, but he had read them so much already he all but had them memorized:

"I'm sorry about this woman who claimed to be your girlfriend. I know you would not be a part of anything like that. I am sorry I had to tell you all of that, but it gave me a chance to do something I've been wanting to do for a long time. I would really like the chance to sit down and talk with you. I know I have made a mess of my life, and my mistakes have hurt so many other people. It is too late to do anything about your mother and sister. I have already lost them, and I will carry that guilt to the grave with me. But I was hoping that you and I could talk and let me tell you how sorry I am, and if you might be willing to give me another try. This time I am not going to mess up. I promise. I do not want to lose you. You are all I have left in this world. If you do not want to, I understand. Call the house. And one last thing. I want to say something to you that I never could bring myself to say before. I love you. Vance

Now, Kris understood why Vance had allowed Manley to kill him. Vance had mailed the letter to Kris and awaited a reply but never received one. He didn't get a reply because Kris had never received the letter. Thinking Kris had no intention of giving him a second chance, Vance allowed Manley to end his life. Something as simple as the wrong address on an envelope had created a disastrous chain of events.

Tears were flowing down Kris' cheek faster than he could wipe them off with his hands. He had neglected to bring any tissues. From the passenger seat of the truck, Kris picked up the small black rectangular box containing Vance's ashes, and said aloud, "Let's go have that talk."

Kris walked to the end of a rickety wooden pier that jutted twenty feet out in the lake and settled the box of ashes into the bottom of a fiberglass rowboat that was unofficially community property. Anyone who wanted to use it could. He paddled out in the middle of the lake, where the depth was around ten feet, and dropped anchor. With the boat gently bobbling up and down, Kris buried his face in his hands and cried long and loudly. He thought about how he, his mother and Becky had hung together to survive Vance's neglect and emotional abuse. He thought about all the nights he had tossed and turned in bed wondering where Vance was and if he would ever come back, or if he did come back, it would be in the back of a hearse. He thought about being embarrassed to be seen with his father and the humiliation of having to get him out of jail or go to a store and make good on a bad check Vance had passed. He thought about all the anger and rage he had built up and held inside over the years. He thought about all the energy he had wasted hating Vance. He thought the time had come to let all that go, to forgive Vance, to give him that second chance, to make peace with him.

Still wiping tears from his eyes, Kris opened the box and slowly started pouring the ashes into the center of Cooter's Lake. "I forgive you, Vance," Kris bawled. "if you'll forgive me for waiting so long for us to have this talk. If you'll forgive me for not telling you I love you."

For five minutes Kris cried uncontrollably, and then suddenly, the tears stopped and he was empowered with a freshness, a clearness of mind and spirit. Kris took a deep breath, smiled and as he looked out on the beautiful little lake, he said, "For the first time in months, I feel in control of my life. I know what I have to do."

Kris had one more important chore to complete before getting on with his life. Rowing back to shore, he hopped into the Ranger and headed directly to Karen who was pleasantly surprised to see him at the front door of her house.

42

"Just in time," she said as she ushered him in. "I'm making lasagna. There's plenty for both of us."

Without saying anything Kris followed her to the kitchen where she poured him a large glass of sweet tea. "I hope you're back for a replay of our recent evening together," she smiled.

"We need to talk," he said.

"I agree. We have lots to talk about, our future and what we're going to do."

"I'm not sure we're on the same page."

"Oh, I understand there will be some compromises to make but..."

Her sentence was interrupted by a boisterous pounding at the front door. "Whoever it is, they'll go away," she said. "As far as you and I talking about the future I'm flexible. Whatever you want to do, wherever you want to go."

Kris did not have time to answer. The banging continued at the front door. Frustrated, Karen told him, "I'll be right back."

Karen opened the door, anticipating telling a salesman to get lost, that his timing was terrible. Instead, she was confronted by Marilyn, whose glare could have hypnotized most meek housewives into buying anything. "I want to see Kris!" she demanded.

"You're supposed to be gone!" Karen snapped back.

"I want to see Kris!" Marilyn insisted, pushing the door open and storming into the living room while clutching a pastel gift bag.

Karen grabbed Marilyn by the arm and twirled her around. "We had a deal, damn you! Now get out of here!"

"Marilyn? I thought you were gone," Kris said. The loud voices had piqued his interest and he had come from the kitchen.

Marilyn placed the gift bag on a coffee table and scurried over to Kris and hugged him. "I was halfway to Atlanta when I realized I had forgotten something. You!" she said. Karen was furious.

"But the letter...you said things would never work out between us."

Marilyn nodded her head toward Karen. "I didn't mean what I said. She made me write the letter. She paid me to write the letter!"

Kris looked at Karen, and before he could say anything, she volunteered, "You don't believe her, do you, Kris? She is just jealous. She's trying to keep you and I apart."

"She gave me two hundred thousand reasons to write that letter," Marilyn said while dumping bundles of bills out of the gift bag onto the coffee table.

Kris looked at the cash in stunned silence and then turned his attention to Karen.

"I think our happiness is worth that much, don't you?" she asked him.

"Where did the money come from?" he asked, still shocked by this new admission.

"From the drugs. Syndicated Delivery," Marilyn responded with no hesitation.

"No! Don't tell me that," Kris pleaded. His voice trailed off and his shoulders slumped.

"All they paid me to do was not to bother them as a reporter and to try to keep other people from bothering them. Is that so wrong?" Karen pleaded.

"Yeah," Kris started, "considering this mess killed Vance and Lonnie and Billy Manley and Popeye and almost killed me."

"None of that was supposed to happen."

"But it did! God! Karen! Why?"

Tears were welling in Karen's eyes. "To get me out of this town. So you and I can be together, with all the money we will ever need. The only way I could get you back in town, to reunite us, was for Vance to screw something up again. Emmy did me a huge favor when she ordered Lonnie to kill Vance. Typical of Lonnie, though, he fouled things up. He didn't have the guts to do it himself and got Manley to do it. Then Manley got all soft, told you that Vance didn't kill himself, and that's when things started falling apart. You may not like the way things unfolded, Kris, but let's face it. You are better off without Vance."

Kris' anger at this woman he had known his entire life was boiling. "Damn you!" he practically screamed. Neither Marilyn nor Karen had seen him this way, almost out of control. He started to speak, opened his mouth, and thought better of it before terrible words came out. He took a deep breath to regain his composure and calmly said, "You don't understand, do you, Karen? The reason I am here this moment is to tell you I'm leaving. There is no future for us, Karen." He hesitated, dropped his head, raised it up to look at her, and said firmly, "You have been a dear friend, but I don't love you. Don't mistake one night of sex for love. I haven't loved you in a long time, certainly not after what has happened here in our hometown. You just admitted that you wanted my father dead. I am leaving, and I have no interest in ever seeing you or this town again."

His words pierced her heart. "You don't mean that. I know you don't. Everything I did, I did because I love you!"

"I'm sorry, Karen, but yes, I mean it!"

"Then I might as well take that whole bottle of sleeping pills."

"Not again," moaned Marilyn.

Karen started whimpering and tears began gathering in her eyes. Kris believed Karen was truly distraught. Marilyn believed she was faking.

"Please," Marilyn mumbled, stretching the word out to about six syllables.

"You might as well turn me over to the police," Karen said between sniffles as the crying increased.

"I won't have to do that. The investigation into what all has happened here has just started. The GBI, FBI, DEA, you know, all those alphabet soup agencies. I have told them all that I'm going to tell them."

"What did you tell them?" a suddenly fearful Karen asked.

"You shouldn't be worried about what I told the authorities. You need to be worried about what Emmy has told them. I've been told she is pointing fingers and naming names. If you have had anything to do with this terrible mess, they will find out. If I were you, Karen, I would get out of town while the getting is good. With some luck, you can have a fresh start. Take whatever of that damn drug money you have left and get the hell out of here. Go somewhere and build a new life. You are beautiful and now you are rich. You won't have any trouble finding a man."

"Please come with me," Karen pleaded.

"I can't do that." Kris sighed deeply and looked directly at Karen. Her face was splotchy and her makeup was a mess. He sighed again and said softly, "Look, I believe I can make a few phone calls and keep the state and federal guys chasing their tails for a few more days. Use that time wisely to tie up any loose ends, complete the sale of the Sentinel to Patrick and say goodbye to people you will never see again. Now is your opportunity to leave this place. Do it!"

Her crying had stopped. Karen knew at that moment she would never be with Kris, but she could not prevent herself from saying, "I love you, Kris. I always have and always will. And you can't convince me that you don't love me."

"We've got to go our separate ways, Karen. If we were together, every time I looked at you, it would bring back the awful memories of what has happened here in Fort Phillips."

"I can make you forget."

"No! Not in a million years, you can't."

"Not a million years but a million dollars. More than a million dollars."

"Go! Please!"

Sobbing, Karen requested, "Can I at least get a hug?"

With no reluctance, Kris hugged Karen but not firmly. It was more like a hug for a retiring co-worker than a hug between two lifelong friends who had been a bit more than just friends.

Marilyn was standing nervously in the room, wanting Kris to end the conversation and his relationship with Karen once and for all.

"Please give some thought to you and I going away together. At least think about it overnight," Karen begged.

"Oh, please!" Marilyn interrupted. Kris held his hand out and shook his head at Marilyn, letting her know she didn't have a say in this conversation.

"I repeat," Kris started explaining to Karen. "You finalize the deal with Patrick for the Sentinel, and then you walk away from this place a free, liberated, rich woman."

"A free, liberated, rich woman who won't have the man she loves," Karen whimpered.

"Do we have a deal?" Kris asked.

Karen stood in the middle of the room, shaking, like a marble statue about to crumble. She was silent for what seemed like an eternity. Kris and Marilyn were waiting for her to say something. Finally, she said, "Deal," barely loud enough to be heard. She did not want to let go of Kris, but she didn't want to run the risk of going to jail either.

"Let's go Marilyn," Kris said. He nudged her by putting his hand on her back, just above the waist. She stopped to slip the money back in the pastel gift bag, but Kris would not let her. "That stays here," he insisted. She groaned but obeyed and followed Kris outside.

They stopped in the driveway next to Marilyn's car. "That was gracious for you to let her go. Gracious, but not very smart. She needs to be locked up," Marilyn said, her words wrapped in ill will.

"She won't get far. The feds will catch up with her quickly. I may not love Karen, but I am indebted to her and her father. I know she has always wanted to get away from here but could not. The least I can do is give her a head start." Kris glanced up to see Karen peeking out the window.

"What about the two of us? Do we have a future?" Marilyn asked.

"I can't give you an answer right now. I still have some serious issues to resolve, and they need to stay my secret for the moment. One of the first things I have to do is find a job. My cash is running low."

"Don't worry. Karen gave me two hundred thousand. I only brought one hundred thousand back. I've got the rest stashed away."

Kris shook his head and looked to the heavens. "Lord, no more surprises today. Please!"

"That money would get us off to a great start," Marilyn said.

"Not now. I've got to put my life back together before I drag anyone else into it," Kris paused, smiled and tenderly took each of her hands in his. "I'll call you when I get my sanity back. I promise. Thank you for saving my life at the Simpson Slacks building."

She smiled at Kris' acknowledgement and said, "I understand you need some time to get your head straight. I get it; I can live with that for now, but you know I don't give up. I'm persistent."

His response was a smile.

"Well," Marilyn sighed, "I guess I'll be on my way to Atlanta. Again. What do I tell people about Emmy?"

"Nothing. They've already heard plenty on the nightly news and they will be hearing more."

Marilyn hugged him, kissed him softly on the lips, got in her car and drove away. Standing on the grass in Karen's front yard, that's what Kris wanted to do as well. Drive away. Get in Vance's Ford Ranger and drive away, as far away from Fort Phillips as possible.

EPILOGUE

It had been six months since all hell broke loose in Fort Phillips. Kris had retreated to a small beach rental near Apalachicola on the Gulf of Mexico. The sun, sand and soothing rhythm of the sea had been cathartic. Sleep was coming swifter; the nightmares were fewer, and the delicious seafood had helped Kris regain his appetite. Considering everything he had endured, Kris knew his life would never return to what it had once been. He accepted that but he was determined to have a new beginning and create a new life.

Marilyn could be a part of that new life. Kris could not understand why Marilyn had chosen to masquerade as a floozy for so long. She was intelligent, articulate, funny and genuinely interested in Kris' well-being. Regularly, Marilyn would fly from Atlanta to Tallahassee where Kris would pick her up and they would drive in Vance's old truck to the beach rental. He discovered they had much in common, including her four years as the shooting guard on her high school basketball team. At Kris' request, they did not talk about Emmy. Marilyn knew about the baby. She quickly recovered from the shock and had pledged to assist Kris in any manner. Kris was not ready for a serious relationship. Marilyn understood and did not pressure him. For the moment, they simply enjoyed each other's company.

Kris had warned Karen to leave Fort Phillips before law enforcement hit town and she did. They caught up with her in Hawaii as she prepared to board a plane for Tahiti. Stateside, a laundry list of charges, state and federal, awaited her. Karen had been smart about her money, depositing most it in Swiss accounts that could not be traced. When and if she was released from prison, she would be able to lead an extremely comfortable life.

Patrick and Margaret had settled comfortably in Fort Phillips. The Sentinel had not missed a beat, in fact had gotten better. Margaret had opened a bakery and combination ice cream and coffee shop which had been an immediate success. As a joke, but also with a sense of pride, Patrick and Margaret had sent Kris a coupon for a free lifetime supply of coffee from the Keller-Cannon Emporium. Eventually, they planned to move the Sentinel office back to Main Street and renovate Vance's house for their permanent residence. Patrick had been fitted with a new right hand that allowed him to do amazing things.

Emmy was working on a plea deal. In exchange for information about the Syndicated Delivery Services operation, which authorities quickly determined was far reaching, she was seeking a lighter sentence. Prosecutors were waiting to see how helpful her information was before agreeing to a deal. The Fort Phillips locals that Emmy implicated had all left town. Several had already been tracked down; the remainder would be shortly.

Emmy still had to be indicted and whether there was a trial or a plea bargain, her case was going to move through the courts slowly. Working in the background with one of the best criminal defense attorneys in Atlanta, Kris had convinced prosecutors to allow Emmy to be under house arrest with her parents. Angry and devastated, the Owens would not allow their only daughter to make any more mistakes. Emmy's bond was not cheap.

About the baby. House arrest meant Emmy would be allowed to have the baby in the hospital or at her parents' home. Realizing she was facing significant prison time even with a plea, she signed over full parental rights to Kris. He offered to allow Emmy to keep the baby until she was incarcerated but she declined, realizing the longer she had possession of the child, the more difficult it would be to let go.

Kris made a promise to himself that he would be a good father. Patrick and Dr. Harrison, the wise pharmacist and long-time friend, had given Kris plenty of advice on parenting. Their words of wisdom: ignore the thousands of self-help books and follow your instincts. Mistakes will be made but you will learn from them. Ironically, Kris was appreciative of Vance who had shown him the type of father *not to be.*

Tests proved Kris to be the baby's father. Other tests showed Kris was having a son. He was naming the child after the two men who had helped Kris grow as a man – Patrick Cannon and Carter Floyd. The name – Patrick Carter Keller.

Kris left Fort Phillips with not a lot of money but that had changed. A publisher had offered him a hefty advance for a first-person account of the Fort Phillips Incident as it came to be called, plus two additional books; one would be true crime, the other fictional crime. Patrick and Margaret had purchased the Keller homeplace and Kris had made a nice profit from that. And then he was brought to tears when he learned Carter Floyd had included Kris in his will. Mr. Floyd had an extensive stock portfolio. It was to be liquidated, with seventy percent going to Karen and thirty percent to Kris.

Kris had decided he loved living on the beach. He had plenty of money to purchase a house, hire a live-in au pair for the baby and write full time. He could do all his writing and research at home and rarely have to leave.

Writing for a living. That was all Kris had ever wanted to do. That time had come. He was ready to tell his stories.

COMING SOON

By Gary Watson
Embedded (Adult Fiction)

Acting on a tip from a dying colleague, reporter Luke Douglas reluctantly begins investigating alleged foreign collusion in Atlanta city council elections. Luke is skeptical at first, believing the tip he received is nothing more than the delusional ramblings of a man wracked with pain and whacked out from morphine. Why would any foreign entity want to get involved with anything as piddling as a city election?

As Luke digs deeper, he uncovers a sinister plot that reaches far beyond Atlanta's municipal election. He forms an alliance with two FBI agents, Assistant Special Agent in Charge Paul Cameron and Special Agent Vicki Borders, to reveal bribes, coerced candidates, money laundering and the true reason behind the election interference.

Luke puts himself and others in harm's way as he races to identify a cold-blooded killer and expose a far-reaching scheme that could elevate U.S. and Russian tension to Cold War status.

COMING SOON

By Gary Watson
Unexpected (Adult Fiction)

In a follow-up to *The Second Chapter of a Bad Dream*, the little south Georgia town of Sanderson is recovering from a series of three ritualistic murders months earlier. For Sanderson residents Jake Martin and Maddie Hampton, recovery has been especially difficult. Both have deep emotional scars from the murders. Jake, editor of the local newspaper, is haunted by the possibility that librarian Janet Wayne, in jail for two of the murders, is innocent and he hasn't done enough to prove her innocence. School teacher Maddie, once a suspect in two of the murders, is secretly being blackmailed by Janet Wayne's daughter Sunny Krause, who believes Maddie should be in jail for the murders rather than her mother. Sunny has her own issues. She is wanted for the murder of her father Regal Krause, who along with the two other murder victims, publicly humiliated Maddie's high school age son, causing him to leave town permanently. Jake and Maddie want to get married but their plans get derailed as they each deal with their personal demons.

Matters get worse when Jake's ex-wife Kathy unexpectedly shows up. She has been involved in Peachtree Mining Opportunity, a gold mining scam that has fleeced millions of dollars from investors. One of her partners in the scam is looking for her, claiming she has money he is owed, and she comes to Sanderson for Jake to help get her out of her predicament.

Jake is tormented, seeking clarity about he really feels about Maddie, Janet Wayne and his ex-wife. Maddie is desperate to get the devious Sunny Krause out of her life. As their lives intersect, they all encounter unexpected developments and the truth becomes very elusive.

Slowly peeling off the layers of the people closest to him, Jakes realizes that even in the small town of Sanderson, everyone has secrets and nothing is really as it seems. His search for the truth may not result in a happy ending for anyone, including himself.

COMING SOON

By Gary Watson

Third Team at Three Creeks (Young Adult)

Josh McAllister, his sister Carly and mother Gina are living paycheck to paycheck in tiny Fanfare, Alabama. Josh offers to drop out of school to help with the family's finances but Gina is adamant that Josh will remain in school because he is set to be the starting quarterback on the football team in the fall. As Josh is approaching his senior year at Fanfare, his grandfather gets sick, and Josh and his mother must move to Three Creeks, a growing community outside Atlanta, to care for him. This improves the family's money issues, but Josh's world is turned upside down.

Josh has to leave behind the opportunity to be a star on the football team and a promising relationship with coed Abby. The situation is made even more upsetting because Carly refuses to move and stays behind in Fanfare with a friend. In Three Creeks, Josh suddenly finds himself at a high school with almost three thousand students, a football team destined for the state championship and an All-American quarterback.

Josh struggles with his role as the seldom-used third team quarterback on his new team. His transition at Three Creeks is further complicated by a teammate who has it in for him and three coeds he has strong feelings for. Abby is the girl who Luke left behind in Fanfare. Monica is a girl who at one time Luke would not have given second though to, and Flannery is the bubbly cheerleader captain who happens to be the girlfriend of stud quarterback Charlie Wade and Luke's nemesis.

As the state championship game approaches, Josh finds himself at the center of a series of events that threaten the team's ability to win. Josh and the Three Creek Cougars face their biggest challenge in the biggest game of the season.

Printed in the United States
by Baker & Taylor Publisher Services

Printed in the United States
by Baker & Taylor Publisher Services